Irresistible Bachelors

Irresistible Bachelors:
Bought for One Night

REESE RYAN

SARA ORWIG

RACHEL BAILEY

MILLS & BOON

First Published in Great Britain 2022
by Mills & Boon, an imprint of HarperCollins*Publishers* Ltd,
1 London Bridge Street, London, SE1 9GF

www.harpercollins.co.uk

HarperCollins*Publishers*
1st Floor, Watermarque Building,
Ringsend Road, Dublin 4, Ireland

IRRESISTIBLE BACHELORS: BOUGHT FOR ONE NIGHT
© 2022 Harlequin Books S.A.

His Until Midnight © 2018 Harlequin Books S.A.
That Night with the Rich Rancher © 2016 Sara Orwig
Bidding on Her Boss © 2015 Rachel Robinson

Special thanks and acknowledgement are given to Reese Ryan for her contribution to the Texas Cattleman's Club: Bachelor Auction series.

ISBN: 978-0-263-30399-5

MIX
Paper from
responsible sources

FSC C007454

HIS UNTIL MIDNIGHT

REESE RYAN

To Johnathan Royal, Stephanie Perkins, Jennifer Copeland, Denise Stokes, Sharon Blount, Stephanie Douglas-Quick and all of the amazing readers in the Reese Ryan VIP Readers Lounge on Facebook. Seriously, y'all rock! I appreciate your readership, engagement, enthusiasm and continued support. Thank you to each and every one of you!

To my infinitely patient and ever-insightful editor, Charles Griemsman, thank you for all you do.

One

Tessa Noble stared at the configuration of high and low balls scattered on the billiard table.

"I'm completely screwed," she muttered, sizing up her next move. After a particularly bad break and distracted play, she was losing badly.

But how on earth could she be expected to concentrate on billiards when her best friend Ryan Bateman was wearing a fitted performance T-shirt that highlighted every single pectoral muscle and his impressive biceps. He could have, at the very least, worn a shirt that fit, instead of one that was a size too small, as a way to purposely enhance his muscles. And the view when he bent over the table in a pair of broken-in jeans that hugged his firm ass like they were made for it...

How in the hell was she expected to play her best?

"You're not screwed," Ryan said in a deep, husky

voice that was as soothing as a warm bath. Three parts sex-in-a-glass and one part confidence out the wazoo.

Tessa's cheeks heated, inexplicably. Like she was a middle schooler giggling over double entendres and sexual innuendo.

"Maybe not, but you'd sure as hell like to be screwed by your best friend over there," Gail Walker whispered in her ear before taking another sip of her beer.

Tessa elbowed her friend in the ribs, and the woman giggled, nearly shooting beer out of her nose.

Gail, always a little too direct, lacked a filter after a second drink.

Tessa walked around the billiard table, pool cue in hand, assessing her options again while her opponent huffed restlessly. Finally, she shook her head and sighed. "You obviously see something I don't, because I don't see a single makeable shot."

Ryan sidled closer, his movements reminiscent of a powerful jungle cat stalking prey. His green eyes gleamed even in the dim light of the bar.

"You're underestimating yourself, Tess," Ryan murmured. "Just shut out all the noise, all the doubts, and focus."

She studied the table again, tugging her lower lip between her teeth, before turning back to him. "Ryan, I clearly don't have a shot."

"Go for the four ball." He nodded toward the purple ball wedged between two of her opponent's balls.

Tessa sucked in a deep breath and gripped the pool cue with one hand. She pressed her other hand to the table, formed a bridge and positioned the stick between her thumb and forefinger, gliding it back and forth.

But the shot just wasn't there.

"I can't make this shot." She turned to look at him. "Maybe you could, but I can't."

"That's because you're too tight, and your stance is all wrong." Ryan studied her for a moment, then placed his hands on either side of her waist and shifted her a few inches. "Now you're lined up with the ball. That should give you a better sight line."

Tessa's eyes drifted closed momentarily as she tried to focus on the four ball, rather than the lingering heat from Ryan's hands. Or his nearness as he hovered over her.

She opened them again and slid the cue back and forth between her fingers, deliberating the position and pace of her shot.

"Wait." Ryan leaned over beside her. He slipped an arm around her waist and gripped the stick a few inches above where she clenched it. He stared straight ahead at the ball, his face inches from hers. "Loosen your grip on the cue. This is a finesse shot, so don't try to muscle it. Just take it easy and smack the cue ball right in the center, and you've got this. Okay?"

"Okay." Tessa nodded, staring at the center of the white ball. She released a long breath, pulled back the cue and hit the cue ball dead in the center, nice and easy.

The cue ball connected with the four ball with a smack. The purple ball rolled toward the corner pocket and slowed, teetering on the edge. But it had just enough momentum to carry it over into the pocket.

"Yes!" Tessa squealed, smacking Ryan's raised palm to give him a high five. "You're amazing. You actually talked me through it."

"You did all the work. I was just your cheering section." He winked in that way that made her tummy flutter.

"Well, thank you." She smiled. "I appreciate it."

"What are best friends for?" He shrugged, picking up his beer and taking a sip from the bottle.

"Thought I was playing Tess," Roy Jensen grumbled. "Nobody said anything about y'all tag-teaming me."

"Oh, quit complaining, you old coot." Tessa stared down her opponent. "I always turn a blind eye when you ask for spelling help when we're playing Scrabble."

Roy's cheeks tinged pink, and he mumbled under his breath as Tessa moved around the table, deciding which shot to take next. She moved toward the blue two ball.

"Hey, Ryan." Lana, the way-too-friendly barmaid, sidled up next to him, her chest thrust forward and a smile as wide as the Rio Grande spread across her face. "Thought you might want another beer."

"Why thank you, kindly." Ryan tipped an imaginary hat and returned the grin as he accepted the bottle.

Tessa clenched her jaw, a burning sensation in her chest. She turned to her friend, whispering so neither Lana nor Ryan could hear her.

"Why doesn't she just take his head and smash it between the surgically enhanced boobs her ex-boyfriend gave her as a consolation prize? It'd be a lot easier for both of them."

"Watch it there, girl. You're beginning to sound an awful lot like a jealous girlfriend." Gail could barely contain her grin.

"There's nothing to be jealous of. Ryan and I are just friends. You know that."

"*Best* friends," her friend pointed out, as she studied Ryan flirting with Lana. "But let's face it. You're two insanely attractive people. Are you really going to try and convince me that neither of you has ever considered—"

"We haven't." Tessa took her shot, missing badly. It was a shot she should've hit, even without Ryan's help. But she was too busy eavesdropping on his conversation with Lana.

"Well, for a person who doesn't have any romantic interest in her best friend, you seem particularly interested in whether or not he's flirting with the big-boobed barmaid." Gail shrugged when Tessa gave her the stink eye. "What? You know it's true."

Tessa scowled at her friend's words and the fact that Roy was taking advantage of her distraction. He easily sank one ball, then another. With no more striped balls left on the table, Roy had a clear shot at the eight ball.

He should be able to make that shot blindfolded.

"Well?" Gail prodded her.

"I'm not jealous of Lana. I just think Ryan could do better. That he *should* do better than to fall for the calculated ploy of a woman who has dollar signs in her eyes. Probably angling for butt implants this time."

Gail giggled. "And why would he want a fake ass when he was mere inches from the real deal?" She nodded toward Tessa's behind, a smirk on her face.

Tessa was fully aware that she'd inherited her generous curves from her mother. She was just as clear about Ryan Bateman's obliviousness to them. To him, she was simply one of the guys. But then again, the comfy jeans and plaid button-down shirts that filled her closet didn't do much to highlight her assets.

Hadn't that been the reason she'd chosen such a utilitarian wardrobe in the first place?

"Dammit!" Roy banged his pool cue on the wooden floor, drawing their attention to him. He'd scratched on the eight ball.

Tessa grinned. "I won."

"Because I scratched." Roy's tone made it clear that he felt winning by default was nothing to be proud of.

"A win's a win, Jensen." She wriggled her fingers, her palm open. "Pay up."

"You won? Way to go, Tess. I told you that you had this game in the bag." Ryan, suddenly beside her, wrapped a big, muscular arm around her shoulder and pulled her into a half hug.

"Well, at least one of us believed in me." Tessa counted the four wrinkled five-dollar bills Roy stuffed in her palm begrudgingly.

"Always have, always will." He beamed at her and took another swig of his beer.

Tessa tried to ignore the warmth in her chest that filtered down her spine and fanned into areas she didn't want to acknowledge.

Because they were friends. And friends didn't get all…whatever it was she was feeling…over one another. Not even when they looked and smelled good enough to eat.

Tessa Noble always smelled like citrus and sunshine. Reminded him of warm summer picnics at the lake. Ryan couldn't peel an orange or slice a lemon without thinking of her and smiling.

There was no reason for his arm to still be wrapped

around her shoulder other than the sense of comfort he derived from being this close to her.

"Take your hands off my sister, Bateman." Tessa's brother Tripp's expression was stony as he entered the bar. As if he was about five minutes away from kicking Ryan's ass.

"Tessa just beat your man, Roy, here." Ryan didn't move. Nor did he acknowledge Tripp's veiled threat.

The three of them had been friends forever, though it was Tessa who was his best friend. According to their parents, their friendship was born the moment they first met. Their bond had only gotten stronger over the years. Still, he'd had to assure Tripp on more than one occasion that his relationship with Tess was purely platonic.

Relationships weren't his gift. He'd made peace with that, particularly since the dissolution of his engagement to Sabrina Calhoun little more than a year ago. Tripp had made it clear, in a joking-not-joking manner, that despite their longtime friendship, he'd punch his lights out if Ryan ever hurt his sister.

He couldn't blame the guy. Tess definitely deserved better.

"Way to go, Tess." A wide grin spread across Tripp's face. He gave his sister a fist bump, followed by a simulated explosion.

The Nobles' signature celebratory handshake.

"Thanks, Tripp." Tessa casually stepped away from him.

Ryan drank his beer, captivated by her delectable scent which still lingered in the air around him.

"You look particularly proud of yourself today, big brother." Tessa raised an eyebrow, her arms folded.

The move inadvertently framed and lifted Tessa's rather impressive breasts. Another feature he tried hard, as her best friend, to not notice. But then again, he was a guy, with guy parts and a guy brain.

Ryan quickly shifted his gaze to Tripp's. "You still pumped about being a bachelor in the Texas Cattleman's Club charity auction?"

Tripp grinned like a prize hog in the county fair, his light brown eyes—identical to his sister's—twinkling merrily. "Alexis Slade says I'll fetch a mint."

"Hmm…" Ryan grinned. "Tess, what do you think your brother here will command on the auction block?"

"Oh, I'd say four maybe even five…dollars." Tessa, Ryan, Gail and Roy laughed hysterically, much to Tripp's chagrin.

Tripp folded his arms over his chest. "I see you all have jokes tonight."

"You know we're just kidding." Ryan, who had called next, picked up a pool cue as Roy gathered the balls and racked them. "After all, I'm the one who suggested you to Alexis."

"And I may never forgive you for creating this monster." Tessa scowled at Ryan playfully.

"My bad, I wasn't thinking." He chuckled.

"What I want to know is why on earth you didn't volunteer yourself?" Gail asked. "You're a moderately good-looking guy, if you like that sort of thing." She laughed.

She was teasing him, not flirting. Though with Gail it was often hard to tell.

Ryan shrugged. "I'm not interested in parading across the stage for a bunch of desperate women to bid on, like I'm a side of beef." He glanced apologetically at his friend, Tripp. "No offense, man."

"None taken." Tripp grinned proudly, poking a thumb into his chest. "This 'side of beef' is chomping at the bit to be taken for a spin by one of the lovely ladies."

Tessa elbowed Ryan in the gut, and an involuntary "oomph" sound escaped. "Watch it, Bateman. We aren't *desperate*. We're civic-minded women whose only interest is the betterment of our community."

There was silence for a beat before Tessa and Gail dissolved into laughter.

Tessa was utterly adorable, giggling like a schoolgirl. The sound—rooted in his earliest memories of her—instantly conjured a smile that began deep down in his gut.

He studied her briefly. Her curly, dark brown hair was pulled into a low ponytail and her smooth, golden brown skin practically glowed. She was wearing her typical winter attire: a long-sleeved plaid shirt, jeans which hid her curvy frame rather than highlighting it, and the newest addition to her ever-growing sneaker collection.

"You're a brave man." Ryan shifted his attention to Tripp as he leaned down and lined his stick up with the cue ball. He drew it back and forth between his forefinger and thumb. "If these two are any indication—" he nodded toward Tess and Gail "—those women at the auction are gonna eat you alive."

"One can only hope." Tripp wriggled his brows and held up his beer, one corner of his mouth curled in a smirk.

Ryan shook his head, then struck the white cue ball

hard. He relished the loud cracking sound that indicated a solid break. The cue ball smashed through the triangular formation of colorful balls, and they rolled or spun across the table. A high and a low ball dropped into the pockets.

"Your choice." Ryan nodded toward Tessa.

"Low." Hardly a surprise. Tessa always chose low balls whenever she had first choice. She walked around the table, her sneakers squeaking against the floor, as she sized up her first shot.

"You know I'm only teasing you, Tripp. I think it's pretty brave of you to put yourself out there like that. I'd be mortified by the thought of anyone bidding on me." She leaned over the table, her sights on the blue two ball before glancing up at her brother momentarily. "In fact, I'm proud of you. The money you'll help raise for the Pancreatic Cancer Research Foundation will do a world of good."

She made her shot and sank the ball before lining up for the next one.

"Would you bid on a bachelor?" Ryan leaned against his stick, awaiting his turn.

He realized that Tess was attending the bachelor auction, but the possibility that she'd be bidding on one of them hadn't occurred to him until just now. And the prospect of his best friend going on a date with some guy whose company she'd paid for didn't sit well with him.

The protective instinct that had his hackles up was perfectly natural. He, Tripp and Tessa had had each others' backs since they were kids. They weren't just friends, they were family. Though Tess was less like a little sister and more like a really hot distant cousin, three times removed.

"Of course, I'm bidding on a bachelor." She sank another ball, then paced around the table and shrugged. "That's kind of the point of the entire evening."

"Doesn't mean you have to. After all, not every woman attending will be bidding on a bachelor," Ryan reminded her.

"They will be if they aren't married or engaged," Gail said resolutely, folding her arms and cocking an eyebrow his way. "Why, Ryan Bateman, sounds to me like you're jealous."

"Don't be ridiculous." His cheeks heated as he returned his gaze to the table. "I'm just looking out for my best friend. She shouldn't be pressured to participate in something that makes her feel uncomfortable."

Tessa was sweet, smart, funny, and a hell of a lot of fun to hang out with. But she wasn't the kind of woman he envisioned with a paddle in her hand, bidding on men as if she were purchasing steers at auction.

"Doesn't sound like Tess, to me. That's all I'm saying." He realized he sounded defensive.

"*Good.* It's about time I do something unexpected. I'm too predictable…too boring." Tessa cursed under her breath when she missed her shot.

"Also known as consistent and reliable," Ryan interjected.

Things were good the way they were. He liked that Tessa followed a routine he could count on. His best friend's need for order balanced out his spontaneity.

"I know, but lately I've been feeling… I don't know…stifled. Like I need to take some risks in my personal life. Stop playing it so safe all the time." She sighed in response to his wide-eyed, slack-jawed stare. "Relax, Rye. It's not like I'm paying for a male escort."

"I believe they prefer the term *gigolo*," Gail, always helpful, interjected, then took another sip of her drink.

Ryan narrowed his gaze at Gail, which only made the woman laugh hysterically. He shifted his attention back to Tessa, who'd just missed her shot.

"Who will you be bidding on?"

Tessa shrugged. "I don't know. No one in particular in mind, just yet. The programs go out in a few days. Maybe I'll decide then. Or... I don't know...maybe I'll wait and see who tickles my fancy when I get there."

"Who *tickles your fancy*?" Ryan repeated the words incredulously. His grip on the pool cue tightened.

He didn't like the sound of that at all.

Two

Tessa followed the sound of moaning down the hall and around the corner to her brother's room.

"Tripp? Are you all right?" She tapped lightly on his partially opened bedroom door.

"No!" The word was punctuated by another moan, followed by, "I feel like I'm dying."

Tessa hurried inside his room, her senses quickly assailed by a pungent scent which she followed to his bathroom. He was hugging the porcelain throne and looking a little green.

"Did you go out drinking last night?"

"No. I think it's the tuna sandwich I got from the gas station late last night on my way back in from Dallas."

"How many times have I told you? Gas station food after midnight? No *bueno*." She stood with her hands on her hips, looking down at her brother who looked like he might erupt again at any minute.

Austin Charles Noble III loved food almost as much as he loved his family. And usually he had a stomach like a tank. Impervious to just about anything. So whatever he'd eaten had to have been pretty bad.

"I'm taking you to Urgent Care."

"No, I just want to go to bed. If I can sleep it off for a few hours, I'm sure I'll be fine." He forced a smile, then immediately clutched his belly and cringed. "I'll be good as new for the bachelor auction."

"Shit. The bachelor auction." Tess repeated the words. It was the next night. And as green at the gills as Tripp looked, there was little chance he'd be ready to be paraded on stage in front of a crowd of eager women by then. The way he looked now, he probably wouldn't fetch more than five dollars and a bottle of ipecac at auction.

"Here, let me help you back to bed." She leaned down, allowing her brother to drape his arm around her and get enough leverage to climb to his feet on unsteady legs. Once he was safely in bed again, she gathered the remains of the tainted tuna sandwich, an empty bottle of beer, and a few other items.

She set an empty garbage can with a squirt of soap and about an inch of water beside his bed.

"Use this, if you need to." She indicated the garbage can. "I'm going to get you some ginger ale and some Gatorade. But if you get worse, I'm taking you to the doctor. Mom and Dad wouldn't be too happy with me if I let their baby boy die of food poisoning while they were away on vacation."

"Well, I am Mom's favorite, so…" He offered a weak smile as he invoked the argument they often teased each other about. "And don't worry about the auction,

I'll be fine. I'm a warrior, sis. Nothing is going to come between me and—" Suddenly he bolted out of bed, ran to the bathroom and slammed the door behind him.

Tessa shook her head. "You're staying right here in bed today and tomorrow, 'warrior.' I'll get Roy and the guys to take care of the projects that were on your list today. And I'll find a replacement for you in the auction. Alexis will understand."

Tripp mumbled his thanks through the bathroom door, and she set off to take care of everything she had promised him.

Tessa had been nursing her brother back to health and handling her duties at the ranch, as well as some of his. And she'd been trying all day to get in touch with Ryan.

Despite his reluctance to get involved in the auction, he was the most logical choice as Tripp's replacement. She was sure she could convince him it was a worthy cause. Maybe stroke his ego and tell him there would be a feeding frenzy for a hot stud like him.

A statement she planned to make in jest, but that she feared also had a bit of truth to it. Tessa gritted her teeth imagining Lana, and a whole host of other women in town who often flirted with Ryan, bidding on him like he was a prize steer.

Maybe getting Ryan to step in as Tripp's replacement in the auction wasn't such a good idea after all. She paced the floor, scrolling through a list of names of other possible options in her head.

Most of the eligible men that came to mind were already participating, or they'd already turned Alexis and Rachel down, from what Tessa had heard.

She stopped abruptly mid-stride, an idea brewing in her head that made her both excited and feel like she was going to toss her lunch at the same time.

"Do something that scares you every single day." She repeated the words under her breath that she'd recently posted on the wall of her office. It was a quote from Eleanor Roosevelt. Advice she'd promised herself that she would take to heart from here on out.

Tessa glanced at herself in the mirror. Her thick hair was divided into two plaits, and a Stetson was pushed down on her head, her eyes barely visible. She was the textbook definition of Plain Jane. Not because she wasn't attractive, but because she put zero effort into looking like a desirable woman rather than one of the ranch hands.

She sighed, her fingers trembling slightly. There was a good chance that Alexis and Rachel would veto her idea for Tripp's replacement. But at least she would ask.

Tessa pulled her cell phone out of her back pocket and scrolled through her contacts for Alexis Slade's number. Her palms were damp as she initiated the call. Pressing the phone to her ear, she counted the rings, a small part of her hoping that Alexis didn't answer. That would give her time to rethink her rash decision. Maybe save herself some embarrassment when Alexis rejected the idea.

"Hey, Tess. How are you?" Alexis's warm, cheerful voice rang through the line.

"I'm good. Tripp? Not so much. I think he has food poisoning." The words stumbled out of her mouth.

"Oh my God! That's terrible. Poor Tripp. Is he going to be okay?"

"I'm keeping an eye on him, but I'm sure he'll be

fine in a few days. I just don't think he's going to recover in time to do the bachelor auction."

"We'll miss having him in the lineup, but of course
we understand. His health is the most important thing."
The concern was evident in Alexis's voice. "Tell him
that we hope he's feeling better soon. And if the auction goes well, maybe we'll do this again next year. I'll
save a spot in the lineup for him then."

"Do you have anyone in mind for a replacement?"
Tessa paced the floor.

"Not really. We've pretty much tapped out our list
of possibilities. Unless you can get Ryan to change his
mind?" She sounded hopeful.

"I considered that, and I've been trying to reach him
all day. But just now, I came up with another idea." She
paused, hoping that Alexis would stop her. Tell her that
they didn't need anyone else. When the woman didn't
respond, she continued. "I was thinking that I might
replace my brother in the lineup." She rushed the words
out before she could chicken out. "I know that this is a
bachelor auction, not a bachelorette—"

"Yes!" Alexis squealed, as if it were the best idea
she'd heard all day. "OMG, I think that's an absolutely
fabulous idea. We'll provide something for the fellas,
too. Oh, Tessa, this is brilliant. I love it."

"Are you sure? I mean, I like the idea of doing something completely unexpected, but maybe we should see
what Rachel thinks." Her heart hammered in her chest.

She'd done something bold, something different, by
offering to take Tripp's place. But now, the thought of
actually walking that stage and praying to God that
someone…anyone…would bid on her was giving her
heart palpitations.

"That's a good idea, but I know she's going to agree with me. Hold on."

"Oh, you're calling her now?" Tessa said to the empty room as she paced the floor.

Rachel Kincaid was a marketing genius and an old college friend of Alexis's. She'd come to Royal as a young widow and the mother to an adorable little girl named Ellie. And she'd fallen in love with one of the most eligible bachelors in all of Texas, oil tycoon Matt Galloway.

"Okay, Rachel's on the line," Alexis announced a moment later. "And I brought her up to speed."

"You weren't kidding about doing something unexpected." There was a hint of awe in Rachel's voice. "Good for you, Tess."

"Thanks, Rachel." She swallowed hard. "But do you think it's a good idea? I mean, the programs have already been printed, and no one knows that there's going to be a bachelorette in the auction. What if no one bids on me? I don't want to cause any embarrassment to the club or create negative publicity for the event."

"Honey, the bachelors who aren't in the auction are going to go crazy when they discover there's a beautiful lady to bid on," Rachel said confidently.

"We'll put the word out that there's going to be a big surprise, just for the fellas. I can email everyone on our mailing list. It will only take me a few minutes to put the email together and send it out," Alexis said.

"Y'all are sure we can pull this off?" Tess asked one last time. "I swear I won't be offended if you think we can't. I rather you tell me now than to let me get up there and make a fool of myself."

"It's going to be awesome," Alexis reassured her.

"But I'm sensing hesitation. Are you second-guessing your decision? Because you shouldn't. It's a good one."

Tessa grabbed a spoon and the pint of her favorite Neapolitan ice cream hidden in the back of the freezer. She sat at the kitchen island and sighed, rubbing her palm on her jeans again. She shook her head, casting another glance in the mirror. "It's just that… I'm not the glamorous type, that's for sure."

"You're gorgeous, girl. And if you're concerned… hey, why don't we give you a whole beauty makeover for the event?" Rachel said excitedly. "It'll be fun and it gives me another excuse to buy makeup."

"That's a fantastic idea, Rachel!" Alexis chimed in. "Not that you need it," she added. "But maybe it'll make you feel more comfortable."

"Okay, yeah. That sounds great. I'd like that." Tessa nodded, feeling slightly better. "I was gonna take tomorrow off anyway. Give myself plenty of time to get ready. But I'm sure you both have a million things to do. I don't want to distract you from preparing for the auction, just to babysit me."

"Alexis is the queen of organization. She's got everything under control. Plus, we have a terrific crew of volunteers," Rachel piped in. "They won't miss us for a few hours. I promise, everything will be fine."

"Have you considered what date you're offering?"

"Date?" Tessa hadn't thought that far in advance. "I'm not sure. I guess…let me think about that. I'll have an answer for you by tomorrow. Is that all right?"

"That's fine. Just let me know first thing in the morning," Alexis said.

"I'll make a few appointments for the makeover

and I'll text you both all the details." Rachel's voice brimmed with excitement.

"Then I guess that's everything," Tessa said, more to herself than her friends. "I'll see you both tomorrow."

She hung up the phone, took a deep breath, and shoveled a spoonful of Neapolitan ice cream into her mouth.

There was no turning back now.

Three

Ryan patted the warm neck of his horse, Phantom, and dismounted, handing the majestic animal off to Ned, one of his ranch hands. He gave the horse's haunches one final pat as the older man led him away to a stall.

Ryan wiped his sweaty forehead with the back of his hand. He was tired, dirty and in desperate need of a shower.

He'd been out on the ranch and the surrounding area since the crack of dawn, looking for several steer that had made their great escape through a break in the fence. While his men repaired the fence, he and another hand tracked down the cattle and drove them back to the ranch.

He'd been in such a hurry to get after the cattle, he'd left his phone at home. Hopefully, his parents hadn't called, worried that he wasn't answering because he'd burned down the whole damn place.

He grumbled to himself, "You nearly burn the barn down as a kid, and they never let you forget it."

Then again, his parents and Tess and Tripp's seemed to be enjoying themselves on their cruise. Their calls had become far less frequent.

Who knows? Maybe both couples would decide it was finally time to retire, give up ranch life, and pass the torch to the next generation. Something he, Tessa and Tripp had been advocating for the past few years. They were ready to take on the responsibility.

When he'd been engaged to Sabrina, his parents had planned to retire to their beach house in Galveston and leave management of the ranch to him. Despite the fact that they hadn't much liked his intended. Not because Sabrina was a bad person. But he and Sabrina were like fire and ice. The moments that were good could be really good. But the moments that weren't had resulted in tense arguments and angry sex.

His mother, in particular, hadn't been convinced Sabrina was the girl for him. She'd been right.

A few months before their wedding, Sabrina had called it off. She just couldn't see herself as a ranch wife. Nor was she willing to sacrifice her well-earned figure to start "popping out babies" to carry on the Bateman name.

He appreciated that she'd had the decency to tell him to his face, well in advance, rather than abandoning him at the altar as Shelby Arthur had done when she'd decided she couldn't marry Jared Goodman.

At least she'd spared him *that* humiliation.

Besides, there was a part of him that realized the truth of what she'd said. Maybe some part of him had always understood that he'd asked her to marry him because it felt like the right thing to do.

He'd been with Sabrina longer than he'd stayed in any relationship. For over a year. So when she'd hinted that she didn't want to waste her time in a relationship that wasn't going anywhere, he'd popped the question.

Neither he nor Sabrina were the type who bought into the fairy tale of romance. They understood that relationships were an exchange. A series of transactions, sustained over time. Which was why he believed they were a good fit. But they'd both ignored an essential point. They were just too different.

He loved everything about ranch life, and Sabrina was a city girl, through and through.

The truth was that he'd been relieved when Sabrina had canceled the wedding. As if he could breathe, nice, deep, easy breaths, for the first time in months. Still, his parents called off their plans to retire.

Maybe this trip would convince them that he and the Bateman Ranch would be just fine without them.

Ryan stretched and groaned. His muscles, taut from riding in the saddle a good portion of the day, protested as he made his way across the yard toward the house.

Helene Dennis, their longtime house manager, threw open the door and greeted him. "There you are. You look an unholy mess. Take off those boots and don't get my kitchen floor all dirty. I just mopped."

Sometimes he wondered if Helene worked for him or if he worked for her. Still, he loved the older woman. She was family.

"All right, all right." He toed off his boots and kicked them in the corner, patting his arms and legs to dislodge any dust from his clothing before entering the house. "Just don't shoot."

Helene playfully punched his arm. "Were you able to round up all of the animals that got loose?"

"Every one of them." Yawning, he kneaded a stubborn kink in his back. "Fence is fixed, too."

"Good. Dinner will be ready in about a half an hour. Go ahead and hop in the shower. Oh, and call Tess when you get the chance."

"Why?" His chest tightened. "Everything okay over at the Noble Spur?"

"Don't worry." She gave him a knowing smile that made his cheeks fill with heat. "She's fine, but her brother is ill. Tess is pretty sure it's food poisoning. She's been trying to reach you all day."

"I was in such a hurry to get out of here this morning, I forgot my phone."

"I know." She chuckled softly "I found it in the covers when I made your bed this morning. It's on your nightstand."

Managing a tired smile for the woman he loved almost as much as his own mother, he leaned in and kissed her cheek. "Thanks, Helene. I'll be down for dinner as soon as I can."

Ryan dried his hair from the shower and wrapped the towel around his waist. The hot water had felt good sluicing over his tired, aching muscles. So he'd taken a longer shower than he'd intended. And though he was hungry, he was tempted to collapse into bed and forgo dinner.

Sighing wearily, he sat on the bed and picked up his phone to call Tess.

She answered in a couple of rings. "Hey, Rye. How'd it go? Were you able to find all the steer you lost?"

Helene had evidently told her where he was and why he hadn't been answering his cell phone.

"Yes, we got them all back and the fence is fixed." He groaned as he reached out to pick up his watch and put it back on. "How's Tripp? Helene said he got food poisoning."

"Wow, you sound like you've been ridden hard and put away wet." She laughed. "And yes, my brother's penchant for late night snacks from suspect eateries finally caught up with him. He looks and feels like hell, but otherwise he's recovering."

"Will he be okay for the auction tomorrow?"

"No." She said the word a little too quickly, then paused a little too long. "He thinks he'll be fine to go through with it, but I'm chalking that up to illness-induced delusion."

"Did you tell Alexis she's a man down?"

"I did." There was another unusual pause. Like there was something she wanted to say but was hesitant.

Ryan thought for a moment as he rummaged through his drawers for something to put on.

"Ahh…" He dragged his fingers through his damp hair. "Of course. She wants to know if I'll take Tripp's place."

Tessa didn't respond right away. "Actually, that's why I was trying so hard to reach you. I thought I might be able to convince you to take Tripp's place…since it's for such a good cause. But when I couldn't reach you, I came up with another option."

"Which is?" It was like pulling teeth to get Tess to just spit it out. He couldn't imagine why that would be…unless he wasn't going to like what she had to say. Uneasiness tightened his gut. "So this other option… are you going to tell me, or should I come over and you can act it out in charades?"

"Smart-ass." She huffed. "No charades necessary. *I'm* the other option. I decided to take Tripp's place in the auction."

"You do know that it's women who will be bidding in this auction, right?" Ryan switched to speakerphone, tossed his phone on the bed, then stepped into his briefs. "Anything you need to tell me, Tess?"

"I'm going to give you a pass because I know you're tired," she groused. "And we've already considered that. If you check your in-box, you'll see that Alexis sent out an email informing all attendees and everyone else on the mailing list that there is going to be a surprise at the end of the auction, just for the gents."

"Oh."

It was the only thing that Ryan could think to say as the realization struck him in the gut like a bull running at full speed. A few days ago, he'd been discomfited by the idea of his friend bidding on one man. Now, there would be who knows how many guys angling for a night with her.

"You sure about this?" He stepped into a pair of well-worn jeans and zipped and buttoned them. "This just doesn't seem much like you."

"That's exactly why I'm doing it." Her voice was shaky. "It'll be good for me to venture outside of my comfort zone."

He donned a long-sleeved T-shirt, neither of them speaking for a moment.

Ryan rubbed his chin and sank on to his mattress.

He slipped on a pair of socks. "Look, I know I said I didn't want to do it, but with Tripp being sick and all, how about I make an exception?"

"You think this is a really bad idea, don't you?" She choked out the words, her feelings obviously hurt.

"No, that's not what I'm saying at all." The last thing he wanted to do was upset his best friend. He ran a hand through his hair. "I'm just saying that it's really last minute. And because of that, it might take people by surprise, that's all."

"I thought of that, too. Alexis and Rachel are positive they can drum up enough interest. But I thought that…just to be safe…it'd be good to have an ace up my sleeve."

"What kind of an ace?"

"I'm going to give you the money to bid on me, in case no one else does. I know it'll still look pretty pathetic if my best friend is the only person who bids on me, but that's a hell of a lot better than hearing crickets when they call my name."

"You want me to bid on you?" He repeated the words. Not that he hadn't heard or understood her the first time. He was just processing the idea. Him bidding on his best friend. The two of them going out on a date…

"Yes, but it'll be my money. And there's no need for us to actually go on the date. I mean, we can just hang out like usual or something, but it doesn't have to be a big deal."

"Sure, I'll do it. But you don't need to put up the money. I'm happy to make the donation myself."

His leg bounced. Despite what his friend believed, Ryan doubted that he'd be the only man there willing to bid on Tessa Noble during her bachelorette auction.

"Thanks, Ryan. I appreciate this." She sounded relieved. "And remember, you'll only need to bid on me if no one else does. If nothing else, your bid might prompt someone else to get into the spirit."

"Got it," he said gruffly. "You can count on me."

"I know. Thanks again, Rye." He could hear the smile in her sweet voice.

"Hey, since Tripp won't be able to make it…why don't we ride in together?"

"Actually, I'm going straight to the auction from… somewhere else. But I'll catch a ride with a friend, so we can ride home together. How's that?"

"Sounds good." He couldn't help the twinge of disappointment he felt at only getting to ride home with her. "I guess I'll see you there."

"I'll be the one with the price tag on her head." Tessa forced a laugh. "Get some rest, Rye. And take some pain meds. Otherwise, your arm'll be too sore to lift the auction paddle."

Her soft laughter was the last thing he heard before the line went dead. Before he could say good-night.

Ryan released a long sigh and slid his feet into his slippers. He didn't like the idea of Tess putting herself on the auction block for every letch in town to leer at. But she was a grown woman who was capable of making her own decisions.

Regardless of how much he disagreed with them.

Besides, he wasn't quite sure what it was that made him feel more uneasy. Tess being bid on by other men, or the idea that he might be the man who won her at the end of the night.

Four

Tessa had never been plucked, primped and prodded this much in her entire life.

She'd been waxed in places she didn't even want to think about and had some kind of wrap that promised to tighten her curves. And the thick head of curls she adored had been straightened and hung in tousled waves around her shoulders. Now Milan Valez, a professional makeup artist, was applying her makeup.

"I thought we were going with a natural look," Tess objected when the woman opened yet another product and started to apply what had to be a third or fourth layer of goop to her face.

"This *is* the natural look." The woman rolled her eyes. "If I had a dime for every client who doesn't realize that what they're calling the natural look is actually a full face." The woman sighed, but her expression softened as she directed Tess to turn her head. "You're a beautiful woman with gorgeous skin. If you're not a makeup wearer, I know it feels like a lot. But I'm just using a few tricks to enhance your natural beauty. We'll make those beautiful eyes pop, bring a little drama to these pouty lips, and highlight your incredible cheek-bones. I promise you won't look too heavily made up. Just trust me."

Tessa released a quiet sigh and nodded. "I trust you."

"Good. Now just sit back and relax. Your friends should be here shortly. They're going to be very pleased, and I think you will, too." The woman smiled. "Now look up."

Tessa complied as Milan applied liner beneath her eyes. "You sure I can't have a little peek?"

"Your friends made me promise. No peeking. And you agreed." She lifted Tess's chin. "Don't worry, honey, you won't have to wait much longer."

"Tessa? Oh my God, you look…incredible." Rachel entered the salon a few minutes later and clapped a hand over her mouth. "I can hardly believe it's you."

Alexis nearly slammed into the back of Rachel, who'd made an abrupt stop. She started to complain, but when she saw Tessa, her mouth gaped open, too.

"Tess, you look…stunning. Not that you aren't always beautiful, but…wow. Just wow."

"You two are making me seriously self-conscious right now." Tessa kept her focus on Milan.

"Don't be," the woman said emphatically. "Remember what we talked about. I've only enhanced what was already there."

Tessa inhaled deeply and nodded. She ignored the butterflies in her stomach in response to the broad grins and looks of amazement on Alexis's and Rachel's faces.

"There, all done." Milan sat back proudly and grinned. "Honey, you look absolutely beautiful. Ready to see for yourself?"

"Please." Even as Tessa said it, her hands were trembling, and a knot tightened in her stomach. How could something as simple as looking in the mirror be so fraught with anxiety? It only proved she wasn't cut out for this whole glamour-girl thing.

Milan slowly turned the chair around and Alexis and Rachel came over to stand closer, both of them bouncing excitedly.

Tessa closed her eyes, took a deep breath and then opened them.

"Oh my God." She leaned closer to the mirror. "I can hardly believe that's me." She sifted her fingers through the dark, silky waves with toffee-colored highlights. "I mean, it looks like me, just...more glamourous."

"I know, isn't it incredible? You're going to be the star of the evening. We need to keep you hidden until you walk across the stage. Really take everyone by surprise." Rachel grinned in the mirror from behind her.

"Oh, that's a brilliant idea, Rachel," Alexis agreed. "It'll have more impact."

"This is only the beginning." Rachel's grin widened. "Just wait until they get a load of your outfit tonight. Every man in that room's jaw will hit the floor."

Tessa took another deep breath, then exhaled as she stared at herself in the mirror. Between her makeover and the daring outfit she'd chosen, there was no way Ryan, or anyone else, would take her for one of the boys.

Her heart raced and her belly fluttered as she antici-pated his reaction. She couldn't wait to see the look of surprise on Ryan's face.

Ryan entered the beautiful gardens where The Great Royal Bachelor Auction was being held. Alexis Slade, James Harris and the rest of the committee had gone out of their way to create a festive and beautiful setting for the event. Fragrant wreaths and sprigs of greenery were strung from the pergolas. Two towering trees dec-orated with gorgeous ornaments dominated the area. Poinsettias, elegant red bows and white lights deco-rated the space, giving it a glowing, ethereal feel. The garden managed to be both romantic and festive. The kind of setting that almost made you regret not having someone to share the night with.

He sipped his Jack and Coke and glanced around the vicinity. Everyone who was anyone was in attendance. He made his way through the room, mingling with Carter Mackenzie and Shelby Arthur, Matt Galloway and Rachel Kincaid, Austin and Brooke Bradshaw, and all of the other members of the club who'd turned out for the event. Several of the bachelors moved around the space, drumming up anticipation for the auction and doing their best to encourage a bidding frenzy.

But Tessa was nowhere to be found. Had she changed her mind? He was looking forward to hang-ing out with her tonight, but he'd understand if she'd gotten cold feet. Hell, there was a part of him that was relieved to think that maybe she'd bailed.

Then again, Tess had said she'd be coming from somewhere else. So maybe she was just running late.

He resisted the urge to pull out his cell phone and

find out exactly where she was. For once in his life, he'd be patient. Even if it killed him.

"Ryan, it's good to see you." James Harris, president of the Texas Cattleman's Club, shook his hand. "I hate that we couldn't convince you to be one of our bachelor's tonight, but I'm glad you joined us just the same."

"Didn't see your name on the list of bachelors either." Ryan smirked, and both men laughed.

"Touché." James took a gulp of his drink and Ryan did the same.

"Looks like y'all are doing just fine without me." Ryan gestured to the space. "I wouldn't have ever imagined this place could look this good."

"Alexis Slade outdid herself with this whole romantic winter wonderland vibe." James's eyes trailed around the space. "To be honest, I wasn't sure exactly how her vision would come together, but she's delivered in spades. I'm glad we gave her free rein to execute it as she saw fit."

"Judging from everyone here's reaction, you've got a hit on your hands." Ryan raised his glass before finishing the last of his drink.

"Let's just hope it motivates everyone to dig deep in their pockets tonight." James patted Ryan on the back. "I'd better go chat with Rose Clayton." He nodded toward the older woman, who looked stunning in her gown. The touch of gray hair at her temples gleamed in the light. "But I'll see you around."

"You bet." Ryan nodded toward the man as he traversed the space and greeted Rose.

"Ryan, how are you?" Gail Walker took a sip of her drink and grinned. "You look particularly handsome tonight. But I see Alexis still wasn't able to talk you into joining the list of eligible bachelors."

"Not my thing, but looks like they've got plenty of studs on the schedule for you to choose from." Ryan sat his empty glass on a nearby tray. "And you clean up pretty well yourself."

"Thanks." She smoothed a hand over the skirt of her jewel-tone green dress. "But I've got my eye on one bachelor in particular." Her eyes shone with mischief. "And I'm prepared to do whatever it takes to get him."

"Well, I certainly wouldn't want to be the woman who has to run up against you." Ryan chuckled. "Good luck."

"Thanks, Ryan. See you around." Gail made her way through the crowd, mingling with other guests.

Ryan accepted a napkin and a few petite quiches from a server passing by. Ignoring the anticipation that made his heart beat a little faster as he considered the prospect of bidding on his friend.

Tessa paced the space that served as the bachelors' green room. Everyone else had spent most of the night mingling. They came to the green room once the start of the auction drew closer. But she'd been stuck here the entire evening, biding her time until she was scheduled to make her grand entrance.

"Tessa Noble? God, you look…incredible." Daniel Clayton shoved a hand in his pocket. "But what are you doing here? Wait…are you the surprise?"

"Guilty." Her cheeks warmed as she bit into another quiche.

She tried her best not to ruin the makeup that Milan had so painstakingly applied. The woman had assured her that she could eat and drink without the lipstick fading or feathering. But Tess still found herself being extra careful.

"Everyone will definitely be surprised," he said, then added, "Not that you don't look good normally."

"It's okay, Daniel. I get it." She mumbled around a mouth full of quiche. "It was a surprise to me, too."

He chuckled, running a hand through his jet-black hair. "You must be tired of people telling you how different you look. How did Tripp and Ryan react?"

"Neither of them has seen me yet." She balled up her napkin and tossed it in the trash. "I'm a little nervous about their reaction."

"Don't be," Daniel said assuredly. "I can't imagine a man alive could find fault with the way you look tonight." He smiled, then scrubbed a hand across his forehead. "Or any night...of course."

They both laughed.

"Well, thank you." She relaxed a little. "You already know why I feel like a fish out of water. But why do you look so out of sorts tonight?"

He exhaled heavily, the frown returning to his face. "For one thing, I'd rather not be in the lineup. I'm doing this at my grandmother's insistence."

"Ms. Rose seems like a perfectly reasonable woman to me. And she loves you like crazy. I'm pretty sure if you'd turned her down she would've gotten over it fairly quickly."

"Maybe." He shrugged. "But the truth is that I owe my grandmother so much. Don't know where I would've ended up if it wasn't for her. Makes it hard to say no." A shadow of sadness passed over his handsome face, tugging at Tessa's heart.

Daniel had been raised by Rose Clayton after his own mother dumped him on her. It made Tessa's heart ache for him. She couldn't imagine the pain Daniel must feel at being abandoned by a woman who preferred drugs and booze to her own son.

"Of course." Tess nodded, regretting her earlier flippant words. She hadn't considered the special relationship that Daniel had with his grandmother and how grateful he must be to her. "I wasn't thinking."

They were both quiet for a moment, when she remembered his earlier words.

"You said 'for one thing.' What's the other reason you didn't want to do this?"

The pained look on Daniel's face carved deep lines in his forehead and between his brows. He drained the glass of whiskey in his hand.

"It's nothing," he said in a dismissive tone that made it clear that they wouldn't be discussing it any further.

She was digging herself deeper into a hole with every question she asked of Daniel tonight. Better for her to move on. She wished him luck and made her way over to the buffet table.

"Hey, Tessa." Lloyd Richardson put another slider on his small plate. "Wow, you look pretty amazing."

"Thanks, Lloyd." She decided against the slider and put some carrots and a cherry tomato on her plate instead.

There wasn't much room to spare in her fitted pantsuit. She wore a jacket over the sleeveless garment to hide the large cutout that revealed most of her back. That had been one idea of Rachel's for which she'd been grateful.

"Hey, you must be plum sick of people saying that

to you by now." Lloyd seemed to recognize the discomfort she felt at all of the additional attention she'd
been getting.

Tess gave him a grateful smile. No wonder her
friend Gail Walker had a crush on Lloyd. He was handsome, sweet and almost a little shy. Which was probably why he hadn't made a move on Gail, since he
certainly seemed interested in her.

"Okay, bachelors and bachelorette." Alexis acknowledged Tess with a slight smile. "The proceedings will
begin in about ten minutes. So finish eating, take a
quick bathroom break, whatever you need to do so
you'll be ready to go on when your number is called."

Alexis had her serious, drill sergeant face on. Something Tessa knew firsthand that a woman needed to
adopt when she was responsible for managing a crew
of men—be they ranchers or ranch hands.

Still, there was something in her eyes. Had she been
crying?

Before she could approach Alexis and ask if she
was all right, she noticed the look Alexis and Daniel Clayton exchanged. It was brief, but meaningful.
Chock full of pain.

Could Alexis be the other reason Daniel hadn't
wanted to be in the bachelor auction? But from the
look of things, whatever was going on between them
certainly wasn't sunshine and roses.

Tessa caught up with Alexis as she grabbed the door
handle.

"Alexis." Tessa lowered her voice as she studied
her friend's face. "Is everything okay? You look like
you've been—"

"I'm fine." Alexis swiped at the corner of one eye,

her gaze cast downward. "I just… I'm fine." She forced a smile, finally raising her eyes to meet Tessa's. "You're going to kill them tonight. Just wait until you come out of that jacket. We're going to have to scrape everyone's jaws off the floor." She patted Tess's shoulder. "I'd tell you good luck, but something tells me that you aren't going to need it tonight."

With that, Alexis dipped out of the green room and was gone.

When Tess turned around, Daniel was standing there, staring after the other woman. He quickly turned away, busying himself with grabbing a bottle of water from the table.

There was definitely something going on with the two of them. And if there was, Tessa could understand why they wouldn't want to make their relationship public. Daniel's grandmother, Rose Clayton, and Alexis's grandfather, Gus Slade, once an item, had been feuding for years.

In recent months, they seemed to at least have found the civility to be decent toward one another. Most likely for the sake of everyone around them. Still, there was no love lost between those two families.

"Looks like Royal has its very own Romeo and Juliet," she muttered under her breath.

Tess took her seat, her hands trembling slightly and butterflies fluttering in her stomach. She closed her eyes, imagining how Ryan would react to seeing her out there on that stage.

Five

Ryan hung back at the bar as the bachelor auction wound down. There were just a couple more bachelors on the list, then Tess would be up.

He gulped the glass of water with lemon he was drinking. He'd talked to just about everyone here. But with neither Tripp nor Tess to hang out with, he'd been ready to leave nearly an hour ago.

Then again, his discomfort had little to do with him going stag for the night and everything to do with the fact that his best friend would be trotted out onto the stage and bid on. His gaze shifted around the garden at the unattached men in attendance. Most of them were members of the Texas Cattleman's Club. Some of them second, third or even fourth generation. All of them were good people, as far as he knew. So why was he assessing them all suspiciously? Wondering which of them would bid on his best friend.

The next bachelor, Lloyd Richardson, was called onto the stage and Alexis read his bio. Women were chomping at the bit to bid on the guy. Including Gail Walker. She'd started with a low, reasonable bid. But four or five other women were countering her bids as quickly as she was making them.

First the bid was in the hundreds, then the thousands. Suddenly, Steena Goodman, a wealthy older woman whose husband had been active in the club for many years before his death, stood and placed her final bid. Fifty-thousand dollars.

Ryan nearly coughed. What was it about this guy that had everyone up in arms?

Steena's bid was much higher than the previous bid of nine thousand dollars. The competing bidders pouted, acknowledging their defeat.

But not Gail. She looked angry and hurt. She stared Steena down, her arms folded and breathing heavily.

Alexis glanced back and forth at the two women for a moment. When Rachel nudged her, she cleared her throat and resumed her duties as auctioneer. "Going once, going twice—"

"One hundred thousand dollars." Gail stared at Steena, as if daring her to outbid her.

The older woman huffed and put her paddle down on the table, conceding the bid.

"Oh my God! One hundred thousand dollars." Alexis began the sentence nearly shrieking but ended with an implied question mark.

Probably because she was wondering the same thing he was.

Where in the hell did Gail Walker get that kind of cash?

Alexis declared Gail the winner of the bid at one hundred thousand dollars.

The woman squealed and ran up on stage. She wrapped her arms around Lloyd's neck and pulled him down for a hot, steamy kiss. Then she grabbed his hand and dragged him off the stage and through the doors that led from the garden back into the main building.

Ryan leaned against the bar, still shocked by Gail's outrageous bid. He sighed. Just one more bachelor, Daniel Clayton. Then Tess was up.

"That was certainly unexpected." Gus Slade ordered a beer from the bar. "Had no idea she was sitting on that kind of disposable cash."

"Neither did I, but I guess we all have our little secrets."

The older man grimaced, as if he'd taken exception to Ryan's words. Which only made Ryan wonder what secrets the old man might be hiding.

"Yes, well, I s'pose that's true." Gus nodded, then walked away.

Ryan turned his attention back to the stage just in time to see Daniel Clayton being whisked away excitedly by an overeager bidder.

There was a noticeable lull as Alexis watched the woman escort Daniel away. Rachel placed a hand on her cohost's back as she took the microphone from Alexis and thanked her for putting on a great event and being an incredible auctioneer.

Alexis seemed to recover from the momentarily stunned look she'd had seconds earlier. She nodded toward Rachel and then to the crowd which clapped appreciatively.

"This has been an amazing night, and thanks to

your generosity, ladies, and to the generosity of our bachelors, we've already exceeded our fund-raising goal for tonight. So thank you all for that. Give yourselves a big hand."

Rachel clapped a hand against the inside of her wrist as the rest of the audience clapped, hooted and shouted.

"But we're not done yet. It's time for the surprise you gents have been waiting for this evening. Fellas, please welcome our lone bachelorette, Miss Tessa Noble."

Ryan pulled out his phone. He'd promised Tripp that he'd record his sister's big debut.

There was a collective gasp in the room as Tessa stepped out onto the stage. Ryan moved away from the bar, so he could get a better view of his friend.

His jaw dropped, and his phone nearly clattered to the ground.

"Tess?" Ryan choked out the word, then silently cursed himself, realizing his stunned reaction would end up on the video. He snapped his gaping mouth shut as he watched her strut across the stage in a glamorous red pantsuit that seemed to be designed for the express purpose of highlighting her killer curves.

Damn, she's fine.

He wasn't an idiot. Nor was he blind. So he wasn't oblivious to the fact that his best friend also happened to be an extremely beautiful woman. And despite her tomboy wardrobe, he was fully aware of the hot body buried beneath relaxed fit clothing. But today…those curves had come out to play.

As if she was a professional runway model, Tess pranced to the end of the stage in strappy, glittery heels, put one hand on her hip and cocked it to the side. She seemed buoyed by the crowd's raucous reaction.

First there was the collective gasp, followed by a chorus of Oh my Gods. Now the crowd was whooping and shouting.

A slow grin spread across her lips, painted a deep, flirtatious shade of red that made him desperate to taste them. She turned and walked back toward where Rachel stood, revealing a large, heart-shaped cutout that exposed the warm brown skin of her open back. A large bow was tied behind her graceful neck.

Tessa Noble was one gift he'd give just about anything to unwrap.

She was incredibly sexy with a fiercely confident demeanor that only made him hunger for her more.

Ryan surveyed the crowd. He obviously wasn't the only man in the room drooling over Tessa 2.0. He stared at the large group of men who were wide-eyed, slack-jawed and obviously titillated by the woman on stage.

Tessa's concerns that no one would bid on her were obviously misplaced. There were even a couple of women who seemed to be drooling over her.

Ryan's heart thudded. Suddenly, there wasn't enough air in the tented, outdoor space. He grabbed his auction paddle and crept closer to the stage.

Rachel read Tessa's bio aloud, as Alexis had done with the bachelors who'd gone before her. Tessa stood tall with her back arched and one hand on her hip. She held her head high as she scanned the room.

Was she looking for him?

Ryan's cheeks flushed with heat. A dozen emotions percolated in his chest, like some strange, volatile mixture, as he studied his friend on stage. Initially, he wanted to rush the stage and drape his jacket over her shoulders. Block the other men's lurid stares. Then there was his own guttural reaction to seeing Tess this way. He wanted to devour her. Kiss every inch of the warm, brown skin on her back. Glide his hands over her luscious bottom. Taste those pouty lips.

He swallowed hard, conscious of his rapid breathing. He hoped the video wasn't picking that up, too.

Rachel had moved on from Tessa's bio to describing her date. "For the lucky gentleman with the winning bid, your very special outing with this most lovely lady will be every man's fantasy come true. Your football-themed date will begin with seats on the fifty-yard line to watch America's team play football against their division rivals. Plus, you'll enjoy a special tailgating meal before the game at a restaurant right there in the stadium. Afterward, you'll share an elegant steak dinner at a premium steak house."

"Shit." Ryan cringed, realizing that, too, would be captured on the video.

There was already a stampede of overly eager men ready to take Tessa up on her offer. Now she'd gone and raised the stakes.

Just great.

Ryan huffed, his free hand clenched in a fist at his side, as her words reverberated through him.

You're only supposed to bid if no one else does.

Suddenly, Tessa's gaze met his, and her entire face lit up in a broad smile that made her even more beautiful. A feat he wouldn't have thought possible.

His heart expanded in his chest as he returned her smile and gave her a little nod.

Tess stood taller. As if his smile had lifted her. Made her even more confident.

And why shouldn't she be? She'd commanded the attention of every man in the room, single or not. Had all the women in the crowd enviously whispering among themselves.

"All right, gentlemen, get your paddles ready, because it's your turn to bid on our lovely bachelorette." Rachel grinned proudly.

He'd bet anything she was behind Tessa's incredible makeover. Ryan didn't know if he wanted to thank her or blame her for messing up a good thing. Back when no one else in town realized what a diamond his Tess was.

He shook his head. *Get it together, Bateman. She doesn't belong to you.*

"Shall we open the bidding at five-hundred dollars?" Rachel asked the crowd.

"A thousand dollars." Clem Davidson, a man his father's age, said.

"Fifteen hundred," Bo Davis countered. He was younger than Clem, but still much older than Tess.

Ryan clenched the paddle in his hand so tightly he thought it might snap in two as several of the men bid furiously for Tess. His heart thumped. Beads of sweat formed over his brow and trickled down his back as his gaze and the camera's shifted from the crowd of enthusiastic bidders to Tessa's shocked expression and then back again.

"Ten thousand bucks." Clem held his paddle high and looked around the room, as if daring anyone else to bid against him. He'd bid fifteen hundred dollars more than Bo's last bid.

Bo grimaced, but then nodded to Clem in concession.

"Twelve thousand dollars." It nearly came as a surprise to Ryan that the voice was his own.

Clem scowled. "Thirteen thousand."

"Fifteen thousand." Now Ryan's voice was the one that was indignant as he stared the older man down.

Clem narrowed his gaze at Ryan, his jaw clenched. He started to raise his paddle, but then his expression softened. Head cocked to the side, he furrowed his brows for a moment. Suddenly, he nodded to Ryan and put his paddle back down at his side.

"Fifteen thousand dollars going once. Fifteen thousand dollars going twice." Rachel looked around the room, excitedly. "Sold! Ryan Bateman, you may claim your bachelorette."

Ryan froze for a moment as everyone in the room looked at him, clapping and cheering. Many of them with knowing smiles. He cleared his throat, ended the recording and slowly made his way toward the stage and toward his friend who regarded him with utter confusion.

He stuffed his phone into his pocket, gave Tess an awkward hug and pressed a gentle kiss to her cheek for the sake of the crowd.

They all cheered, and he escorted Tess off the stage. Then Rachel and Alexis wrapped up the auction.

"Oh my God, what did you just do?" Tessa whispered loudly enough for him to hear her over all the noise.

"Can't rightly say I know," he responded, not looking at her, but fully aware of his hand on her waist, his thumb resting on the soft skin of her back. Electricity sparked in his fingertips. Trailed up his arm.

"I appreciate what you did, Rye. It was a very generous donation. But I thought we agreed you would only bid if no one else did." Tessa folded her arms as she stared at him, searching his face for an answer.

"I know, and I was following the plan, I was. But I just couldn't let you go home with a guy like Clem."

Tessa stared up into his green eyes, her own eyes widening in response. Ryan Bateman was her oldest and closest friend. She knew just about everything there was to know about him. But the man standing before her was a mystery.

He'd gone beyond his usual protectiveness of her and had landed squarely into possessive territory. To be honest, it was kind of a turn-on. Which was problematic. Because Rye was her best friend. Emphasis on *friend*.

She folded her arms over her chest, suddenly self-conscious about whether the tightening of her nipples was visible through the thin material.

"And what, exactly, is it that you have against Clem?"

Ryan shook his head. "Nothing really." He seemed dazed, maybe even a little confused himself. "I just didn't want you to go out with him. He's too old for you."

"That's ageist." She narrowed her gaze.

It was true that she'd certainly never considered Clem Davidson as anything other than a nice older man. Still, it wasn't right for Ryan to single him out because of his age. It was a football date. Plain and simple. There would be no sex. With anyone.

"Clem isn't that much older than us, you know. Ten or fifteen years, tops." She relaxed her arms and ran her fingers through the silky waves that she still hadn't gotten accustomed to.

Ryan seemed to tense at the movement. He clenched his hand at his side, then nodded. "You're right on both counts. But what's done is done." He shrugged.

"What if it had been Bo instead? Would you have outbid him, too?"

"Yes." He seemed to regret his response, or at least the conviction with which he'd uttered the word. "I mean...yes," he said again.

"You just laid down fifteen grand for me," Tess said as they approached the bar. "The least I can do is buy you a drink."

She patted her hips, then remembered that her money and credit cards were in her purse backstage.

"Never mind. I've got it. Besides, I'm already running a tab." Ryan ordered a Jack and Coke for himself and one for her, which she turned down, requesting club soda with lime instead. "You...uh...you look pretty incredible."

"Thanks." She tried to sound grateful for the compliment, but when everyone fawned over how good she looked tonight, all she heard was the implication that her everyday look was a hot mess.

Her tomboy wardrobe had been a conscious choice, beginning back in grade school. She'd developed early. Saw how it had changed the other kids' perception of her. With the exception of Ryan, the boys she'd been friends with were suddenly more fascinated with her budding breasts than anything she had to say. And they'd come up with countless ways to cop an "accidental" feel.

Several of the girls were jealous of her newfound

figure and the resulting attention from the boys. They'd said hateful things to her and started blatantly false rumors about her, which only brought more unwanted attention from the boys.

Tess had recognized, even then, that the problem was theirs, not hers. That they were immature and stupid. Still, it didn't stop the things they'd said from hurting.

She'd been too embarrassed to tell Tripp or Ryan, who were a few grades ahead of her. And she was worried that Ryan's temper would get him in serious trouble. She hadn't told her parents, either. They would've come to her school, caused a scene and made her even more of a social pariah.

So she'd worn bulky sweaters, loose jeans and flannel shirts that masked her curves and made her feel invisible.

After a while, she'd gotten comfortable in her wardrobe. Made it her own. Until it felt like her daily armor.

Wearing a seductive red pantsuit, with her entire back exposed and every curve she owned on display, made her feel as vulnerable as if she'd traipsed across the stage naked.

But she was glad she'd done it. That she'd reclaimed a little of herself.

The bartender brought their drinks and Ryan stuffed a few dollars into the tip jar before taking a generous gulp of his drink.

"So, is this your new look?" An awkward smile lit Ryan's eyes. "'Cause it's gonna be mighty hard for you to rope a steer in that getup."

"Shut it, Rye." She pointed a finger at him, and they both laughed.

When they finally recovered from their laughter, she took his glass from his hand and took a sip of his drink. His eyes darkened as he watched her, his jaw tensing again.

"Not bad. Maybe I will have one." She handed it back to him.

Without taking his eyes off of her, Ryan signaled for the bartender to bring a Jack and Coke for her, too. There was something in his stare. A hunger she hadn't seen before.

She often longed for Ryan to see her as more than just "one of the boys." Now that it seemed he was finally seeing her that way, it was unsettling. His heated stare made her skin prickle with awareness.

The prospect of Ryan being as attracted to her as she was to him quickened her pulse and sent a shock of warmth through her body. But just as quickly, she thought of how her relationship with the boys in school had changed once they saw her differently.

That wasn't something she ever wanted to happen between her and Ryan. She could deal with her eternal, unrequited crush, but she couldn't deal with losing his friendship.

She cleared her throat, and it seemed to break them both from the spell they'd both fallen under.

They were just caught up in emotions induced by the incredibly romantic setting, the fact that she looked like someone wholly different than her everyday self, and the adrenaline they'd both felt during the auction. Assigning it meaning…that would be a grave mistake. One that would leave one or both of them sorely disappointed once the bubble of illusion burst.

"So…since it's just us, we don't need to go out on a

date. Because that would be…you know…weird. But, I'm totally down for hanging out. And seats on the fifty-yard line…so…yay."

"That's what I was really after." Ryan smirked, sipping his drink. "You could've been wearing a brown potato sack, and I still would've bid on those tickets. It's like the whole damned date had my name written all over it." His eyes widened with realization. "Wait… you did tailor it just for me, didn't you?"

Tessa's cheeks heated. She took a deep sip of her drink and returned it to the bar, waving a hand dismissively.

"Don't get ahead of yourself, partner. I simply used your tastes as a point of reference. After all, you, Tripp and my dad are the only men that I've been spending any significant time with these days. I figured if you'd like it, the bidders would, too."

"Hmm…" Ryan took another sip of his drink, almost sounding disappointed. "Makes sense, I guess."

"I'm glad you get it. Alexis and Rachel thought it was the least romantic thing they could imagine. They tried to talk me into something else. Something grander and more flowery."

"Which neither of us would've enjoyed." Ryan nodded. "And the makeover… I assume that was Rachel's idea, too."

"Both Alexis and Rachel came up with that one. Alexis got PURE to donate a spa day and the makeover, so it didn't cost me anything." Tessa tucked her hair behind her ear and studied her friend's face. "You don't like it?"

"No, of course I do. I love it. You look…incredible.

You really do. Your parents are going to flip when they see this." He patted the phone in his pocket.

"You recorded it? Oh no." Part of her was eager to see the video. Another part of her cringed at the idea of watching herself prance across that stage using the catwalk techniques she'd studied online.

But no matter how silly she might feel right now, she was glad she'd successfully worked her magic on the crowd.

The opening chords of one of her favorite old boy band songs drew her attention to the stage where the band was playing.

"Oh my God, I love that song." Tessa laughed, sipping the last of her drink and then setting the glass on the bar. "Do you remember what a crush I had on these guys?"

Rye chuckled, regarding her warmly over the rim of his glass as he finished off his drink, too. "I remember you playing this song on repeat incessantly."

"That CD was my favorite possession. I still can't believe I lost it."

Ryan lowered his gaze, his chin dipping. He tapped a finger on the bar before raising his eyes to hers again and taking her hand. "I need to make a little confession."

"You rat!" She poked him in the chest. "You did something to my CD, didn't you?"

A guilty smirk curled the edges of his mouth. "Tripp and I couldn't take it anymore. We might've trampled the thing with a horse or two, then dumped it."

"You two are awful." She realized that she'd gone a little overboard in her obsession with the group. But trampling the album with a horse? That was harsh.

"If I'm being honest, I've always felt incredibly

guilty about my role in the whole sordid affair." Ryan placed his large, warm hand on her shoulder. The tiny white lights that decorated the space were reflected in his green eyes. "Let me make it up to you."

"And just how do you plan to do that?" Tessa folded her arms, cocking a brow.

He pulled out his phone, swiped through a few screens. "First of all, I just ordered you another copy of that album—CD and digital."

She laughed. "You didn't need to do that, Rye."

"I did, and I feel much better now. Not just because it was wrong of us to take away something you loved so much. Because I hated having that secret between us all these years. You're the one person in the world I can tell just about anything. So it feels pretty damn good to finally clear my conscience." He dropped his hand from her shoulder.

"All right." She forced a smile, trying her best to hide her disappointment at the loss of his touch. "And what's the second thing?"

He held his large, open palm out to her. "It seems I've bought myself a date for the night. Care to dance?"

"You want to dance to this sappy, boy band song that you've always hated?"

He grabbed her hand and led her to the dance floor. "Then I guess there's one more confession I need to make... I've always kind of liked this song. I just didn't want your brother to think I'd gone soft."

Tessa laughed as she joined her best friend on the dance floor.

Six

Gus Slade watched as Tessa Noble and Ryan Bateman entered the dance floor, both of them laughing merrily. Gus shook his head. Ryan was one of the prospects he'd considered as a good match for his granddaughter Alexis. Only it was clear that Ryan and Tess were hung up on each other, even if the self-proclaimed "best friends" weren't prepared to admit it to themselves.

It was no wonder Ryan's brief engagement to that wannabe supermodel he'd met in the city didn't last long enough for the two of them to make it to the altar.

Encouraging Alexis to start something with the Bateman boy would only result in heartache for his granddaughter once Ryan and Tess finally recognized the attraction flickering between them.

He'd experienced that kind of hurt and pain in his life when the woman he'd once loved, whom he thought truly loved him, had suddenly turned against him, shutting him out of her life.

It was something he'd never truly gotten over. Despite a long and happy marriage that lasted until the death of his dear wife.

Gus glanced over at Rose Clayton, his chest tightening. Even after all these years, the woman was still gorgeous. Just a hint of gray was visible at her temples. The rest of her hair was the same dark brown it was when she was a girl. She wore it in a stylish, modern cut that befit a mature woman. Yet, anyone who didn't know her could easily mistake her for a much younger woman.

And after all these years, Rose Clayton still turned heads, including his. The woman managed to stay as slim now as she had been back when she was a young girl. Yet, there was nothing weak or frail about Rose Clayton.

Her every move, her every expression, exuded a quiet confidence that folks around Royal had always respected. And tonight, he had to admit that she looked simply magnificent.

Gus glanced around the tented garden area again. The space looked glorious. Better than he could ever have imagined when the club first decided to undertake a major renovation of this space and a few other areas of the club, which had been in operation since the 1920s.

Alexis had headed up the committee that put on the auction. And his granddaughter had truly outdone herself.

Gus searched the crowd for Alexis. Her duties as

Mistress of Ceremony appeared to be over for the night. Still, he couldn't locate her anywhere.

Gus walked toward the main building. Perhaps she was in the office or one of the other interior spaces. But as he looked through the glass pane, he could see Alexis inside, hemmed up by Daniel Clayton. From the looks of it, they were arguing.

Fists clenched at his sides, Gus willed himself to stay where he was rather than rushing inside and demanding that Daniel leave his granddaughter alone. If he did that, then Alexis would defend the boy.

That would defeat the purpose of the elaborate plan he and Rose Clayton had concocted to keep their grandkids apart.

So he'd wait there. Monitor the situation without interfering. He didn't want his granddaughter marrying any kin to Rose Clayton. Especially a boy with a mother like Stephanie Clayton. A heavy drinker who'd been in and out of trouble her whole life. A woman who couldn't be bothered to raise her own boy. Instead, she'd dumped him off on Rose who'd raised Daniel as if he was her own son.

From where he stood, it appeared that Daniel was pleading with Alexis. But she shoved his hand away when he tried to touch her arm.

Gus smirked, glad to see that someone besides him was getting the sharp end of that fierce stubborn streak she'd inherited from him.

Suddenly, his granddaughter threw her arms up and said something to Daniel that he obviously didn't like. Then she turned and headed his way.

Gus moved away from the door and around the corner to the bar as quickly and quietly as he could. He waited for her to pass by.

"Alexis!" Gus grabbed hold of her elbow as she hurried past him. He chuckled good-naturedly. "Where's the fire, darlin'?"

She didn't laugh. In fact, the poor thing looked dazed, like a wounded bird that had fallen out of the nest before it was time.

"Sorry, I didn't see you, Grandad." Her eyes didn't meet his. Instead, she looked toward the office where she was headed. "I'm sorry I don't have time to talk right now. I need to deal with a major problem."

"Alexis, honey, what is it? Is everything all right?"

"It will be, I'm sure. I just really need to take care of this now, okay?" Her voice trembled, seemed close to breaking.

"I wanted to tell you how proud I am of you. Tonight was magnificent and you've raised so much money for pancreatic cancer research. Your grandmother would be so very proud of you."

Alexis suddenly raised her gaze to his, the corners of her eyes wet with tears. Rather than the intended effect of comforting her, his words seemed to cause her distress.

"Alexis, what's wrong?" Gus pleaded with his darling girl. The pain in her blue eyes, rimmed with tears, tore at his heart. "Whatever it is, you can talk to me."

Before she could answer, Daniel Clayton passed by. He and Alexis exchanged a long, painful look. Then Daniel dropped his gaze and continued to the other side of the room.

"Alexis, darlin', what's going on?"

The tears spilled from her eyes. Alexis sucked in a deep breath and sniffled.

"It's nothing I can't handle, Grandad." She wiped away the tears with brusque swipes of her hand and shook her head. "Thank you for everything you said. I appreciate it. Really. But I need to take care of this issue. I'll see you back at home later, okay?"

Alexis pressed a soft kiss to his whiskered cheek. Then she hurried off toward the clubhouse offices.

Gus sighed, leaning against the bar. He dropped on to the stool, tapped the bar to get the bartender's attention, and ordered a glass of whiskey, neat. He gripped the hard, cold glass without moving it to his lips.

Their little plan was a partial success. Neither he nor Rose had been able to match their grandchildren up with an eligible mate. Yet, they'd done exactly what they'd set out to do. They'd driven a wedge between Daniel and Alexis.

So why didn't he feel good about what they'd done?

Because their grandkids were absolutely miserable.

What kind of grandfather could rejoice in the heartbreak of a beautiful girl like Alexis?

"Hello, Gus." Rose had sidled up beside him, and ordered a white wine spritzer. "The kids didn't look too happy with each other just now."

"That's an understatement, if ever I've heard one." He gripped his glass and gulped from it. "They're in downright misery."

"Is it that bad?" She glanced over at him momentarily, studying his pained look, before accepting her glass of wine and taking a sip.

"Honestly? I think it's even worse." He scrubbed a hand down his jaw. "I feel like a heel for causing baby girl so much pain. And despite all our machinations, neither of us has found a suitable mate for our respective grandchildren."

She nodded sagely. Pain dimmed the light in her gray eyes. And for a moment, the shadow that passed over her lovely face made her look closer to her actual years.

"I'm sorry that they're both hurting. But it's better that they have their hearts broken now than to have it happen down the road, when they're both more invested in the relationship." She glanced at him squarely. "We've both known that pain. It's a feeling that never leaves you. We're both living proof of that."

"I guess we are." Gus nodded, taking another sip of his whiskey. "But maybe there's something we hadn't considered." He turned around, his back to the bar.

"And what's that?" She turned on her bar stool, too, studying the crowd.

"Daniel and Alexis share our last names, but that doesn't make them us. And it doesn't mean they're doomed to our fates."

Rose didn't respond as she watched her grandson Daniel being fawned over by the woman who'd bought him at auction. He looked about as pleased by the woman's attentions as a man getting a root canal without anesthesia.

"We did what was in their best interests. The right thing isn't always the easiest thing. I know they're hurting now, but when they each find the person they were meant to be with, they'll be thankful this happened."

Rose paid for her drink and turned to walk away.

"Rose."

She halted, glancing over her shoulder without looking directly at him.

"What if the two of them were meant to be together? Will they be grateful we interfered then?"

A heavy sigh escaped her red lips, and she gathered her shawl around her before leaving.

His eyes trailed the woman as she walked away in a glimmering green dress. The dress was long, but form-fitting. And despite her age, Rose was as tantalizing in that dress as a cool drink of water on a hot summer day.

After all these years he still had a thing for Rose Clayton. What if it was the same for Daniel and Alexis?

He ordered another whiskey, neat, hoping to God that he and Rose hadn't made a grave mistake they'd both regret.

Seven

Ryan twirled Tessa on the dance floor and then drew her back into his arms as they danced to one of his favorite upbeat country songs. Everyone around them seemed to be singing along with the lyrics which were both funny and slightly irreverent.

Tessa turned her back to him, threw her hands up, and wiggled her full hips as she sang loudly.

His attention was drawn to the sway of those sexy hips keeping time to the music. Fortunately, her dancing was much more impressive than her singing. Something his anatomy responded to, even if he didn't want it to. Particularly not while they were in the middle of a crowded dance floor.

Ryan swallowed hard and tried to shove away the rogue thoughts trying to commandeer his good sense. He and Tessa were just two friends enjoying their night together. Having a good time.

Nothing to see here, folks.

"Everything okay?" Tessa had turned around, her beautiful brown eyes focused on him and a frown tugging down the corners of her mouth.

"Yeah, of course." He forced a smile. "I was just... thinking...that's all." He started to dance again, his movements forced and rigid.

Tessa regarded him strangely, but before she could probe further, Alexis appeared beside them looking flustered. Her eyes were red, and it looked like she'd been crying.

"Alexis, is something wrong?" Tessa turned to her friend and squeezed her hand.

"I'm afraid so. I've been looking everywhere for you two. Would you mind meeting with James and me in the office as soon as possible?" Alexis leaned in, so they could both hear her over the blaring music.

"Of course, we will." Tessa gave the woman's hand another assuring squeeze. "Just lead the way."

Alexis made her way through the crowd with Tessa and Ryan following closely behind.

Ryan bit back his disappointment at the interruption. If the distress Alexis appeared to be experiencing was any indication, the situation was one level below the barn being on fire. Which triggered a burning in his gut.

Whatever Alexis and James wanted with the two of them, he was pretty sure neither of them was going to like it.

"Tessa, Ryan, please, have a seat." James Harris, president of the Texas Cattleman's Club, gestured to the chairs on the other side of the large mahogany desk in his office.

After such a successful night, he and Alexis looked incredibly grim. The knot that had already formed in her gut tightened.

She and Ryan sat in the chairs James indicated while Alexis sat on the sofa along one wall.

"Something is obviously wrong." Ryan crossed one ankle over his knee. "What is it, James?"

The other man hesitated a moment before speaking. When he did, the words he uttered came out in an anguished growl.

"There was a problem with one of the bids. A *big* problem."

"Gail." Tessa and Ryan said her name simultaneously.

"How does something like this happen?" Ryan asked after James had filled them both in. "Can anyone just walk in off the street and bid a bogus hundred K?"

James grimaced.

Tessa felt badly for him. James hadn't been president of the Texas Cattleman's Club for very long. She could only imagine how he must be feeling. He'd been riding high after putting on what was likely the most successful fund-raiser in the club's history. But now he was saddled with one of the biggest faux pas in the club's history.

"It's a charity auction. We take folks at their word when they make a bid," James replied calmly, then sighed. "Still, I don't like that this happened on my watch, and I'll do everything I can to remedy the situation."

Tessa's heart broke for the man. She didn't know James particularly well, but she'd heard the tragic story about what had happened to his brother and his sister-in-law. They'd died in an accident, leaving behind their orphaned son, who was little more than a year old, to be raised by James.

He was a nice enough guy, but he didn't seem the daddy type. Still, he was obviously doing the best he could to juggle all the balls he had in the air.

Tessa groaned, her hand pressed to her forehead. "I knew Gail had a thing for Lloyd Richardson, but I honestly never imagined she'd do something so reckless and impulsive."

"No one thinks you knew anything about it, Tess. That's not why we asked you here," Alexis assured her.

"Then why are we here?" Ryan's voice was cautious as he studied the other man.

"Because we have another dilemma that could compound the first problem." James heaved a sigh as he sat back in his chair, his hands steepled over his abdomen. "And we could really use your help to head it off."

"Was there another bid that someone can't make good on?" Ryan asked.

"No, but there is a reporter here, whom I invited." Alexis cringed as she stood. "He's intrigued by that one-hundred thousand dollar bid, and he wants to interview Gail and Lloyd."

"Damn. I see your dilemma." Ryan groaned sympathetically. "Instead of getting good press about all of the money the club did raise, all anyone will be talking about is Gail and her bogus bid."

"It gets even worse," Alexis said. She blew out a frustrated breath as she shook her head, her blond locks flipping over her shoulder. "We can't find hide nor hair of either Gail or Lloyd. It's like the two of them simply vanished."

Ryan shook his head. "Wow. That's pretty messed up."

"What is it that you want Ryan and me to do?" Tessa looked at James and then Alexis.

"The reporter was also very intrigued by everyone's reaction to you and all the drama of how Ryan beat out Clem and Bo's bids." A faint smile flickered on Alexis's mouth. "So we suggested that he follow the two of you on your little date."

"What?"

Panic suddenly seized Tessa's chest. It was one thing to play dress up and strut on the stage here at the club. Surrounded mostly by people she'd known her entire life. It was another to be followed by a reporter who was going to put the information out there for the entire world to see.

"We hadn't really intended to go on a date," Tessa said. "Ryan and I were just going to hang out together and have fun at the game. Grab a bite to eat at his favorite restaurant. Nothing worthy of reporting on."

"I know." There was an apology in Alexis's voice. "Which is why I need to ask another big favor..."

"You want us to go on a real date after all." Ryan looked from Alexis to James.

"Going out with a beautiful woman like Tess here, who also just happens to be your best friend...not the worst thing in the world that could happen to a guy." James forced a smile.

"Only...well, I know that the date you'd planned is the perfect kind of day for hanging with the guys." Alexis directed her attention toward Tess. "But this needs to feel like a big, romantic gesture. Something worthy of a big write-up for the event and for our club."

"I d-don't know, Alexis," Tessa stuttered, her heart

racing. "I'm not sure how comfortable either of us would feel having a reporter follow us around all day."

"We'll do it," Ryan said suddenly. Decisively. "For the club, of course." He cleared his throat and gave Tess a reassuring nod. "And don't worry, I know exactly what to do. I'll make sure we give him the big, romantic fantasy he's looking for."

"I'm supposed to be the one who takes you out on a date," Tess objected. "That's how this whole thing works."

"Then it'll make for an even grander gesture when I surprise you by sweeping you off your feet."

He gave her that mischievous half smile that had enticed her into countless adventures. From searching for frogs when they were kids to parasailing in Mexico as an adult. After all these years, she still hadn't grown immune to its charm.

"Fine." Tessa sighed. "We'll do it. Just tell him we'll need a day or two to finalize the arrangements."

"Thank you!" Alexis hugged them both. "We're so grateful to you both for doing this."

"You're saving our asses here and the club's reputation." James looked noticeably relieved, though his eyebrows were still furrowed. "I can't thank you enough. And you won't be the only ones on the hot seat. Rose Clayton persuaded her grandson Daniel to give the reporter an additional positive feature related to the auction."

Alexis frowned at the mention of Daniel's name, but then she quickly recovered.

"And about that bid of Gail's...no one outside this room, besides Gail and Lloyd, of course, knows the situation." James frowned again. "We'd like to keep it that way until we figure out how we're going to resolve this. So please, don't whisper a word of this to anyone."

"Least of all the reporter," Alexis added, emphatically.

Tessa and Ryan agreed. Then Alexis introduced them to the reporter, Greg Halstead. After Greg gathered some preliminary information for the piece, Ryan insisted that he be the one to exchange contact information with Greg so they could coordinate him accompanying them on their date.

Every time Greg repeated the word *date*, shivers ran down Tessa's spine.

The only thing worse than having a thing for her best friend was being shanghaied into going on a fake date with him. But she was doing this for the club that meant so much to her, her family and the community of Royal.

Alexis had worked so hard to garner positive publicity for the club. And she'd raised awareness of the need to fund research for a cure for pancreatic cancer—the disease that had killed Alexis Slade's dear grandmother. Tess wouldn't allow all of her friend's hard work to be squandered because of Gail's selfish decision. Not if she could do something to prevent it.

Maybe she hadn't been aware of what Gail had planned to do tonight. But she'd been the one who'd invited Gail to tonight's affair. Tess couldn't help feeling obligated to do what she could to rectify the matter.

Even if it meant torturing herself by going on a pretend date that would feel very real to her. No matter how much she tried to deny it.

Eight

Ryan and Tessa finally headed home in his truck after what felt like an incredibly long night.

He couldn't remember the last time he and Tessa had danced together or laughed as much as they had that evening. But that was *before* James and Alexis had asked them to go on an actual date. Since then, things felt…different.

First, they'd politely endured the awkward interview with that reporter, Greg Halstead. Then they'd gone about the rest of the evening dancing and mingling with fellow club members and their guests. But there was a strange vibe between them. Obviously, Tessa felt it, too.

Why else would she be rambling on, as she often did when she was nervous.

Then again, lost in his own thoughts, he hadn't been very good company. Ryan drummed his fingers on the steering wheel during an awkward moment of silence.

"This date…it isn't going to make things weird between us, is it?" Tess asked finally, as if she'd been inside his head all along.

One of the hazards of a friendship with someone who knew him too well.

He forced a chuckle. "C'mon, Tess. We've been best buds too long to let a fake date shake us." His eyes searched hers briefly before returning to the road. "Our friendship could withstand anything."

Anything except getting romantically involved. Which is why they hadn't and wouldn't.

"Promise?" She seemed desperate for reassurance on the matter. Not surprising. A part of him needed it, too.

"On my life." This time, there was no hesitation. There were a lot of things in this world he could do without. Tessa Noble's friendship wasn't one of them.

Tessa nodded, releasing an audible sigh of relief. She turned to look out the window at the beautiful ranches that marked the road home.

His emphatic statement seemed to alleviate the anxiety they'd both been feeling. Still, his thoughts kept returning to their date the following weekend. The contemplative look on Tess's face, indicated that hers did, too.

He changed the subject, eager to talk about anything else. "What's up with your girl bidding a hundred K she didn't have?"

"I don't know." Tess seemed genuinely baffled by Gail's behavior.

Tessa and Gail certainly weren't as close as he and

Tess were. But lately, at her mother's urging, Tessa had tried to build stronger friendships with other women in town.

She and Gail had met when Tessa had used the woman's fledgling grocery delivery business. They'd hit it off and started hanging out occasionally.

He understood why Tess liked Gail. She was bold and a little irreverent. All of the things that Tess was not. But Ryan hadn't cared much for her. There was something about that woman he didn't quite trust. But now wasn't the time for I told you so's. Tessa obviously felt badly enough about being the person who'd invited Gail to the charity auction.

"I knew she had a lightweight crush on Lloyd Richardson," Tessa continued. "Who doesn't? But I certainly didn't think her capable of doing something this crazy and impulsive."

"Seems there was a lot of that going around," Ryan muttered under his breath.

"Speaking of that impulsiveness that seemed to be going around…" Tessa laughed, and Ryan chuckled, too.

He'd obviously uttered the words more to himself than to her. Still, she'd heard them, and they provided the perfect opening for what she'd been struggling to say all night.

"Thank you again for doing this, Rye. You made a very generous donation. And though you did the complete opposite of what I asked you to do—" they both laughed again "—I was a little…no, I was a *lot* nervous about going out with either Clem or Bo in such a high pressure situation, so thank you."

"Anything for you, Tess Noble." His voice was deep and warm. The emotion behind his words genuine. Something she knew from their history, not just as theory.

When they were in college, Ryan had climbed into his battered truck, and driven nearly two thousand miles to her campus in Sacramento after a particularly bad breakup with a guy who'd been an all-around dick. He'd dumped her for someone else a few days before Valentine's Day, so Ryan made a point of taking her to the Valentine's Day party. Then he kissed her in front of everyone—including her ex.

The kiss had taken her breath away. And left her wanting another taste ever since.

Tessa shook off the memory and focused on the here and now. Ryan had been uncharacteristically quiet during the ride home. He'd let her chatter on, offering a grunt of agreement or dissension here or there. Otherwise, he seemed deep in thought.

"And you're sure I can't pay you back at least some of what you bid on me?" Tessa asked as he slowed down before turning into the driveway of the Noble Spur, her family's ranch. "Especially since you're commandeering the planning of our date."

"Oh, we're still gonna use those tickets on the fifty-yard line, for sure," he clarified. "And there's no way I'm leaving Dallas without my favorite steak dinner. I'm just going to add some flourishes here and there. Nothing too fancy. But you'll enjoy the night. I promise." He winked.

Why did that small gesture send waves of electricity down her spine and make her acutely aware of her nipples prickling with heat beneath the jacket she'd put on to ward against the chilly night air?

"Well, thank you again," she said as he shifted his tricked out Ford Super Duty F-350 Platinum into Park. Ryan was a simple guy who didn't sweat the details—except when it came to his truck.

"You're welcome." Ryan lightly gripped her elbow when she reached for the door. "Allow me. Wouldn't want you to ruin that fancy outfit of yours."

He hopped out of the truck and came around to her side. He opened the door and took her hand.

It wasn't the first time Ryan had helped her out of his vehicle. But something about this time felt different. There was something in his intense green eyes. Something he wouldn't allow himself to say. Rare for a man who normally said just about anything that popped into his head.

When she stepped down onto the truck's side rail, Ryan released her hand. He gripped her waist and lifted her to the ground in a single deft move.

Tessa gasped in surprise, bracing her hands on his strong shoulders. His eyes scanned her once more. As if he still couldn't believe it was really her in the sexiest, most feminine item of clothing she'd ever owned.

Heat radiated off his large body, shielding her from the chilliness of the night air and making her aware of how little space there was between them.

For a moment, the vision of Ryan's lips crashing down on hers as he pinned her body against the truck flashed through her brain. It wasn't an unfamiliar image. But, given their positions and the way he was looking at her right now, it felt a little too real.

Tessa took short, shallow breaths, her chest heaving.

She needed to get away from Ryan Bateman before she did something stupid. Like lift on to her toes and press a hot, wet kiss to those sensual lips.

She needed to get inside and go to her room. The proper place to have ridiculously inappropriate thoughts about her best friend. With her battery-operated boyfriend buried in the nightstand drawer on standby, just in case she needed to take the edge off.

But walking away was a difficult thing to do when his mouth was mere inches from hers. And she trembled with the desire to touch him. To taste his mouth again. To trace the ridge behind the fly of his black dress pants.

"Good night." She tossed the words over her shoulder as she turned and headed toward the house as quickly as her feet would carry her in those high-heeled silver sandals.

"Tessa." His unusually gruff voice stopped her dead in her tracks.

She didn't turn back to look at him. Instead, she glanced just over her shoulder. A sign that he had her full attention, even if her eyes didn't meet his. "Yes?"

"I'm calling an audible on our date this weekend." Ryan invoked one of his favorite football terms.

"A last-minute change?" Tessa turned slightly, her curiosity piqued.

She'd planned the perfect weekend for Ryan Bateman. What could she possibly have missed?

"I'll pick you up on Friday afternoon, around 3:00 p.m. Pack a bag for the weekend. And don't forget that jumpsuit."

"We're spending the entire weekend in Dallas?" She turned to face him fully, stunned by the hungry look on his face. When he nodded his confirmation, Tessa focused on slowing her breath as she watched the cloud her warm breath made in the air. "Why? And since when do you care what I wear?"

"Because I promised Alexis I'd make this date a big, grand gesture that would keep the reporter preoccupied and off the topic of our missing bachelor and his hundred-thousand-dollar bidder." His words were matter of fact, signaling none of the raw, primal heat she'd seen in his eyes a moment ago.

He shut the passenger door and walked around to the driver's side. "It doesn't have to be that same outfit. It's just that you looked mighty pretty tonight. Neither of us gets much of a chance to dress up. Thought it'd be nice if we took advantage of this weekend to do that." He shrugged, as if it were the most normal request in the world.

This coming from a man who'd once stripped out of his tuxedo in the car on the way home from a mutual friend's out-of-town wedding. He'd insisted he couldn't stand to be in that tuxedo a moment longer.

"Fine." Tessa shrugged, too. If it was no big deal to Ryan, then it was no big deal to her either. "I'll pack a couple of dresses and skirts. Maybe I'll wear the dress I'd originally picked out for tonight. Before I volunteered to be in the auction."

After all that waxing, she should show her baby smooth legs off every chance she got. Who knew when she'd put herself through that kind of torture again?

"Sounds like you got some packing to do." A restrained smirk lit Ryan's eyes. He nodded toward the house. "Better get inside before you freeze out here."

"'Night, Ryan." Tessa turned up the path to the

house, without waiting for his response, and let herself in, closing the door behind her. The slam of the heavy truck door, followed by the crunch of gravel, indicated that Ryan was turning his vehicle around in the drive and heading home to the Bateman Ranch next door.

Tessa released a long sigh, her back pressed to the door.

She'd just agreed to spend the weekend in Dallas with her best friend. Seventy-two hours of pretending she didn't secretly lust after Ryan Bateman. Several of which would be documented by a reporter known for going after gossip.

Piece of cake. Piece of pie.

Nine

"Tessa, your chariot is here," Tripp called to her upstairs. "Hurry up, you're not gonna believe this."

Tripp was definitely back to his old self. It was both a blessing and a curse, because he hadn't stopped needling her and Ryan about their date ever since.

She inhaled deeply, then slowly released the breath as she stared at herself in the mirror one last time.

It's just a weekend trip with a friend. Ryan and I have done this at least a dozen times before. No big deal.

Tessa lifted her bag on to her shoulder, then made her way downstairs and out front where Tripp was handing her overnight suitcase off to Ryan.

Her eyes widened as she walked closer, studying the sleek black sedan with expensive black rims.

"Is that a black on black Maybach?"

"It is." Ryan took the bag from her and loaded it into the trunk of the Mercedes Maybach before closing it and opening the passenger door. He gestured for her to get inside. "You've always said you wanted to know what it was like to ride in one of these things, so—"

"You didn't go out and buy this, did you?" Panic filled her chest. Ryan wasn't extravagant or impulsive. And he'd already laid out a substantial chunk of change as a favor to her.

"No, of course not. You know a mud-caked pickup truck is more my style." He leaned in and lowered his voice, so only she could hear his next words. "But I'm supposed to be going for the entire illusion here, remember? And Tess…"

"Yes?" She inhaled his clean, fresh scent, her heart racing slightly from his nearness and the intimacy of his tone.

"Smile for the camera." Ryan nodded toward Greg Halstead who waved and snapped photographs of the two of them in front of the vehicle.

Tess deepened her smile, and she and Ryan stood together, his arm wrapped around her as the man clicked photos for the paper.

When Greg had gotten enough images, he shook their hands and said he'd meet them at the hotel later and at the restaurant tomorrow night to get a few more photos.

"Which hotel? And which restaurant?" Tessa turned to Ryan.

A genuine smile lit his green eyes and they sparkled in the afternoon sunlight. "If I tell you, it won't be a surprise, now will it?"

"Smart-ass." She folded her arms and shook her

head. Ryan knew she liked surprises about as much as she liked diamondback rattlesnakes. Maybe even a little less.

"There anything I should know about you two?" Tripp stepped closer after the reporter was gone. Arms folded over his chest, his gaze shifted from Ryan to her and then back again.

"You can take the protective big brother shtick down a notch," she teased. "I already explained everything to you. We're doing this for the club, and for Alexis."

She flashed her I'm-your-little-sister-and-you-love-me-no-matter-what smile. It broke him. As it had for as long as she could remember.

The edge of his mouth tugged upward in a reluctant grin. He opened his arms and hugged her goodbye before giving Ryan a one-arm bro hug and whispering something to him that she couldn't hear.

Ryan's expression remained neutral, but he nodded and patted her brother on the shoulder.

"We'd better get going." Ryan helped her into the buttery, black leather seat that seemed to give her a warm hug. Then he closed her door and climbed into the driver's seat.

"God, this car is beautiful," she said as he pulled away from the house. "If you didn't buy it, whose is it?

"Borrowed it from a friend." He pulled on to the street more carefully than he did when he was driving his truck. "The guy collects cars the way other folks collect stamps or Depression-era glass. Most of the cars he wouldn't let anyone breathe on, let alone touch. But he owed me a favor."

Tessa sank back against the seat and ran her hand along the smooth, soft leather.

"Manners would dictate that I tell you that you shouldn't have, but if I'm being honest, all I can think is, Where have you been all my life?" They both chuckled. "You think I can have a saddle made out of this leather?"

"For the right price, you can get just about anything." A wide smile lit his face.

Tessa sighed. She was content. Relaxed. And Ryan seemed to be, too. There was no reason this weekend needed to be tense and awkward.

"So, what did my brother say to you when he gave you that weird bro hug goodbye?"

The muscles in Ryan's jaw tensed and his brows furrowed. He kept his gaze on the road ahead. "This thing has an incredible sound system. I already synced it to my phone. Go ahead and play something. Your choice. Just no more '80s boy bands. I heard enough of those at the charity auction last week."

Tessa smirked. "You could've just told me it was none of my business what Tripp said."

His wide smile returned, though he didn't look at her. "I thought I just did."

They both laughed, and Tessa smiled to herself. Their weekend was going to be fun. Just like every other road trip they'd ever taken together. Things would only be uncomfortable between them if she made them that way.

Ryan, Tessa and Greg Halstead headed up the stone stairs that led to the bungalow of a fancy, art-themed boutique hotel that he'd reserved. The place was an easy drive from the football stadium.

Tessa had marveled at the hotel's main building and

mused about the expense. But she was as excited as
a little kid in a candy store, eager to see what was on
the other side of that door. Greg requested to go in
first, so he could set up his shot of Tessa stepping inside the room.

When he signaled that he was ready, Ryan inserted
the key card into the lock and removed it quickly. Once
the green light flashed, he opened the door for her.

Tessa's jaw dropped, and she covered her mouth
with both hands, genuinely stunned by the elegant
beauty of the contemporary bungalow.

"So…what do you think?" He couldn't shake the
nervousness he felt. The genuine need to impress her
was not his typical MO. So what was going on? Maybe
it was the fact that her impression would be recorded
for posterity.

"It's incredible, Ryan. I don't know what to say."
Her voice trembled with emotion. When she glanced
up at him, her eyes were shiny. She wiped quickly at
the corners of her eyes. "I'm being silly, I know."

"No, you're not." He kissed her cheek. "That's exactly the reaction I was hoping for."

Ryan stepped closer and lowered his voice. "I want
this to be a special weekend for you, Tess. What you
did last week at the charity auction was brave, and I'm
proud of you. I want this weekend to be everything the
fearless woman who strutted across that stage last Saturday night deserves."

His eyes met hers for a moment and his chest filled
with warmth.

"Thanks, Rye. This place is amazing. I really appreciate everything you've done." A soft smile curled the
edges of her mouth, filling him with the overwhelm-

ing desire to lean down and kiss her the way he had at that Valentine's Day party in college.

He stepped back and cleared his throat, indicating that she should step inside.

Tessa went from room to room of the two-bedroom, two-bath hotel suite, complete with two balconies. One connected to each bedroom. There was even a small kitchen island, a full-size refrigerator and a stove. The open living room boasted a ridiculously large television mounted to the wall and a fireplace in both that space and the master bedroom, which he insisted that she take. But Tessa, who could be just as stubborn as he was, wouldn't hear of it. She directed the bellman to take her things to the slightly smaller bedroom, which was just as beautiful as its counterpart.

"I think I have all the pictures I need." Greg gathered up his camera bag and his laptop. "I'll work on the article tonight and select the best photos among the ones I've taken so far. I'll meet you guys at the restaurant tomorrow at six-thirty to capture a few more shots."

"Sounds good." Ryan said goodbye to Greg and closed the door behind him, glad the man was finally gone. Something about a reporter hanging around, angling for a juicy story, felt like a million ants crawling all over his skin.

He sank on to the sofa, shrugged his boots off, and put his feet up on the coffee table. It'd been a short drive from Royal to Dallas, but mentally, he was exhausted.

Partly from making last-minute arrangements for their trip. Partly from the effort of reminding himself that no matter how much it felt like it, this wasn't a real date. They were both just playing their parts. Making the TCC look good and diverting attention from the debacle of Gail's bid.

"Hey." Tess emerged from her bedroom where she'd gone to put her things away. "Is Greg gone?"

"He left a few minutes ago. Said to tell you good-bye."

"Thank goodness." She heaved a sigh and plopped down on the sofa beside him. "I mean, he's a nice guy and everything. It just feels so... I don't know..."

"Creepy? Invasive? Weird?" he offered. "Take your pick."

"All of the above." Tessa laughed, then leaned forward, her gaze locked on to the large bouquet of flowers in a glass vase on the table beside his feet.

"I thought these were just part of the room." She removed the small envelope with her name on it and slid her finger beneath the flap, prying it open. "These are for me?"

"I hope you like them. They're—"

"Peonies. My favorite flower." She leaned forward and inhaled the flowers that resembled clouds dyed shades of light and dark pink. "They're beautiful, Ryan. Thank you. You thought of everything, didn't you?" Her voice trailed and her gaze softened.

"I meant it when I said you deserve a really special weekend. I even asked them to stock the freezer with your favorite brand of Neapolitan ice cream."

"Seriously?" She was only wearing a hint of lip gloss in a nude shade of pink and a little eyeshadow and mascara. But she was as beautiful as he'd ever seen her. Even more so than the night of the auction when she'd worn a heavy layer of makeup that had covered her creamy brown skin. Sunlight filtered into the room, making her light brown eyes appear almost golden. "What more could I possibly ask for?"

His eyes were locked on her sensual lips. When he finally tore his gaze away from them, Tess seemed disappointed. As if she'd expected him to lean in and kiss her.

"I like the dress, by the way."

"Really?" She stood, looking down at the heather-gray dress and the tan calf-high boots topped by knee socks. The cuff of the socks hovered just above the top of the boot, drawing his eye there and leading it up the side of her thigh where her smooth skin disappeared beneath the hem of her dress.

His body stiffened in response to her curvy silhouette and her summery citrus scent.

Fucking knee socks. *Seriously*? Tess was *killing* him.

For a moment he wondered if she was teasing him on purpose. Reminding him of the things he couldn't have with her. The red-hot desires that would never be satisfied.

Tess seemed completely oblivious to her effect on him as she regarded the little gray dress.

Yet, all he could think of was how much he'd like to see that gray fabric pooled on the floor beside his bed.

Ryan groaned inside. This was going to be the longest seventy-two hours of his life.

Ten

"Is that a bottle of champagne?" Tessa pointed to a bottle chilling in an ice bucket on the sideboard along the wall.

She could use something cold to tamp down the heat rising in her belly under Ryan's intense stare. It also wouldn't be a bad idea to create some space between them. Enough to get her head together and stop fantasizing about what it would feel like to kiss her best friend again.

"Even better." Ryan flashed a sexy, half grin. "It's imported Italian Moscato d'Asti. I asked them to chill a bottle for us."

Her favorite. Too bad this wasn't a real date, because Ryan had ticked every box of what her fantasy date would look like.

"Saving it for something special?"

"Just you." He winked, climbing to his feet. "Why don't we make a toast to kick our weekend off?"

Tessa relaxed a little as she followed him over to the ice bucket, still maintaining some distance between them.

Ryan opened the bottle with a loud pop and poured each of them a glass of the sparkling white wine. He handed her one.

She accepted, gratefully, and joined him in holding up her glass.

"To an unforgettable weekend." A soft smile curved the edges of his mouth.

"Cheers." Tessa ignored the beading of her nipples and the tingling that trailed down her spine and sparked a fire low in her belly. She took a deep sip.

"Very good." Tessa fought back her speculation about how much better it would taste on Ryan's lips.

Ryan returned to the sofa. He finished his glass of moscato in short order and set it on the table beside the sofa.

Tessa sat beside him, finishing the remainder of her drink and contemplating another. She decided against it, setting it on the table in front of them.

She turned to her friend. God, he was handsome. His green eyes brooding and intense. His shaggy brown hair living in that space between perfectly groomed and purposely messy. The ever-present five o'clock shadow crawling over his clenched jaw.

"Thanks, Rye." She needed to quell the thoughts in her head. "This is all so amazing and incredibly thoughtful. I know this fantasy date isn't real, but you went out of your way to make it feel that way, and I appreciate it."

Tessa leaned in to kiss his stubbled cheek. Something she'd done a dozen times before. But Ryan turned his head, likely surprised by her sudden approach, and her lips met his.

She'd been right. The moscato did taste better enmeshed with the flavor of Ryan's firm, sensual lips.

It was an accidental kiss. So why had she leaned in and continued to kiss him, rather than withdrawing and apologizing? And why hadn't Ryan pulled back either?

Tessa's eyes slowly drifted closed, and she slipped her fingers into the short hair at the nape of Ryan's neck. Pulled his face closer to hers.

She parted her lips, and Ryan accepted the unspoken invitation, sliding his tongue between her lips and taking control. The kiss had gradually moved from a sweet, inadvertent, closed-mouth affair to an intense meshing of lips, teeth and tongues. Ryan moved his hands to her back, tugging her closer.

Tessa sighed softly in response to the hot, demanding kiss that obliterated the memory of that unexpected one nearly a decade ago. Truly kissing Ryan Bateman was everything she'd imagined it to be.

And she wanted more.

They'd gone this far. Had let down the invisible wall between them. There was nothing holding them back now.

Tessa inhaled deeply before shifting to her knees and straddling Ryan's lap. He groaned. A sexy sound that was an undeniable mixture of pain and pleasure. Of intense wanting. Evident from the ridge beneath his zipper.

As he deepened their kiss, his large hand splayed against her low back, his hardness met the soft, warm space between her thighs, sending a shiver up her spine. Her nipples ached with an intensity she hadn't experienced before. She wanted his hands and lips on her naked flesh. She wanted to shed the clothing that prevented skin-to-skin contact.

She wanted…sex. With Ryan. Right now.

Sex.

It wasn't as if she'd forgotten how the whole process worked. Obviously. But it'd been a while since she'd been with anyone. More than a few years. One of the hazards of living in a town small enough that there was three degrees or less of separation between any man she met and her father or brother.

Would Ryan be disappointed?

Tessa suddenly went stiff, her eyes blinking.

"Don't," he whispered between hungry kisses along her jaw and throat that left her wanting and breathless, despite the insecurities that had taken over her brain.

Tess frowned. "Don't do what?"

Maybe she didn't have Ryan Bateman's vast sexual experience, but she was pretty sure she knew how to kiss. At least she hadn't had any complaints.

Until now.

"Have you changed your mind about this?"

"No." She forced her eyes to meet his, regardless of how unnerved she was by his intense stare and his determination to make her own up to what she wanted. "Not even a little."

The edge of his mouth curved in a criminally sexy smirk. "Then for once in your life, Tess, stop overthinking everything. Stop compiling a list in your head of all the reasons we shouldn't do this." He kissed her again, his warm lips pressed to hers and his large hands gliding down her back and gripping her bottom as he pulled her firmly against him.

A soft gasp escaped her mouth at the sensation of his hard length pressed against her sensitive flesh. Ryan swept his tongue between her parted lips, tangling it with hers as he wrapped his arms around her.

Their kiss grew increasingly urgent. Hungry. Desperate. His kiss made her question whether she'd ever *really* been kissed before. Made her skin tingle with a desire so intense she physically ached with a need for him.

A need for Ryan's kiss. His touch. The warmth of his naked skin pressed against hers. The feel of him inside her.

Hands shaking and the sound of her own heartbeat filling her ears, Tessa pulled her mouth from his. She grabbed the hem of her dress and raised it. His eyes were locked with hers, both of them breathing heavily, as she lifted the fabric.

Ryan helped her tug the dress over her head and he tossed it on to the floor. He studied her lacy, gray bra and the cleavage spilling out of it.

Her cheeks flamed, and her heart raced. Ryan leaned in and planted slow, warm kisses on her shoulder. He swept her hair aside and trailed kisses up her neck.

"God, you're beautiful, Tess." His voice was a low growl that sent tremors through her. He glided a callused hand down her back and rested it on her hip. "I think it's pretty obvious how much I want you. But I need to know that you're sure about this."

"I am." She traced his rough jaw with her palm. Glided a thumb across his lips, naturally a deep shade of red that made them even more enticing. Then she crashed her lips against his as she held his face in her hands.

He claimed her mouth with a greedy, primal kiss that strung her body tight as a bow, desperate for the release that only he could provide.

She wanted him. More than she could ever remember wanting anything. The steely rod pressed against the slick, aching spot between her thighs indicated his genuine desire for her. Yet, he seemed hesitant. As if he were holding back. Something Ryan Bateman, one of the most confident men she'd ever known, wasn't prone to do.

Tess reached behind her and did the thing Ryan seemed reluctant to. She released the hooks on her bra, slid the straps down her shoulders and tossed it away.

He splayed one hand against her back. The other glided up and down her side before his thumb grazed the side of her breast. Once, twice, then again. As if testing her.

Finally, he grazed her hardened nipple with his open palm, and she sucked in a sharp breath.

His eyes met hers with a look that fell somewhere between asking and pleading.

Tessa swallowed hard, her cheeks and chest flushed with heat. She nodded, her hands trembling as she braced them on his wide shoulders.

When Ryan's lips met her skin again, she didn't fight the overwhelming feelings that flooded her senses, like a long, hard rain causing the creek to exceed its banks. She leaned into them. Allowed them to wash over her. Enjoyed the thing she'd fantasized about for so long.

Tessa gasped as Ryan cupped her bottom and pulled her against his hardened length. As if he was as desperate for her as she was for him. He kissed her neck, her shoulders, her collarbone. Then he dropped tender, delicate kisses on her breasts.

Tessa ran her fingers through his soft hair. When he raised his eyes to hers, she leaned down, whispering in his ear.

"Ryan, take me to bed. Now."

Before she lost her nerve. Before he lost his.

Ryan carried her to his bed, laid her down and settled between her thighs. He trailed slow, hot kisses down her neck and chest as he palmed her breast with his large, work-roughened hand. He sucked the beaded tip into his warm mouth. Grazed it with his teeth. Lathed it with his tongue.

She shuddered in response to the tantalizing sensation that shot from her nipple straight to her sex. Her skin flamed beneath Ryan's touch, and her breath came in quick little bursts. He nuzzled her neck, one large hand skimming down her thigh and hooking behind her knee. As he rocked against the space between her thighs, Tessa whimpered at the delicious torture of his steely length grinding against her needy clit.

"That's it, Tess." Ryan trailed kisses along her jaw. "Relax. Let go. You know I'd never do anything to hurt you." His stubble scraped the sensitive skin of her cheek as he whispered roughly in her ear.

She did know that. She trusted Ryan with her life. With her deepest secrets. With her body. Ryan was sweet and charming and well-meaning, but her friend could sometimes be a bull in the china shop.

Would he ride roughshod over her heart, even if he didn't mean to?

Tessa gazed up at him, her lips parting as she took

in his incredibly handsome form. She yanked his shirt from the back of his pants and slid her hands against his warm skin. Gently grazed his back with her nails. She had the fleeting desire to mark him as hers. So that any other woman who saw him would know he belonged to her and no one else.

Ryan moved beside her, and she immediately missed his weight and the feel of him pressed against her most sensitive flesh. He kissed her harder as he slid a hand up her thigh and then cupped the space between her legs that throbbed in anticipation of his touch.

Tessa tensed, sucking in a deep breath as he glided his fingertips back and forth over the drenched panel of fabric shielding her sex. He tugged the material aside and plunged two fingers inside her.

"God, you're wet, Tess." The words vibrated against her throat, where he branded her skin with scorching hot kisses that made her weak with want. He kissed his way down her chest and gently scraped her sensitive nipple with his teeth before swirling his tongue around the sensitive flesh.

Tessa quivered as the space between her thighs ached with need. She wanted to feel him inside her. To be with Ryan in the way she'd always imagined.

But this wasn't a dream; it was real. And their actions would have real-world consequences.

"You're doing it again. That head thing," he muttered in between little nips and licks. His eyes glinted in the light filtering through the bedroom window. "Cut it out."

God, he knew her too well. And after tonight, he would know every single inch of her body. If she had her way.

Eleven

Ryan couldn't get over how beautiful Tessa was as she lay beside him whimpering with pleasure. Lips parted, back arched and her eyelashes fluttering, she was everything he'd imagined and more.

He halted his action just long enough to encourage her to lift her hips, allowing him to drag the lacy material down her legs, over her boots, and off. Returning his attention to her full breasts, he sucked and licked one of the pebbled, brown peaks he'd occasionally glimpsed the outline of through the thin, tank tops she sometimes wore during summer. He'd spent more time than he dared admit speculating about what her breasts looked like and how her skin would taste.

Now he knew. And he desperately wanted to know everything about her body. What turned her on? What would send her spiraling over the edge, his name on her lips?

He eagerly anticipated solving those mysteries, too.

Ryan inserted his fingers inside her again, adding a third finger to her tight, slick channel. Allowed her body to stretch and accommodate the additional digit.

He and Tess had made it a point not to delve too deeply into each other's sex lives. Still, they'd shared enough for him to know he wouldn't be her first or even her second. She was just a little tense, and perhaps a lot nervous. And she needed to relax.

Her channel stretched and relaxed around his fingers as he moved to her other nipple and gave it the same treatment he'd given the first. He resumed the movement of his hand, his fingers gliding in and out of her. Then he stroked the slick bundle of nerves with his thumb.

Tessa's undeniable gasp of pleasure indicated her approval.

The slow, small circles he made with his thumb got wider, eliciting a growing chorus of curses and moans. Her grip on his hair tightened, and she moved her hips in rhythm with his hand.

She was slowly coming undone, and he was grateful to be the reason for it. Ryan wet his lips with a sweep of his tongue, eager to taste her there. But he wanted to take his time. Make this last for both of them.

He kissed Tessa's belly and slipped his other hand between her legs, massaging her clit as he curved the fingers inside her.

"Oh god, oh god, oh god, Ryan. Right there, right there," Tess pleaded when he hit the right spot.

He gladly obliged her request, both hands moving with precision until he'd taken Tess to the edge. She'd called his name, again and again, as she dug the heels of her boots into the mattress and her body stiffened.

Watching his best friend tumble into bliss was a thing of beauty. Being the one who'd brought her such intense ecstasy was an incredible gift. It was easily the most meaningful sexual experience he'd ever had, and he was still fully clothed.

Ryan lay down, gathering Tess to him and wrapping her in his arms, her head tucked under his chin. He flipped the cover over her, so she'd stay warm.

They were both silent. Tessa's chest heaved as she slowly came down from the orgasm he'd given her.

When the silence lingered on for seconds that turned to minutes, but felt like hours, Ryan couldn't take it.

"Tess, look, I—"

"You're still dressed." She raised her head, her eyes meeting his. Her playful smile eased the tension they'd both been feeling. "And I'm not quite sure why."

The laugh they shared felt good. A bit of normalcy in a situation that was anything but normal between them.

He planted a lingering kiss on her sweet lips.

"I can fix that." He sat up and tugged his shirt over his head and tossed it on to the floor unceremoniously.

"Keep going." She indicated his pants with a wave of her hand.

"Bold and bossy." He laughed. "Who is this woman and what did she do with my best friend?"

She frowned slightly, as if what he'd said had hurt her feelings.

"Hey." He cradled her face in one hand. "You know that's not a criticism, right? I like seeing this side of you."

"Usually when a man calls a woman bossy, it's code for bitchy." Her eyes didn't quite meet his.

Ryan wanted to kick himself. He'd only been teasing when he'd used the word bossy, but he hadn't been thinking. He understood how loaded that term was to Tess. She'd hated that her mother and grandmother had constantly warned her that no ranch man would want a bossy bride.

"I should've said assertive," he clarified. "Which is what I've always encouraged you to be."

She nodded, seemingly satisfied with his explanation. A warm smile slid across her gorgeous face and lit her light brown eyes. "Then I'd like to assert that you're still clothed, and I don't appreciate it, seeing as I'm not."

"Yes, ma'am." He winked as he stood and removed his pants.

Tessa gently sank her teeth into her lower lip as she studied the bulge in his boxer briefs. Which only made him harder.

He rubbed the back of his neck and chuckled. "Now I guess I know how the fellas felt on stage at the auction."

"Hmm…" The humming sound Tess made seemed to vibrate in his chest and other parts of his body. Specifically, the part she was staring at right now.

Tess removed her boots and kneeled on the bed in front of him, her brown eyes studying him. The levity had faded from her expression, replaced by a heated gaze that made his cock twitch.

She looped her arms around his neck and pulled his mouth down toward hers. Angling her head, she kissed him hard, her fingers slipping into his hair and her naked breasts smashed against his hard chest.

If this was a dream, he didn't want to wake up.

Ryan wrapped his arms around Tess, needing her body pressed firmly against his. He splayed one hand against the smooth, soft skin of her back. The other squeezed the generous bottom he'd always quietly admired. Hauling her tight against him, he grew painfully hard with the need to be inside her.

He claimed her mouth, his tongue gliding against hers, his anticipation rising. He'd fantasized about making love to Tess long before that kiss they'd shared in college.

He'd wanted to make love to her that night. Or at the very least make out with her in his truck. But he'd promised Tripp he wouldn't ever look at Tess that way.

A promise he'd broken long before tonight, despite his best efforts.

Ryan pushed thoughts of his ill-advised pledge to Tripp and the consequences of breaking it from his mind.

Right now, it was just him and Tess. The only thing that mattered in this moment was what the two of them wanted. What they needed from each other.

Ryan pulled away, just long enough to rummage in his luggage for the condoms he kept in his bag.

He said a silent prayer, thankful there was one full strip left. He tossed it on the nightstand and stripped out of his underwear.

Suddenly she seemed shy again as his eyes roved every inch of her gorgeous body.

He placed his hands on her hips, pulling her close to him and pressing his forehead to hers.

"God, you're beautiful, Tess." He knew he sounded like a broken record. But he was struck by how breathtaking she was and by the fact that she'd trusted him with something as precious as her body.

"You're making me feel self-conscious." A deep blush stained Tess's cheeks and spread through her chest.

"Don't be." He cradled her cheek, hoping to put her at ease. "That's not my intention. I just…" He sighed, giving up on trying to articulate what he was feeling.

One-night stands, even the occasional relationship… those were easy. But with Tess, everything felt weightier. More significant. Definitely more complicated. He couldn't afford to fuck this up. Because not having Tess as his friend wasn't an option. Still, he wanted her.

"Ryan, it's okay." She wrapped her arms around him. "I'm nervous about this, too. But I know that I want to be with you tonight. It's what I've wanted for a long time, and I don't want to fight it anymore."

He shifted his gaze to hers. A small sigh of relief escaped his mouth.

Tess understood exactly what he was feeling. They could do this. Be together like this. Satisfy their craving for each other without ruining their friendship.

He captured her mouth in a bruising kiss, and they both tumbled on to the mattress. Hands groping. Tongues searching. Hearts racing.

He grabbed one of the foil packets and ripped it open, sheathing himself as quickly as he could.

He guided himself to her slick entrance, circling his hips so his pelvis rubbed against her hardened clit. Tessa gasped, then whimpered with pleasure each time he ground his hips against her again. She writhed against him, increasing the delicious friction against the tight bundle of nerves.

Ryan gripped the base of his cock and pressed its head to her entrance. He inched inside, and Tess whimpered softly. She dug her fingers into his hips, her eyes meeting his as he slid the rest of the way home. Until he was nestled as deeply inside her as the laws of physics would allow.

When he was fully seated, her slick, heated flesh surrounding him, an involuntary growl escaped his mouth at the delicious feel of this woman who was all softness and curves. Sweetness and beauty. His friend and his lover.

His gaze met hers as he hovered above her and moved inside her. His voice rasping, he whispered to her. Told her how incredible she made him feel.

Then, lifting her legs, he hooked them over his shoulders as he leaned over her, his weight on his hands as he moved.

She gasped, her eyes widening at the sensation of him going deep and hitting bottom due to the sudden shift in position.

"Ryan… I…oh… God." Tessa squeezed her eyes shut.

"C'mon, Tess." He arched his back as he shifted his hips forward, beads of sweat forming on his brow and trickling down his back. "Just let go. Don't think. Just feel."

Her breath came in quick pants, and she dug her nails in his biceps. Suddenly, her mouth formed a little *O* and her eyes opened wide. The unmistakable expression of pure satisfaction that overtook her as she called his name was one of the most beautiful things he'd ever seen. Something he wanted to see again and again.

Her flesh throbbed and pulsed around him, bringing

him to his peak. He tensed, shuddering as he cursed and called her name.

Ryan collapsed on to the bed beside her, both of them breathing hard and staring at the ceiling overhead for a few moments.

Finally, she draped an arm over his abdomen and rested her head on his shoulder.

He kissed the top of her head, pulled the covers over them, and slipped an arm around her. He lay there, still and quiet, fighting his natural tendency to slip out into the night. His usual MO after a one-night stand. Only he couldn't do that. Partly because it was Tess. Partly because what he'd felt between them was something he couldn't quite name, and he wanted to feel it again.

Ryan propped an arm beneath his head and stared at the ceiling as Tessa's soft breathing indicated she'd fallen asleep.

Intimacy.

That was the elusive word he'd been searching for all night. The thing he'd felt when his eyes had met hers as he'd roared, buried deep inside her. He'd sounded ridiculous. Like a wounded animal, in pain. Needing someone to save him.

Ryan scrubbed a hand down his face, one arm still wrapped around his best friend. Whom he'd made love to. The woman who knew him better than anyone in the world.

And now they knew each other in a way they'd never allowed themselves to before. A way that made him feel raw and exposed, like a live wire.

While making love to Tess, he'd felt a surge of power as he'd teased her gorgeous body and coaxed her over the edge. Watched her free-fall into ecstasy, her body trembling.

But as her inner walls pulsed, pulling him over the cliff after her, he'd felt something completely foreign and yet vaguely familiar. It was a thing he couldn't name. Or maybe he hadn't wanted to.

Then when he'd startled awake, his arm slightly numb from being wedged beneath her, the answer was on his tongue.

Intimacy.

How was it that he'd managed to have gratifying sex with women without ever experiencing this heightened level of intimacy? Not even with his ex—the woman he'd planned to marry.

He and Sabrina had known each other. What the other wanted for breakfast. Each other's preferred drinks. They'd even known each other's bodies. *Well.* And yet he'd never experienced this depth of connection. Of truly being known by someone who could practically finish his sentences. Not because Tessa was so like him, but because she understood him in a way no one else did.

Ryan swallowed the hard lump clogging his throat and swiped the backs of his fingers over his damp brow.

Why is it suddenly so goddamned hot in here?

He blew out a long, slow breath. Tried to slow the rhythm of his heart, suddenly beating like a drum.

What the hell had he just done?

He'd satisfied the curiosity that had been simmering just below the surface of his friendship with Tessa. The desire to know her intimately. To know how it would feel to have her soft curves pressed against him as he'd surged inside her.

Now he knew what it was like for their bodies to move together. As if they were a single being. How it made his pulse race like a freight train as she called his name in a sweet, husky voice he'd never heard her use before. The delicious burn of her nails gently scraping his back as she wrapped her legs around him and pulled him in deeper.

And how it felt as she'd throbbed and pulsed around his heated flesh until he could no longer hold back his release.

Now, all he could think about was feeling all of those things again. Watching her shed the inhibitions that had held her back at first. Taking her a little further.

But Tessa was his best friend, and a very good friend's sister. He'd crossed the line. Broken a promise and taken them to a place they could never venture back from. After last night, he couldn't see her and not want her. Would never forget the taste and feel of her.

So what now?

Tess was sweet and sensitive. Warm and thoughtful. She deserved more than being friends with benefits. She deserved a man as kind and loving as she was.

Was he even capable of being that kind of man?

His family was nothing like the Nobles. Hank and Loretta Bateman weren't the doting parents that kissed injured knees and cheered effort. They believed in tough love, hard lessons and that failure wasn't to be tolerated by anyone with the last name Bateman.

Ryan knew unequivocally that his parents loved him, but he was twenty-nine years old and could never recall hearing either of them say the words explicitly.

He'd taken the same approach in his relationships.

It was how he was built, all he'd ever known. But Tess could never be happy in a relationship like that.

Ryan sucked in another deep breath and released it quietly. He gently kissed the top of her head and screwed his eyes shut. Allowed himself to surrender to the sleep that had eluded him until now.

They'd figure it all out in the morning. After he'd gotten some much-needed sleep. He always thought better with a clear head and a full stomach.

Twelve

Tessa's eyes fluttered opened. She blinked against the rays of light peeking through the hotel room curtain and rubbed the sleep from her eyes with her fist. Her leg was entwined with Ryan's, and one of her arms was buried beneath him.

She groaned, pressing a hand to her mouth to prevent a curse from erupting from her lips. She'd made love with her best friend. Had fallen asleep with him. She peeked beneath the covers, her mouth falling open.

Naked. Both of them.

Tessa snapped her mouth shut and eased the cover back down. Though it didn't exactly lie flat. Not with Ryan Bateman sporting a textbook definition of morning wood.

She sank her teeth into her lower lip and groaned internally. Her nipples hardened, and the space between her thighs grew incredibly wet. Heat filled her cheeks.

She'd been with Ryan in the most intimate way imaginable. And it had been…incredible. Better than anything she'd imagined. And she'd imagined it more than she cared to admit.

Ryan had been intense, passionate and completely unselfish. He seemed to get off on pleasing her. Had evoked reactions from her body she hadn't believed it capable of. And the higher he'd taken her, the more desperate she became to shatter the mask of control that gripped his handsome face.

Tessa drew her knees to her chest and took slow, deep breaths. Willed her hands to stop shaking. Tried to tap into the brain cells that had taken a siesta the moment she'd pressed her lips to Ryan's.

Yes, sex between them had been phenomenal. But the friendship they shared for more than two decades— that was something she honestly couldn't do without.

She needed some space, so she could clear her head and make better decisions than she had last night. Last night she'd allowed her stupid crush on her best friend to run wild. She'd bought into the Cinderella fantasy. Lock, stock and barrel.

What did she think would happen next? That he'd suddenly realize she was in love with him? Maybe even realize he was in love with her, too?

Not in this lifetime or the next.

She simply wasn't that lucky. Ryan had always considered her a friend. His best friend, but nothing more. A few hours together naked between the sheets wouldn't change that.

Besides, as her mother often reminded her, tigers don't change their stripes.

How many times had Ryan said it? *Sex is just sex.* A way to have a little fun and let off a little steam. Why would she expect him to feel differently just because it was her?

Her pent-up feelings for Ryan were her issue, not his.

Tessa's face burned with an intense heat, as if she was standing too close to a fire. Waking up naked with her best friend was awkward, but they could laugh it off. Blame it on the alcohol, like Jamie Foxx. Chalk it up to them both getting too carried away in the moment. But if she told him how she really felt about him, and he rejected her...

Tessa sighed. The only thing worse than secretly lusting after her best friend was having had him, knowing just how good things could be, and then being patently rejected. She'd never recover from that. Would never be able to look him in the face and pretend everything was okay.

And if, by some chance, Ryan was open to trying to turn this into something more, he'd eventually get bored with their relationship. As he had with every relationship he'd been in before. They'd risk destroying their friendship.

It wasn't worth the risk.

Tessa wiped away tears that stung the corners of her eyes. She quietly climbed out of bed, in search of her clothing.

She cursed under her breath as she retrieved her panties—the only clothing she'd been wearing when they entered the bedroom. Tessa pulled them on and grabbed Ryan's shirt from the floor. She slipped it on and buttoned a few of the middle buttons. She glanced back at his handsome form as he slept soundly, hoping everything between them would be all right.

Tessa slowly turned the doorknob and the door creaked open.

Damn.

Wasn't oiling door hinges part of the planned maintenance for a place like this? Did they not realize the necessity of silent hinges in the event a hotel guest needed a quiet escape after making a questionable decision with her best friend the night before?

Still, as soundly as Ryan was sleeping, odds were, he hadn't heard it.

"Tess?" Ryan called from behind her in that sexy, sleep-roughened voice that made her squirm.

Every. Damn. Time.

She sucked in a deep breath, forced a nonchalant smile and turned around. "Yes?"

"Where are you going?"

He'd propped himself up in bed on one elbow as he rubbed his eyes and squinted against the light. His brown hair stood all over his head in the hottest damn case of bed head she'd ever witnessed. And his bottle-green eyes glinted in the sunlight.

Trying to escape before you woke up. Isn't it obvious?

Tessa jerked a thumb over her shoulder. "I was about to hop into the shower, and I didn't want to wake you."

"Perfect." He sat up and threw off the covers. "We can shower together." A devilish smile curled his red lips. "I know how you feel about conserving water."

"You want to shower…together? The two of us?" She pointed to herself and then to him.

"Why? Were you thinking of inviting someone else?"

"Smart-ass." Her cheeks burned with heat. Ryan was in rare form. "You know what I meant."

"Yes, I do." He stalked toward her naked, at more than half-mast now. Looking like walking, talking sex-on-a-stick promising unicorn orgasms.

Ryan looped his arms around her waist and pressed her back against the wall. He leaned down and nuzzled her neck.

Tessa's beaded nipples rubbed against his chest through the fabric of the shirt she was wearing. Her belly fluttered, and her knees trembled. Her chest rose and fell with heavy, labored breaths. As if Ryan was sucking all the oxygen from the room, making it harder for her to breathe.

"C'mon, Tess." He trailed kisses along her shoulder as he slipped the shirt from it. "Don't make this weird. It's just us."

She raised her eyes to his, her heart racing. "It's already weird *because* it's just us."

"Good point." He gave her a cocky half smile and a micro nod. "Then we definitely need to do something to alleviate the weirdness."

"And *how* exactly are we going to do—" Tess squealed as Ryan suddenly lifted her and heaved her over his shoulder. He carried her, kicking and wiggling, into the master bathroom and turned on the water.

"Ryan Bateman, don't you dare even think about it," Tessa called over her shoulder, kicking her feet and holding on to Ryan's back for dear life.

He wouldn't drop her. She had every confidence of that. Still...

"You're going to ruin my hair."

"I like your curls better. In fact, I felt a little cheated that I didn't get to run my fingers through them. I always wanted to do that."

Something about his statement stopped her objections cold. Made visions dance in her head of them together in the shower with Ryan doing just that.

"Okay. Just put me down."

Ryan smacked her bottom lightly before setting her down, her body sliding down his. Seeming to rev them both up as steam surrounded them.

She slowly undid the three buttons of Ryan's shirt and made a show of sliding the fabric down one shoulder, then the other.

His green eyes darkened. His chest rose and fell heavily as his gaze met hers again after he'd followed the garment's descent to the floor.

Ryan hooked his thumbs into the sides of her panties and tugged her closer, dropping another kiss on her neck. He gently sank his teeth into her delicate flesh, nibbling the skin there as he glided her underwear over the swell of her bottom and down her hips.

She stepped out of them and into the shower. Pressed her back against the cool tiles. A striking contrast to the warm water. Ryan stepped into the shower, too, closing the glass door behind him and covering her mouth with his.

Tessa lay on her back, her hair wound in one of Ryan's clean, cotton T-shirts. He'd washed her hair and taken great delight in running a soapy loofah over every inch of her body.

Then he'd set her on the shower bench and dropped to his knees. He'd used the removable shower head as a makeshift sex toy. Had used it to bring her to climax twice. Then showed her just how amazing he could be with his tongue.

When he'd pressed the front of her body to the wall, lifted one of her legs, and taken her from behind, Tessa honestly hadn't thought it would be possible for her to get there again.

She was wrong.

She came hard, her body tightening and convulsing, and his did the same soon afterward.

They'd gone through their morning routines, brushing their teeth side by side, wrapped in towels from their shower together. Ryan ordered room service, and they ate breakfast in bed, catching the last half of a holiday comedy that was admittedly a pretty crappy movie overall. Still, it never failed to make the two of them laugh hysterically.

When the movie ended, Ryan had clicked off the television and kissed her. A kiss that slowly stoked the fire low in her belly all over again. Made her nipples tingle and the space between her thighs ache for him.

She lay staring up at Ryan, his hair still damp from the shower. Clearly hell-bent on using every single condom in that strip before the morning ended, he'd sheathed himself and entered her again.

Her eyes had fluttered closed at the delicious fullness as Ryan eased inside her. His movements were slow, deliberate, controlled.

None of those words described the Ryan Bateman

she knew. The man she'd been best friends with since they were both still in possession of their baby teeth.

Ryan was impatient. Tenacious. Persistent. He wanted everything five minutes ago. But the man who hovered over her now, his piercing green eyes boring into her soul and grasping her heart, was in no hurry. He seemed to relish the torturously delicious pleasure he was giving her with his slow, languid movements.

He was laser-focused. His brows furrowed, and his forehead beaded with sweat. The sudden swivel of his hips took her by surprise, and she whimpered with pleasure, her lips parting.

Ryan leaned down and pressed his mouth to hers, slipping his tongue inside and caressing her tongue.

Tessa got lost in his kiss. Let him rock them both into a sweet bliss that left her feeling like she was floating on a cloud.

She held on to him as he arched his back, his muscles straining as his own orgasm overtook him. Allowed herself to savor the warmth that encircled her sated body.

Then, gathering her to his chest, he removed her makeshift T-shirt turban and ran his fingers through her damp, curly hair.

She'd never felt more cherished or been more satisfied in her life. Yet, when the weekend ended, it would be the equivalent of the clock striking twelve for Cinderella. The dream would be over, her carriage would turn back into a pumpkin, and she'd be the same old Tessa Noble whom Ryan only considered a friend.

She inhaled his scent. Leather and cedar with a hint of patchouli. A scent she'd bought him for Christmas three years ago. Ryan had been wearing it ever since.

Tess was never sure if he wore it because he truly liked it or because he'd wanted to make her happy.

Now she wondered the same thing about what'd happened between them this weekend. He'd tailored the entire weekend to her. Had seemed determined to see to it that she felt special, pampered.

Had she been the recipient of a pity fuck?

The possibility of Ryan sleeping with her out of a sense of charity made her heart ache.

She tried not to think of what would happen when the weekend ended. To simply enjoy the moment between them here and now.

Tessa was his until "midnight." Then the magic of their weekend together would be over, and it would be time for them to return to the real world.

Thirteen

Ryan studied Tessa as she gathered her beauty products and stowed them back into her travel bag in preparation for checkout. They'd had an incredible weekend together. With the exception of the time they spent politely posing for the reporter at dinner and waxing poetic about their friendship, they'd spent most of the weekend just a few feet away in Ryan's bed.

But this morning Tessa had seemed withdrawn. Before he'd even awakened, she'd gotten out of bed, packed her luggage, laid out what she planned to wear to the football game, and showered.

Tessa opened a tube of makeup.

"You're wearing makeup to the game?" He stepped behind her in the mirror.

"Photos before the game." She gave his reflection a cursory glance. "Otherwise, I'd just keep it simple. Lip gloss, a little eye shadow. Mascara."

She went back to silently pulling items out of her makeup bag and lining them up on the counter.

"Tess, did I do something wrong? You seem really... I don't know...distant this morning."

A pained look crimped her features, and she sank her teeth into her lower lip before turning to face him. She heaved a sigh, and though she looked in his direction, she was clearly looking past him.

"Look, Rye, this weekend has been amazing. But I think it's in the best interest of our friendship if we go back to the way things were. Forget this weekend ever happened." She shifted her gaze to his. "I honestly feel that it's the only way our friendship survives this."

"Why?"

His question reeked of quiet desperation, but he could care less. The past two days had been the best days of his life. He thought they had been for her, too. So her request hit him like a sucker punch to the gut, knocking the wind out of him.

She took the shower cap off her head, releasing the long, silky hair she'd straightened with a blow-dryer attachment before they'd met Greg at the restaurant for dinner the night before.

"Because the girl you were attracted to on that stage isn't who I am. I can't maintain all of this." She indicated the makeup on the counter and her straightened hair. "It's exhausting. More importantly, it isn't me. Not really."

"You think all of this is what I'm attracted to? That I can't see...that I haven't always seen you?"

"You never kissed me before, not seriously," she added before he could mention that kiss in college. "And we certainly never..." She gestured toward the bed, as if she was unable to bring herself to say the words or look at the place where he'd laid her bare and tasted every inch of her warm brown skin.

"To be fair, you kissed me." Ryan stepped closer.

She tensed, but then lifted her chin defiantly, meeting his gaze again. The rapid rise and fall of her chest, indicated that she was taking shallow breaths. But she didn't step away from him. For which he was grateful.

"You know what I mean," she said through a frustrated little pout. "You never showed any romantic interest in me before the auction. So why are you interested now? Is it because someone else showed interest in me?"

"Why would you think that?" His voice was low and gruff. Pained.

Her accusation struck him like an openhanded slap to the face. It was something his mother had often said to him as a child. That he was only interested in his old toys when she wanted to give them to someone else.

Was that what he was doing with Tess?

"Because if I had a relationship…a life of my own, then I wouldn't be a phone call away whenever you needed me." Her voice broke slightly, and she swiped at the corners of her eyes. "Or maybe it's a competitive thing. I don't know. All I know is that you haven't made a move before now. So what changed?"

The hurt in her eyes and in the tremor of her voice felt like a jagged knife piercing his chest.

She was right. He was a selfish bastard. Too much of a coward to explore his attraction to her. Too afraid of how it might change their relationship.

"I… I…" His throat tightened, and his mouth felt dry as he sought the right words. But Tessa was his best friend, and they'd always shot straight with each other. "Sex, I could get anywhere." He forced his gaze to meet hers. Gauged her reaction. "But what we have... I don't have that with anyone else, Tess. I didn't want to take a chance on losing you. Couldn't risk screwing up our friendship like I've screwed up every relationship I've ever been in."

She dropped her gaze, absently dragging her fingers through her hair and tugging it over one shoulder. Tess was obviously processing his words. Weighing them on her internal bullshit meter.

"So why risk it now? What's changed?" She wrapped her arms around her middle. Something she did to comfort herself.

"I don't know." He whispered the words, his eyes not meeting hers.

It was a lie.

Tess was right. He'd been prompted to action by his fear of losing her. He'd been desperate to stake his claim on Tess. Wipe thoughts of any other man from her brain.

In the past, she had flirted with the occasional guy. Even dated a few. But none of them seemed to pose any real threat to what they shared. But when she'd stood on that stage as the sexiest goddamn woman in the entire room with men falling all over themselves to spend a few hours with her...suddenly everything was different. For the first time in his life, the threat of losing his best friend to someone else suddenly became very real. And he couldn't imagine his life without her in it.

Brain on autopilot, he'd gone into caveman mode. Determined to win the bid, short of putting up the whole damn ranch in order to win her.

Tessa stared at him, her pointed gaze demanding further explanation.

"It felt like the time was right. Like Fate stepped in and gave us a nudge."

"You're full of shit, Ryan Bateman." She smacked her lips and narrowed her gaze. Arms folded over her chest, she shifted to a defensive stance. "You don't believe in Fate. 'Our lives are what we make of them.' That's what you've always said."

"I'm man enough to admit when I'm wrong. Or at least open-minded enough to explore the possibility."

She turned to walk away, but he grasped her fingertips with his. A move that was more of a plea than a demand. Still, she halted and glanced over her shoulder in his direction.

"Tess, why are you so dead set against giving this a chance?"

"Because I'm afraid of losing you, too." Her voice was a guttural whisper.

He tightened his grip on her hand and tugged her closer, forcing her eyes to meet his. "You're not going to lose me, Tess. I swear, I'm not going anywhere."

"Maybe not, but we both know your MO when it comes to relationships. You rush into them, feverish and excited. But after a while you get bored, and you're ready to move on." She frowned, a pained look furrowing her brow. "What happens then, Ryan? What happens once you've pulled me in deep and then you decide you just want to go back to being friends?" She shook her head vehemently. "I honestly don't think I could handle that."

Ryan's jaw clenched. He wanted to object. Promise to never hurt her. But hadn't he hurt every woman he'd ever been with except the one woman who'd walked away from him?

It was the reason Tripp had made him promise to leave his sister alone. Because, though they were friends, he didn't deem him good enough for his sister. Didn't trust that he wouldn't hurt her.

Tessa obviously shared Tripp's concern.

Ryan wished he could promise Tess he wouldn't break her heart. But their polar opposite approaches to relationships made it seem inevitable.

He kept his relationships casual. A means of mutual satisfaction. Because he believed in fairy-tale love and romance about as much as he believed in Big Foot and the Loch Ness Monster.

Tess, on the other hand, was holding out for the man who would sweep her off her feet. For a relationship like the one her parents shared. She didn't understand that Chuck and Tina Noble were the exception, rather than the rule.

Yet, despite knowing all the reasons he and Tess should walk away from this, he couldn't let her go.

Tessa's frown deepened as his silent response to her objection echoed off the walls in the elegant, tiled bathroom.

"This weekend has been amazing. You made me feel like Cinderella at the ball. But we've got the game this afternoon, then we're heading back home. The clock is about to strike midnight, and it's time for me to turn back into a pumpkin."

"You realize that you've just taken the place of the Maybach in this scenario." He couldn't help the smirk that tightened the edges of his mouth.

Some of the tension drained from his shoulders as

her sensual lips quirked in a rueful smile. She shook her head and playfully punched him in the gut.

"You know what I mean. It's time for me to go back to being me. Trade my glass slippers in for a pair of Chuck Taylors."

He caught her wrist before she could walk away. Pulling her closer, he wrapped his arms around her and stared deep into those gorgeous brown eyes that had laid claim on him ever since he'd first gazed into them.

"Okay, Cinderella. If you insist that things go back to the way they were, there's not much I can do about that. But if you're mine until midnight, I won't be cheated. Let's forget the game, stay here and make love."

"But I've already got the tickets."

"I don't care." He slowly lowered his mouth toward hers. "I'll reimburse you."

"But they're on the fifty-yard line. At the stadium that's your absolute favorite place in the world."

"Not today it isn't." He feathered a gentle kiss along the edge of her mouth, then trailed his lips down her neck.

"Ryan, we can't just blow off the—" She dug her fingers into his bare back and a low moan escaped her lips as he kissed her collarbone. The sound drifted below his waist and made him painfully hard.

"We can do anything we damn well please." He pressed a kiss to her ear. One of the many erogenous zones he'd discovered on her body during their weekend together. Tessa's knees softened, and her head lolled slightly, giving him better access to her neck.

"But the article…they're expecting us to go to the game, and if we don't…well, everyone will think—"

"Doesn't matter what they think." He lifted her chin and studied her eyes, illuminated by the morning sunlight spilling through the windows. He dragged a thumb across her lower lip. "It only matters what you and I want."

He pressed another kiss to her lips, lingering for a moment before reluctantly pulling himself away again so he could meet her gaze. He waited for her to open her eyes again. "What do you want, Tess?"

She swallowed hard, her gaze on his lips. "I want both. To go to the game, as expected, and to spend the day in bed making love to you."

"Hmm…intriguing proposition." He kissed her again. Tess really was a woman after his own heart. "One that would require us to spend one more night here. Then we'll head back tomorrow. And if you still insist—"

"I will." There was no hesitation in her voice, only apology. She moved a hand to cradle his cheek, her gaze meeting his. "Because it's what's best for our friendship."

Ryan forced a smile and released an uneasy breath. Tried to pretend that his chest didn't feel like it was caving in. He gripped her tighter against him, lifting her as she wrapped her legs around him.

If he couldn't have her like this always, he'd take every opportunity to have her now. In the way he'd always imagined. Even if that meant they'd be a little late for the game.

Fourteen

They'd eaten breakfast, their first meal in the kitchen since they'd arrived, neither of them speaking much. The only part of their conversation that felt normal was their recap of some of the highlights during their team's win the day before. But then the conversation had returned to the stilted awkwardness they'd felt before then.

Ryan had loaded their luggage into the Maybach, and they were on the road, headed back to Royal, barely two words spoken between them before Tessa finally broke their silence.

"This is for the best, Rye. After all, you were afraid to tell my brother about that fake kiss we had on Valentine's Day in college." Tessa grinned, her voice teasing.

Ryan practically snorted, poking out his thumb and holding it up. "A… I am *not* afraid of your brother."

Not physically, at least. Ryan was a good head taller than Tripp and easily outweighed him by twenty-five pounds of what was mostly muscle. But, in all honesty, he *was* afraid of how the weekend with Tessa would affect his friendship with Tripp. It could disrupt the connection between their families.

The Batemans and Nobles were as thick as thieves now. Had been since their fathers were young boys. But in the decades prior, the families had feuded over land boundaries, water rights and countless other ugly disputes. Some of which made Ryan ashamed of his ancestors. But everything had changed the day Tessa's grandfather had saved Ryan's father's life when he'd fallen into a well.

That fateful day, the two families had bonded. A bond which had grown more intricate over the years, creating a delicate ecosystem he dared not disturb.

Ryan continued, adding his index finger for effect. "B… Yes, I think it might be damaging to our friendship if Tripp tries to beat my ass and I'm forced to defend myself." He added a third finger, hesitant to make his final point. An admission that made him feel more vulnerable than he was comfortable being, even with Tess. "And C…it wasn't a fake kiss. It was a little too real. Which is why I've tried hard to never repeat it."

Ryan's pulse raced, and his throat suddenly felt dry. He returned his other hand to the steering wheel and stared at the road ahead. He didn't need to turn his head to know Tessa was staring at him. The heat of her stare seared his skin and penetrated his chest.

"Are you saying that since that kiss—" Her voice was trembling, tentative.

"Since that kiss, I've recognized that the attraction between us went both ways." He rushed the words out, desperate to stop her from asking what he suspected she might.

Why hadn't he said anything all those years ago? Or in the years since that night?

He'd never allowed himself to entertain either question. Doing so was a recipe for disaster.

Why court disaster when they enjoyed an incomparable friendship? Shouldn't that be good enough?

"Oh." The disappointment in her voice stirred heaviness in his chest, rather than the ease and lightness he usually felt when they were together.

When Ryan finally glanced over at his friend, she was staring at him blankly, as if there was a question she was afraid to ask.

"Why haven't you ever said anything?"

Because he hadn't been ready to get serious about anyone back then. And Tessa Noble wasn't the kind of girl you passed the time with. She was the genuine deal. The kind of girl you took home to mama. And someone whose friendship meant everything to him.

"Bottom line? I promised your brother I'd treat you like an honorary little sister. That I'd never lay a hand on you." A knot tightened in his belly. "A promise I've obviously broken."

"Wait, you two just decided, without consulting me? Like I'm a little child and you two are my misfit parents? What kind of caveman behavior is that?"

Ryan winced. Tessa was angry, and he didn't blame her. "To be fair, we had this conversation when he and I were about fourteen. Long before you enlightened us on the error of our anti-feminist tendencies. Still, it's a promise I've always taken seriously. Especially since, at the time, I did see you as a little sister. Obviously, things have changed since then."

"When?" Her tone was soft, but demanding. As if she needed to know.

It wasn't a conversation he wanted to have, but if they were going to have it, she deserved his complete honesty.

"I first started to feel some attraction toward you when you were around sixteen." He cleared his throat, his eyes steadily on the road. "But when I left for college I realized how deep that attraction ran. I was miserable without you that first semester in college."

"You seemed to adapt pretty quickly by sleeping your way across campus," she huffed. She turned toward the window and sighed. "I shouldn't have said that. I'm sorry. I…" She didn't finish her statement.

"Forget it." Ryan released a long, slow breath. "This is uncharted territory for us. We'll learn to deal with it. Everything'll be fine."

But even as he said the words, he couldn't convince himself of their truth.

After Ryan's revelations, the ride home was awkward and unusually quiet, even as they both tried much too hard to behave as if everything was fine.

Everything most certainly was *not* fine.

Strained and uncomfortable? *Yes.* Their forced conversation, feeble smiles and weak laughter were proof they'd both prefer to be anywhere else.

And it confirmed they'd made the right decision by not pursuing a relationship. It would only destroy their friendship in the end once Ryan had tired of her and was ready to move on to someone polished and gorgeous, like his ex.

This was all her fault. She'd kissed Ryan. Tessa clenched her hands in her lap, willing them to stop trembling.

She only hoped their relationship could survive this phase of awkwardness, so things could go back to the way they were.

Tessa's phone buzzed, and she checked her text messages.

Tripp had sent a message to say that he'd landed a meeting with a prospect that had the potential to become one of their largest customers. His flight to Iowa would leave in a few days, and she would be in charge at the Noble Spur.

She scrolled to the next text and read Bo's message reminding her that she'd agreed to attend a showing of *A Christmas Carol* with him at the town's outdoor, holiday theater.

Tessa gripped her phone and turned it over in her lap, looking over guiltily at Ryan. After what had happened between them this weekend, the thought of going out with someone else turned her stomach, but she'd already promised Bo.

And even though she and Bo were going to a movie together, it could hardly be considered a date. Half the town of Royal would be there.

Would it be so wrong for them to go on a friendly outing to the movies?

Besides, maybe seeing other people was just the thing to alleviate the awkwardness between them and prompt them to forget about the past three days.

Tessa worried her lower lip with her teeth. Deep

down, she knew the truth. Things would never be the same between them.

Because she wanted Ryan now more than ever.

No matter how hard she tried, Tessa would never forget their weekend together and how he'd made her feel.

Fifteen

Gus sat in his favorite recliner and put his feet up to watch a little evening television. Reruns of some of his favorite old shows. Only he held the remote in his hand without ever actually turning the television on.

The house was quiet. Too quiet.

Alexis was in Houston on business, and her brother Justin was staying in Dallas overnight with a friend.

Normally, he appreciated the solitude. Enjoyed being able to watch whatever the hell he wanted on television without one of the kids scoffing about him watching an old black-and-white movie or an episode of one of his favorite shows that he'd seen half a dozen times before. But lately, it had been harder to cheerfully bear his solitude.

During the months he and Rose had worked together to split up Daniel and Alexis, he'd found himself enjoying her company. So much so that he preferred it mightily to being alone in this big old house.

Gus put down the remote and paced the floor. He hadn't seen Rose since the night of the bachelor auction at the Texas Cattleman's Club. They'd spoken by phone twice, but just to confirm that their plan had worked.

As far as they could tell, Alexis and Daniel were no longer seeing each other. And both of them seemed to be in complete misery.

Gus had done everything he could to try and cheer Alexis up. But the pain in her eyes persisted. As did the evidence that she'd still been crying from time to time.

He'd tried to get his granddaughter to talk about it, but she'd insisted that it wasn't anything she couldn't handle. And she said he wouldn't understand anyway.

That probably hurt the most. Especially since he really did understand how she was feeling. And worse, he and Rose had been the root cause of that pain.

The guilt gnawed at his gut and broke his heart.

Rose had reminded him of why they'd first hatched the plan to break up Daniel and Alexis. Their families had been mortal enemies for decades. Gus and Rose had hated each other so much they were willing to work together in order to prevent their grandchildren from being involved with each other. Only, Gus hadn't reckoned on coming to enjoy the time he spent with Rose Clayton. And he most surely hadn't anticipated that he'd find himself getting sweet on her again after all these years.

He was still angry at Rose for how she'd treated him all those years ago, when he'd been so very in love with her. But now he understood that because of her cruel father, holding the welfare of her ill mother over Rose's head, she'd felt she had no choice but to break it off with him and marry someone Jedediah Clayton had deemed worthy.

He regretted not recognizing the distress Rose was in back then. That her actions had been a cry for help. Signs he and his late wife, Sarah, who had once been Rose's best friend, had missed.

Gus heaved a sigh and glanced over his shoulder at the television. His reruns could wait.

Gus left the Lone Wolf Ranch and headed over to Rose's place, The Silver C, one last time to say goodbye. Maybe share a toast to the success of their plan to look out for Alexis and Daniel in the long run, even if the separation was hurting them both now.

The property had once been much vaster than his. But over the years, he'd bought quite a bit of it. Rose had begrudgingly sold it to him in order to pay off the gambling debts of her late husband, Ed.

Rose's father must be rolling over in his grave because the ranch hand he'd judged unworthy of his daughter was now in possession of much of the precious land the man had sought to keep out of his hands. Gus didn't normally think ill of the dead. But in Jedediah's case, he was willing to make an exception.

When Gus arrived at The Silver C, all decked out in its holiday finest, Rose seemed as thrilled to see him as he was to see her.

"Gus, what on earth are you doing here?" A smile lighting her eyes, she pulled the pretty red sweater she was wearing around her more tightly as cold air rushed in from outside.

"After all these months working together, I thought

it was only right that we had a proper goodbye." He held up a bottle of his favorite top-shelf whiskey.

Rose laughed, a joyful sound he still had fond memories of. "Well, by all means, come on in."

She stepped aside and let Gus inside. The place smelled of pine from the two fresh Christmas trees Rose had put up. One in the entry hall and another in the formal living room. And there was the unmistakable scent of fresh apple pie.

Rose directed Gus to have a seat on the sofa in the den where she'd been watching television. Then she brought two glasses and two slices of warm apple pie on a little silver tray.

"That homemade pie?" Gus inquired as she set the tray on the table.

"Wouldn't have it any other way." She grinned, handing him a slice and a fork. She opened the bottle of whiskey and poured each of them a glass, neat.

She sat beside him and watched him with interest as he took his first bite of pie.

"Hmm, hmm, hmm. Now that's a little slice of heaven right there." He grinned.

"I'm glad you like it. And since we're celebrating our successful plot to save the kids from a disastrous future, pie seems fitting." She smiled, but it seemed hollow. She took a sip of the whiskey and sighed. "Smooth."

"That's one of the reasons I like it so much." He nodded, shoveling another bite of pie into his mouth and chewing thoughtfully. He surveyed the space and leaned closer, lowering his voice. "Daniel around today?"

"No, he's gone to Austin to handle some ranch business." She raised an eyebrow, her head tilted. "Why?"

"No reason in particular." Gus shrugged, putting down his pie plate and sipping his whiskey. "Just wanted to ask how the boy is doing. He still as miserable as my Alexis?"

Pain and sadness were etched in Rose's face as she lowered her gaze and nodded. "I'm afraid so. He's trying not to show how hurt he is, but I honestly don't think I've ever seen him like this. He's already been through so much with his mother." She sighed, taking another sip of whiskey. Her hands were trembling slightly as she shook her head. "I hope we've done the right thing here. I guess I didn't realize how much they meant to each other." She sniffled and pulled a tissue out of her pocket, dabbing at her eyes.

Rose forced a laugh. "I'm sorry. You must think me so ridiculous sitting here all teary-eyed over having gotten the very thing we both wanted."

Gus put down his glass and took Rose's hand between his. It was delicate and much smaller than his own. Yet, they were the hands of a woman who had worked a ranch her entire life.

"I understand just what you're feeling." He stroked her wrist with his thumb. "Been feeling pretty guilty, too. And second-guessing our decision."

"Oh, Gus, we spent so many years heartbroken and angry. It changed us, and not for the better." Tears leaked from Rose's eyes, and her voice broke. "I just hope we haven't doomed Alexis and Daniel to the same pain and bitterness."

"It's going to be okay, Rose." He took her in his arms and hugged her to his chest. Tucked her head beneath his chin as he swayed slowly and stroked her hair.

"We won't allow that to happen to Alexis and Daniel. I promise."

"God, I hope you're right. They deserve so much more than that. Both of them." She held on to him. One arm wrapped around him and the other was pressed to his chest.

He should be focused on Daniel and Alexis and the dilemma that he and Rose had created. Gus realized that. Yet, an awareness of Rose slowly spread throughout his body. Sparks of electricity danced along his spine.

He rubbed her back and laid a kiss atop her head. All of the feelings he'd once experienced when he'd held Rose in his arms as a wet-behind-the-ears ranch hand came flooding back to him. Overwhelmed his senses, making his heart race in a way he'd forgotten that it could.

After all these years, he still had a thing for Rose Clayton. Still wanted her.

Neither of them had moved or spoken for a while. They just held each other in silence, enjoying each other's comfort and warmth.

Finally, Rose pulled away a little and tipped her head, her gaze meeting his. She leaned in closer, her mouth hovering just below his, her eyes drifting closed.

Gus closed the space between them, his lips meeting hers in a kiss that was soft and sweet. Almost chaste.

He slipped his hands on either side of her face, angling it to give him better access to her mouth. Ran his tongue along her lips that tasted of smooth whiskey and homemade apple pie.

Rose sighed with satisfaction, parting her lips. She

clutched at his shirt, pulling him as close as their position on the sofa would allow.

She murmured with pleasure when he slipped his tongue between her lips.

Time seemed to slow as they sat there, their mouths seeking each other's out in a kiss that grew hotter. Greedier. More intense.

There was a fire in his belly that he hadn't felt in ages. One that made him want things with Rose he hadn't wanted in so long.

Gus forced himself to pull away from Rose. He gripped her shoulders, his eyes searching hers for permission.

Rose stood up. She switched off the television with the remote, picked up their two empty whiskey glasses, then walked toward the stairs that led to the upper floor of The Silver C. Looking back at him, she flashed a wicked smile that did things to him.

"Are you coming or not?"

Gus nearly knocked over the silver tray on the table in front of him in his desperation to climb to his feet. He hurried toward her but was halted by her next words.

"Don't forget the bottle."

"Yes, ma'am." Grinning, he snatched it off the table before grabbing her hand and following her up the stairs.

Sixteen

When he heard his name called, Ryan looked up from where Andy, his farrier, was shoeing one of the horses.

It was Tripp.

The muscles in Ryan's back tensed. He hadn't talked to Tess or Tripp in the three days since they'd been back from their trip to Dallas. He could tell by his friend's expression that Tripp was concerned about something.

Maybe he had come to deliver a much-deserved asswhipping. After all, Ryan had broken his promise by sleeping with Tess.

"What's up, Tripp?" Ryan walked over to his friend, still gauging the man's mood.

"I'm headed to the airport shortly, but I need to ask a favor."

"Sure. Anything."

"Keep an eye on Tess, will you?"

Ryan hadn't expected that. "Why, is something wrong?"

"Not exactly." Tripp removed his Stetson and adjusted it before placing it back on his head. "It's just that Mom and Dad are still gone, and I'm staying in Des Moines overnight. She'll be kicking around that big old house by herself mostly. We let a few hands off for the holidays. Plus… I don't like that Bo and Clem have been sniffing around the last few days. I'm beginning to think that letting Tessa participate in that bachelor auction was a mistake."

Ryan tugged his baseball cap down on his head, unsettled by the news of Bo and Clem coming around. He'd paid a hefty sum at the auction to ward those two off. Apparently, they hadn't gotten the hint.

"First, if you think you *let* your sister participate in that bachelor's auction, you don't know your sister very well. Tess has got a mind of her own. Always has. Always will."

"Guess you're right about that." Tripp rubbed the back of his neck. "And I'm not saying that Bo or Clem are bad guys. They're nice enough, I guess."

"Just not when they come calling on your sister." Ryan chuckled. He knew exactly how Tripp felt.

"Yeah, pretty much."

"Got a feeling the man you'll think is good enough for your little sister ain't been born yet."

"And probably never will be." Tripp chuckled. "But as her big brother, it's my job to give any guy who comes around a hard time. Make him prove he's worthy."

"Well, just hold your horses there, buddy. It's not like she's considering either of them." Ryan tried to appear nonchalant about the whole ordeal. Though on the inside he felt like David Banner in the midst of turning into the Incredible Hulk. He wanted to smash both Bo and Clem upside the head and tell them to go sniffing around someone else. "I think you're getting a little ahead of yourself."

"You haven't been around since you guys got back." The statement almost sounded accusatory. "Looks like the flower show threw up in our entry hall."

"Clem and Bo have been sending Tessa flowers?" Ryan tried to keep his tone and his facial expression neutral. He counted backward from ten in his head.

"Clem's apparently determined to empty out the local florist. Bo, on the other hand, has taken Tessa out to some play and this afternoon they're out riding."

Ryan hoped like hell that Tripp didn't notice the tick in his jaw or the way his fists clenched at his sides.

Tripp flipped his wrist, checking his watch. "Look, I'd better get going. I'll be back tomorrow afternoon, but call me if you need anything."

"Will do." Ryan tipped the brim of his baseball hat. "Safe travels."

He watched his friend climb back into his truck and head toward the airport in Dallas.

Jaw clenched, Ryan uncurled his fists and reminded himself to calm down. Then he saddled up Phantom, his black quarter horse stallion, and went for a ride.

For the past few days, he hadn't been able to stop thinking about his weekend with Tess. The moments they'd shared replayed again and again in his head. Distracted him from his work. Kept him up staring at the ceiling in the middle of the night.

He knew Tess well. Knew she'd been as affected by

their weekend together as he had. So how could she dismiss what they'd shared so easily and go out with Bo, or for God's sake, Clem?

Phantom's hooves thundered underneath him as the cold, brisk air slapped him in the face. He'd hoped that his ride would calm him down and help him arrive at the same conclusion Tess had. That it would be better for everyone if they remained friends.

But no matter how hard and fast he'd ridden, it didn't drive away his desire for Tess. Nor did it ease the fury that rose in his chest at the thought of another man touching her the way he had. The way he wanted to again.

He recognized the validity of Tessa's concerns that he wasn't serious and that he'd be chasing after some other skirt in a few months. He couldn't blame her for feeling that way. After all, as Helene was fond of saying, the proof was in the pudding.

He wouldn't apologize for his past. Because he'd never lied to or misled any of the women he'd dated. So he certainly wouldn't give his best friend any sense of false hope that he'd suddenly convert to the romantic suitor he'd been over the course of the weekend, for the sake of the Texas Cattleman's Club.

Ryan wasn't that guy any more than Tessa was the kind of woman who preferred a pair of expensive, red-bottomed heels to a hot new pair of sneakers.

So why couldn't he let go of the idea of the two of them being together?

He'd asked himself that question over and over the past few days, and the same answer kept rising above all the bullshit excuses he'd manufactured.

He craved the intimacy that they shared.

It was the thing that made his heart swell every time he thought of their weekend together. The thing that made it about so much more than just the sex.

He'd even enjoyed planning their weekend. And he'd derived a warm sense of satisfaction from seeing her reaction to each of his little surprises.

Ryan had always believed that people who made a big show of their relationships were desperate to make other people believe they were happy. But despite his romantic gestures being part of a ruse to keep the club from being mired in scandal, they had brought him and Tess closer. Shown her just how much he valued her.

Maybe he didn't believe that love was rainbows and sugarplums. Or that another person was the key to his happiness. But he knew unquestionably that he would be miserable if Tess got involved with someone else.

He couldn't promise her that he'd suddenly sweep her off her feet like some counterfeit Prince Charming. But he sure as hell wanted to try, before she walked into the arms of someone else.

Ryan and Phantom returned to the stables, and he handed him off to Andy. Then he hurried into the house to take a shower. He needed to see Tess right away.

Seventeen

Tessa checked her phone. The only messages were from Tripp, letting her know that his plane had landed safely, and from Clem asking if she'd received his flowers ahead of their casual dinner date later that night.

She tossed the phone on the counter. No messages from Ryan. They'd maintained radio silence since he'd set her luggage in the entry hall, said goodbye, and driven off.

Tessa realized that the blame wasn't all his. After all, the phone worked both ways. On a typical day, she would've called her best friend a couple of times by now. She was clearly avoiding him, as much as he was avoiding her.

She was still angry that Ryan and Tripp had made a pact about her. As if she were incapable of making her own decisions. Mostly, she was hurt that Ryan hadn't countered her accusation that he'd eventually tire of her and move on to someone else.

She wanted him to deny it. To fight for her. But Ryan hadn't raised the slightest objection. Which meant what he really wanted was a no-strings fuck buddy until something better came along.

For her, that would never be enough with Ryan. She was already in way too deep. But the truth was, she would probably never be enough for him. She was nothing like the lithe, glamorous women who usually caught Ryan's eye. Women like Sabrina Calhoun who was probably born wearing a pair of Louboutins and carrying an Hermès bag. Or women like Lana, the overly friendly barmaid. Women who exuded sex and femininity rather than looking like they shopped at Ranchers R Us.

Headlights shone in the kitchen window. Someone was in the driveway. As soon as the vehicle pulled up far enough, Tess could see it clearly.

It was Ryan's truck.

Her belly fluttered, and her muscles tensed. She waited for him to come to the kitchen door, but he didn't. Instead, he made a beeline for the stables.

Ryan had likely come to check on the stables at Tripp's request. He was obviously still avoiding her, and she was over it.

Nervousness coiled through her and knotted in her belly. They both needed to be mature about this whole thing. Starting right now.

She wouldn't allow the fissure between them to crack open any wider. If that meant she had to be the one to break the ice, she would.

Tessa's hair, piled on top of her head in a curly bun,

was still damp from the shower. She'd thrown on an old graphic T-shirt and a pair of jeans, so she could run out and double-check the stables.

Not her best look.

Tess slipped on a jacket and her boots and trudged out to the stables.

"Hey." She approached him quietly, her arms folded across her body.

"Hey." Ryan leaned against the wall. "Sorry, I haven't called. Been playing catch-up since we returned."

"I've been busy, too." She pulled the jacket tighter around her.

"I heard. Word is you've got a date tonight." The resentment in his voice was unmistakable. "You spent the weekend in my bed. A few days later and suddenly you and Bo are a thing and Clem is sending you a houseful of flowers?"

"Bo and I aren't *a thing*. We've just gone out a couple times. As friends." Her cheeks were hot. "And despite what happened this weekend, you and I *aren't* a thing. So you don't get a say in who I do or don't spend time with." The pitch of her voice was high, and the words were spilling out of her mouth. Tessa sucked in a deep breath, then continued. "Besides, are you going to tell me you've never done the same?"

Crimson spread across his cheeks. He stuffed his hands in his pockets. "That was different."

"Why? Because you're a guy?"

"Because it was casual, and neither of us had expectations for anything more."

"How is that different from what happened between us?"

Ryan was playing mind games with her, and she didn't appreciate it.

"Because I *do* expect more. That is, I want more. With you." He crept closer.

Tessa hadn't expected that. She shifted her weight from one foot to the other, her heart beating faster. "What are you saying?"

"I'm saying I want more of what we had this past weekend. That I want it to be me and you. No one else. And I'm willing to do whatever you need in order to make it happen."

"Whatever *I* need?" The joy that had been building in her chest suddenly slammed into a brick wall. "As in, you'd be doing it strictly for my benefit, not because it's what you want?"

"You make it sound as if I'm wrong for wanting you to be happy." His brows furrowed, and his mouth twisted in confusion. "How does that make me the bad guy?"

"It doesn't make you a bad person, Ryan. But I'm not looking for a fuck buddy. Not even one who happens to be my best friend." She pressed a hand to her forehead and sighed.

"I wouldn't refer to it that way, but if it makes us happy, why not?" Ryan's voice was low, his gaze sincere. He took her hand in his. "Who cares what anyone else thinks as long as it's what we want?"

"But it isn't what *I* want." Tears stung Tessa's eyes, and her voice wavered.

Ryan lifted her chin, his green eyes pinning her in place. "What *do* you want, Tess?"

"I want the entire package, Ryan. Marriage. Kids, eventually." She pulled away, her back turned to him for a moment before turning to face him again. "And I'll never get any of that if I settle for being friends with benefits."

"How can you be so sure it wouldn't work between us?" he demanded.

"Because you can't even be honest about what you want in bed with me." She huffed, her hands shaking.

There, she'd said it.

"What the hell are you talking about, Tess?"

Her face and chest were suddenly hot, and the vast barn seemed too small a space for the two of them. She slipped off her jacket and hung it on a hook.

Though the remaining ranch staff had left for the day and Tripp was gone, she still lowered her voice. As if the horses would spread gossip to the folks in town.

"I know you like it…rough. You weren't like that with me."

"Really? You're complaining about my performance?" He folded his arms, his jaw clenched.

"No, of course not. It was amazing. *You* were amazing. But I overheard Sabrina talking to a friend of hers on the phone when you two were still together. She was saying that she liked rough sex, and there was no one better at it than you."

Tessa's heart thumped. Her pulse, thundering in her ears, seemed to echo throughout the space.

"You overheard her say that on the phone?"

Tessa nodded.

"You know that wasn't an accident, right? She got a kick out of rattling your cage."

Tess suspected as much. Sabrina had never much liked her.

"You didn't answer my question." She looked in his

direction, but her eyes didn't quite meet his. "No judgment. I just want to know if it's true."

"Sometimes." He shrugged. "Depends on my mood, who I'm with. And we're not talking whips and chains, if that's what you're imagining." He was clearly uncomfortable having this discussion with her. Not that she was finding it to be a walk in the park either. "Why does it matter?"

"Because if that's what you like, but with me you were…"

"Not rough," he offered tersely. "And you're angry about that?"

"Not angry. Just realistic. If you can't be yourself with me in bed, you're not going to be happy. You'll get bored and you'll want out."

Ryan stared down at her, stepping closer. "I responded to you. Gave you what I thought you wanted."

"And you did." She took a step backward, her back hitting the wall. She swallowed hard. "But did it ever occur to you that I would've liked the chance to do the same for you?"

Sighing heavily, Ryan placed one hand on the wall behind her and cradled her cheek with the other. "It's not like that's the only way I like it, Tess. I don't regret anything about my weekend with you."

"But the point was you felt you *couldn't*. Because of our friendship or maybe because of your promise to Tripp. I don't know. All I know for sure is that pretending that everything will be okay is a fool's game." She forced herself to stand taller. Chin tipped, she met his gaze.

"So that's it? Just like that, you decide that's reason enough for us to not be together?" His face was red, and anger vibrated beneath his words, though his expression remained placid.

"Isn't that reason enough for you?"

"Sex isn't everything, Tess."

"For you, it always has been. Sex is just sex, right? It's not about love or a deeper connection." The knot in Tessa's stomach tightened when Ryan dropped his gaze and didn't respond. She sighed. "Tigers can't change their stripes, Ryan. No matter how hard they might try."

She turned to dip under his arm, but he lowered it, blocking her escape from the heated look in his eyes. His closeness. His scent. Leather. Cedar. Patchouli.

Damn that patchouli.

"Ryan, what else is there for us to say?"

"Nothing." He lowered his hands to her waist and stepped closer, his body pinning hers to the wall.

Time seemed to move in slow motion as Ryan dipped his head, his lips hovering just above hers. His gaze bored into hers. She didn't dare move an inch. Didn't dare blink.

When she didn't object, his lips crushed hers in a bruising, hungry kiss that made her heart race. He tasted of Helene's famous Irish stew—one of Ryan's favorite meals—and an Irish ale.

His hands were on her hips, pinning her in place against the wall behind her. Not with enough force to hurt her, but he'd asserted himself in such a way that it was crystal clear that he wanted her there, and that she shouldn't move.

She had no plans to.

As much as she'd enjoyed seeing a gentler side of Ryan during their weekend together, the commanding look in his eye and the assertiveness of his tone revved her up in a way she would never have imagined.

He trailed his hands up her sides so damned slowly she was sure she could count the milliseconds that passed. The backs of his hands grazed her hips, her waist, the undersides of her breasts.

The apex of her thighs pulsed and throbbed with such power she felt like he might bring her over the edge just from his kiss and his demanding touch.

Her knees quivered, and her breaths were quick and shallow. His kisses grew harder, hungrier as he placed his large hands around her throat. Not squeezing or applying pressure of any real measure. But conveying a heightened sense of control.

Ryan pulled back, his body still pinning hers, but his kiss gone. After a few seconds, her eyes shot open. He was staring at her with an intensity that she might have found scary in any other situation. But she knew Ryan. Knew that he'd never do anything to hurt her.

"You still with me, Tess?"

She couldn't pry her lips open to speak, so she did the only thing she could. Her impression of a bobble-head doll.

His eyes glinted, and he smirked. Ryan leaned in and sucked her bottom lip. Gently sank his teeth into it. Then he pushed his tongue between her lips and swept it inside the cavern of her mouth. Tipped her head back so that he could deepen the kiss. Claimed her mouth as if he owned every single inch of her body and could do with it as he pleased.

Her pebbled nipples throbbed in response, and she made a small gasp as his hard chest grazed the painfully hard peaks.

His scorching, spine-tingling kiss coaxed her body into doing his bidding, and his strong hands felt as if they were everywhere at once.

Tessa sucked in a deep breath when Ryan squeezed her bottom hard, ramping up the steady throb between her thighs.

When she'd gasped, he sucked her tongue into his mouth. He lifted her higher on the wall, pinning her there with his body as he settled between her thighs.

She whimpered as his rock-hard shaft pressed against the junction of her thighs. He seemed to enjoy eliciting her soft moans as she strained her hips forward, desperate for more of the delicious friction that made her belly flutter and sent a shudder up her spine.

"Shirt and bra off," he muttered against her lips, giving her barely enough room to comply with his urgent request. But she managed eagerly enough and dropped the garments to the floor.

He lifted her higher against the wall until her breasts were level with his lips. She locked her legs around his waist, anchoring herself to the wall.

Ryan took one heavy mound in his large hand. Squeezed it, then savagely sucked at her beaded tip, upping the pain/pleasure quotient. He gently grazed the pebbled tip with his teeth, then swirled his tongue around the flesh, soothing it.

Then he moved to the other breast and did the same. This time his green eyes were locked with hers. Gauging her reaction. A wicked grin curved the edge of his mouth as he tugged her down, so her lips crashed against his again.

Could he feel the pooling between her thighs through her soaked underwear and jeans? Her cheeks heated, momentarily, at the possibility. But her embarrassment was quickly forgotten as he nuzzled her ear and whispered his next command.

"When I set you down again I want you out of every single stitch of clothing you're wearing."

"Out here? In the stable? Where anyone could see us?" she stuttered, her heart thudding wildly in her chest.

"There's no one but us here," he said matter-of-factly. "But if you want me to stop…"

"No, don't." Tess was shocked by how quickly she'd objected to ending this little game. The equivalent of begging for more of him. For more of this.

At least he hadn't made her undress alone. Ryan tugged the beige plaid shirt over his head and on to the floor, giving her a prize view of his hard abdomen. She wanted to run the tip of her tongue along the chiseled lines that outlined the rippled muscles he'd earned by working as hard on the ranch as any of his hands. To kiss and suck her way along the deep V at his hips that disappeared below his waist. Trace the ridge on the underside of his shaft with her tongue.

Ryan toed off his work boots, unzipped his jeans and shoved them and his boxers down his muscular thighs, stepping out of them.

Tess bit into her lower lip, unable to tear her gaze from the gentle bob of his shaft as he stalked toward her and lifted her on to the edge of the adjustable, standing desk where she sometimes worked.

He raised the desk, which was in a seated position, until it was at just the right height.

"I knew this table would come in handy one day." She laughed nervously, her hands trembling slightly.

He didn't laugh, didn't smile. "Is this why you came out here, Tess? Why you couldn't be patient and wait until I came to your door?"

Before she could respond, he slid into her and they both groaned at the delicious sensation of him filling her. His back stiffened and he trembled slightly, his eyes squeezed shut.

Then he cursed under his breath and pulled out, retrieving a folded strip of foil packets from the back pocket of his jeans.

They'd both lost control momentarily. Given into the heat raging between them. But he'd come prepared. Maybe he hadn't expected to take her here in the stable or that he'd do so with such ferocity. But he had expected that at some point he'd be inside of her.

And she'd caved. Fallen under the hypnotic spell of those green eyes which negated every objection she'd posed up till then.

Sheathed now, Ryan slid inside her, his jaw tensed. He started to move slowly, but then he pulled out again.

"On your knees," he growled, before she could object.

Tessa shifted onto all fours, despite her self-consciousness about the view from behind as she arched her back and widened her stance, at his request.

Ryan adjusted the table again until it was at the perfect height. He grabbed his jeans and folded them, putting them under her knees to provide cushion.

Then suddenly he slammed into her, the sound of his skin slapping against hers filling the big, empty space. He pulled back slowly and rammed into her again. Then he slowly built a rhythm of rough and gentle strokes. Each time the head of his erection met the perfect spot deep inside her she whimpered at the pleasure building.

When he'd eased up on his movement, stopping just short of that spot, she'd slammed her hips back against him, desperate for the pleasure that the impact delivered.

Ryan reached up and slipped the tie from her hair, releasing the damp ringlets so that they fell to her shoulders and formed a curtain around her face.

He gathered her hair, winding it around his fist and tugging gently as he moved inside her. His rhythm was controlled and deliberate, even as his momentum slowly accelerated.

Suddenly, she was on her back again. Ryan had pulled out, leaned forward, and adjusted the table as high as it would go.

"Tell me what you want, Tess," he growled, his gaze locked with hers and his eyes glinted.

"I… I…" She couldn't fix her mouth to say the words, especially here under the harsh, bright lights in the stable. She averted her gaze from his.

He leaned in closer. His nostrils flared and a subtle smirk barely turned one corner of his mouth. "Would it help if I told you I already know *exactly* what you want. I just need to hear you say it. For you to beg for it."

His eyes didn't leave hers.

"I want…" Tessa swallowed hard, her entire body trembling slightly. "Your tongue."

He leaned in closer, the smirk deepening. "Where?"

God, he was really going to make her say it.

"Here." She spread her thighs and guided his free hand between her legs, shuddering at his touch. Tess hoped that show-and-tell would do, because she was teetering on the edge, nearly ready to explode. "Please."

"That wasn't so hard, now, was it?" He leaned down and lapped at her slick flesh with his tongue.

She quivered from the pleasure that rippled through her with each stroke. He gripped her hips, holding her in place to keep her bottom at the edge of the table, so she couldn't squirm away. Despite the pleasure building to a crescendo.

Tess slid her fingers in his hair and tugged him closer. Wanting more, even as she felt she couldn't possibly take another lash of his tongue against her sensitive flesh.

Ryan sucked on the little bundle of nerves and her body stiffened. She cursed and called his name, her inner walls pulsing.

Trailing kisses up her body, he kissed her neck. Then he guided her to her feet and turned her around, so her hands were pressed to the table and her bottom was nestled against his length.

He made another adjustment of the table, then lifted one of her knees on to it. He pressed her back down so her chest was against the table and her bottom was propped in the air.

He slid inside her with a groan of satisfaction, his hips moving against hers until finally he'd reached his own explosive release. As he gathered his breath, each pant whispered against her skin.

"Tess, I didn't mean to…" He sighed heavily. "Are you all right?"

She gave him a shaky nod, glancing back at him over her shoulder. "I'm fine."

He heaved a long sigh and placed a tender kiss on

her shoulder. "Don't give up on this so easily, Tess. Or do something we'll both regret."

Ryan excused himself to find a trash can where he could discreetly discard the condom.

Tessa still hadn't moved. Her limbs quivered, and her heart raced. Slowly, she gathered her bra, her jeans and her underwear. Her legs wobbled, as if she were slightly dazed.

She put on the clothing she'd managed to gather, despite her trembling hands.

When he returned, Ryan stooped to pick up her discarded shirt. Glaring, he handed it to her.

She muttered her thanks, slipping the shirt on. "You're upset. Why? Because I brought up your sex life with Sabrina?"

"Maybe it never occurred to you that the reason Sabrina and I tended to have rough, angry sex is because we spent so much of our relationship pissed off with each other.

He put his own shirt on and buttoned it, still staring her down.

Tessa felt about two inches tall. "I hadn't considered that."

She retrieved the hair tie from the standing desk, that she'd never be able to look at again without blushing. She pulled her hair into a low ponytail, stepped into her boots, and slipped her jacket back on.

"It can be fun. Maybe even adventurous. But in the moments when you're not actually having sex, it makes for a pretty fucked-up relationship. That's not what I want for you, Tess. For us." He shook his head, his jaw still clenched. "And there's something else you failed to take into account."

"What?"

"Rough sex is what got Sabrina off. It was her thing, not mine. What gets me off is getting you there. But I guess you were too busy making your little comparisons to notice." He stalked away, then turned back, pointing a finger at her for emphasis. "I want something more with you, Tess, because we're good together. We always have been. The sex is only a small component of what makes us fit so well together. I would think that our twenty plus years of friendship should be evidence enough of that."

Tessa wished she could take back everything she'd said. That she could turn back time and get a do-over.

"Rye, I'm sorry. I didn't mean to—"

"If you don't want to be with me, Tess, that's fine. But just be honest about it. Don't make up a bunch of bullshit excuses." He tucked his plaid shirt into his well-worn jeans, then pulled on his boots before heading toward the door. "Enjoy your date with Clem."

"It's not a date," she yelled after him, her eyes stinging with tears.

He didn't respond. Just left her standing there shaking. Feeling like a fool.

And she deserved it. Every angry stare. Every word uttered in resentment.

She'd been inventing reasons for them not to be together. Because she was terrified of the truth. That she wanted to be with Ryan more than anything. She honestly did want it all—marriage, a house of her own, kids. And she wanted them with her best friend. But she wouldn't settle for being in a relationship where she was the only one in love.

And she was in love with Ryan.

But as much as she loved him, she was terrified of the deafening silence she'd face if she confessed the truth to him. Because Ryan didn't believe in messy, emotional commitments.

He'd never admitted to being in love with a single one of his girlfriends. In fact, he'd never even said that he loved Sabrina. Just that there was a spark with her that kept things exciting between them. Something he hadn't felt with anyone else.

Tessa's sight blurred with tears and she sniffled, angrily swiping a finger beneath each eye. She'd done this, and she could fix it. Because she needed Ryan in her life. And he needed her, too. Even if all they'd ever be was friends.

Tessa's phone buzzed. She pulled it from her pocket. *Clem.*

She squeezed her eyes shut, her jaw clenched. Tess hated to bail on him, but after what had happened between her and Ryan, the thought of going out with someone else made her physically ill.

She answered the phone, her fingers pressed to her throbbing temple.

"Hey, Clem, I was just about to call you. Suddenly, I'm not feeling very well."

Eighteen

Ryan hopped into his truck and pulled out of the Noble Spur like a bat out of hell. He was furious with Tess and even madder that he'd been so turned on by her when she was being completely unreasonable.

He pulled into the drive of the Bateman Ranch and parked beside an unfamiliar car. A shiny red BMW.

As Ryan approached the big house, Helene hurried to the door to meet him. By the way she was wringing that dish towel in her hand, he wasn't going to like what she had to say one bit.

He glanced at the car again, studying the license plate. Texas plates, but it could be a rental car. And only one person he knew would insist on renting a red BMW.

Hell.

This was the last thing he needed.

"Ryan, I am so sorry. I told her that you weren't home, but she insisted on waiting for you. No matter how long you were gone." She folded her arms, frowning.

"It's okay, Helene." Ryan patted the woman's shoulder and forced a smile.

"Well, well, well. Look who finally decided to come home." His ex-fiancée, Sabrina Calhoun, sashayed to the front door. "Surprised to see me, baby?"

The expression on Helene's face let him know she was fit to be tied. Never a fan of the woman, his house manager would probably sooner quit than be forced to deal with his ex's condescending attitude again.

Ryan gave Helene a low hand signal, begging her to be civil and assuring her that everything would be all right.

Sabrina was the kind of mistake he wouldn't make twice. No matter how slick and polished she looked. Outrageously expensive clothes and purse. A haircut that cost more than most folks around here made in a week. A heavy French perfume that costed a small mint.

His former fiancée could be the dictionary illustration for high maintenance. He groaned internally, still kicking himself for ever thinking the two of them could make a life together.

Sabrina wasn't a villain. They just weren't right for each other. A reality that became apparent once she'd moved to Texas and they'd actually lived together.

Suddenly, her cute little quirks weren't so cute anymore.

"What brings you to Royal, Sabrina?" Ryan folded

his arms and reared back on his heels. He asked the question as politely as he could manage.

"I happened to be in Dallas visiting a friend, and I thought it would be rude not to come by and at least say hello." She slid her expensive sunglasses from her face and batted her eyelashes. "You think we can chat for a minute? Alone?"

She glanced briefly at Helene who looked as if she was ready to claw the woman's face off.

"Do you mind, Helene?" He squeezed her arm and gave her the same smile he'd been using to charm her out of an extra slice of pie since he was a kid.

She turned and hurried back into the house, her path littered with a string of not-so-complimentary Greek terms for Sabrina.

Ryan extended an arm toward the front door and followed Sabrina inside.

Whatever she was here for, it was better that he just let her get it out, so she could be on her merry way.

They sat down in the living room, a formal space she was well aware that his family rarely used. An indication that he didn't expect her visit to last long. And that he didn't consider her visit to be a friendly one.

"The place looks great." Sabrina glanced around.

He crossed his ankle over his knee and waited a beat before responding. "I don't mean to be rude, Brie, but we both know you're not the kind of person who'd drop by unannounced without a specific purpose in mind. I'm pressed for time today. So, it'd be great if we could just skip to the part where you ask whatever it is you came to ask."

"You know me well. Probably better than anyone."

Sabrina moved from the sofa where she was seated to the opposite end of the sofa where he was situated.

Ryan watched her movement with the same suspicion with which he'd regard a rattlesnake sidling up to him. Turning slightly in his seat, so that he was facing her, he pressed a finger to his temple and waited.

He knew from experience that his silence would drive Sabrina nuts. She'd spill her guts just to fill the empty void.

"I have a little confession to make. I visited my friend in Dallas because she emailed that article about you."

He'd nearly forgotten about that article on the bachelor's auction featuring him and Tess. Helene had picked up a few copies for his parents, but he hadn't gotten around to reading the piece. Between issues on the ranch and everything that had been going on with Tess, the article hadn't seemed important.

"And that prompted you to come to Royal because…?"

Sabrina stood, walking over to the fireplace, her back to him for a moment. She turned to face him again.

"It made me think about you. About us. I know we didn't always get along, but when we did, things were really great between us. I miss that." She tucked her blond hair behind her ears as she stepped closer. "I miss you. And I wondered if maybe you missed me, too."

Ryan sighed heavily. Today obviously wasn't his day. The woman he wanted insisted they should just be friends, and the woman he didn't want had traveled halfway across the country hoping to pick up where they'd left off.

He couldn't catch a break.

Ryan leaned forward, both feet firmly on the floor. "Sabrina, we've been through all this. You and I, we're just too different."

"You know what they say." She forced a smile after her initial frown in response to his rejection. "Opposites attract."

"True." He had been intrigued by their differences and because she'd been such a challenge. It had made the chase more exciting. "But in our case, it wasn't enough to maintain a relationship that made either of us happy. In fact, in the end, we were both miserable. Why would you want to go back to that?"

"I'm a different person now. More mature." She joined him on the sofa. "It seems you are, too. The time we've spent away from each other has made me realize what we threw away."

"Sabrina, you're a beautiful woman and there are many things about you that I admire." Ryan sighed. "But you just can't force a square peg into a round hole. This ranch is my life. Always has been, always will be. That hasn't changed. And I doubt that you've suddenly acquired a taste for country living."

"They do build ranches outside of Texas, you know." She flashed her million-dollar smile. "Like in Upstate New York."

"This ranch has been in my family for generations. I have no interest in leaving it behind and starting over in Upstate New York." He inhaled deeply, released his breath slowly, then turned to face her. "And I'm certainly not looking to get involved."

"With me, you mean." Sabrina pushed to her feet and crossed her arms, the phony smile gone. She peered up at him angrily. "You sure seemed eager to 'get involved' with your precious Tess. You went all out for her."

"It was a charity thing. Something we did on behalf of the Texas Cattleman's Club."

"And I suppose you two are still *just* friends?" The question was accusatory, but she didn't pause long enough for him to respond either way. "Suddenly you're a romantic who rents her fantasy car, knows exactly which flowers she likes, and which wine she drinks?" She laughed bitterly. "I always suspected you two were an item. She's the real reason our relationship died. Not because we're so different or that we want different things."

"Wait. What do you mean Tess is the reason we broke up?"

Sabrina flopped down on the sofa and sighed, shaking her head. "It became painfully obvious that I was the third wheel in the relationship. That I'd never mean as much to you as she does. I deserve better."

Ryan frowned, thinking of his time with Sabrina. Especially the year they'd lived together in Royal before their planned wedding.

He hadn't considered how his relationship with Tessa might have contributed to Sabrina's feelings of isolation. At the time, he'd thought her jealousy of Tess was unwarranted. There certainly hadn't been anything going on between him and Tess back then. Still, in retrospect, he realized the validity of her feelings.

He sat beside Sabrina again. "Maybe I did allow my relationship with Tess to overshadow ours in some ways. For that, I'm sorry. But regardless of the reason for our breakup, the bottom line is, we're just not right for each other. In my book, finding that out before we got married is a good thing."

"What if I don't believe it. What if I believe..." She inhaled deeply, her stormy blue eyes rimmed with tears. "What if I think it was the biggest mistake I ever made, walking away from us?"

"We never could have made each other happy, Brie." He placed his hand over hers and squeezed it. "You would've been miserable living in Royal, even if we had been a perfect match. And God knows I'd be miserable anywhere else. Because this is where my family and friends are. Where my future lies."

"Your future with Tessa?" She pulled her hand from beneath his and used the back of her wrist to wipe away tears.

"My future with Tessa is the same now as it was back then." Regardless of what he wanted. "We're friends."

Sabrina's bitter laugh had turned caustic. She stalked across the floor again. "The sad thing is, I think you two actually believe that."

"What do you mean?"

"You've been in love with each other for as long as I've known you. From what I can tell, probably since the day you two met in diapers. What I don't understand is why, for the love of God, you two don't just admit it. If not to everyone else, at least to yourselves. Then maybe you'd stop hurting those of us insane enough to think we could ever be enough for either of you."

Ryan sat back against the sofa and dragged a hand across his forehead. He'd tried to curtail his feelings for Tess because of his promise to Tripp and because he hadn't wanted to ruin their friendship. But what lay at the root of his denial was his fear that he couldn't be the man Tess deserved. A man as strong as he was loving and unafraid to show his affection for the people he loved.

A man like her father.

In his family, affection was closely aligned with weakness and neediness. In hers, it was just the opposite. With their opposing philosophies on the matter, it was amazing that their parents had managed to become such good friends.

He'd been afraid that he could never measure up to her father and be the man she deserved. But what he hadn't realized was the time he'd spent with Tessa and her family had taught him little by little how to let go of his family's hang-ups and love a woman like Tess.

Sabrina was right. He *was* in love with Tess. Always had been. And he loved her as much more than just a friend. Tessa Noble was the one woman he couldn't imagine not having in his life. And now, he truly understood the depth of his feelings. He needed her to be his friend, his lover, his confidante. He wanted to make love to her every night and wake up to her gorgeous face every morning.

He'd asked Tess to give their relationship a chance, but he hadn't been honest with her or himself about *why* he wanted a relationship with her.

He loved and needed her. Without her in his life, he felt incomplete.

"It wasn't intentional, but I was unfair to you, Sabrina. Our relationship was doomed from the start, because I do love Tess that way. I'm sorry you've come all this way for nothing, but I need to thank you, too.

For helping me to realize what I guess I've known on some level all along. That I love Tess, and I want to be with her."

"As long as one of us is happy, right?" Her bangs fluttered when she blew out an exasperated breath.

Ryan stood, offering her an apologetic smile. "C'mon, it's getting late. I'll walk you to your car."

Ryan gave Sabrina a final hug, grateful to her. He'd ask Tess again to give them a chance.

This time, he wouldn't screw it up.

Nineteen

Tessa had been going crazy, pacing in that big old house all alone. She hadn't been able to stop thinking about Ryan. Not just what had happened in the stables, but she'd replayed everything he'd said to her.

She hadn't been fair to him, and she needed to apologize for her part in this whole mess. But first, she thought it best to let him cool off.

Tessa got into her truck and drove into town to have breakfast at the Royal Diner. It was a popular spot in town, so at least she wouldn't be alone.

She ordered coffee and a short stack of pancakes, intending to eat at the counter of the retro diner owned by Sheriff Battle's wife, Amanda. The quaint establishment was frozen in the 1950s with its red, faux-leather booths and black-and-white checkerboard flooring. But Amanda made sure that every surface in the space was gleaming.

"Tessa?"

She turned on her stool toward the booth where someone had called her name.

It was the makeup artist from PURE. Milan Valez.

"Milan. Hey, it's good to see you. How are you this morning?"

"Great. I always pass by this place. Today, I thought I'd stop in and give it a try." Milan's dark eyes shone, and her pecan brown skin was flawless at barely eight in the morning. "I just ordered breakfast. Why don't you join me?"

Tessa let the waitress know she'd be moving, then she slid across from Milan in the corner booth where the woman sat, sipping a glass of orange juice.

When the waitress brought Milan's plate, she indicated that she'd be paying for Tess's meal, too.

"That's kind of you, really, but you're the one who is new in town. I should be treating you," Tess objected.

"I insist." Milan waved a hand. "It's the least I can do after you've brought me so much business. I'm booked up for weeks, thanks to you and that article on the frenzy you caused at the charity auction. Good for you." Milan pointed a finger at her. "I told you that you were a beautiful woman."

"I'm glad everything worked out for at least one of us." Tess muttered the words under her breath, but they were loud enough for the other woman to hear.

"Speaking of which, how is it that you ended up going on this ultra-romantic weekend with your best friend?" Milan tilted her head and assessed Tessa. "And if you two are really 'just friends'—" she used air quotes "—why is it that you look like you are nursing a broken heart?"

Tessa's cheeks burned, and she stammered a bit before taking a long sip of her coffee.

"Don't worry, hon. I don't know enough folks in town to be part of the gossip chain." Milan smiled warmly. "But I've been doing this long enough to recognize a woman having some serious man troubles."

Tessa didn't bother denying it. She took another gulp of her coffee and set her cup on the table. She shook her head and sighed. "I really screwed up."

"By thinking you and your best friend could go on a romantic weekend and still remain just friends?" Milan asked before taking another sip of her orange juice.

"How did you—"

"I told you, been doing this a long time. Makeup artists are like bartenders or hairdressers. Folks sit there in that chair and use it as a confessional." Milan set her glass on the table and smiled. "Besides, I saw those pictures in the paper. That giddy look on your face? That's the look of a woman in love, if ever I've seen it."

"That obvious, huh?"

"Word around town is there's a pool on when you two finally get a clue." Milan laughed.

Tessa buried her face in her hands and moaned. "It's all my fault. He was being a perfect gentleman. I kissed him and then things kind of took off from there."

"And how do you feel about the shift in your relationship with…?"

"Ryan," Tess supplied. She thanked the waitress for her pancakes, poured a generous amount of maple syrup on the stack and cut into them. "I'm not quite sure how to feel about it."

"I'm pretty sure you are." Milan's voice was firm, but kind. "But whatever you're feeling right now, it scares the hell out of you. That's not necessarily a bad thing."

Milan was two for two.

"It's just that we've been best friends for so long. Now everything has changed, and yeah, it is scary. Part of me wants to explore what this could be. Another part of me is terrified of what will happen if everything falls apart. Besides, I'm worried that..." Tessa let the words die on her lips, taking a bite of her pancakes.

"You're worried that...what?" One of Milan's perfectly arched brows lifted.

"That he'll get bored with a Plain Jane like me. That eventually he'll want someone prettier or more glamorous than I could ever be." She shrugged.

"First, glammed up or not, you're nobody's Plain Jane," Milan said pointedly, then offered Tess a warm smile. "Second, that look of love that I saw...it wasn't just in your eyes. It was there in his, too."

Tessa paused momentarily, contemplating Milan's observation. She was a makeup artist, not a mind reader, for goodness' sake. So it was best not to put too much stock in the woman's words. Still, it made her hopeful. Besides, there was so much more to the friendship she and Rye had built over the years.

They'd supported one another. Confided in each other. Been there for each other through the best and worst of times. She recalled Ryan's words when he'd stormed out of the stables the previous night.

They *were* good together. Compatible in all the ways that mattered. And she couldn't imagine her life without him.

"Only you can determine whether it's worth the risk to lean into your feelings for your friend, or if you're better off running as fast as you can in the opposite direction." Milan's words broke into her thoughts. The woman took a bite of her scrambled eggs. "What's your gut telling you?"

"To go for the safest option. But that's always been my approach to my love life, which is why I haven't had much of one." Tessa chewed another bite of her pancakes. "In a perfect world, sure I'd take a chance. See where this relationship might lead. But—"

"There's no such thing as a perfect world, darlin'." A smile lit Milan's eyes. "As my mama always said, nothing ventured, nothing gained. You can either allow fear to prevent you from going for what you really want, or you can grow a set of lady *cojones*, throw caution to the wind, and confess your feelings to your friend. You might discover that he feels the same way about you. Maybe he's afraid of risking his heart, too."

Milan pointed her fork at Tessa. "The question you have to ask yourself is—is what you two could have together worth risking any embarrassment or hurt feelings?"

"Yes." The word burst from her lips without a second of thought. Still, its implication left her stunned, her hands shaking.

A wide smile lit the other woman's face. "Then why are you still sitting here with me? Girl, you need to go and get your man, before someone else does. Someone who isn't afraid."

Tess grabbed two pieces of bacon and climbed to her feet, adrenaline pumping through her veins. "I'm sorry, Milan. Rain check?"

"You know where to find me." She nodded toward the door. "Now go, before you lose your nerve."

Tessa gave the woman an awkward hug, then she hurried out of the diner, determined to tell Ryan the truth.

She was in love with him.

Ryan was evidently even angrier with Tessa than she'd thought. She'd called him repeatedly with no answer. She'd even gone over to the Bateman Ranch, but Helene said he'd left first thing in the morning and she didn't expect him until evening. Then she mentioned that his ex, Sabrina, had been at the house the day before.

Tess's heart sank. Had her rejection driven Ryan back into the arms of his ex?

She asked Helene to give her a call the second Ryan's truck pulled into the driveway, and she begged her not to let Ryan know.

The woman smiled and promised she would, giving Tess a huge hug before she left.

Tessa tried to go about her day as normally as possible. She started by calling Bo and Clem and apologizing for any misunderstanding. Both men were disappointed, but gracious about it.

When Tripp arrived back home from the airport, he brought her up to speed on the potential client. He'd landed the account. She hugged her brother and congratulated him, standing with him when he video conferenced their parents and told them the good news.

Tripp wanted to celebrate, but she wasn't in the mood to go out, and he couldn't get a hold of Ryan, either. So he called up Lana, since it was her day off.

Tessa had done every ranch chore she could think of

to keep her mind preoccupied, until finally Roy Jensen ran her off, tired of her being underfoot.

When Roy and the other stragglers had gone, she was left with nothing but her thoughts about what she'd say to Ryan once she saw him.

Finally, when she'd stepped out of the shower, Helene called, whispering into the phone that Ryan had just pulled into the drive of the Bateman Ranch.

Tessa hung up the phone, dug out her makeup bag and got ready for the scariest moment of her life.

Ryan hopped out of the shower, threw on a clean shirt and a pair of jeans. He picked up the gray box and stuck it in his pocket, not caring that his hair was still wet. He needed to see Tess.

He hurried downstairs. The entire first floor of the ranch smelled like the brisket Helene had been slow-cooking all day. But as tempted as he was by Helene's heavenly cooking, his stomach wasn't his priority. It would have to wait a bit longer.

"I was beginning to think you'd dozed off up there. And this brisket smells so good. It took every ounce of my willpower not to nab a piece." Tessa stood in the kitchen wearing a burgundy, cowl-neck sweater dress that hit her mid-thigh. "I mean, it would be pretty rude to start eating your dinner before you've had any."

"Tessa." He'd been desperate to see her, but now that she was here, standing in front of him, his pulse raced and his heart hammered against his ribs. "What are you doing here?"

She frowned, wringing her hands before forcing a smile. "I really needed to talk to you. Helene let me in before she left. Please don't be mad at her."

"No, of course I'm not mad at Helene."

"But you are still angry with me?" She stepped closer, peering up at him intensely.

"I'm not angry with you, Tess. I…" He sighed, running a hand through his wet hair.

He'd planned a perfect evening for them. Had gone over the words he wanted to say again and again. But seeing her now, none of that mattered. "But I do need to talk to you. And, despite the grand plans that I'd made, I just need to get this out."

"What is it, Rye?" Tessa worried her lower lip with her teeth. "What is it you need to tell me?" When he didn't answer right away, she added, "I know Sabrina was here yesterday. Did you two…are you back together?"

"Sabrina and me? God, no. What happened with us was for the best. She may not see it now, but one day she will."

Tessa heaved a sigh of relief. "Okay, so what do you need to tell me?"

Ryan reached for her hand and led her to the sofa in the family room just off the kitchen. Seated beside her, he turned his body toward hers and swallowed the huge lump in his throat.

"Tess, you've been my best friend since we were both knee-high to a grasshopper. The best moments of my life always involve you. You're always there with that big, bright smile and those warm, brown eyes, making me believe I can do anything. That I deserve everything. And I'm grateful that you've been my best friend all these years."

Tess cradled his cheek with her free hand. The corners of her eyes were wet with tears. She nodded. "Me, too. You've always been there for me, Ryan. I guess we've both been pretty lucky, huh?"

"We have been. But I've also been pretty foolish. Selfish even. Because I wanted you all to myself. Was jealous of any man who dared infringe on your time, or God forbid, command your attention. But I was afraid to step up and be the man you deserved."

"'*Was* afraid?'" Now the tears flowed down her face more rapidly. She wiped them away with the hand that had cradled his face a moment ago. "As in past tense?"

"*Am* terrified would be more accurate." He forced a smile as he gently wiped the tears from her cheek with his thumb. "But just brave enough to tell you that I love you, Tessa Noble, and not just as a friend. I love you with all my heart. You're everything to me, and I couldn't imagine my life without you."

"I love you, too, Rye." Tessa beamed. "I mean, I'm in love with you. I have been for so long, I'm not really even sure when it shifted from you being my best friend to you being the guy I was head over heels in love with."

"Tess." He kissed her, then pulled her into his arms. "You have no idea how happy I am right now."

Relief flooded his chest and his heart felt full, as if it might burst. He loved this woman, who also happened to be his best friend. He loved her more than anything in the world. And he wanted to be with her.

Always.

For the first time in his life, the thought of spending the rest of his days with the same woman didn't give him a moment's pause. Because Tessa Noble had laid claim to his heart long ago. She was the one woman whose absence from his life would make him feel incomplete. Like a man functioning with only half of his heart.

"Tessa, would you…" He froze for a moment. His tongue sticking to the roof of his mouth. Not because he was afraid. Nor was he having second thoughts. There were a few things he needed to do first.

"What is it, Ryan?" She looked up at him, her warm, brown eyes full of love and light. The same eyes he'd been enamored with for as long as he could remember.

"I'd planned to take you out to dinner. Maybe catch a movie. But since Helene has already made such an amazing meal…"

"It'd be a shame to waste it." A wicked smile lit her beautiful face. "So why don't we eat dinner here, and then afterward…" She kissed him, her delicate hands framing his face. "Let's just say that dinner isn't the only thing I'm hungry for."

"That makes two of us." He pulled her into the kitchen and made them plates of Helene's delicious meal before they ended up naked and starving.

After their quick meal, Ryan swept Tessa into his arms and kissed her. Then he took her up to his bedroom where he made love to his best friend.

This time there was no uncertainty. No hesitation. No regrets. His heart and his body belonged to Tessa Noble. Now and always.

Ryan woke at nearly two in the morning and patted the space beside him. The space where Tess had lain, her bottom cuddled against his length. Her spot was still warm.

He raised up on his elbows and looked around. She

was in the corner of the room, wiggling back into her dress.

"Hey, beautiful." He scrubbed the sleep from his eye. "Where are you going?"

"Sorry, I didn't mean to wake you." She turned a lamp on beside the chair.

"You're leaving?" He sat up fully, drawing his knees up and resting his arms on them when she nodded in response. "Why?"

"Because until we talk to our families about this, I thought it best we be discreet."

"But it's not like you haven't spent the night here before," he groused, already missing the warmth of her soft body cuddled against his. It was something he'd missed every night since their return from Dallas.

"I know, but things are different now. I'm not just sleeping in the guest room." She gave him a knowing look.

"You've slept in here before, too."

"When we fell asleep binge-watching all the Marvel movies. And we both fell asleep fully dressed." She slipped on one of her boots and zipped it. "Not when I can't stop smiling because we had the most amazing night together. Tripp would see through that in two seconds."

He was as elated by her statement as he was disappointed by her leaving. What she was saying made sense. Of course, it did. But he wanted her in his bed, in his life. Full stop.

Tessa deserved better than the two of them sneaking around. Besides, with that came the implication that the two of them were doing something wrong. They weren't. And he honestly couldn't wait to tell everyone in town just how much he loved Tessa Noble.

"I'll miss you, too, babe." She sat on the edge of the bed beside him and planted a soft kiss on his lips.

Perhaps she'd only intended for the kiss to placate him. But he'd slipped his hands beneath her skirt and glided them up to the scrap of fabric covering her sex.

She murmured her objection, but Ryan had swallowed it with his hungry kiss. Lips searching and tongues clashing. His needy groans countered her small whimpers of pleasure.

"Rye… I really need to go." Tess pulled away momentarily.

He resumed their kiss as he led her hand to his growing length.

"Guess it would be a shame to waste something that impressive." A wicked smile flashed across Tess's beautiful face. She encircled his warm flesh in her soft hand as she glided it up and down his straining shaft. "Maybe I could stay a little longer. Just let me turn off the light."

"No," he whispered against the soft, sweet lips he found irresistible. "Leave it on. I want to see you. All of you."

He pulled the dress over her head and tossed it aside. Then he showed Tess just how much he appreciated her staying a little while longer.

Twenty

Ryan waved Tripp to the booth he'd secured at the back of the Daily Grind.

Tripp was an uncomplicated guy who always ordered the same thing. At the Royal Diner, a stack of pancakes, two eggs over easy, crispy bacon and black coffee. Here at the Daily Grind, a bear claw that rivaled the size of one's head and a cup of black coffee, two sugars.

Ryan had placed their order as soon as he'd arrived, wanting to get right down to their conversation.

His friend slid into the booth and looked at the plate on the table and his cup of coffee. "You already ordered for me?"

"Don't worry. It's still hot. I picked up our order two minutes ago."

Tripp sipped his coffee. "Why do I have the feeling that I'm about to get some really bad news?"

"Depends on your point of view, I guess." Ryan shoved the still warm cinnamon bun aside, his hands pressed to the table.

"It must be really bad. Did something happen to our parents on the cruise?"

"It's nothing like that." Ryan swallowed hard, tapping the table lightly. He looked up squarely at his friend. "I just… I need to tell you that I broke my promise to you…about Tess." Ryan sat back in the booth. "Tripp, I love her. I think I always have."

"I see." Tripp's gaze hardened. "Since you're coming to me with this, it's probably safe to assume you're already sleeping with my little sister."

Ryan didn't respond either way. He owed Tripp this, but the details of their relationship, that was between him and Tess. They didn't owe anyone else an explanation.

"Of course." Tripp nodded, his fists clenched on the table in front of him. "That damn auction. The gift that keeps on giving."

Ryan half expected his friend to try to slug him, as he had when they were teenagers and the kids at school had started a rumor that Ryan was Tess's boyfriend. It was the last time the two of them had an honest-to-goodness fight.

That was when Tripp had made him promise he'd never lay a hand on Tess.

"Look, Tripp, I know you didn't think I was good enough for your sister. Deep down, I think I believed that, too. But more than anything I was afraid to ruin my friendship with her or you. You and Tess…you're more than just friends to me. You're family."

"If you were so worried about wrecking our friend-

ships, what's changed? Why are you suddenly willing to risk it?" Tripp folded his arms as he leaned on
the table.

"I've changed. Or at least, my perspective has. I
can't imagine watching your sister live a life with
someone else. Marrying some other guy and raising
their children. Wishing they were ours." Ryan shook
his head. "That's a regret I can't take to my grave. And
if it turns out I'm wrong, I honestly believe my friendship with you and Tess is strong enough to recover. But
the thing is… I don't think I am wrong about us. I love
her, Tripp, and I'm gonna ask her to marry me. But I
wanted to come to you first and explain why I could
no longer keep my promise."

"You're planning to propose? Already? God, what
the hell happened with you guys in Dallas?" Tripp shut
his eyes and shook his head. "Never mind. On second
thought, don't *ever* tell me what happened in Dallas."

"Now that's a promise I'm pretty sure I can keep."
Ryan chuckled.

"I guess it could be worse. She could be marrying
some dude I hate instead of one of my best friends."

It was as close to a blessing as he was likely to get
from Tripp. He'd gladly take it.

"Thanks, man. That means a lot. I promise, I won't
let you or Tess down."

"You'd better not." Tripp picked up his bear claw
and took a huge bite.

It was another promise he had every intention of
keeping.

Ryan, Tessa, Tripp and both sets of their parents,
had dinner at the Glass House restaurant at the exclu-

sive five-star Bellamy resort to celebrate their parents'
return and Tripp landing the Noble Spur's biggest customer account to date.

The restaurant was decked out in festive holiday
decor. Two beautiful Douglas firs. Twinkling lights
everywhere. Red velvet bows and poinsettias. Then
there were gifts wrapped in shiny red, green, gold and
silver foil wrapping paper.

Tessa couldn't be happier. She was surrounded by
the people who meant the most to her. And both her
parents and Ryan's had been thrilled that she and Ryan
had finally acknowledged what both their mothers
claimed to have known all along. That she and Ryan
were hopelessly in love.

Ryan had surprised her with an early Christmas
gift—the Maybach saddle she'd mused about on their
drive to Dallas.

Even Tripp was impressed.

The food at the Glass House was amazing, as always. And a live act, consisting of a vocalist and an
acoustic guitar player, set the mood by serenading the
patrons with soft ballads.

When they started to play Christina Perri's "A
Thousand Years," Ryan asked her to dance. Next, the
duo performed Train's song, "Marry Me."

"I love that song. It's so perfect." Tessa swayed hap-
pily to the music as the vocalist sang the romantic lyrics.

"It is." He grinned. "And so are you. I'm so lucky
that the woman I love is also my best friend. You, Tess,
are the best Christmas gift I could ever hope for."

"That's so sweet of you to say, babe." Her cheeks

flushed and her eyes shone with tears. She smiled: "Who says you're not romantic?"

"You make me want to be. Because you deserve it all. Romance, passion, friendship. A home of our own, marriage, kids. You deserve all of that and more. And I want to be the man who gives that to you."

Tessa blinked back tears. "Ryan, it sounds a lot like you're asking me to marry you."

"Guess that means I ain't doing it quite right." Ryan winked and pulled a gray velvet box from his pocket. He opened it and Tessa gasped, covering her mouth with both hands as he got down on one knee and took her left hand in his.

"Tessa Marie Noble, you're my best friend, my lover, my confidante. You've always been there for me, Tess. And I always want to be there for you, making an incredible life together right here in the town we both love. Would you please do me the great honor of being my wife?"

"Yes." Tessa nodded, tears rolling down her cheeks. "Nothing would make me happier than marrying my best friend."

Ryan slipped on the ring and kissed her hand.

He'd known the moment he'd seen the ring that it was the one for Tess. As unique and beautiful as the woman he loved. A chocolate diamond solitaire set in a strawberry gold band of intertwined ribbons sprinkled with vanilla and chocolate diamonds.

Tessa extended her hand and studied the ring, a wide grin spreading across her gorgeous face. "It's my Neapolitan engagement ring!"

"Anything for you, babe." Ryan took her in his arms

and kissed her with their families and fellow diners cheering them on.

But for a few moments, everyone else disappeared, and there was only Tessa Noble. The woman who meant everything to him, and always would.

* * * * *

THAT NIGHT WITH
THE RICH RANCHER

SARA ORWIG

With many thanks to Stacy Boyd, Senior Editor

With many thanks to Stacy Boyd, Senior Editor

One

Tony Milan felt ridiculous. Standing in the wings of the wide stage of the elegant Dallas country club ballroom, he promised himself that next time, he would be more careful making bets with his oldest brother. Losing at saddle bronc riding in a rodeo last April had put him backstage tonight at this gala charity event, which included a dinner dance as well as an auction. One that would auction *him* off. At least it was all for a good cause, he reminded himself. The funds raised would go to Parkinson's disease research.

As he'd made his way to the stage earlier, he had seen some of the attendees: beautiful women dressed in designer gowns accompanied by men in tailored tuxedos. The highest bidders would win a night with "Texas's most desirable bachelors," according to the brochure that had been mailed to a select group wealthy enough to afford the event. He couldn't imagine any woman bidding much for an evening out with a guy she won in an auction, but after the opening bid, he realized he was wrong. The Texas ranchers who'd gone before him had stirred up high prices.

Looking out at the latest bachelor who now pranced offstage, Tony could not recall ever feeling more out of place. And then he heard his name called.

Taking a deep breath and forcing himself to smile broadly, he stepped forward, striding out of the darkened shadows into the blinding spotlights in front of a glittering audience. Applause was loud as he waved at the audience, most of which he could no longer clearly see because of the spotlights shining in his eyes.

After a spiel about his bachelor status, the master of ceremonies opened up the bidding. Tony was startled by the number of women who jumped into the bidding, but as the amount climbed, first one and then another dropped out until only three women were left.

Shocked yet pleased by the amount he was going to draw, he grinned and walked around the stage as the bidding climbed.

When a woman in a front table bid, he glanced down and saw it was an ex-girlfriend. He hoped she didn't win. As far as he was concerned, he'd said a final goodbye to her when she'd started getting serious. No long-term relationships for Tony Milan. He liked to flirt, play the field, just have a good time with no strings attached. Thankfully, after a flurry of bidding, his ex-girlfriend dropped out and only two women were left.

Tony couldn't see either one of the women, hidden by the blinding lights, but he heard their competitive bids. They were calling outrageous sums of money—all for an evening with him. When one graciously dropped out, the MC brought down the gavel.

"We have a winner," he said, not able to hide his out-right glee at the final amount for the charity. "Would our lucky woman please come up onto the stage?"

Tony couldn't contain his curiosity. He scanned the audience for a glimpse at her, and then a spotlight found her at a table off to the right. His pulse jumped when a stunning blonde stood up. Her hair was piled atop her head with a few spiral curls falling about her face, and she wore a fiery red dress as she threaded her way to the stage. Even from a distance he could see the dress clung to a breathtaking figure. Jeweled straps glittered on her slender shoulders and her full breasts pillowed above the low-cut neckline.

One of the auction's ushers took her hand as she climbed the steps to the stage and Tony's gaze finally swept over her from head to toe, taking in her long, shapely legs revealed by a high slit in the skirt. Instantly Tony began to feel immensely better about the entire auction and the upcoming evening.

As the blonde crossed the stage, his gaze swept over her features. She wasn't a local resident, he thought, because he didn't recognize her. But then as she neared center stage to give the MC her name, he had a niggling feeling that he did indeed know her. He looked at her again. Something about her features seemed familiar. Perhaps... There was a faint resemblance to a local—his neighbor and lifetime enemy, Lindsay Calhoun.

He shrugged away that notion. The woman talking to the MC could not be Lindsay Calhoun. For one brief moment, a memory flashed through his mind of Lindsay dressed in skintight jeans and driving her muddy pickup, her long sandy braid bouncing beneath her floppy old hat. That was followed by another memory—Lindsay wag-ging her finger at him and accusing him of taking her ranch's water—something unethical he would never do to any neighbor, even Lindsay. She was mule stubborn, never took his advice and wouldn't agree with him if he said the sun set in the west.

Most of all, she was serious in every way, all business all the time. With their many confrontations, he had wondered if she'd ever had any fun in her life. So there was no way on earth that the vision who had won an evening with him was Lindsay.

Curiosity ran rampant as the MC took the mystery woman's hand and she turned to the audience, shooting a quick glance at Tony and then smiling at the audience while the MC held her hand high like a boxer at a heavyweight fight.

"Our winner—a beautiful Texan, Miss Lindsay Calhoun!"

Tony was stunned. His gaze raked over her again. Why had she done this? Their families had maintained a perpetual feud since the first generation of Milans and Calhouns had settled in Texas, and he and Lindsay kept that feud alive. Besides, she didn't even date. Nor would she spend a dime for an evening with him. She never even spoke to him unless she was accusing him of something.

He squeezed his eyes shut as if to clear them, and then looked at her again. Actually, he stared, transfixed. Not one inch of her looked like his neighbor.

She turned as another man in a black tux came forward to escort her toward Tony while the MC began to talk about the next bachelor.

"Lindsay?" Tony's voice came out a croak. The woman he faced was breathtaking. He wouldn't have guessed all the makeup in Texas could have made such a transformation.

Her huge blue eyes twinkled and she leaned close, giving him a whiff of an exotic perfume—another shock.

"Close your mouth, Tony," she whispered so only he could hear. "And stop staring."

The tuxedo-clad man stepped forward. "Lindsay, it seems you've already met your bachelor, Tony Milan. Tony, this is Lindsay Calhoun."

"We know each other." Tony hoped he said it out loud. His brain felt all jumbled and he couldn't force his gaze from Lindsay. He still couldn't believe what he was seeing. He had known her all his life. Not once had she even caused him to take a second glance. Nor had he ever seen her as anything except a colossal pest. Saying she wasn't his type was an understatement.

But was there another side to her? Why was Lindsay here? Why had she bid a small fortune to get the evening with him? No doubt she wanted something from him—and wanted it badly.

Would she go to this length to get water? He ruled that out instantly, remembering her fury and harsh words when she had accused him of buying bigger pumps for his wells to take more groundwater from the aquifer they shared. He had told her what she should do—dig her wells deeper. She had charged right back, saying she wouldn't have to go to the added expense if he wasn't depleting her water with bigger pumps. And there it went. Once again her usual stubborn self refused to take his advice or believe him.

Then she had started calling him devious, a snake and much worse. She pushed him to the edge and he knew he had to just walk away, which he did while she hurled more names at him.

That was the Lindsay Calhoun he knew. This Lindsay tonight had to be up to something, too. Surprisingly, though, he couldn't bring himself to care much. Thoughts of ranching and feuding fled from his mind. He was too busy enjoying looking at one of the most beautiful women he had ever seen.

How could she possibly look so good? They were being given the details of their evening, beginning with a limousine waiting at the country club entrance to take them to the airport where a private jet would fly them to Houston for dinner. He barely registered a word said to him; he couldn't focus on anything but the sight of her.

"Excuse me a moment. I'll be right back," their host said, leaving them alone momentarily.

"You've got to give me a moment to come out of my shock," Tony said with a shake of his head.

"You take all the time you want. I've been waiting for this," she drawled. "If necessary, I would have paid a lot more to get this night with you."

"If you'd come over to the ranch dressed the way you are now and just knocked on the door, you could have had my full attention for an evening without paying a nickel, but this is for a good cause."

"It's for two good causes," she said in a sultry voice, and his heartbeat quickened. He still couldn't quite believe what was happening. Before tonight, he would have bet the ranch he could never be dazzled or even take a second look, let alone willingly go out with his stubborn neighbor.

"Lindsay, I've never fainted in my life, but I might in the next thirty seconds, except I don't want to stop looking at you for anything."

"When you saw I had won, I was afraid you'd turn down this evening."

"I wouldn't turn down tonight if I had to pay twice

what you did," he said without thinking, and her smile widened, a dazzling smile he had never seen in his life.

"If you two will follow me, I can show you to the front entrance," their host said, returning to join them. "First, Miss Calhoun, you need to step to the desk to make arrangements about payment."

"Certainly," she answered. "See you in a few minutes, Tony," she added in a soft, breathless voice.

Where had that sexy tone come from? He recalled times when he had heard her shout instructions to hands on her ranch. She had a voice that could be heard a long stretch away and an authoritative note that got what she wanted done. As he watched her, she turned to look at him. She smiled at him, another dazzling, knee-weakening smile, and he couldn't breathe again.

Holy saints, where had Lindsay gotten that enticing smile? It muddled his thoughts, sent his temperature soaring and made him want to please her enough to get another big smile.

He had seen her stomping around horses, yelling instructions and swearing like one of the men, the sandy braid flopping with her steps. He had faced her when she had yelled furious accusations at him about dumping fertilizer. How could that be the breathtaking woman walking away from him? His gaze ran down her bare back to her tiny waist, down over her flared hips that shifted slightly in a provocative walk.

With the tight dress clinging to her every curve, he caught a flash of long legs when she turned and the slit in her skirt parted. That's when he noticed the stiletto heels. He would have sworn she had never worn heels in her life, yet she moved as gracefully as a dancer. He wiped his heated brow. This was rapidly turning into the most impossible night of his life.

Befuddled, totally dazzled by her, he tried to remind himself she was Lindsay, and he should pull his wits together. That might not be so easy. He would never again view her in the same manner.

Why hadn't he ever really looked at her before? He knew full well the answer to his question. He had been blinded by their fights over every little thing, from her tree falling on his truck to his fence on her property line. Not to mention her usual raggedy appearance when she worked.

If she had gone to such lengths tonight to wring something she wanted out of him, he had better get a grip, because it was going to be all but impossible to say no to the fantastic woman in red standing only yards away and writing a check for thousands of dollars for an evening with him. Not even a night— just a dinner date and maybe some dancing.

But Lindsay Calhoun wasn't interested in dinner dates and ballroom dancing, boot scooting or even barn dances. He eyed her skeptically. To what lengths was she prepared to go tonight to get what she wanted?

He gave up trying to figure her out.

Still, he couldn't take his eyes off her. The skintight red dress left little to the imagination. Why had she hidden her gorgeous figure all these years? Why had she always pulled her hair back in a braid or ponytail? He looked at the beautiful silky blond hair arranged on her head, some strands falling loosely in back. He had never seen her hair falling freely around her face—would he before this night was over?

She looked seductive, like pure temptation, and he knew he should be on his guard, but there was no way he could be defensive with the woman standing only yards away. He wanted her in his arms. He wanted to kiss her.

And, if he was truthful with himself, he wanted to make love to her.

When she finished writing and handing over her check, their host led them to a garden, where they had pictures taken together. As he slipped his arm around her tiny waist while they posed for the camera, the physical contact sizzled. He was so heated he thought he would go up in flames.

He made a mental note to get a picture. His brother-in-law and sister were in the audience, so they had seen her tonight. So was his oldest brother, Wyatt. He was certain Jake Calhoun had seen his sister look this way before, but Wyatt was probably as shocked as he had been.

Talking constantly, their host escorted Lindsay and Tony through the wide front doors of the country club, where a long white limousine waited.

As soon as the door closed on the limo, they were alone, except for the driver on the other side of a partition.

"Maybe you've been using the wrong approach," Tony remarked.

She smiled another full smile that revealed even, white teeth that made him inclined to agree with whatever she said.

"That's what I decided. So we'll see how it helps letting my hair down, getting out of my jeans and into a dress, smiling and being friendly. So far, it seems to be working rather well, don't you think?"

"Absolutely. I don't know why you waited this long. I keep reminding myself not to give you the deed to my ranch tonight."

She laughed with a dazzling, irresistible smile on her lips. "The other way is a more direct approach. You know where you stand."

"And this is a sugarcoated enticement to get what you want?"

"Oh, my, yes. I'm just getting started. When I walked up on stage, I'm sure you wanted to refuse keeping your part of the bargain."

"You're wrong. Not the way you look tonight," he said in a husky voice. "With you in that red dress, there's nothing that would cause me to turn down an evening with you."

When had he reacted like this to a woman? He escorted beautiful women, was friends with them, had them continually around in his life and yet never had he been dazzled senseless as he was tonight. He wouldn't ever have guessed Lindsay could generate such attraction and make him overlook all their battles.

It had to be the shock of who she was that was setting him ablaze. He'd better get a grip on reality and see her as the person he knew her to be. But that wasn't going to happen tonight. His thought processes worked clearly enough to know that.

She smiled sweetly. "Penny for your thoughts."

"I'm wondering why I haven't ever heard from anyone about how gorgeous you can be."

"I suppose because I rarely go out on dates and never with anyone in these parts."

"Why not?"

She shrugged. "I've just never met anyone around here I wanted to go out with very much. And there's nowhere close by here to go dressed up."

"There's Dallas."

With a twinkle in her blue eyes, she answered, "In Dallas, our paths probably wouldn't cross."

"I've known you all my life and I know your family

well. Tonight I feel as if I'm spending the evening with a complete stranger I've just met."

She looked amused. "In some ways, Tony, we are strangers. There's a lot you don't know about me," she said in the breathless, sultry voice that made the temperature in the limo climb again.

"I should have asked you out long ago," he said.

"You know how likely that was to have happened, and what my response would have been."

He nodded. "Our past is better left alone and forgotten tonight."

"We fully agree on that one," she answered as the limo slowed. "Tonight is filled with illusions."

"The way you look is no illusion. You're gorgeous," he said, and was rewarded with another coaxing smile.

The limo turned into the airport and in minutes they slowed to a stop. While the chauffeur held the door, Tony took her arm to escort her to the waiting private jet. The moment he touched her, awareness burned in a fiery current. Her arm was warm, her skin silky smooth. He caught another whiff of her exotic perfume, and he couldn't wait to get her to their destination so he could ask her to dance and have an excuse to hold her in his arms.

In the plane he was aware of how close she sat. It was difficult to keep from staring because her red dress had fallen open, revealing those beautiful, long shapely legs. He took a deep breath.

"I need to keep pinching myself to make sure this is actually happening," he said. "And I keep reminding myself you're the same neighbor I see across the fence with your horses."

"I love my horses. You should come visit and really look at them sometime. I have some fine horses."

"I've seen them across the fence. Everyone in the county knows you have some of the finest horses."

"They're working horses or horses for my riding. I like to ride."

"We have that in common, Lindsay."

"I've never seen you riding just for pleasure."

"If it's for pleasure, I don't ride in the direction of your ranch." He smiled sheepishly. "I figure we're both better off that way."

"We're in agreement there, too," she remarked in a tone that was light and held no rancor.

"Have you attended one of these charity bachelor auctions before?"

"Sure, because it's a good cause." She held up a hand but stopped before it touched his arm. "I don't need to ask, I know you haven't. What prompted you to agree to participate in the auction tonight? You seem to be more the type to just donate the money."

"I lost a bet with Wyatt over bronc riding in an Abilene rodeo."

She laughed. "So because of your brother you're trapped into a night with me now."

"I was filled with thoughts of revenge until you stood up to walk to the stage. Since then, this night has taken the best possible turn."

She smiled. "I must admit I'm pleasantly surprised by your reaction. I never, ever thought I'd hear you say that. But you know, underneath this red dress, I'm still me."

He inhaled deeply, his temperature spiking at her mention of what was beneath the red dress, even though she had intended a different meaning.

He cleared his throat. "I have a feeling I better not say anything about what's underneath your red dress."

She looked as if she held back a laugh. "I knew there

had to be another side to you besides the one I always see. I've wondered how the evening would go and so far, so good. I think, Tony, we've set a record already for the length of time we've been civil to each other."

"I intend to be more than 'civil to each other.' We're just getting started," he said. "Frankly, Lindsay, it's damn difficult to remember that you're the same woman whose ranch adjoins mine. I feel as if I'm with a beautiful woman I've just met," he said softly, taking her hand in his and rubbing her knuckles lightly with his thumb. His brows arched and he turned her hand over to open her palm, looking up at her.

"You have soft hands. I know how you work with the cowboys. You should have hands like mine—with scars, calluses and crooked bones from breaks. How did you get these?" he asked, running his thumb lightly over her palm.

"I wear gloves most of the time," she said. "And I haven't been out working quite as much for the past two weeks because I was shopping for a dress and getting ready for tonight."

Her voice had changed, becoming throaty, losing the humor, and he wondered if she had a reaction to his touch. That idea made the temperature in the limo climb again. He gazed into her big blue eyes. "I hope tonight will be far better than you dreamed possible and worth all the effort you put into it," he said softly, and raised her hand to brush her palm with his lips.

His thumb brushed across her wrist and he felt her racing pulse, making his own pulse jump again in response. As he looked into Lindsay's eyes, he wanted to pull her close and kiss her. He couldn't help the thought that came to mind. How much was this night going to complicate his life?

He couldn't answer his question, but he was glad for the auction and thankful she hoped to win him over with sweet talk. It was a dazzling prospect.

He tried to pour on the charm and avoid any topics about the ranch, their relationship or their families. The feud between their families had been far stronger when they had been children and their grandparents had influenced the families. As a small child, Tony was taught to avoid speaking to any Calhoun, and she'd been taught the same about the Milans. In fact, they hadn't spoken to each other until they became neighboring ranchers and had their first dispute over her tree falling on his fence and hitting his truck.

The plane ride seemed to take mere minutes. Before he knew it, they touched down in Houston and were ushered to another waiting limo. A short while later, they pulled into a circular drive lined by manicured shrubs strung with tiny white lights and stopped in front of a sprawling stone building he recognized as an exclusive club.

When they stepped out of the limo, Tony took her arm to walk through the canopied entrance. Inside, when he told the maître d' they were from the Dallas auction, they were welcomed and led to a linen-covered table by a window overlooking the wide patio that held hundreds more twinkling lights and a splashing water fountain.

A piano player sang as he played a familiar old ballad and several couples danced on a small dance floor.

In minutes they were presented a bottle of Dom Pérignon champagne. As soon as they were alone with drinks poured, Tony raised his glass in a toast. "Here's to the most beautiful woman in Texas."

She smiled. "A very nice exaggeration, Tony," she said, touching his glass lightly with hers and taking a sip. "Actually, you look rather handsome yourself."

He smiled and wondered if she felt any real attraction. "Lindsay, I can't imagine why you've been hiding that beauty all these years."

She laughed. "Not so many years, Tony. And thank you. I'm far from the most beautiful woman in Texas, but it's nice to hear."

"You could have had most of the single guys in the county asking you out if you'd wanted," he said.

"Actually, that's not my aim in life," she remarked. "And I do get asked out."

"To talk about someone's horses. If they could see you tonight, though, horses wouldn't come up in the conversation." He waited a second and then asked the question that flitted into his mind. "Speaking of which, Lindsay, will you go to dinner with me next Friday night?"

She grinned at him. "Aren't you jumping the gun? You don't know if we can make it through tonight and get along the entire time."

He leaned across the table to take her hand again. "I promise you, we're going to get along tonight," he said, his tone lowering as it did when he was aroused. "A lot of people saw you at the auction tonight. I think you'll be inundated with invitations from guys when you get home. I want you to myself," he added softly, and something flickered in the depths of her eyes as her smile vanished and she gazed at him solemnly. Electricity flashed between them, and he wanted to be alone with her and kiss her more than ever.

As their waiter appeared, Tony released her hand and leaned back in his chair, listening to a menu recited by the waiter. When they were alone again, Tony raised his flute of champagne. "Here's to a fabulous evening that we'll both remember and want to repeat."

With a seductive smile, she touched his glass with hers

lightly, causing a faint clink, and sipped again, watching him the whole time with a look that made him want to forget dinner and find somewhere to be alone with her.

"I'm beginning to see that you have a sensual side you've kept well hidden."

"Well, yes, Tony. I've kept it hidden from *you*," she said with good humor, and he laughed.

"I suppose I brought that on," he said, wondering whom she had allowed to see this aspect of herself. He sat back to study her. "As well as I know your family, I really don't know much about you. You went to Texas Tech, didn't you? And you were an agriculture major?"

"Yes, with a minor in business. I knew I'd come home to run a ranch."

"Good background. Do you ever feel overwhelmed with the ranch?"

"Sometimes the problems seem a little overwhelming, but I love the ranch too much to feel at odds with it. It's my life."

"I agree, but it's different for you. Don't you want a family someday?"

"Owning the ranch doesn't mean I can't have a family," she retorted.

"I suppose." He nodded as he considered her remark. "Everyone in the county knows you work as hard as the guys who work for you. It's difficult to look at you now and remember how tough and resilient you are."

"Did you know my big brother came out to the ranch, sat me down and lectured me to try to get me to be nicer to you?"

"The hell you say. Is that why you're here tonight?" he asked. Still, he couldn't believe that the gorgeous creature flirting with him now was only here to make nice.

She leaned over the table, reaching out to take his

hand in hers, and his heart jumped again. Every touch, her flirting, the looks she was giving him, all stirred responses that shocked him. No other woman had ever had the same instant effect on him from the slightest contact.

"No," she replied, her voice lowering. "Before the night is over, you'll know this was all my idea and not one of my brothers had anything to do with my plans for tonight."

Her plans? His mind began to race with the possibilities and they were all X-rated. His blood pulsed hot through his veins. "I'm beginning to wish we were alone right now."

With a satisfied expression, she sat back. "Mike and Josh weren't at the auction and I haven't talked to them lately. They have no idea what I'm doing tonight. Jake was in the audience, with Madison, but across the room from me. Otherwise, I'm sure he would have tried to stop my bidding because he would have suspected my motives. But he more than any of my brothers should know you can take care of yourself."

Tony nodded. "I'll bet it was Jake who tried to talk you into being nicer. Mike has had his own problems with losing his first wife, caring for four-year-old Scotty and getting married to Savannah. And Josh is too busy making money with his hotels."

"You're right about all three." She glanced down to their joined hands. "Although I don't think this was exactly what Jake had in mind when he told me to be civil to you."

Tony couldn't help but smile. "I'm sure it wasn't." He turned his hand so that his was holding hers and rubbed his thumb across her smooth skin. "You know, I've heard little Scotty adores his aunt Lindsay. I'm beginning to see how that's possible."

"I don't think Scotty sees me the way you do."

He laughed. "No, I'm sure he doesn't. But you have a whole different side to you that I'm seeing tonight." And he was still having quite a time wrapping his mind around this Lindsay. If this auction night had happened when she first moved to her ranch, would they have avoided their big clashes? Or would that same stubborn Lindsay still have been lurking beneath this beauty?

"I've gotten the same lecture from my brother Wyatt about cooling our fights," he told her. "As county sheriff, he just wants peace and quiet in his life and he doesn't want to have to continually deal with our battles—which will be less in the future, I promise you."

"I hope we can end the clashes altogether."

"If you're like this, you'll have my complete cooperation. You know, I have to tell you. Over the years, some things you've wanted or accused me of destroying, I had nothing to do with. Hopefully, after this, you'll listen to my side a little more. But enough about our past. It doesn't exist tonight, Lindsay."

"That suits me fine," she said softly as she licked her lower lip.

"That does it." He pushed back his chair and went around to her. "If you do one more sexy thing, I may go up in spontaneous combustion." He held out his hand to her. "Let's dance. I don't want the table between us anymore." He also needed to move around and cool down.

Her blue eyes sparkled. "Ah, so I have your attention."

"You've had my full attention since that spotlight revealed you."

He led her to the dance floor, where he turned to take her into his arms. He was intensely aware of her enticing perfume, of her soft hand in his, of her other hand skimming the back of his neck. She was soft, lithe and a good dancer, one more surprise for the evening.

"You have really hidden yourself away from a lot of fun and a lot of attention."

"I have a life. Around the ranch and in Verity, I don't think I've missed a thing. You don't know what I do when I go to Dallas, Houston or New York."

"No, I don't, but I'm curious now."

"I have a lovely time. I have friends in other places besides Verity and the ranch, you know."

"I'll bet you do," he said, smiling at her.

He had seen Lindsay in one of the bars in Verity, playing poker and downing whiskey like one of the men. Now he had a hard time reconciling that image with the woman in his arms. He stared at her, amazed it was her and wondering how long this facade would last.

Even when she returned to her normal self—and she eventually would—he knew he'd never look at her in the same way again. Discovering there was an enticing side to her changed his entire view of the woman who took life too seriously.

For once, she wasn't so serious and earnest. He knew that was her nature, though, and he warned himself not to have high expectations of partying or lovemaking. She was not the type of woman he wanted to get entangled with, but for tonight he was going to break one of his basic rules of life.

Tonight he was going to stop thinking about the past and their problems. Tonight he was simply going to enjoy being with a stunning woman whose intention was to please him. And he wanted to return the favor.

When the dance ended, he took her hand. "I think our salads have been served. Shall we go back?"

As they ate, he listened attentively while she talked about growing up a Calhoun. She avoided mentioning the family feud or any touchy subject. Instead, she related childhood memories, college incidents and ranch success stories. The whole time she spoke, he couldn't stop picturing her blond hair long and soft over her shoulders. He wondered if she would let him take it down later. He wanted to run his fingers through the long strands, hold her close and kiss her. He wanted seduction.

Again, he wondered about her plans for the night. She had surprised him constantly since the bidding began back at the auction. In a way she was being her most devious self, but he hoped she never stopped. So far, he had loved every minute of this night since the spotlight first picked her out of the crowd.

Over their dinners, which were a thick, juicy steak cooked to perfection for him and a lobster for her, she asked about his life, and he shared some stories.

Finally, their desserts were brought out, fancy, beautifully crafted dishes that they both ignored because they were more interested in each other.

"Would you like to dance again?" he asked when she sat back.

"Of course."

The piano player had been joined by four more musicians, and the group played a ballad that allowed him to hold Lindsay close in his arms.

"Remember," he whispered in her ear, "for tonight, we'll forget our battles."

"I already have," she said, squeezing his hand lightly and making his breath catch.

The band changed to a fast number and he released Lindsay reluctantly. Instead of returning to her seat, she began to dance in front of him, and he followed suit. As he watched her, he could feel his body heat rising. She was like a flame, her hips gyrating sensuously, her blue eyes languid and heated as if thoughts of making love were inspiring her every movement. She was sexy—another shocking discovery. She had to know the effect she was having on him. While her eyes glittered, a faint, satisfied smile hovered on her face. He wanted to yank her into his arms, lean over her until she held him tightly and plunder her soft mouth.

He danced near the wide glass doors overlooking the veranda. He opened the doors and whirled her through them onto the patio, where warm night air enveloped them.

"We can dance out here?"

"The night has cooled enough and we have this to ourselves," he said, moving to the music that was only slightly muted. He danced out of the light spilling through the glass doors, into the shadows and stopped, looking down at her as she tilted her face up.

She was taller than most women he had gone out with, but still shorter than he was. His eyes adjusted to the August night and he could see her looking up at him as he tightened his arm around her, feeling her softness press against him.

"Ever since you walked across the stage at the country club, I've been wanting to do this." Slowly, inch by inch, he leaned in closer, taking his time to steal the kiss he craved.

He wondered if it would be worth the wait.

Two

As Lindsay gazed into Tony's eyes, her heart thudded—
and not just from desire. Wanting his kiss disturbed her
because it was not part of her plans for enticing him.
Still, there was no denying it. Some crazy chemistry
burned between them. Actually being attracted to Tony
Milan had not even occurred to her as a remote possibility when she'd initially come up with her plan to get him
to be friendly and to influence him to stop overpumping
his groundwater, which was taking water from her wells.
Somewhere in the back of her mind, a question formed
in the sultry haze. Could he have been truthful when he
said he wasn't using bigger water pumps?

From the first encounter they were at odds. The initial confrontation was over the boundary between their
neighboring ranches. Each had come armed with over
a century's worth of documents to prove their property
lines. Tony had been the condescending Mr. Know-It-

All, telling her she was wrong and how to run her ranch. He'd changed little since that first meeting. He was still a classic alpha male who had to control everything and when it came to ranching, that attitude was annoying. Tonight, though, was a whole different matter.

She was in control.

Or so she planned.

Right now she had to admit she was nearly speechless, because she had never planned or considered an attraction to Tony. She thought she could have a fun, pleasant evening and get on better footing with him. He had lots of friends, so she figured he had to have a nice side and that's what she hoped to get to know tonight with her bachelor-auction ploy.

She had hoped to entice him, make him see her as a desirable woman, have fun and maybe even share some kisses with him so their battles would not be so bitter and he would stop doing annoying things. Instead, she was breathless around him. An attraction between them that she had not expected had flared to life.

How could he be so attractive to her? She knew already that it was because of his charm, his seductive ways, his same alpha male that annoyed her with his know-it-all, take-charge attitude, but now it thrilled her. It was aimed at her, like a missile locked on its target, and, incredibly, she found it appealing…and sexy. She was definitely seeing him in a whole new way tonight.

Still, she couldn't help feeling her carefully laid-out plan was going off the rails a bit. Now wasn't the time to analyze her feelings, though. Not while she was in his arms. She knew this could never continue past tonight. Feelings for Tony Milan could complicate her life big-time. But for one night only, she would go where her heart and body led her. She could only tilt her head back and go with them. And right now they were taking her closer and closer to Tony. She wanted his kiss.

Her heartbeat raced as her gaze lowered to Tony's mouth, and she closed her eyes when his lips finally touched hers.

All thoughts fled and her heart slammed against her ribs as Tony's warm mouth moved on hers. His lips brushed hers lightly, a tantalizing touch that heightened her need for his kiss. Every inch of her tingled as desire electrified her nerves, hot and intense.

Another warm brush of his lips and she tightened her arm around his waist, sliding her hand behind his neck to wind her fingers in his thick, short hair. Every contact was unique, special, something she'd never expected and would never forget.

His mouth settled on hers, parting her lips as his tongue thrust deep and stroked hers, slowly. It was a kiss to make her moan and cling to him, to make her want him more than was sensible and beyond what she had set as limits for tonight's "date." His kiss set her ablaze with desire, making her quiver for his touch and dare to touch him in kind. How could Tony's kisses do this to her? How could he cause responses that no other man ever had?

Her knees felt weak while desire was too strong. Her heart pounded and she moaned softly against his lips. She felt as if she could kiss him for hours and still want so much more from him. As her hand slipped down over his arm, she felt the hard bulge of solid muscle even through the sleeves of his tux and shirt. The feel of that strength, that powerful maleness, rocked her. She felt as if she was hanging on to her senses by a thread.

What she was doing? Somewhere in her mind the question formed, but her thoughts were too scrambled and hungry with need to articulate an answer.

Nearby voices dimly reached her ears, barely registering in her thought processes. Tony released her slightly and for a few seconds they stared at each other. He looked as dazed as she felt, his half-lidded eyes smoky and dark, his lips wet and smeared with her lip gloss.

His voice was thick and deep when he finally spoke. "Damn, Lindsay, there's another side to you I never knew. You're a stranger that I've never met before tonight."

"I think I can say the same thing about you," she whispered. "All I hoped was to get you to talk to me."

He dragged his eyes away from hers and cast a glance to the side of the veranda. He frowned slightly as voices grew louder.

"We're not alone out here anymore," he whispered, still studying her solemnly as if she were the first woman he had ever kissed. But she knew better than that.

"Logic says we should go inside," she replied without moving. For seconds they continued to stare at each other until Tony took her arm and led her silently back inside. The small band was playing another fast number and they moved to the dance floor, stepping out in time to the throbbing beat. Still stunned by his kiss, she watched him dance, his black tux jacket swinging open as he moved with a masculine grace that was sensual, sexy, his hips gyrating and making her think of being in bed with him.

She felt her cheeks flame and looked up to meet his gaze. It was as if he read her mind. Desire was blatant in his eyes.

The band slipped into a slow ballad and Tony took her hand, drawing her into his arms to dance close. Their bodies were pressed together, his hardness against her curves, and she didn't know how long she'd be able to stay in his arms like this before she would combust. He pulled back ever so slightly to look down at her, and she was caught in his solemn gaze. For the first time, she realized his eyes were blue, with green flecks in their depths. He had thick dark brown eyelashes, straight brown hair that was neatly cut and short.

Tony Milan was *handsome*.

Down deep she had always thought that, in spite of how annoyed she had usually been with him. But up close like this now, she could no longer view him in any such detached manner. Not after that kiss. Tony Milan wasn't dime a dozen "handsome." No. He was drop-dead gorgeous.

And she wanted him to kiss her again.

The realization surprised her on top of the other jolting shocks of this night. Was she going to regret her decision to see if she could win him over with enticement and sweetness? It wasn't sweetness Tony was bringing out in her tonight. It was desire. She wanted to be alone with him and she wanted him to kiss her again. She wanted to kiss and hold him, to run her hands over him. There was no way she was going to bed with him—she'd established that boundary from the start—but she wanted more than she'd originally planned.

The night had lost its sense of reality and become a moment out of time. Everything had changed. Desire was hot, constant. Tony was sexy, virile, charming, appealing, and tonight he was the most desirable man she had ever known.

She had never expected or planned on a night like this one. Since she had decided to own a ranch, she had never wanted to date other ranchers or cowboys. She knew them too well and she didn't want them telling her how to conduct her business on the Rocking L Ranch. She loved her ranch—it was her whole life. No one had the right to come along and tell her how to run it. How many times had Tony done exactly that?

Tonight was different, though. Tony was different. How much would tonight change their relationship as neighboring ranchers? Or would they go back home with the same attitudes they had always had?

She knew she wouldn't and she didn't think he would, either.

And then she couldn't think anymore. Tony moved her hand against his chest and covered it with his own, pulling her even closer, as if wrapping their joined hands in the heat from their bodies. She inhaled the scent of his woodsy aftershave, a musky scent that was all male. She gave herself over to him and let him lead her with his sure steps. They were totally in sync as they moved, their long legs pressed against each other's. The contact was electrifying. She wanted to keep dancing with him for hours, almost as much as she wanted to be alone with him, in his arms and kissing him. Was that where the evening would lead, or would he follow the auction itinerary and go back to the Dallas country club, kiss her goodnight and each of them drive away? To her surprise, that wasn't the way she wanted to end the evening.

For the next hour they danced and she realized Tony was fun to be with when he wanted to be. He had her laughing over things he had done with her brothers over the years. She knew he was friends with them even though they were older. She was the only Calhoun who actively fought with him, but she had always blamed Tony for being such a know-it-all and so uncooperative as a neighbor. For tonight, though, she saw none of that. Far from it. He looked as if he was having a wonderful time and he helped her to have a wonderful time.

There was one rational part of her that cried out a

warning: she needed to remember why she bid on him. She couldn't let her plan backfire on her. When this night was over, she'd still need what she came here for—and that wasn't a relationship with Tony Milan. A relationship was the one thing she needed to avoid at all costs, because it would vastly complicate her life. She was here only to win his friendship so he would discuss their problems with her. If possible, even talk about their water situation.

From her earliest memories she had been taught by her grandparents not to trust Milans. Now her brother had married one and he was blissfully happy. She had to admit that she liked and trusted her sister-in-law Madison. And a distant Calhoun cousin—Destiny—had married a Milan—Wyatt, who was sheriff of Verity. Wyatt had been a shock because he proved untrue everything Lindsay had been taught by her grandparents and mother about Milans. In all her dealings with Wyatt, she had found him to be honest, friendly, fair and definitely trustworthy.

She gazed at Tony's handsome features and wondered if he could be trusted, as well. As they danced, he constantly touched her, looked intently at her. He paid her compliments, got her whatever refreshment she wanted. All his attention, his casual touches, increased her awareness of him, as well as her desire for him. She fought the temptation to tell him that she wanted to go someplace where they could be alone. She had a hotel room in Dallas for the night provided by the auction board. She could invite him back for a drink.

As much as she told herself she wanted to kiss him again, she knew where the kissing might lead. And she couldn't make love with Tony. Difficult as it was to curb her desire, she had no other choice.

Finally, as the band took a break, Tony turned to her.

"It's time for us to meet our chauffeur so we can take the plane back to Dallas. It's all arranged to get us back by midnight, so we should go now."

"Let me pick up my purse," she said.

On their flight home, Tony embodied the perfect gentleman, continuing to surprise her. She'd known he had to have a good side to him, but she'd never expected to be charmed by him or even find him such enjoyable company. Certainly not once had she thought she would be attracted to him or see him as a sexy, exciting man whose kiss set her heart pounding.

As they flew back to Dallas, Tony reached for her hand, holding it in his. "The evening will still be young when we get home. We can go dancing or just go have a drink and talk. Better yet, I have a condo in Dallas. Come back with me. I'll take you to your hotel whenever you want. We can have the place to ourselves."

Eagerness to draw out the evening made it easy to answer. "Let's go to your place," she said. "I don't want tonight to end yet. It's been fun, Tony. I know things will go back somewhat to the way they were because that's reality, but this has been a special night."

"You have no idea how special it has been. Things may go back to sort of like they were, but they won't ever again be the same as before. You'll no longer have an antagonistic neighbor. I promise."

"Dare I hope," she gasped, clutching her heart, making him laugh. Shaking her head, she smiled. "There's no way this truce is going to last."

"I'll try if you will," he said, his eyes twinkling with mischief, and she had to laugh in return.

"I promise I'll try, too," she said, looking into his eyes and again feeling an electrifying current spark between them.

"I keep waiting for a pitch from you to get me to agree to something. You all but admitted that's the purpose of your bidding for me tonight."

"Maybe I've delayed that original agenda," she said in a sultry voice. "I'm having fun, Tony. Fun that I don't want to spoil. The night is magical, a trip into a world that doesn't really exist. But for a few hours, we can pretend it does and enjoy it."

He raised her hand and brushed a light kiss on her knuckles, his breath warm on her hand.

"I'm glad," he said. "I'm not ready to tell you good-night and watch you walk away." He placed his hands on the arms of her seat, facing her and leaning close, his voice dropping to a whisper as he said, "I want to hold you and kiss you again."

Her heart thudded and for the first time she realized she might be in trouble. Was Tony the one who would get what he wanted out of tonight instead of her? She'd planned to wring concessions from him, but now it seemed he was once again in control and she was under his spell. Not once had it crossed her mind that she could be so beguiled by him.

And she was powerless to stop it.

His gaze lowered to her mouth and suddenly she couldn't get her breath. She tingled, feeling as if she strained to lean closer to him while she actually didn't move at all. He moved closer, until his mouth settled on hers. He kissed her, another kiss that set her heart racing and made her want to move into his lap, wrap her arms around him and kiss for the rest of the flight.

Instead, in seconds—or was it minutes?—she shifted away. "This plane isn't the place," she whispered reluctantly. She had to keep her wits about her. Had to mind her goal of working out her water problem, at least partially. Still, her breath came quick and shallow, matching his own.

Looking at her mouth, he didn't move for a moment and her heart continued to drum a frantic rhythm. He leaned closer to whisper in her ear, "I want to kiss you for hours." His words caused a tremor to rock her. Another shock added to the continual shocks of the night. She had no choice but to admit the truth—she wanted him to kiss her for hours.

As his gaze met hers, he scooted back into his seat and buckled his seat belt again.

When her breathing returned to normal, she tried for conversation.

"Why do you have a condo in Dallas? I thought you were as much into ranching as my brother Mike, that both of you had devoted your lives solely to ranching."

"I'm on two boards that meet in Dallas—for my brothers. Wyatt has recently acquired a bank and I'm on that board. Nick recently became owner of a trucking company with two close friends and I'm on that board, too. In Dallas, I have a small condo and I like having a place of my own I can go relax when I'm in the city. It's convenient even though I don't spend a lot of time there. I don't have a regular staff in Dallas unless I plan to stay a long time, which rarely happens. Then I hire from a local agency to cook and clean."

"That makes sense."

"I spend most of my time on my ranch. When we're back in our regular routines, I'd like for you to come over to the MH Ranch sometime. I have a new horse and I'm boarding a new quarter horse that Josh bought. You're welcome to come see them, ride them and tell me what you think."

"Sure," she said. "I suspect you better let all the guys

who work for you know that you invited me or they'll tell me I'm trespassing and toss me off your ranch."

He laughed. "I'll tell them. Now if you'll come wearing a dress with your hair down, they'll be so dazzled, there's no way they'll mention trespassing. Far from it. We'll all welcome you with open arms."

Smiling, she shook her head. "Nice try, but I don't wear a dress to ride a horse." She shrugged. "In fact, I don't wear a dress anywhere around home. But you can tell them I'm coming."

"Sure. Better yet, let me know beforehand and I'll pick you up. I probably should do that anyway, so they all know we have a truce of sorts." He turned more so that he faced her in his seat. "And it is a truce, Lindsay. Definite and permanent. I'll never again be able to fight with you."

"Don't say things you don't mean, Tony. Your intentions might be good, but there is no way this side of hell that you'll be able to stick by that statement."

Once again he leaned in closer and her heartbeat quickened as it had before. "Yes, there is definitely a way that I can be influenced to stick by that statement. You can wind me around your little finger if you really want to."

"I don't believe that one."

"You should," he said, settling back in his seat again. "Before tonight, did you ever think we would get along as well as we have?"

"Of course not." She tilted her head to study him. "In some ways, we're strangers. There's a lot I don't know about you."

"That's true and a lot I don't know about you. But strangers? No way, Lindsay. There is much I want to explore and discover about you and I intend to do that tonight," he said in a husky voice that made her heartbeat jump again.

Cutting into their conversation, their pilot announced descent into Dallas, and in a short time Lindsay looked out at the twinkling city lights spread far into the distance.

"Do you have your car at the club?" Tony asked.

"No. I left it at the hotel and took a cab."

"Good thinking," he said.

Once they arrived back at the country club, a valet brought Tony's car around and in minutes they drove through the iron gates to his condo complex.

As soon as Lindsay entered his unit, she walked through his entry hall to cross the spacious living room and look out over the sparkling lights of downtown Dallas.

"You have a gorgeous view."

"Do I ever," he said, and she smiled when she turned to see him looking at her.

"I meant the city lights," she explained, knowing he understood exactly what she had referred to.

"Want a drink?" he asked.

"Yes. White wine, please."

He removed his jacket and tie, dropping them on a chair, and walked to a bar in a corner of the room.

"This is a large living area. It's very nice," she said, looking at comfortable brown leather chairs and a long leather sofa.

"It's convenient when I'm here, which is not too often. A few days here and I'm ready for the ranch."

"That I understand," she said, crossing to the bar to perch on a stool and watch him pour her wine.

"I have a full bar if you prefer something else."

"The wine is good."

He handed her the glass and picked up a cold beer. "I figured you for a cold brew," he said, smiling at her.

He set his bottle on the counter, his gaze skimming over her legs when her skirt fell open just above her knees. "Lindsay, it's a crime to hide legs like yours all the time."

"You have no idea what I do all the time. We see each other about once every four or five months at best."

"That I intend to change."

She shook her head. "You know as well as I do that we'll go right back to our usual way of life when the sun rises in the morning."

"I hope to hell not," he said, holding up his bottle of beer in a toast. "Here's to the most beautiful neighbor I'll ever have and to a night I'll never forget."

Laughing softly, she touched his bottle with her wineglass and sipped her wine.

"Here's to the day we can both be civil to each other," she said.

"I'll drink to that." He touched her glass, took a sip of beer and set his bottle on the bar. "But we're going to be much more than civil to each other," he said, the amusement no longer visible in his expression. With his deep blue eyes gazing intently at her, he took her drink from her hand and placed it on the bar. Her heartbeat quickened in anticipation while desire burned in the depths of his eyes.

"I've waited all evening for this moment—to be alone with you," he said, stepping closer. His arm circled her waist and he lifted her off the bar stool easily, standing her on her feet and drawing her into his embrace as his gaze lowered to her mouth.

Desire made her draw a deep breath as he leaned closer, and then she closed her eyes, winding her arms around his neck, surrendering to his kiss.

The moment his mouth settled on hers, her heart slammed against her ribs as passion ignited and desire overwhelmed her. Tony was hard, his chest sculpted with muscles, his biceps like rocks from constant ranch work. She breathed in his scent and knew she would remember it forever. She wound her fingers through his short hair and returned his kiss, wanting to stir him as much as he did her. She tightened her arms around him without having to stand on tiptoe to kiss him because her heels added inches to her height.

As Tony drew her more tightly against him, his warm hand played over her bare back and then up to her shoulders. Dimly she felt him push away her straps as they slipped down on her arms. In seconds she was aware of slight tugs to her scalp when he removed the pins and her hair fell over her shoulders and down on her back.

Slowly, while he kissed her senseless, he drew away each pin until finally her hair framed her face.

He raised his head to look at her, running his fingers slowly through the long locks. "You're so beautiful. You take my breath away, Lindsay," he whispered, sounding as if he meant every word. How could she find this pleasure with Tony? Or want him so desperately?

She had meant this night to be lighthearted, friendly, seductive, so afterward he would be civil to her and try to cooperate with her. She hadn't considered there could be this unbelievable, fiery attraction that he seemed to feel as much as she did.

No matter what he said, they'd go back to their old ways after tonight, though maybe not as contentious. This blazing attraction was for one night only. Tonight she wanted this time with him because she had never before desired or reacted to a man the way she did Tony.

His gaze shifted to her mouth and he leaned down to kiss her again. How long they stood kissing, she didn't know, but at some point, Tony picked her up to carry her to the sofa, switching off the overhead lighting, leaving only the bar light glowing softly.

She planned on some kisses and caresses and then she'd stop. Truthfully, she had never even planned on this much. Dancing, some laughs, a good time, maybe some flirting as she tried to soften him up so he would be more receptive to what she wanted.

She had never dreamed it was possible for Tony's kisses to turn her world upside down, to make her heartbeat race and cause her to desire him more than any other man. She was on fire. As if of their own accord, her hips shifted slightly against him, pressing tightly and feeling his hardness. He was ready for her.

Astounded by the need she felt for him and the response his kisses evoked in her, she kissed him wildly, her fingers unfastening the studs on his shirt, finally pushing away the fabric. Wanting to touch him, she ran her hands over his warm, rock-hard chest, growing bolder when she heard him take a deep, trembling breath. He set her on her feet while he continued to kiss her.

She felt his fingers at her waist at the back of her dress and then felt him tug down the zipper. He ran his hand lightly over her bottom and she moaned softly as her desire intensified.

While he kissed her, his hands slipped lightly up her back and across her shoulders and then came down to push her red dress over her hips so it fell softly around her ankles.

Tony stepped back to look at her. She wore only lacy bikini panties.

His eyes had darkened to a stormy blue-green and he let out a ragged breath. "I'll never forget this moment," he whispered, and stepped to her to crush her against him, kissing her deeply, a kiss that made her feel wanted and loved. She knew she wasn't loved by him, but he made her feel that way, as if he needed her more than he had ever needed any other woman.

He showered kisses on her throat while his hands cupped her full breasts and his thumbs circled their tips. His kisses moved lower until his lips met one breast while his hands caressed the other.

Running her fingers in his hair, she gasped with pleasure when his tongue circled her nipple. She was awash in desire, wanting him more than she had ever dreamed possible. She wanted his loving; she wanted all of him.

She had made a decision much earlier to end this night before it led to lovemaking, and she'd stuck with it even as they flew back to Dallas. But now desire forced her to rethink her decision, instinctively feeling that this moment would not come again.

Common sense told her that, come morning, they would go back, at least partially, to the arguments they had had all their adult lives. Tonight was special, a once-in-a-lifetime magical night that would never come again, and what they did tonight, all their loving, would carry no ties after dawn.

Tony was incredible. No man had ever excited her the way he had, and no man would ever make love to her the way she knew he would. Beyond that, she was unable to think when his hands and mouth were on her. But she was able to make a decision. She pulled back and looked into his eyes.

"Tony, I'm not protected."

He raised his head, kissing her lightly. "I'll take care of it," he whispered, and leaned down to kiss and fondle her other breast.

She wanted him with all her being, wanted to make love with him for the rest of the night. With deliberation her fingers unfastened his trousers. He grasped her wrist and she paused as he released her to yank off his boots and then his socks. He dropped them carelessly to the floor and returned to kissing her while she pushed down his trousers and then peeled away his briefs.

Her heartbeat raced as her gaze swept over his muscled body. His manhood was thick and hard, ready to love. Stepping closer, she caressed him while he stroked and showered her with kisses.

He picked her up again, kissing her when he carried her through his condo. She clung to him with her eyes closed as they kissed. He touched a light and she glanced quickly to see they were in a bedroom. She returned to kissing him until he stood her on her feet. He reached down to yank away the comforter covering his high, king-size bed.

Watching him, she felt her heart drum in anticipation of the pleasure he would give her. As her gaze swept over his muscled body, she trembled. He stepped back, looking at her in a slow, thorough study that made her tingle as much as if his fingers had moved over her in feathery caresses.

"So beautiful, so perfect," he whispered, drawing her into his embrace as he leaned over her to kiss her hungrily. His hard erection pressed against her, his hard body hot and solid against her.

Why did she want him so desperately and respond to him so intensely? His slightest touch set her quivering and his kisses rocked her, building in her a need unlike she had ever felt before. How could she have found this with Tony?

She couldn't answer her question. Nor did she care. She just wanted Tony and his loving for the rest of the night.

He lifted her into his arms again and placed her on the white sheets, kneeling beside her, his knees lightly pressing against her thighs. Then, as if in a dream—or a fantasy—he rained kisses from her ankles to her mouth.

She writhed, her hips moving slightly as blinding need built inside her until she wanted him more than she ever thought possible.

"Tony, make love to me," she whispered.

"Not so fast, darlin'. We're going to take our time and love for hours," he whispered, still showering her with kisses.

His endearment, spoken in a tender voice that she had never heard before from him, was as effective as his caresses.

"Tony," she gasped, sitting up to grasp his shoulders. "Make love to me. Let me love you."

"Shh, darlin'," he said softly while he kissed her breasts between his words. "Lie down and turn over, let me kiss you," he said, pushing gently.

She rolled onto her stomach and he picked up her foot to kiss her ankle lightly and then brush kisses higher up the back of her leg. He traced circles with his tongue on the back of her knee.

Digging her fingers into the bed, she raised her head slightly to look over her shoulder. "Tony, I can't touch or kiss you this way."

"You will soon," he whispered, and returned to his tender ministrations, trailing his tongue slowly up the back and then along the inside of her thigh.

Aflame with longing, she twisted and rolled over, sitting up to wrap her arms around his neck and kiss him, pouring all her hunger for him into her kiss, wanting to drive him as wild as he had her.

They fell back on the bed with Tony over her, his weight welcome against her. While she moved her hips against him, he kissed her as he rolled beside her. "Do you like me to touch you here?" he whispered, fondling her breast. "Do you want me to kiss you here?" he whispered, moving to brush kisses on her inner thigh, watching her as he did. "You're beautiful."

His words heightened the moment, making her more aware of him and what he was doing while she was lost in sensation and desire.

While he kissed her, his hand trailed up her leg to the inside of her thighs. When he stroked her she gasped with pleasure.

His hand moved against her, driving her to new heights. She didn't think she could take more and she reveled in the feelings he evoked in her. Needing him, she reached out and took him in one hand as her other played over his chest.

She wanted him to feel the same heady sensations he was strumming in her, so she caressed him, eliciting a growl deep in his throat. He stopped her, but he continued to love her, driving her to the brink, lifting her to the precipice of release. And then, when she was about to fall over, he pulled his touch away, shifting his hands to caress her breasts as he also showered them with kisses.

Her fingers wound in his hair. "Tony, I want you. I'm ready," she gasped, moaning with pleasure as he continued to kiss each breast, his tongue drawing lazy circles over each nipple. His fingers dallied on her stomach, but when they slipped lower, she arched against him, thrusting her hips and spreading her legs to give him access.

That was all the urging he needed. Or so she thought. He moved between her legs and she clutched his buttocks, pulling him toward her. "Tony, I want you now," she whispered. But he didn't enter her.

The warm, solid weight of him pressed against her as he stretched over her and kissed her with a hunger that made her heart pound even harder. She wrapped her long legs around him, wanting him more with each second that ticked past. Never before had she wanted to make love as much as she did now.

"Tony," she whispered again, the rest of her words smothered by his mouth covering hers and his tongue entwining with hers.

How could she want him so much? She couldn't answer her own question, she just knew she did. She ached for him, her pulse pounding. "Tony, I can't keep waiting…"

"Yes, you can and it'll be better than ever," he said. He laved her breasts, teasing her nipples between his teeth, and she felt a tug between her legs. All the while, his hands caressed her, binding them in one night of love-making that she would always remember. Though this night could not be repeated, she knew this was the time to make memories she'd carry with her forever.

"I want you now," she finally gasped, tugging him closer.

He stepped off the bed to open a night table drawer and then he watched her, his eyes burning her, as he stood beside the bed to slowly put on the condom.

As she caressed his thigh, her hips shifted slightly in anticipation. She wished he would hurry. Then, he knelt between her legs, his eyes still on hers, as he finally entered her. She wrapped her legs around him again, caressing his smooth, muscled back and hard buttocks, as he slowly thrust into her. She cried out, arching to meet him, wanting him to move with her to give her release for all the tension that coiled tightly in her.

Hot and hard, his manhood filled her, moving slowly, driving her to greater need as she clung to him and moved beneath him in perfect sync.

"Now," she cried, running her hands over his muscled thighs. He obeyed her, and her hips moved faster, her head thrashing as she was lost in the throes of passion, until finally he gave one last thrust, deep and hard, and she cried out. Arching under him, her fingers raking his back, her hips thrusting against him, she found that elusive release and he followed her, bursting within her.

"Tony," she cried.

"Ah, darlin'…" He ground out the words through clenched teeth as his body continued to move over hers.

Finally, satiated, they stilled.

"You're fantastic in every way," he whispered, kissing her temple lightly, trailing light kisses down her cheek and sighing as he lowered his weight carefully onto her.

Gasping for breath, she clung to him while her heartbeat and breathing returned to normal. Tony rolled to his side. He kept her with him, his legs entwined with hers.

"I don't want to let you go."

"You don't have to right now. I want to stay here in your arms, against you. Tony, this has been a wonderful, once-in-a-lifetime night."

"I agree," he said, hugging her lightly and kissing her forehead. "Our lives have changed."

"Not really. It may not ever again be as bad or as hateful, but tonight doesn't really change what we'll face tomorrow. My water problems, you telling me what I should or should not do, not to mention the next thing that'll come up between us."

There was silence while he toyed with locks of her hair. It seemed to her that many minutes went by until he finally spoke. "There's one question I'd like you to answer. Is water what was behind your high bid tonight? You wanted something from me, Lindsay, and I haven't heard one word about what it is."

Three

At his question, she felt her very core stiffen. She didn't want to get into that with him lying beside her and her wrapped in his arms. She didn't want to say anything that would upset him and break the spell that had been woven around them.

"We'll talk about that tomorrow. Tonight is special, Tony. I want to keep it magical until the sun rises and brings the reality of our regular lives back to us. Is that okay with you?"

"Sure, because I have plans for the rest of this magical night. Big plans."

"I do hope they involve me and your sexy body and your wild kisses."

"My sexy body and wild kisses? Wow. Definitely back to my plans for tonight," he said, leaning down to kiss her again. In minutes he propped his head on his hand to look at her again.

She couldn't tell from his eyes what he was thinking. "What?" she asked him.

He toyed with a strand of her hair as he answered. "At this moment I can't imagine ever returning to the way we were. All I'll have to do is remember tonight. All of it, darlin'."

"You better stop calling me darlin' when we go back to real life."

"I can call you that if I want."

"I suspect you won't really want to, but it's very nice tonight under the circumstances."

He smiled at her. "As you said, this is a magical night. One giant surprise after another. And deep down, I know you're right. We'll go back to our ordinary lives and our usual fights, except maybe they won't be quite so bad. After tonight I'll listen, I'll try to cooperate with you and maybe even do what you want."

She couldn't hold back a laugh. "Like hell you will!"

He chuckled, a deep throaty sound that she could feel in her hand as it lay on his muscled chest. Her fingers traced the solid muscles in his shoulders, chest and arms. Occasionally, she would feel the rough line of a scar. His daily outdoor work not only showed in the strength of his fit body but in his scars, as well.

He pulled her close against his side. "Do you have to go home tomorrow? I hope not. I want to stay right here."

"I suppose I don't, until late afternoon. I'll need to be home early Monday morning," she answered, thinking more about his flat stomach, hard with muscles and dusted with hair, over which she ran her fingers.

"Good. I have plans and they involve staying right here and not talking to anyone except each other."

"I have to check out of the hotel tomorrow by noon,

though. That room was paid for by the auction board."
She drew another circle slowly on his stomach.

"I'll call and have tomorrow night put on my card, so
you can get your things whenever you're ready," he said,
rolling over and stretching out his long arm to retrieve
his phone. "What hotel?"

"I can do that."

"Don't argue. We're not going to disagree with each
other this weekend."

She smiled as she told him the name of her hotel and
watched him get the number on his phone. Once again she
thought his take-charge attitude was delightful when he
focused on her. When he finished and she had the room
for another night, he turned to take her into his arms again.

"Thanks, Tony. That was nice of you," she said, running her fingers over the dark stubble on his jaw. "I have
to say, I didn't know I could ever be quite so fascinated
by a cowboy's body."

"I guarantee you, I'm totally fascinated by a cowgirl's
body," he said, trailing his fingers lightly over her breasts.
Even though she had a sheet pulled up over her, she felt
his feathery caresses, and her rapidly heating body responded to them.

"A beautiful blonde cowgirl," he continued, as his eyes
seemed to feast on her. "I want you here with me as long
as possible."

She felt the same way and had no desire to get up and
leave him. Though her heart wished the night could go
on forever, she couldn't get her head around the fact that
she was in Tony Milan's bed. "My family would never
believe we're together tonight. No one would."

"All those people who heard what you paid for a night
with me will believe it."

She laughed. "I suppose you're right." She rolled over

and sat up slightly to look down at him. "You're really amazing, you know that? Tonight is astonishing. I never dreamed it would be like this."

"I promise you that I didn't, either." His face took on a sheepish look. "When I stepped out on that auction stage earlier, I didn't really think anyone would bid for me."

"Now that is ridiculous."

"I'm just a cowboy."

"A cowboy named Milan—a name that's well known in these parts. And a very wealthy rancher," she remarked. "With all the ranches and businesses owned by your family, I think you could count on someone bidding for an evening with you."

"Who bid against you? I couldn't see either one of you because of the lights in my eyes, not until you stood to come to the stage and a spotlight picked you out. As soon as I laid eyes on you, my attitude about the evening did an immediate reversal."

She smiled at him. "I don't know who bid against me. There were people from Dallas and Lubbock there, and from other places, as well. Probably one of your old girlfriends who wasn't ready to say goodbye," she said.

"Let's not discuss my old girlfriends," he said through a grin. "I'd much rather talk about you anyway. I still say if you'd wear a dress to town, you'd have a slew of guys asking you out."

"I don't want a 'slew' of locals asking me out, thank you very much."

"Why not? There are nice guys out there."

"Sure there are, but they're ranchers and cowboys. I don't want to go out with ranchers or cowboys."

"You could've fooled me. You paid a small fortune to go out with a rancher tonight, in case you've forgotten."

"I won't ever forget you," she said, hoping she kept

her voice light, but a shiver slithered down her spine because she suspected she had spoken the absolute truth. This had turned into the best night of her life because of Tony. He'd charmed her, seduced her and become the most appealing man she had ever known—as long as she didn't think about him as a rancher.

He didn't let the subject drop. Instead, he questioned her. "Why don't you want to go out with ranchers or cowboys? We're nice guys."

"I know you guys are nice. It's just that—" She stopped, hesitating to tell him the truth. But Tony deserved an answer to his question. "I'm a ranch owner, remember? I'm not a party girl out for fun. I'm also not a sweetie who'll go dancing and come home and cook and have a family and kiss a cowboy goodbye every morning while he goes out to work and listen politely to him at night while he tells me bits and pieces about what he had to do at work. Even worse, I don't want to fall for another rancher and have him tell me how to run my ranch."

"I should have guessed. Two bosses can't run a ranch."

"Not my ranch," she said.

"If you don't marry a rancher or a cowboy, the guy is going to want to move you to the city."

"Now you're beginning to get the picture—the complete picture—of why I never wear dresses. I can't imagine marrying a city guy, either, so there you are." She gave a nod of her head, then shrugged. "I have a nice life. I have my nephew, Scotty, who stays with me a lot, and soon there will be another baby in Mike's family."

"But, Lindsay, you were meant for marriage in so many ways. I hope some guy comes along and sweeps you off your feet and you can't say no. Rancher or city guy."

She giggled. "My, oh, my. Is this a sideways proposal?"

He grinned. "You know better than that. We're doing

well together tonight, but for a lifetime…? Would you want that?"

She studied him, knowing she had to make light of his question, but another shiver ran down her spine and she couldn't explain why. She squeezed his biceps. "Mmm, you do make good husband material. You have all your teeth and they look in good shape and you're healthy and strong and light on your feet. And you're incredibly sexy." She gave an exaggerated sigh. "Given our past and probably our future, I think I have to answer…no."

"Incredibly sexy? Oh, darlin', come here." He drew her closer, but she resisted and placed her hand against his chest.

"Whoa, cowboy. Don't let that compliment go to your head…or other parts," she said, and he grinned.

"I told you our future will not be like our past."

She had to agree. "I don't think it will, either."

"Right now I want to relish the present. How about a soak in the tub?"

"A splendid idea," she said, already eager to be naked in the water with him.

He stood and picked her up. She yelped in surprise as she slid her arm around his neck. "I never dreamed you could be so much fun or so charming."

"I promise you, I have to say the same about you. And, to boot, you're breathtakingly beautiful and hot and sexy. I guarantee that sentiment will not end when morning comes," he added with an intent look that made her heart skip a beat.

He carried her to a huge two-room bathroom. One room held plants, mirrors, two chaise longues with a glass-topped iron table between them, plus dressing tables, a shower and an oversize sunken Jacuzzi tub.

Soon they were soaking in a tub of swirling hot water while she sat between his legs, leaning back against him.

"Tony, this is decadent. It feels wonderful."

"I suspect you're referring to the hot water and not my naked body pressed against yours. Right?"

"I won't answer that question."

"An even better choice than I expected from you. Also, I seem to remember a short time ago hearing you say something about my sexy body and wild kisses," he whispered, fondling her breasts as he kissed her nape.

"That I did and I meant it," she concurred, running her hands over his strong legs.

In no time, desire overwhelmed her, and their playful moment transformed. She turned to sit astride him. Placing her hands on both sides of his face, she leaned forward to kiss him, long and thoroughly, her hair falling over his shoulders. He was ready to love her again, too—she felt it. His hands caressed her breasts, then slid down over her torso to her inner thigh. His fingers glided higher, stroking her intimately until she closed her eyes and clung to him, her hips moving as he loved her.

"Tony, you need protection," she said, her eyes flying open.

"So I do," he said, reaching behind him for his terry robe on the footstool. He took a condom out of the pocket and, in seconds, he was sheathed and ready. He pulled her close again, lifting her so he could enter her in one smooth stroke. She locked her legs around him and lowered herself onto his hard shaft.

Her climax came fast, as if they hadn't made love earlier, and she achieved another before Tony reached his. When he was sated, he watched her with hooded eyes and she wondered what he thought.

She picked up a towel to dry herself, her gaze running

over broad shoulders that glistened with drops of water. "I'll see you in bed," she said, leaning close to kiss him. His arm snaked out to wrap around her neck.

"I want to keep you right here in my arms," he said between kisses. Damp locks of his hair clung to his forehead and he felt warm and wet.

"I'll see you in bed," she repeated with amusement. "You're insatiable. When do you run out of energy?"

"With you, I hope never."

She laughed, snatching up another towel to wrap around herself as she got out of the tub and headed to bed.

She felt as if she was having an out-of-body experience. The night continued to shock her—Tony continued to shock her. She couldn't believe he'd given her the best sex of her life, three bone-shattering orgasms—and the night wasn't over yet.

She walked into a big closet and looked at his clothes so neatly hanging. Boots were lined in rows. She found what she wanted—a navy terry robe—and she pulled it on, belting it around her waist.

She climbed into bed, detecting a faint scent of Tony's aftershave, wondering how long it would be before he joined her.

In minutes he walked through the door and her heart skipped a beat. With a navy towel knotted around his waist, he oozed sex appeal as he crossed the room.

"I couldn't wait to be with you. You look more gorgeous than ever," he said, discarding his towel and scooting beneath the sheet. "Want a drink? Something to eat? Music and dancing?"

She laughed out loud. "You've got to be kidding. Relax, Tony. Sit back and enjoy the moment." She sobered and ran her fingers over his smooth jaw. "You shaved."

"Just for you." Turning on his side, he pulled her close against him. "This is better. I like your hair down best."

"I rarely wear it that way, but I'll keep that in mind."

"No, you won't. You'll forget." He ran his fingers through the damp locks. "You know you never gave me an answer to my invitation to go to dinner next Friday night."

She was silent, mulling over his question. She had wanted to accept instantly when he had asked her the first time, but reluctance had filled her. It still did. "I think when we go back to our real lives, you'll wish you hadn't asked me."

"Not so."

"Call me next week and ask me again if you still want to go out. I don't think you will."

"Darlin', if I didn't want you to go, I wouldn't ask you."

"Just call me next week."

He gave her a long look and she wondered what was running through his mind. Had their mild clash reminded him of the big fights they'd had? From the shuttered look that had come to his eyes, she suspected it had. She didn't want any such intrusion on this night. She scooted close against him. "In the meantime, I intend to keep you happy with me," she said, hoping for a sultry voice.

The shuttered look was replaced by blatant desire, and she guessed she had succeeded in making things right between them again. When he turned to kiss her, she was certain she had.

It was midafternoon the next day when she walked out of the shower. Wearing the navy robe again, she roamed through his sprawling condo into a big kitchen that had an adjoining sitting room with a fireplace.

Exploring the refrigerator and his freezer, she saw

some drinks, a few covered dishes and an assortment of berries. She had leaned down to look at the lower shelves when Tony's arms circled her waist to draw her back against him. He nuzzled her neck.

"I know what I want," he said.

She turned to wrap her arms around his neck. He wore another thick navy robe that fell open over his broad chest.

Aware their idyll was about to end, she kissed him passionately. She dreaded stepping back into reality, where she would have to wrangle with him again.

He released her. "Hold that thought and let me put something in the oven so I can feed us."

"At last…food," she said, clutching her heart and batting her eyelashes dramatically at him. When she licked her lips slowly as she watched him remove the covered casserole dish from the fridge and nudge the door closed, he placed the dish on the counter and turned to draw her into his arms.

"You were going to get fed until you did that," he said in a husky voice, pulling her close.

"Did what?"

"You know what," he said, leaning closer to kiss her, a hungry kiss that ignited fires more swiftly than ever.

In minutes she wriggled out of his grasp. "I think we should eat. Whatever I did, I won't do again. How can I help?"

He was breathing hard, looking down, and she realized the top of her robe was pulled apart enough to reveal her breasts. She closed the robe more tightly. "As I was saying, what can I do to help?"

He seemed to not even hear her, but in seconds he looked up. "If you want to eat, I suggest you go sit over there on the sofa and talk to me while I get something heated up. If you stay within arm's reach, I'm reaching."

She smiled and left him alone, watching him put the dish into the oven and get plates, pour juice, wash berries. Her gaze raked over him. He was a gorgeous man. Sexy, strong, successful. Why hadn't some woman snatched him up already? As far as she knew from local gossip, there had never been a long-term girlfriend. Just a trail of girlfriends who'd come and gone. Apparently, he didn't go in for serious affairs.

"Tony, you really should let me help you. I feel silly sitting here doing nothing except watching you work."

"This isn't hard work. You stay where you are so I'm not too distracted to get breakfast on the table."

"I do that to you? Distract you?"

"Lindsay," he said in a threatening tone, "do you want breakfast or do you want to go back to bed?"

She laughed. "Breakfast. I'm famished. And I'll help any way I can."

"You know what you can do, so do it," he said.

"Yes, sir," she answered demurely, teasing him. When his gaze raked over her, she became aware of the top of her robe gaping open enough to give a another glimpse of her breasts and the lower half of her robe falling open over her crossed legs. She closed her robe and belted it tightly, glancing up to find him still watching her.

"Show's over," she said.

He nodded and turned to finish preparing the meal.

After a breakfast of egg-and-bacon casserole and fruit, he turned on music as they cleared the table, and took her wrist. "Stop working and come dance with me," he said, moving to a familiar lively rock number.

Unable to resist him, she danced with him, aware as

she did that her robe gaped below her waist, revealing her legs all the way to her thighs.

Next a ballad came on and he drew her into his arms to slow dance. He was aroused, ready to make love again. His arms tightened around her and he shifted closer to kiss her. Dimly she was aware they had stopped dancing.

His hand trailed down between them to untie her robe while he continued kissing her. When she reached out to do the same, his belt was tightly knotted and she needed his help, but soon both robes were open. He shoved them aside, pulling her naked body against his.

Her soft moan was a mixture of pleasure and desire as he kissed her and picked her up to carry her back to bed.

It was almost two hours later when he held her close beside him in bed and rolled over to look at her. He wound his fingers in the long strands of her hair, toying with her locks.

"I know you have to go home soon," he said. "I think it's time we get to the reason behind this weekend and your incredible bid for me at the auction. You paid a mind-boggling sum to get my attention, so now you have it. What's behind this? What did you want me to agree to do?"

Tony looked into her big eyes that were the color of blue crystal. His gaze went to her mouth and he wanted to kiss her again. He stifled the urge, difficult as it was. Their time together had been fabulous, a dream, but it would end shortly and they would go back to their regular lives. How much would it change because of the auction? For a moment a memory flashed in his mind of the second and most direct encounter they had, when a big tree on her property fell during a storm in the night. It had fallen on his fence, taking it down and also smashing one of his trucks, which had stalled in the rainstorm.

One of the men had called to tell him. When he drove out to view the damage, she was already there with a crew working to cut up the fallen tree and haul it away. She held a chain saw and had a battered straw hat on her head with a long braid hanging over her shoulder. He'd known her all his life but rarely paid any attention to her. He knew she was two years younger than he was, but right then he thought she looked five years younger. The noise of chain saws was loud, the ground spongy from the rain when he stepped out of his truck.

Even though she had to pay for the damage because it was her tree, he'd tried to curb his anger that she hadn't called him first. She saw him and walked over.

"My tree fell in the storm. Sorry about the damage. But I'm insured."

"Did you call your agent?"

"No, I will. I want to get the fence up as soon as possible so I don't lose any livestock."

"Lindsay, that's my fence and I'll fix it. You should have called me. Your insurance should cover the damages when a tree falls on something, but only if you have notified your company. They would have sent someone out to see what happened, take pictures and write a report. Now the tree is back on your property, cut up as we speak, and I doubt if you can collect anything."

She had looked surprised. "I haven't had a tree fall on anything before. I'll check with my insurance company, and I'll pay you for the damage."

"Stop cutting up the tree. I'm going to call and see if my adjustor wants to come out anyway."

She'd frowned but agreed.

"And leave the fence alone. It's my fence and I'll get it replaced today."

She had scowled at him. "Today?"

"This morning," he said. "As soon as we can. If you have livestock grazing here, move them. Don't let them in this pasture. That's simple enough," he said, wondering if she knew how to run that ranch of hers.

"I know that," she snapped.

"Leave the fence to me. Stop cutting up and hauling away the tree. I'll get someone out here to look this over," he repeated, suspecting she was stubborn enough to keep cutting up the tree.

She had clamped her mouth closed as her blue eyes flashed. "Anything else you want to tell me to do?" she snapped, and his temper rose a notch.

"Probably a lot, but I'm not going to," he answered evenly.

"Why was your truck parked right by my property?"

He had been annoyed by her question, though he tried to hang on to his temper. "It was on my property and we can park the truck wherever we want on this side of that fence. If you want to know, one of the men was headed back in the storm and checking to see if the fences were okay. He'd been driving through high water in several low places and the truck quit running here. Unfortunately, near your tree."

She'd been silent a moment as if thinking about what he had said. "I know it was my tree on your truck. My word should be good enough for the insurance."

Impatiently, he shook his head. "No, it's not good enough. Next time, remember to call your adjustor before you do anything else. You may have a hard time collecting."

He remembered her raising her chin defiantly and he'd

wondered if she would argue, but then she looked around and seemed lost in thought until she turned back to him. "That isn't a new truck. Get three estimates in Verity for the repairs and I'll cover the lowest bidder's charges."

"Look, I can't get that kind of damage fixed in Verity. At least not at three different places and you know it. The truck will be totaled."

"I'm not buying you a brand-new truck."

"Tell your guys to stop working and then go home, Lindsay, and call your insurance company. They'll tell you what to do next."

Her cheeks had grown red and fire had flashed in her eyes, but he hadn't cared if his instructions made her angry. She had already annoyed the hell out of him.

Yes, Lindsay Calhoun had that unique ability to boil his blood.

Right now, though, as he reined his thoughts back to the present and looked down at her naked body, she had the ability to heat his blood in a different way.

Tony pushed aside the past to gaze into her big blue eyes. He didn't expect what they'd had this weekend to last much longer because the real world was settling back into their lives.

Last night he hadn't cared what she wanted from him. He'd been totally focused on her as he adjusted to his new discoveries about her. Now, though, curiosity reared its ugly head and he wanted to learn her purpose behind the evening.

"You should know what I want to talk about," she said, scooting to sit up in bed and lean back against pillows, pulling the sheet demurely high and tucking it beneath her arms. Her pale yellow hair spilled over her shoulders. She looked tousled, warm and soft, and he wanted to wrap his arms around her and kiss her again, but he refrained. It was time he heard her out and learned what was so important to her that she would pay several thousand dollars just to get his attention.

"Two things, Tony," she said, and he sighed, trying to be quiet and listen, to be patient and talk to her calmly. He had already given her the solution to her water problem, but she didn't believe him. He could deal with this in a civilized manner, but underneath all her sex appeal, breathtaking beauty and their dream weekend, there still was the real woman who was mule-stubborn and did not take advice well.

Lindsay was all he avoided in women—stubborn, far too serious and constantly stirring conflict.

The irony of the fact that she was now sharing his bed was not lost on him. But he ignored it as he focused on her.

She continued her explanation. "First and foremost I hope that we have some sort of truce where we can be civil to each other, with no tempers flaring."

"I'd say we can be mighty civil to each other. You should have some of your money's worth there," he said, caressing her throat, letting his fingers drift down lightly over her breast.

"I hope so," she said solemnly.

"I'm willing," he said. "So continue."

She squared her shoulders and fussed with the sheet. Then she cleared her throat and spoke. "My wells are running dry and I figured you've replaced your old pumps with bigger ones that are drawing on the aquifer and depleting my groundwater. I can get bigger pumps, too, but that might take water from other neighbors and I don't want to do that."

He held up his hand. "I told you, Lindsay, I do not have bigger pumps."

"Well, for some reason, my water is dwindling away to almost nothing."

"It's a record drought," he said, as if having to explain the obvious to a child.

"I've asked Cal Thompson and he doesn't have bigger pumps. Neither does Wendell Holmes. I figured it was you."

"It is not. According to the weather experts, this is the worst drought in these parts in the past almost sixty years—before you and I were born, much less before we became owners of neighboring ranches. I told you the solution to my problem. You can do the same. Just dig deeper wells and you'll have much more water. Then when it rains, the aquifer will fill back up again. If you don't want to dig deeper, buy water and have it piped in. That's what Wendell is doing."

She stared at him thoughtfully in silence for several minutes. It was difficult to keep his attention on her water worries while she sat beside him in bed, naked, with only a sheet pulled up beneath her arms. He couldn't resist reaching out to caress her throat again, letting his hand slide down and slip beneath the sheet to caress her bare breasts. It took an effort to sit quietly and wait when all he wanted to do was take her in his arms and kiss her thoroughly. Well, that wasn't all he wanted to do.

The instant his fingers brushed her nipple, he saw a flicker in her eyes.

"You really had them dug deeper?"

Thinking more about her soft skin and where his fingers wanted to go, he hung on to his patience. "Yes, I did. When we get home, come over anytime and I'll show you my old pumps."

When she merely nodded, he felt a streak of impatience with her for being so stubborn. She didn't seem convinced he was telling the truth, and he suspected she wasn't going to take his advice. With every passing minute he could see her sliding back into her serious, stubborn self, stirring up conflict unnecessarily. Lindsay seemed to thrive on conflict. Except for last night. For that brief time she had been sexy, appealing, cooperative and wonderful. Now they were drifting back to reality and he had to hang on to his patience once again.

"I might do that."

As his gaze ran over her, it was difficult to think about anything else except how sexy she was and how the minutes were running out on this brief truce. She looked incredibly enticing with her bare shoulders and just the beginning of luscious curves revealed above the top of the sheet. How could she be this appealing and he had never noticed? He knew his answer, but it still amazed him that he hadn't had a clue about her beauty. In the past, once she started arguing he couldn't see beyond his anger. He saw now.

He was unable to resist trailing his fingers lightly over her alluring bare shoulder, looking so soft and smooth. If his life depended on it, he couldn't stop touching her or looking at her. He wanted to pull away the sheet, place her in his lap and kiss her senseless. They were wasting their last few moments together talking about the drought, when he had other things he wanted to do.

He leaned forward to brush a kiss on that perfect shoulder.

"Tony, you're not even listening," she snapped, her voice taking on the stubborn note he had heard her use too many times. Right now, he didn't care, because he knew how to end her annoyance.

He trailed kisses to her throat and up to her ear while his hands traveled over her, pulling the sheet down as they set out in exploration. Suddenly, she pushed him down and moved over him to sit astride him. She had tossed aside the sheet completely and was naked. It still startled him to realize what a sexy body she had.

"This weekend has opened possibilities I never thought of when I was bidding," she said in a throaty voice while her hands played over his chest.

He cupped her full breasts, their softness sending his temperature soaring. He was fully aroused, hard and ready and wanting her as if they hadn't made love ever.

"I'll leave you with memories that will torment you," she whispered, leaning down to shower kisses over his chest.

He sighed as she moved down his body, her hand stroking his thick rod as she trailed kisses over his abdomen and lower. When she reached his erection, he groaned.

He relished her ministrations, but he didn't want their last time to be like this. He wanted to be inside her. In one smooth motion he rolled her over so he was on top. His mouth covered hers in a demanding, possessive kiss at the same time that he grabbed a condom from the bedside table.

In seconds he entered her, taking her hard and fast while she locked her legs around him and rocked wildly against him in return.

He wanted to bring her to more than one climax, as he'd done before, but this time was too unbridled, too untamed. The second he sent her flying over the edge of an orgasm, he joined her, reaching the stars together on a hell of a ride.

When they slowed and their breathing became regular, he stayed inside her, too exhausted to move. Finally he kissed her lips and said softly, "You can't imagine how beautiful and sexy I think you are."

A smile lit up her eyes, though it did not grace her mouth. "I hope so. I don't want you to forget this weekend," she whispered.

He gazed into her eyes and doubted if he ever would.

This time with her had been special, but now they would be going back to their real lives. While they should be more neighborly in the future, they were still the same people, with the same personalities. Lindsay was not his type—she was way too serious for him and far too stubborn. He suspected today would be goodbye.

He pulled out of her and rolled over.

"I should get ready to go home," she said.

He turned to her. "I'll fly you home if you want to have someone pick up your car. Or I can take you home when I go."

She shook her head. "Thank you, but I'll drive home. I'd better get in the shower now. It's time," she said.

He caught her arm and she pulled up a sheet to cover herself while she paused getting out of bed.

"Lindsay, more water is a poor return on your money. For your bid and for this weekend, you should get a whole lake of water in return."

To his surprise she smiled, standing to wrap the sheet around herself in toga fashion. She walked to the other side of the bed to put her arms around his neck. When she did, he placed his hands on her tiny waist, wanting to kiss her instead of listening to whatever she had to say.

"Maybe not such a poor return," she said in the throaty voice that conjured up images of them in bed together. "We've made some inroads on our fighting that will make a huge change in our relationship. At least the fights in the future might not be so bitter."

He grinned. "We'll see how long we can both hold on to our tempers. All I have to do is remember you like this," he said, leaning down to kiss her lightly as he ran his hands over her back.

"I need to shower," she said, stepping away from him.

"Shucks. I hoped I was irresistible," he drawled, and she smiled.

"You are, Tony. Far too much," she said as she walked away from him, picking up the navy bathrobe on her way to the shower.

After her last statement he was tempted to catch up with her and kiss her again. He wanted to hold her, to see how truly irresistible he could be. But they were getting ready to go home and return to their regular lives and there would be no lovemaking in their future. With a sigh he pulled out some fresh clothes and went down the hall to another bathroom.

All the time she showered, Lindsay wondered how much this weekend would change how they treated each other at home. Tony was still Tony, telling her what to do. She hadn't said anything to him, but she wanted to check his pumps by herself. She wouldn't put it past him to be bluffing with his invitation to come look. After all, he was a Milan.

One of her earliest memories had been her grandmother telling her to never trust a Milan. Could she trust Tony now?

The Tony she had just been with for the past twenty hours was a man she would trust with her life. That thought startled her; it was completely at odds with how she'd been raised. Then again… Had her grandmother just been passing down family opinions that could have gone back generations?

Thirty minutes later, dressed and ready to go, Lindsay joined Tony in the living room. He came to his feet when she entered, his gaze sweeping over her, making her tingle. To her surprise, reluctance to see the weekend end filled her. After all, she and Tony had always known it wouldn't—couldn't—last.

Even in jeans, boots and a navy Western shirt, Tony looked sexy and handsome. A short while ago, as they'd talked about ranching, she'd felt the old annoyance with him for telling her what she should do. Now, simply looking at him made her heart beat faster.

She looked down at the red dress she'd worn last night and wore again now. "I have to go back to my hotel in this. It's four in the afternoon, so I may turn heads," she said, forcing a grin that never made it fully to her lips.

He crossed the room to place his hands on her shoulders. "Lindsay, in that dress, you'll turn heads any hour of the day or night. You're gorgeous." He reached out to play with her hair, which fell about her shoulders. "I like your hair down."

For some reason she hadn't put it up when she got ready. She couldn't say why.

"Thank you. I'm ready to go. You know what the drive is like back to the ranch. Are you going home today?" She knew he was driving her to her hotel, but wasn't sure where he was headed after that.

"No, I have an appointment in Dallas in the morning. Otherwise, I would have pushed harder to go home together."

"I see." She gave one nod. "Well, now we go back to our real lives and the real world. But it was a wonderful, magical weekend that I never, ever expected."

"My sentiments exactly," he said. "I don't want you

to go. I don't want this to end, but I know it has to and it won't be the same."

"Afraid not," she agreed with him. "I'm ready. Shall we go?"

"Yes. But how about one last kiss?" He took her in his arms and he kissed her, hard, as if his kiss was sealing a bond that had been established between them this weekend. His lips were making sure that she would never forget his lovemaking, even though she knew it wouldn't happen again.

She kissed him in kind, wanting just as much to make certain he couldn't forget her, either.

He raised his head. "How about a picture of the two of us to commemorate the occasion?" he asked, pulling out his phone. "Do you know how few selfies I've taken? I think one—with a friend and my horse at a rodeo."

She laughed. "I rank right up there with your horse. Wow."

He grinned as he held out the phone and took the shot, then he showed it to her. "You're gorgeous, Lindsay."

"Look at that picture the next time you think about dumping trash on the entrance to my ranch."

He shook his head. "I'm still telling you that I did not do any such thing. You might have annoyed someone else, you know."

Startled, she studied him. "You really mean that?"

"I really mean it."

"If you didn't do it, then I owe you an apology," she said, still staring at him. But, even if she had accused him of something he didn't do, there was bound to have been things he did do. And he still had those take-charge ways that drove her nuts. Besides, he liked to play the field and never get serious. No, Tony was not for her.

"One picture, Lindsay, just of you, so I can look and

remember. Okay?" he asked, stepping away and taking her picture as she placed her hand on her hip and smiled.

"We have to go. I need to get home," she said, shouldering a delicate, jeweled purse that matched the straps on her dress.

"Sure thing," he said, taking her arm to walk her out to the car. As she slid onto the passenger seat, her skirt fell open and she glanced up to see him looking at her legs. She tucked her skirt around her while he closed the door and walked around to his side of the car.

He was quiet on the ride to the hotel, and so was she. As he drew up to the front entrance a short while later, he stepped out and talked to a valet, then came around to escort her into the lobby. "I'm glad you were the high bidder. But I don't want to say goodbye."

"We both know the weekend is over. Really over. Reality sets in now, Tony. As we've already agreed, it might be a little better than it was."

He nodded. "You take care."

"You, too. Thanks for a weekend that was worth my bid."

"That'll go to my head. I didn't dream I could bring such a price." He smiled as he stepped away. "Goodbye," he said, turning and walking out of the hotel.

She stood watching him, unable to understand the feelings of sadness and loss as he walked away.

Four

When he vanished from sight, she turned to go to her room to change to jeans and get her things to drive back to her real life at her ranch. She wished she had gotten a selfie for herself and then she laughed at herself. If she had, at the first ornery thing he did, she would have erased it. And she didn't expect one weekend to change Tony's alpha-male ways or his flitting from woman to woman.

Even if he changed, which couldn't happen, she didn't care to break her rule about avoiding entanglements with cowboys and ranchers. Tony would be the last man on earth she would want to fall in love with because it would be disaster for each of them from the first minute. They were both ranchers, with clear ideas of how they wanted to run things and opposing ideas on most everything. Life with Tony would be a continual battle. Unless he retired and just stayed in the bedroom. That thought made her laugh out loud as she drove all alone in her car, heading west out of Dallas and back to her ranch.

Midmorning on Tuesday as Tony sat at his ranch desk and worked at his computer, trying to find Texas water sources, his phone rang and he answered to hear his brother Wyatt.

"I thought I better call and see if you survived Saturday night. I heard you didn't come home until Monday evening."

"Keane, my foreman, always knows how to get hold of me. You didn't know I was worth so much money, did you?" Tony asked.

Wyatt laughed. "You brought in a fortune at the auction. And it was all for a good cause, so thanks. You really contributed, but don't let it go to your head. Even though this is bound to bring another slew of admiring females into your life."

Tony hadn't thought of that. "Maybe, but there's one thing I do know. I will never bet with you on saddle bronc riding events again."

Wyatt gave a belly laugh. "How'd the date with Lindsay go, bro? I was worried what she might want to do with you. I gotta tell you, I had no idea she could look like she did."

Tony recalled the blonde beauty who was such a surprise. "Lindsay's looks sent me into shock, and once I caught sight of that red dress, the evening instantly improved. But you shouldn't worry. We did fine together."

"I figured her looks would smooth things over. Don't know if you know yet, but the two of you are all the gossip in Verity and in the sheriff's office. I've been asked more than a few questions. I think around my office, they're waiting for a report from me about how the evening went."

"Civilized. That's what you tell them. We just set aside our differences—for charity."

"I'll bet you did," Wyatt said, and Tony could hear the amusement in his brother's voice. "No way in hell would you fight with someone who looked like she did Saturday night. And she must have wanted something from you badly to pay that kind of money."

"Yeah, she wants more water."

"Don't we all. She should know you can't help her out there. No rain in the forecast, either. Hang on a sec, Tony." Wyatt put him on hold while he consulted with one of his deputies. When he returned, he was back on what appeared to be his favorite subject. "Like I was saying, some people will never look at Lindsay the same way. Those who didn't see her at the auction are curious as hell. I don't know why she keeps those looks hidden."

"She's not interested in dating cowboys or ranchers. She doesn't want anyone telling her how to run her ranch. You can figure that one out."

"Definitely. I was shocked to see who had won the bid," Wyatt remarked drily.

Tony would agree with that. "We had a good time Saturday night, but she's still Lindsay, all stubborn and serious. But we did agree to ease off the fights from now on."

"Thank heaven for that one. My life will get a hell of a lot more peaceful. Call when you come to town."

"Sure, Wyatt."

After he hung up, he stared at the phone, thinking about Lindsay, and he was tempted to pick up the phone and call her. Then reason reared its head. Beneath all that beauty, he reminded himself, she was still the stubborn, obstreperous woman she had always been. She was as wise to avoid ranchers as they were to avoid her. She was not his type. Still…that weekend with her had been the sexiest in his life, and she had been the sexiest woman he'd ever been with.

He had to shake his head to get rid of the images that flooded his mind. The two of them in bed, in the Jacuzzi… No, he had to leave things alone. The weekend was over and it wouldn't happen again.

Breathing a sigh, he turned to the ledger he needed to work on and tried to forget her and the steamy memories of their weekend.

The next few days slipped by without a cloud in the bight blue sky, the drought growing more severe as water dwindled in the creeks and riverbeds and strong, hot winds warmed the parched earth. Lindsay threw herself into work, trying to forget the weekend with Tony, but she was unable to do so. It surprised her how much she thought about him. Even worse, she finally admitted to herself that she missed seeing him. She gritted her teeth at the thought. She didn't want to miss Tony. She didn't want him or the weekend they'd had to be important. Her reactions to him continually shocked her.

All her adult life she had avoided going out with men who would want to tell her how to run her ranch. She had managed, until Tony. That was the road straight to disaster. She didn't want to marry a take-charge male— and a Milan, to boot!—and then fight over running everything. There was no way she would be in agreement on everything or turn her ranch over to someone else to run. She shook her head, knowing she needn't worry. Tony wouldn't ever get close to proposing to her. He wasn't going to propose to any woman. He was not even the type of person she wanted to go out with again, and she was certain he felt the same way about her.

It was done. They were done. It was that simple.

Turning back to work, she forced him out of her mind. Soon she wouldn't even think about him.

But that resolve didn't stop her from mulling over his property. That afternoon when she drove her pickup along the boundary between her ranch and Tony's, she stopped, switched off the engine, got binoculars and climbed up on her pickup to find out if she was close enough to see his pump on the water well nearest her land.

It was visible in the distance, but she couldn't tell whether it was old or new. Damn. Time was running out for her.

How much longer could she go without rain?

Her other neighbors were buying water and having it piped or shipped in.

Tony had told her to come look at his pumps. If he still had the old pumps and he had dug deeper—if he was telling the truth—then that would be the best thing for her to do. She frowned. Why did it rankle so much to do what he told her to do?

As she looked at his land, she couldn't keep from moving her binoculars in a wide swing, curious whether Tony worked in the area. She didn't see him and she hated to admit to herself that she was disappointed. She missed his company. Now she was sorry she hadn't accepted his dinner invitation for Friday night, instead telling him to call her this week if he still wanted to take her out again. She hadn't expected to hear from him and so far, she had been right. It was Thursday and he hadn't called, so he must have had second thoughts when he got home.

She hated to admit that she was disappointed, but she told herself it was for the best. Still, she couldn't stop the memories… She remembered being in his arms, his kisses, his blue-green eyes that darkened to the color of a stormy sea when he was in the throes of passion. How could he be so handsome and so sexy? Maybe it had been the tux. Or his naked body that was male perfection. Or his—

Her ringing phone cut off that steamy train of thought. Shaking her head as she wiped her brow, she yanked her cell out of her pocket expecting Abe, her foreman, but the caller ID read T. Milan. Her heart missed a beat as she stared at the phone until the next ring jolted her out of her surprise. She said hello and heard Tony's deep voice.

"How are you?" he asked politely, and suddenly she was suspicious of why he was calling, but at the same time, she was happy to hear his voice.

"I'm fine. Actually, I'm at our boundary line and looking at your closest well trying to see your pump."

"Hey, are you really? I'm not far. Stay where you are and I'll join you and give you a closer look."

She laughed. "You don't need to."

"Of course I don't need to, but I'm already headed that way, so don't drive off."

"I wouldn't think of it."

"Oh, I almost forgot. I called to ask about dinner tomorrow night."

So he hadn't had second thoughts after all. She couldn't stop the smile from spreading across her lips.

"How about something simpler than last weekend?" he continued before he had her answer. "Like Marty's Roadhouse? I know it's two counties away, but if we go anywhere around here, you'll be besieged by cowboys wanting to take you out. Also, we'll be the top of the list for local gossip."

"I don't want either to happen."

"We'll do a little two-steppin' and eat some barbecue and discuss what you can do to get water."

She should say no. They could talk about water on the phone or when he arrived in a few minutes. Common sense told her to decline. But then she thought about dancing with him. If she just had some self-discipline and had him bring her home after dinner, an evening with him couldn't hurt. "That would be good," she said.

"Great. I'll pick you up at six. We'll have a good time dancing."

She heard a motor. "I think I hear you approaching."

"You do. Stay where you are."

"See you in seconds," she said, and broke the connection. Amused, she pulled on leather gloves and parted strands of barbed wire that formed the fence that divided their property. She had been climbing through or over barbed wire since she was little. She straightened to watch him approach.

He drove up in a red pickup, stopped and jumped down. As he came into view, she saw that he wore a light blue long-sleeved shirt with the sleeves rolled up, tight jeans, boots and a black broad-brimmed hat.

She knew she was going against good sense getting involved any more deeply with Tony. So why did her entire body tingle at the sight of him?

"You look great," Tony said as he approached her and reached out to tug her braid. "I never realized how good you look in jeans."

She laughed. "Until last weekend, I never realized you could look at me without getting annoyed."

Grinning, his gaze roamed down her legs again and every inch of her felt his eyes on her. "Oh, darlin', those jeans do fit you. I just should have taken a second look." He looked into her eyes and her breath caught. How could he cause such a reaction in her now? She had known him all her life and until last weekend she'd never once had this kind of response to him just saying hello.

"I'm glad you said yes to tomorrow night," he said, the amusement fading from his expression.

Her smile vanished when his did. "Tony, we're probably doing something we shouldn't. You and I have no future with each other in a social way."

He didn't argue with her and, instead, continued to stare at her. He shrugged and stepped closer to run his finger along her cheek. The feathery touch sizzled and she had to draw a deep breath and resist walking into his arms.

"It's just a fun Friday night, Lindsay. Surely we can do that just one more time."

She knew the more time she spent with him, the more she could get hurt. Tony would not change, and neither would she. At the next problem to come up between them, he would be telling her what to do and she would be angry with him all over again. She needed to stay rooted in reality for the good of her ranch, because she couldn't afford to be sidetracked by him. "Come on," he urged. "We'll have a good time dancing. Marty's on Friday night is fun."

"Until the fights break out."

"That doesn't happen often and if it does, we'll get out of there. I have no intention of spending any part of my night in a brawl."

"So it's two-stepping and eating."

He caught her braid in his hand again as he gazed into her eyes. "Plus some kissing."

She drew a deep breath, wanting him to lean closer and kiss her now yet knowing at the same time that she shouldn't want any such thing.

His phone rang and he looked at it. "I have to go, so let's look at the pumps another time. I have an appointment, but I thought as long as I was close, I'd come say hello. Tomorrow night can't come soon enough." He looked at her as if he still had something he wanted to say. Silence settled between them and she wondered what it was and what was keeping him from saying it.

"I've missed being with you," he finally said. He placed his hands on her shoulders, and an odd expression came over his face. "You seem shorter."

She laughed. "I am. I'm not in my high heels like last weekend."

"Oh, yeah," he said, still staring at her. "But you weren't always wearing heels last weekend," he added in a low voice. "Oh, dang," he said, on a ragged exhale. "I shouldn't, but I'm going to anyway." Pulling her closer, he kissed her.

Her heart thudded and she couldn't catch her breath. His kiss was thorough and sexy, making her heart race. And she responded to it instantly.

When he released her, he was breathing hard. "I have to go. I'll see you tomorrow night at six. Leave your hair down so I can see if it looks as good as I think it did last weekend." As she laughed, he grinned while he placed his hands on her waist to pick her up and set her on the other side of the fence. She remembered how easily he'd carried her in his arms Saturday night. He went back to his pickup in long strides, climbed in, waved and drove away.

Her lips still tingled as she stood there staring after him in a daze. "I should have said no," she whispered to herself. "I should not be going out with him. He's still Tony, all alpha male, a man I've always fought with."

Each hour she spent with him only meant more trouble. She knew that as well as she knew her own name. But she'd already accepted, and besides, it was just dinner and dancing, in a place with lots of people. And talking about water. Far from romantic. She wasn't going back to his ranch afterward. Their evening together would be meaningless.

So why couldn't she wait for tomorrow night?

Lindsay studied herself in the mirror while her two Australian shepherd dogs lay nearby on the floor. It was ten to six; Tony would be here any minute. Time for a last check in the mirror. She'd brushed her hair, curled it slightly in long, spiral curls and finally tied it behind her head with a blue silk scarf. She wore a black Resistol, a denim blouse with bling, washed jeans with bling on the hip pockets and her fancy black hand-tooled boots.

She turned to her dogs and each raised his head.

"I promise you, Tony Milan will not be invited inside tonight. When he comes to the door, don't bark at him and don't bite him."

Both animals thumped their tails as she patted their heads and left the room. The dogs followed her to the front room, where she could watch the drive.

In minutes she heard Tony's pickup approach the house. Hurrying to the door, she turned to tell the dogs to sit. As soon as they did, she opened the door. The sight of Tony took her breath away, just as it had when she had seen him yesterday. His black hat, long-sleeved black Western shirt, tight jeans and black boots made him look 100 percent gorgeous cowboy.

She kept a smile on her face as he approached, even as she silently reassured herself there was no way an attraction between them could possibly develop into anything meaningful. With Tony that was impossible and she was certain he felt the same way. As the dogs barked, she gave them commands that caused them to stop, and they came forward quietly to meet Tony, who patted their heads.

"Hi, cowboy," she said.

"Oh, yeah, you don't go out with cowboys. Well, consider this a business dinner," he said, his eyes twinkling.

"Of course. And business kisses."

"Who said one word about kisses?" he asked, his voice lowering a notch as he placed his hand on the jamb over her head. While she looked up at him, her pulse raced.

"I thought there might be a few kisses as well as dinner."

"We could just skip dinner and go inside and you can show me your bedroom."

She smiled and tapped his chest. "What finesse. I think not. You promised dancing and barbecue."

"Whatever the beautiful lady wants," he said, sounding serious, as if he had stopped joking and flirting. She wanted to step into his arms and kiss him. Then she remembered Tony had broken more than a couple of hearts with his "love 'em and leave 'em" ways.

"Let me turn on the alarm, lock up and we can go," she said in a breathless voice that she hoped he wouldn't notice.

"Sure thing." As she moved back, his eyes raked her body. "Each time I see you, you look fantastic."

"Thank you." She said goodbye to the dogs, who now sat near his feet. "You must have a way with dogs. They don't usually take to strangers."

"Women, children and dogs," Tony said.

"I suppose I have to agree on the women and dogs because that's definitely proven. I don't know about children."

"They love me, too," he said with humor in his voice. "Ask your nephew, Scotty."

Smiling, she switched on the alarm and stepped out with him, hearing the lock click.

He linked her arm in his and they walked to his red pickup.

"Allow me," he said as he held the door for her. She climbed in, aware of his constant scrutiny.

"I do love tight jeans," he said, closing the door behind her.

Laughing, she watched him walk around the pickup, feeling excitement mount as she looked forward to being with him again.

"Some of my family has called me to ask about our evening. My guess is that yours has called you," she said, turning toward him as much as her seat belt allowed. She could hardly believe she was sitting here next to him. Her anticipation of this night with him had built all day.

There still was no danger of it becoming a habit for either of them, just one more night—only a few hours of dancing and talking and, maybe, kisses at her door. As they turned on the road toward the county highway, she gripped his arm. "Tony, look over there in the trees. That's a wolf."

Tony followed the direction of her hand and looked toward a stand of scrub oaks. He didn't see any animal. "I don't see anything and there are no wolves in Texas."

"There's one on my ranch. Look."

She was insistent, so he slowed and backed up, stretching his arm over the back of the seat as he reversed the car around the curve. He saw a furry gray animal at the edge of the trees.

"That has to be a coyote," he said. "It looks like a wolf, but it's not. There aren't any in Texas."

"It's too big and furry to be a coyote," she said. As they

watched, the animal turned and disappeared into the darkness of the trees.

"That animal didn't really look like a dog," Tony said, putting the car in gear and continuing to drive. "Well, we've always got wild animals around here. My money's on a coyote."

"It's a gray wolf. They have them now in New Mexico, and a wolf doesn't know state boundaries. They could easily roam into Texas and probably already have. That was only a matter of time. Remember, there's an old legend around these parts about a gray wolf roaming West Texas and anyone who tames him will have one wish granted."

Tony glanced at her with an exaggerated leer. "I know what my wish would be," he said, his gaze sweeping over her.

She laughed. "You lusty man. You've got no chance of taming it. You'd have to catch the wolf first." She returned to her earlier topic. "About our families…"

"Yeah," Tony said. "Wyatt called me Tuesday morning and said we're the hot topic in Verity."

"Imagine that. Me—the hot topic in Verity. Well, let them talk. It'll die down soon because there won't be enough to talk about."

He cast a glance at her. "I'll bet some new guys have asked you out since last Saturday night."

"They have," she said, "but I turned each one down. A couple were at the auction and a couple heard about the auction," she said, having no intention of telling him six guys who saw her Saturday night had asked her out and three who had simply heard about the auction had called and one more had dropped by the ranch.

"All ranchers, I suppose."

"Ranchers, cowboys and an auctioneer from Fort Worth. No way will I get involved with any of them."

"I can understand that, except you're with me tonight."

She smiled. "Maybe you've moved into the classification of an old friend. Besides, there's no danger of involvement for either one of us. I figure this for our last time together."

"You're probably right," he said.

"You can dance, you're fun, and after last weekend, we're civil to each other. I'm sure we'll have a good time."

"I agree about the good time. I can't wait to get you on the dance floor."

"Also, I want something from you."

He shot her a quick glance and then his attention went back to the road. "What can I do for you?" he asked evenly, but his voice had changed, taken on the all-business tone that she was more familiar with.

"I'm trying to see if I can finagle an invitation to your ranch."

He smiled. "Darlin', I thought you'd never ask! I'll take you home with me tonight."

"Cool it, cowboy. I just want to take you up on your earlier offers to look at one of your water pumps."

His smile disappeared and she wondered if he wanted to turn around now and take her home. "Sure, Lindsay. Tell me when you want to come."

His voice had turned solemn and a muscle now worked in his jaw. She knew she was annoying him, but she wanted to see for herself if he still had his old water pumps.

"Thanks, Tony. I appreciate your offer. You told me to come look."

"So I did," he answered, and then he became silent as they drove on the empty road.

After they reached the county road, he glanced at her

once again. "Lindsay, if that's what you wanted tonight, and why you accepted, do you still want to go?"

"But, Tony," she said in a sultry voice, "that wasn't the sole purpose of accepting your offer to go dancing tonight." She ran her fingers lightly along his thigh. "I also remember how much fun and sexy you can be."

She received another one of his glances and saw him inhale deeply. "Then I'm glad you're here, darlin'. That makes the evening much better. 'Fun and sexy,' huh? I'll try to live up to that description."

She laughed. "I'm sure you will," she said.

Flirting with him made the drive seem shorter, and he flirted in return, causing her to forget about water pumps.

When they reached the roadside honky-tonk, loud music greeted them outside the log building. Inside, they found a booth in the dark, crowded room that held a few local people she knew but more that she didn't.

As soon as they had two beers on the table, Tony asked her to dance. The band, made up of a fiddler, drummer and piano player, had couples doing a lively two-step. As they stepped into the group, Tony held her hands, staying close beside her as they circled the room, and then he turned her, so she danced backward as he led. His gaze locked with hers. Desire was evident in the depths of his eyes as he watched her while they danced. She had his full attention and she tingled beneath his gaze and forgot about her problems.

They danced past midnight and after they returned to their table, he leaned closer. "Ready to leave? We can't talk in here anyway."

When she nodded, he stood, waiting as she slid out of the booth to walk out with him. The air was warm outside, the music fading as they climbed into his pickup.

Light from the dash highlighted his prominent cheekbones, but his eyes were in shadow. The ambience reminded her of their night together, when the dim light of his condo bedroom had shielded his eyes from her view. The memories stirred her as she recalled making love with him. She had tried to avoid thinking about him all week, yet here she was with him. This was crazy. She had to get over Tony, forget him and go on with her life. No way did she want to think about their lovemaking or give him a hint that she would ever want to make love to him again.

As they approached her ranch house, lights blazed from it. "Looks like you have a house filled with people."

"I leave it that way. I don't like to come home to a dark, empty house. And I leave some lights for the dogs," she explained. "Drive around to the back door. It'll be easier for me."

He drove through her wrought iron gates, which closed automatically, and did as she instructed. "I can tell you a better way to avoid a dark, empty house. Come home with me." He unbuckled his seat belt and turned to her. "My house will be neither dark nor empty, and I promise you some fun."

She smiled at him, able to see his eyes now; their blue depths seemed to sparkle even in the darkness. "Thanks, but I belong here. Besides, we agreed on the parameters for tonight."

"It's temptation. You're temptation, Lindsay. Beyond my wildest imaginings," he said, leaning forward to unlock her seat belt. As he did, his lips nuzzled her throat while his fingers caressed her nape. Then he turned to get out of the truck and strode around to open her door for her.

He draped his arm across her shoulders as they walked to her door. "Tonight was fun. I could dance with you for hours. There are a lot of things I could do with you for hours."

Her insides tightened and heated, but she forced a grin. "Is playing chess one of them?" she asked, trying to lighten the moment and get his mind off making love.

"No, chess is not what I had in mind at all," he said as he stopped and turned her to face him in the yard under the darkness of a big oak. As he slipped his arm around her waist, her heart thudded. He leaned close to trail kisses on her neck, her ear. "No, what I want to do is hold you close, kiss you until you melt," he said in a deep, husky voice.

His words worked the same magic on her as his lips and hands. Her knees felt weak and she wanted his mouth on hers. Forgetting all her intentions to keep the evening light, she slipped her arm around his neck and raised her mouth for his kiss.

"Why do I find you so damn irresistible?" she asked.

The moment his mouth touched hers, her heart thudded out of control. More than anything she wanted a night with him, wanted to ask him in, but she intended to stick with her promise to herself to say goodbye to him at her door. He deepened the kiss, his tongue stroking hers, slowly and sensually, and she could barely remember what promise she was thinking about. He was aroused, ready to make love, and she, too, ached to take him to her bedroom and have another night like before.

She didn't know how long they had kissed when she finally looked up at him. She had no idea where her next words came from. "I better go in now."

He stared at her, his hot gaze filled with desire that wrapped itself around her and held her in its spell. Stepping out of its heat, she turned to walk onto her porch. Reluctantly he followed.

When they entered the house, the dogs greeted them. She turned them into the fenced yard, closed the door and faced him.

Though he didn't ask for one, she wanted to give him an explanation.

"Tony, we both agreed last weekend was an anomaly. As special as it was, it's over and we need to leave it over. I don't want an affair and I don't think you do, either. With our families intermarried, we would complicate our lives. We're not really all that compatible anyway. I'm too serious for you and you're too much a playboy for me. If I have an affair, I want it long-term, with commitment. You're not the type for that."

"Don't second-guess me, Lindsay. You're incredibly desirable."

"Do you really want us to get deeply involved?"

He inhaled and gazed at her while seconds ticked past.

"I think that's an answer," she said, "and I agree with it."

"There will never be a time when I can look at you and honestly say I don't want you. I—" He stopped when she placed her fingers against his lips.

"Shh. Don't say things that you don't really know."

Kissing her fingers before she took them away, he nodded as he released a breath. "Okay, so we say good-night now. But I'm not going without a goodbye kiss."

He reached out to take off her hat and toss it onto a nearby chair along with his. "Hats get in the way sometimes," he said as he pulled loose the silk scarf that held her hair behind her head and dropped it into her hat. She shook her head and her hair swung across her shoulders to frame her face.

"You're beautiful, Lindsay," he whispered before his mouth covered hers. He kissed her hard, a passionate kiss that tempted her to throw away common sense and invite him upstairs for one more fabulous night.

She felt his arousal, knew he was as ready to make love as she.

But suddenly, before she could speak, he released her. "Good night, Lindsay. If I don't go right now, I won't go at all. I know what you really want is for me to leave." Before she could move, he turned and hurried out the door.

She fled to her bedroom before she called him to come back. Her heart pounded and she ached with longing for him. How could she feel this way about Tony? A Milan, and her nemesis for so many years?

She had to get beyond this heart-pounding reaction she had to him. She couldn't afford to see him again because each time bound her more closely to him.

He had walked out of her life tonight and there wasn't any reason for him to come back into it. At least not in the immediate future. Things would always happen that would cause them to see each other, but her usual encounters with Tony had been only three or four times a year.

When she had asked him if she could come to his ranch and look at one of his pumps, the question had made him angry. Would he be even angrier if she actually went to his ranch? He probably would, but she was going anyway to see for herself whether he had been truthful. It had been ingrained in her by her family not to trust a Milan and she found it difficult to trust Tony on ranch matters.

And personal matters? After last weekend, she might have to answer that question differently.

She lay across the bed, the lights out, and as thoughts of Tony swirled in her mind, she knew she'd never sleep tonight. Not when she was wishing she were with him, in his arms, naked beside him. Would he sleep? Knowing him, she figured he'd sleep like a bear in winter.

She closed her eyes against the tears that stung them. Tony was out of her life—where he should be. There was no way they had any future as a couple. She'd accomplished all she'd set out to do that night at the bachelor auction. She'd bid on him to butter him up, to make him more amenable. At least that seemed to have worked. With any luck, the fights had stopped or at least changed to simple quarrels. If that had happened, it all would have been worthwhile.

There'd be no more calls from Tony after tonight. The thought swept her with a sense of loss. She shook her head as if she could shake away the feeling. How long would it take her life to get back to normal?

Five

He hadn't been ready to tell her goodbye tonight. The whole time he'd cruised down the driveway he'd watched her house in the rearview mirror, fighting the urge to turn around.

If he let himself, Tony could envision the scene clearly. He'd stop sharply, his tires spewing dirt and gravel as he spun around and gunned his engine. When he pulled up at her back porch, she'd be there throwing open the door, and she'd run to him just as he stepped out of the truck. He'd pick her up in his arms and carry her back into her house, right up to her bedroom. They wouldn't say a word to each other; they wouldn't need to. They'd simply make love. And it would be amazing.

A nice image, he had to admit. But one that wouldn't happen.

Instead, he drove the pickup onto the county road toward his own ranch.

He couldn't help but feel tense, and not just sexually.

He'd been looking forward to this night with Lindsay, and to say it hadn't ended the way he'd hoped would be an understatement. But she was right. They had no future. And Lindsay wasn't the type of woman to have an affair without a future.

And she was too serious, just as she said.

Not to mention the whole business with her wanting to see his water pumps. Damn, she still didn't believe that he hadn't installed bigger pumps to steal her water. She wanted to see it with her own two eyes. Because he was a Milan, no doubt, and Milans never told the truth!

He banged the palm of his hand on the steering wheel. He needed to forget her.

As he drove along the darkened road, he turned on the radio, but the guy who sang—some guy who'd won one of those ubiquitous TV reality shows—strummed a soulful guitar and sang about the cute filly he was pining for. Tony didn't want to hear it. He shut it off. He had enough of his own problems with his own cute filly. A spirited one, at that.

He had to let out a laugh at the thought of Lindsay knowing he had referred to her as a filly. She'd probably take out her shotgun and fill him with buckshot.

The drive home seemed endless, but by the time he pulled onto the long driveway up to his ranch house, he knew what he had to do. He had to forget everything about Lindsay Calhoun, starting with last Saturday night. From the moment he'd seen her in that red dress all the way to tonight. As sexy, as enticing, as appealing as Lindsay was, she wasn't the woman for him. They could never be together. She was commitment with a capital *C*, and that was one thing he couldn't—wouldn't—ever be willing to give.

He entered the house and went up to bed, not even bothering to turn on a light.

* * *

She hadn't bothered to turn on the light.

For some reason, that thought struck her as she woke up. She remembered running up to her room, in the dark, after Tony left, and throwing herself on the bed, sad and uncharacteristically near tears. She thought she'd never sleep tonight, but apparently she had.

She felt beside her and at her feet, but the dogs weren't in their usual position. Then she remembered. She'd let them out when she got home and then forgotten about them. They'd probably gone over to the bunkhouse for the night.

She sat up, glancing at the clock on her bedside table to see it was after three in the morning. A long, sad howl sent chills down her spine and she ran to the window to look out. Another sad howl filled the night.

Moonlight splashed over open spaces and something moved. Chills ran down her spine again as she saw the wolf standing at the edge of a grove of trees. As she watched, it threw back its head and howled again.

She shivered. For the first time since being on the ranch, she felt alone and didn't like it. She wished she had kept the dogs with her and hoped no one at the bunkhouse turned them out, because she didn't want them tangling with a wolf. She also hoped no one at the bunkhouse got his gun. The men were good shots. If they wanted to kill the wolf, they would surely succeed. She grabbed her phone to call her foreman, thought about it and decided it would be ridiculous to wake him. When morning came, she would talk to Abe about the four-legged intruder.

Another lonely howl caused a fresh batch of shivers to crawl up her spine. Impulsively, telling herself she shouldn't, she called the one person she thought of.

She felt silly when Tony answered, and she suddenly

wished she hadn't called him. But she'd awakened him and she had to explain why.

"Sorry, Tony. I know I woke you."

"Lindsay? Are you okay?" he asked, in a surprisingly clear, alert voice.

"I'm fine, Tony." Now that she had him on the phone she couldn't seem to tell him about the wolf. What did she expect him to do about it?

"Okay then, darlin', what's on your mind at…3:17 a.m.?"

"I feel really silly now."

"Lindsay, you didn't call me in the middle of the night to tell me you feel silly."

"The wolf/coyote/dog—except it looks like a wolf—is howling near my bedroom. I can see it and the animal sounds hurt."

"All animals sound hurt when they howl. So? I know you're a crack shot even with that big .45 you own. Take him out and go back to sleep."

"A gunshot would wake everyone on the ranch and create an uproar. Anyway, I can't kill him. Or her. He or she sounds pitiful and eerie, and for the first time since I've owned the ranch I don't like being here alone."

"I'm coming over."

"No, Tony. I just wanted to hear your voice. Don't get up and come over."

"I can be there in a few minutes."

"Stay in bed," she said, hearing another long howl and looking at the animal standing half in the moonlight and half in shadow. "I feel sorry for it. It sounds hurt and lonesome."

"I'll be over in a flash. I can really take your mind off the wolf, howls or no howls."

She smiled and sat back in the chair by the window.

"You're succeeding right now and you just stay home. We'll both be better off."

She didn't want a repeat of the scene they'd endured only hours ago at her back door. Watching him walk away was hard enough then; she couldn't go through seeing him—and losing him—again.

"That may be true for you, but if I come over, I would definitely be better off."

Despite herself, she laughed softly. "You make me feel so much better. But I still think you should stay home."

"Lindsay, I'm already pulling on my jeans."

"Don't. I really mean it. I feel better now and I can go back to sleep, and I know you can roll over and go to sleep the minute your head is on the pillow." She refused to picture him taking off his jeans and getting back into bed, shirtless and sexy.

"Fine," he said. "The guys will take care of the animal for you and, hereafter, you won't have to listen to it howl again."

"I don't know why, but I feel sorry for it. Unless it kills some of the livestock, I'd hate for them to shoot it."

"Well, this is a change. You're usually pretty damn tough and I know you've shot plenty of wildlife."

"Now how would you know that?"

"The guys talk. And I remember a few marksmanship competitions over the years. Come to think of it, you haven't participated in any in a long time."

"Nope. It doesn't seem to matter any longer. When I first got the ranch, I felt I had to prove that I could handle running the place and a few other things. I don't feel that way any longer."

"I would think not. Half the ranchers around here call you about their animals."

"Not really half, but a few have," she said. She settled

back in the chair to talk, forgetting about everything but the sound of his voice, soothing and smooth as it settled around her in the darkness. It was an hour later when they finally said goodbye and she went to bed. That's when she realized the howls had stopped long ago, but she hadn't actually noticed when, thanks to Tony.

As the next week passed, Lindsay tried to keep busy and struggled to stop thinking about Tony, but that was impossible. She heard nothing from him for eight more days, but, instead of forgetting about him—something she once could easily do—she thought about him constantly, to the point where she had been distracted at work.

It was Thursday, in the middle of a hot, dry afternoon, after she'd helped move steers to another pasture, when her phone rang and she saw it was Tony. She pulled her truck off the road into the shade of an oak and opened the windows.

"It's Tony. I thought it was time to see if you want to come look at the pumps on my water wells."

She was surprised, to say the least. Even though he'd offered, she'd never really expected him to have her over to his ranch—because she still figured he had installed new and bigger pumps. She glanced at her watch. "Give me about two hours and I'll be there. Tell everyone I'm coming so they don't send me away if they see me."

"Nobody's going to send you away and my foreman knows I was going to call you. Come on over. See you in two hours," he said, and ended the connection.

She looked at her phone for seconds, as if she could see Tony. Was he up to some trickery to convince her that he still had his old pumps and had just dug deeper?

She would never tell Tony, but she had already started checking into having her wells dug deeper, and Tony had been right. If she went deeper, there was still water in the aquifer, and when the rains finally came, that depleted water would be replenished and everything would be like it was.

She had already told the men she was headed home, so she started her truck and drove back to her house to shower. She changed into washed jeans, boots and a short-sleeved blue cotton shirt. She knew Tony liked her hair down and not fastened, but she was back at home and she didn't care to change her appearance, so she braided her hair and got her wide-brimmed black hat.

She hadn't been to Tony's ranch house even though she had seen pictures of it on the web, along with a map of his ranch land. As she approached, she looked at the sprawling two-story ranch house that appeared even larger than hers. A porch ran across the front and a wide circle drive joined a walk leading to the front porch.

Flower beds surrounded the house with rock and cactus gardens, plants well adapted to the drought that usually hit West Texas. As she approached, Tony crossed his porch, coming to meet her, his long legs covering the distance. His hair was combed and he had on a clean short-sleeved blue-and-red-plaid shirt, tucked into his jeans. She smiled, happy to see him again.

Tony opened the door of her truck and watched her step out.

"Oh, lady, you do look great," he said, his gaze sweeping over her and making her tingle and momentarily forget why she was here.

"And hello to you. Thank you."

"You've never been to my home, have you?"

"Nope, I haven't. And you haven't been in mine, yet. Not really," she amended, as she thought about last week and how he'd barely made it through her back door before he left.

"Well, I hope to remedy that soon," he said.

"We'll see."

They stepped into an entry foyer that held a full-length mahogany mirror, two hat racks, hooks for coats, shelves that housed several pairs of boots. Stepping through the hallway, they came to a huge kitchen with state-of-the-art-equipment and luxurious dark wood cabinetry. The adjoining family room held a stone fireplace, a big-screen television, a game table, as well as a desk with two computers and other electronic devices.

"All the comforts of home, huh?" she asked. "It's a marvelous home."

"I suspect you have one to match," he remarked.

"Odd that we've never been in each other's houses in all the years we've known each other," she said.

"There's a lot we didn't do in all the years we've known each other," he said, setting her nerves on edge. "C'mon, I'll show you more."

They walked down a wide hall with Western paintings and beautiful tapestries that surprised her. The hall held finely crafted furniture, double front doors where floor-to-ceiling windows let in light and offered a grand view of the front of his property.

"Very beautiful, Tony. And a little surprising."

"You probably pictured me in a log cabin with brass spittoons and bawdy paintings," he said grinning.

She smiled. "Not that extreme, just maybe a little more rustic than this. After all, you're a rancher at heart. This fancy home could belong to a Chicago stockbroker."

He shrugged. "It's comfortable, what I like and a haven when I come home."

"That I understand." She followed him as he directed her down another hallway.

"I don't really know much about you as a person," she

said when he stopped outside a closed door. "Just as an annoyance in my life—until this month," she said.

"I'm glad you added that last part. Here, Lindsay," he said, ushering her into a suite with a sitting room that held floor-to-ceiling windows affording a panoramic view of a terrace and fields beyond it where horses grazed. "Here's my living room. Want to see my bedroom next?"

Smiling at him, she shook her head. "I think we're skirting the edge of temptation too much as it is. Thanks, I'll pass."

"Okay, then, on to the study."

They went down the hall to another room, as elegant as the last, with leather furniture, oils on the walls, heavy shelves and polished cherrywood floors.

As she looked around, he said, "We can finish the tour later." He glanced out the window. "Because I want you to see one of the pumps before the sun goes down."

"Good idea," she said. She wanted to see it in daylight, too, because if it really was his old pump, it would have rust.

"I'm ready."

He placed a hand on the small of her back. "So am I," he said in the husky tone he'd had when making love.

She stepped back. "You're not helping the situation. We agreed that we were not pursuing…" She searched but couldn't find the word she wanted. "Not pursuing this," she said, "any further." She tried to sound forceful, but her words sounded hollow, even to herself.

Tony must have thought so, too, because he said nothing. He merely stepped close and placed his hands on her waist. Her breathing became shallow and erratic as his steady gaze met her eyes and then lowered to her mouth.

Dimly the thought nagged at her that it had been a

mistake to come here, but she wanted to see if he had been truthful with her.

She couldn't step away or protest. She saw the desire in the blue-green depths of his eyes and her mouth went dry. She wanted his kiss just one more time.

He leaned down to kiss her, a hot, possessive kiss that made her feel he wanted her with all his being. Her heart pounded as she wrapped her arms around his neck and kissed him back, once again trying to make him remember this moment and be as conflicted as she was.

Her world spun away, lost in Tony's kisses that set her ablaze. She felt his hands drifting up her back, then moving forward to lightly caress her breasts.

"Tony," she whispered, unable to tell him to stop, yet knowing they should.

She caught his wrists and leaned back. "This isn't why I came," she whispered, and then stepped away. "Water well pump, remember?" she asked, unable to get any firmness in her voice.

"When you're ready, we'll go," he said. He stood so close that her heart pounded and it took all the willpower she had to move away.

"We both have to do better than this tonight."

"I intend to do a lot better," he said, teasing and leering at her, causing her to laugh.

"You're hopeless and headed for trouble, and you're taking me with you." She smoothed down her shirt and stood tall. "I'm ready to look at that pump now."

"One thing—in case you think I might have one old pump for moments like this and the rest are new, I'll let you select which one we go see," he said. She went with him to his desk, a massive cherry table. He opened a drawer and pulled out a map, which he unfolded. "This is a map of the ranch with the water wells circled in yellow. You can select one. If you want to look at all of them, we can."

She gave him a searching look. "I'm beginning to believe you and feel really foolish."

"This is why you came. Pick the wells, Lindsay," he instructed.

She looked again and pointed to one the shortest distance from the house.

"Is that all? I want you totally satisfied when you go home." He said the last words in the tone of voice he used when he was flirting with her. He was back to sexy innuendos, which kept her thinking about his kisses and lovemaking.

"Tony, you've got to stop that," she said, unable to suppress another laugh. He grinned and took her arm.

"I don't think you really want me to. You say those words, but your body, your eyes, your voice are giving you away, darlin'."

"Time to go, Tony," she said, trying to resist him, the sensible thing to do.

They drove to the well and she could see the rust on the pump from yards away. She turned to place her hand on his arm. "Tony, I'm sorry. I've misjudged you and accused you of things you didn't do."

He turned to face her. "You don't want to see another well?"

She shook her head, "No. I apologize."

"Apology accepted."

"I've already taken your advice and called to see about digging my wells deeper."

"Good. C'mon, let's go home and have some juicy steaks."

She knew she should say no, but she couldn't. She

had been wrong about him—he had been telling her the truth all along.

She thought of all the times she had been told not to trust a Milan. Her grandmother had practically drummed it into her head. But her brother had married Tony's sister and trusted her fully. Shouldn't she have learned anything from Jake?

They rode back in silence, but when they stepped into his kitchen, she had to apologize again. She felt that bad.

"Tony, again, I'm so sorry. I—"

He turned to her and put his hands on her waist. "Don't worry about it, it doesn't matter now. This is all that matters."

He tilted her chin up, and she saw the flicker in his eyes and knew when the moment changed. He drew her into his embrace and kissed her, holding her tightly and kissing her thoroughly until she was breathless. With a moan of pleasure, she slipped her arm around his neck and another around his waist to hold him tightly, wanting his kiss in spite of all her intentions of resisting him.

When he released her, he smiled. "That's better," he said. "Let's have a drink and I'll start the steaks."

Though she knew she should go home for a quiet dinner alone, she nodded instead. She tingled from his kiss and wanted more. Each kiss was a threat to her heart and she promised herself she would stop seeing him after this evening. It was just one more night.

She drew a deep breath as her throat went dry. "We weren't going to do this."

"So we're together three times instead of two. Seeing each other will end and we both know it, so what does tonight hurt?" he asked.

"You make it sound like something silly for me to protest."

"You know I want you to stay. It won't be a big deal, Lindsay."

With her heart drumming, she watched him walk to a bar. Who would have thought it? A cowboy who could turn her world upside down, who had become the sexiest, most handsome man she had ever known. How could Tony have become important to her, able to set her heart pounding just by walking into a room where she was?

What seemed worse, the more she knew him, the better she liked him and the more she thought of him. That realization scared her. She didn't want to respect him, admire him and like him. He was still Tony, who had to run everything all the time. Physically, she was intensely attracted to him, but it was beginning to spill over into other aspects of their lives and that scared her.

Never in her life had she been attracted to someone who could put her way of life at risk—until now.

To protect her own lifestyle, she had to make tonight the last time she would socialize with him. She had to break off seeing him before her life was in shambles and her heart broken.

Could she adhere to that…or was it too late?

Six

He wasn't in the kitchen when she came back from freshening up in the powder room. Where had he gone?

She saw a column of gray smoke spiraling skyward and followed it to the glassed-in sitting room where she saw him outside at a grill. When she went out, he turned to smile at her. Tall, lean and strong, he kept her heart racing. His blue-eyed gaze drifted over her and she could see his approval.

"The steak smells wonderful," she said.

"Thanks. We have tossed salad and twice-baked potatoes, too."

"When did you fix all that? Twice-baked potatoes? You planned this?"

"No. I have Gwynne, a cook who has gone home now. She fixes dinners and leaves them for me. The potatoes were frozen and easy to thaw and heat. She lives in her own place here on the ranch and cooks five days a week."

"And what do you do the other two days?"

"Eat alone," he said.

"I can imagine," she remarked, thinking of women she knew he had taken out.

He chuckled as he turned to look at the steaks.

The terrace was broad, running across the back of the house and along the bright blue swimming pool that looked so inviting.

"What do you want to drink? Iced tea, wine, cold beer, martini—you name what you'd like."

"With a drive home tonight, I think iced tea is a good choice."

"I'll get you that, but I'd be happy to drive you home tonight."

"I'll take the tea," she answered, smiling at him, wanting to accept his offer, wanting to stay all night, but determined to do what she should.

In minutes he brought her a tall glass of tea and he held a cold beer. "Shall we sit where I can keep an eye on the steaks?"

All the time they talked, she was aware of him sitting close. His hand rested on her shoulder, rubbing it lightly, or on her nape, his warm fingers drifting in feathery caresses, all small touches that were heightening desire. Was it going to be easy to forget the times spent with him? Was she going to miss him or think about him when they parted for good? She knew the answers to both questions. What she was uncertain about was whether she could resist him.

Soon they sat down to eat in his cool, informal dining area.

"Once again, I'm surprised and impressed. You're quite a cook, Tony. The steaks are delicious."

"Thank you. Our own beef and my own cooking. Ta-da."

When she laughed, he shook his head.

"I need to make an improvement," he said, reaching out to unfasten one more button of her shirt and push it open to reveal her lush curves. His warm fingers brushed her lightly and she drew a sharp breath, longing for his touch.

She hoped what she wanted didn't show. She could barely eat. All she wanted was to be in his arms. In some part of her mind she wondered if he had an ulterior motive for inviting her to see the pumps.

He turned on the charm during dinner, smiling and telling her stories about his family and funny incidents when he started as a rancher. They sat for hours after they finished their steaks, laughing and talking over coffee, until she realized the sun had gone down a long time ago. She stood. "It's getting late, Tony. I should go home." She picked up her plate. Instantly Tony took her dish from her hands.

"None of that. Gwynne will be here in the morning and will take care of it."

"So then I should be going," she said, trying to stick to what she felt she should do.

Placing his hands on her shoulders, making her tingle in anticipation, he turned her to face him.

"Don't go home tonight, Lindsay. You have choices—you can sleep downstairs alone or upstairs with me, but stay. I don't want you to drive back tonight."

"Tony," she said, her heart drumming as she looked into his blue-green eyes, "you know I should go. We've talked about this."

He stepped closer to wrap his arms around her and kiss her. When she knew she was on the verge of agreeing to stay, she stepped out of his embrace.

"I have to go home," she said breathlessly.

He nodded and watched as she straightened her blouse and turned for the door.

Draping his arm across her shoulders, he walked her to her pickup.

"I know you're doing what's sensible. We have different lifestyles. Even so, I don't want you to go."

"I have to," she said and turned to climb into her pickup. She smiled at him. "Thanks for dinner and for showing me your water pump."

"Sure. I'll call you," he said, and closed the pickup door.

He stood on the driveway watching her as she drove away. She glanced several times at the rearview mirror and he still stood watching. Then she rounded a curve and he was gone from view.

She trembled with longing, wanting to stay, telling herself over and over that she was doing the right thing and the smart thing. She had no future with Tony. Far from it, he would be a threat to her and her ranch. Why didn't that knowledge make her feel better?

She tried to stop thinking about his kisses, the laughs they had shared. What she was doing was for the best. She missed him, but she was not brokenhearted after an affair that Tony had ended, something she wanted to avoid with all her being.

The auction had been worth the money if she got friendliness and cooperation from him. She knew he would never stop telling her what she should do, but they could have a more neighborly relationship. In a week she would probably feel differently about him if she stopped seeing him and talking to him.

Tony stood a few minutes after Lindsay drove out of sight. Longing for her tore at him and was impossible for him to ignore.

How could he have so much fun with her now, find her

so desirable when not long ago they were at each other's throats over every issue?

He knew the answer to his question. She was the sexiest, best-looking, most fun woman he had ever known. The realization still shook him.

Feeling empty, he stared at the road, wishing she would turn around and come back. Back into his arms and into his bed tonight.

He shouldn't miss her—he had never missed a woman this much or given one this much thought when he wasn't with her.

Of all the women in Texas, why did it have to be Lindsay who had turned his life topsy-turvy?

With a long sigh, he turned to go inside, knowing he wouldn't be able to stop thinking about her or sleep peacefully tonight.

As he walked back to his house, he saw a light in one of the barns. On impulse, to avoid being alone, he changed direction and strolled to the barn, where he found Keane nailing up more shelves in the tack room.

"I wondered who was working. Need help?"

"Yep. In a minute. I need a break. If you have time, four hands will be better than two trying to get these shelves in place," Keane said as he sat on a crate.

Tony sat on a bale of hay and stretched out his legs. "Lindsay just left and she's happy about my water pumps. She is going to look into doing the same, as we have to get water."

"She can be a nice lady. Good for neighbors to get along."

"It should be more peaceful. I hope it lasts, because she still can be her stubborn self."

"She's not so bad, but you know that now. The people who work for her like her."

"For a time it will probably be better between us."

"I'd bet money on that one," Keane remarked drily. "She's a strong woman who knows what she wants."

"Amen to that. Actually, I don't think we'll see any more of each other in the future."

"Maybe so. You'll work it out, I'm sure."

Tony focused on his foreman because it sounded as if Keane was trying to hold back laughter. "Ready to get back to work?" Tony asked, standing because he wanted to end the conversation about his private life.

"Sure. You can hold one of these boards in place for me."

Silently, Tony followed directions from Keane, but his thoughts drifted to Lindsay. He didn't want to go back to his empty house. He missed her and didn't want to think about her staying or having her in his arms in his bed tonight.

Once Keane stopped to look at him.

"What?"

"You're getting ready to hammer that board in and it's in the wrong place."

Startled, Tony looked at the narrow board he held in his hands. "Sorry," he said, adjusting it as he felt his face heat. He had been lost in thoughts about Lindsay. He made an effort to stop thinking about her and focus on the job at hand.

Tony managed to keep his thoughts on the task and, in minutes, Keane stepped back to look at his completed shelves.

"With your help, we're through," Keane said. "Thanks, boss. That went quickly. I'll put away the tools."

"I'll help," Tony stated, acting quickly. In minutes they parted, Keane for his house and Tony walking back to his, which was dark and empty.

He stepped inside, locked the door and went to the kitchen to get a beer. He carried it out to the patio to sit and gaze at the pool, gardens and fountain while he thought about Lindsay.

He had to get her out of his thoughts. They had no future together and neither one wanted a future together. It still amazed him how much she was in his thoughts.

"Goodbye, Lindsay," he said aloud, as if he could get her out of his thoughts that way. He didn't expect to see her again soon. He tried to ignore the pang that caused.

Lindsay stood in front of the calendar the next morning counting the days. Once and again. No matter how many times she counted it, the results were the same. She had missed her period by almost a couple of weeks now, and that had never happened before. Common sense said there could be a host of reasons and she should give it more time. But could she be pregnant? Tony had taken precautions, but there was always a chance. She knew the statistics.

Anxiety washed over her with the force of a tidal wave, and she pulled out her desk chair to sit down.

After a few minutes, she reminded herself that women were late all the time without it meaning they were pregnant and she should give it a few more days. No sense worrying needlessly. She simply put it out of her mind and got ready for work.

But when the next two days passed with no change, she had to get a home pregnancy test. She couldn't get it in Verity or any town in the surrounding counties where she knew nearly everyone.

She was having Tony's baby. She knew it. Shock buffeted her. How could she deal with it?

She was going to have to figure out how to deal with

it. She picked up her phone to send a text to her foreman. *Something's come up. I'll call later.*

In a minute she received a reply: *Okay.* She put her head in her hands. If only she could undo everything and go back to the way she and Tony had been before the auction. She didn't want to be pregnant with Tony's baby. She'd always thought someday she would marry and have a family. Now she was going to have the family without the marriage.

She didn't want Tony to know yet. She had to have plans in place so he couldn't take over.

She ran her hands through her hair. She wasn't ready for this. Tony would want to be part of his child's life, and he would take charge and tell her what to do the moment he learned she was carrying his baby.

Telling her how to run her ranch would be nothing compared to telling her how to raise a baby.

Their baby.

A Milan baby.

A Milan baby fathered by a man she could never marry.

But their families would want them to marry. Hers would pressure her, just as his would pressure him. She knew he was the family type who would think they should marry for this baby's sake. She would have a bigger fight with Tony than she had ever had before. Running two big ranches and raising a baby together. They wouldn't have a battle—they'd have a war! She put her head in her hands to cry, something she rarely did. How would she cope with this? For once in her life she felt overwhelmed.

For a few minutes as she cried, she let go, swamped by a looming disaster. She raised her head and her gaze fell on a picture of her nephew she had taken when Scotty was two. He was laughing, sitting astride a big horse and holding the reins. She loved the picture and she loved Scotty with all her heart and had always hoped she would have a little boy just like him.

She sat up, dried her eyes and stared at Scotty's picture, pulling it close. She was going to have a baby and maybe her child would be as wonderful as Scotty. And her family would stand by her. She had no doubts about that.

She had always avoided dating ranchers until Tony. When she bought a night with him at the auction, she had not expected to fall into bed with him or to even want to see him again.

She should have stuck to her rule of not dating a rancher, no matter the circumstances. But it had never once occurred to her that she could be attracted to Tony, not until she had seen him in that tux, looking so sexy, those eyes that could convey enough desire to melt her.

Logic said to make a doctor's appointment and have her pregnancy verified by a lab and a professional. She could get a home kit, but she wanted a doctor's results to be certain. That was step one. Telling Tony would be step two and the one that she could not cope with thinking about now.

Why had she ever bid for him in the damn auction? No undoing that night now, but it was coming back to haunt her. She needed to plan and to find a good doctor. She couldn't go to a doctor in Verity or anywhere around the area. Texas might not even be big enough. She didn't want word getting to Tony until she was ready to tell him herself. She should fly to a big city, like Tulsa or Albuquerque, but she didn't know any doctors there. She thought about Savannah, Mike's pregnant wife who was from Arkansas.

If Savannah gave her an Arkansas doctor's name, she

could drive to Dallas and then fly to Arkansas without anyone else in the family knowing where she had gone or why. As she thought about her older brother, Mike, she wanted to talk to him and to Savannah. Because of Scotty, she had gotten where she felt close to Mike, and now that he had married Savannah, they would be the ones to talk to about her situation. Savannah had never intended to become pregnant and when her ex-fiancé in Arkansas found out, he had been hateful and hadn't wanted his baby. Lindsay sighed. At least she would never have to worry about that with Tony. It would be just the opposite with Tony. He would want this baby in his life all the time.

Madison, Jake's wife, was expecting, too. That would help soften Jake's attitude about her situation. And Jake liked Tony. Her brothers liked him and their wives did, too. She had been the sole member of her generation to fight him. In fact, it was the older generations of Calhouns that didn't like the Milans. She had heard Destiny talk about her grandmother's intense dislike of Milans. Maybe that had eased up now that Wyatt and Destiny were married, as well as Jake and Madison.

She had always been close to all her brothers, particularly Josh when they were young, so Josh and Abby would give her support. Abby had a heart of gold and would be as kind as Josh.

Looking again at the calendar, she picked up her phone and called Savannah and in minutes made arrangements to see her.

By noon she was showered and dressed. She studied herself in the mirror, turning first one way and then another, knowing it was ridiculous to expect to see any change yet. Her cell phone rang. When she saw it was Tony, she ignored the call.

* * *

Smiling, Savannah opened the back door. "Come in. Mike is out on the ranch somewhere and you said not to call him, so I didn't. Scotty is napping."

"I'll make this short, Savannah. I wanted to talk to just you. Not Mike. And not Scotty right now."

"Sure. Come in," Savannah said, stepping back out of the way and shaking her blond hair away from her face. "Want a cool drink?" Savannah asked.

"Ice water would be fine, and you sit and let me get it and whatever you want to drink. I know this kitchen almost as well as my own."

"I'm a little clumsy, but I'm not feeble. I can get us glasses of water," Savannah said as she turned to wash her hands and get down glasses. Lindsay's gaze ran over Savannah's navy T-shirt and jeans. She knew Savannah's baby was due in October, which was only weeks away now that it was already the first day of September. Savannah's round belly didn't look big enough to deliver in another month. "You don't look very pregnant."

"I feel very, very pregnant. And believe me, there's no such thing as not very pregnant."

Lindsay laughed politely, but she still couldn't cope with the prospect of being pregnant or joke about it. Each time she thought about it, she also wondered how she would ever tell Tony. She had no answer to that one.

In minutes they had glasses of water and sat in the family room. Savannah gazed at her. "I heard you and Tony got along fine on your auction date. And you've been out with him since."

"I suppose it's impossible to keep our going out together private as long as we go out in Texas."

"I don't imagine you can. Both of you know many

people," Savannah said. She sipped her water. "Are you okay, Lindsay?" she asked finally.

"I don't know. That's why I think you're the one to talk to. I do need to keep this secret awhile and I thought about you being from Little Rock. I need to see an obstetrician without my family or anyone else around here knowing except you and Mike. Savannah, I think I'm pregnant with Tony's baby."

"Oh, my word," Savannah said, her blue eyes growing wide. "I know that's a shock."

"It is a shock that I haven't adjusted to, but I want it officially confirmed."

"Maybe you're worrying needlessly."

"I don't think so. I feel it to my bones."

"Oh, my. It'll be better than what I went through, although it led me to Mike. With Tony, it'll be good. He'll marry you, Lindsay. It's obvious you have made peace with each other. And the whole Calhoun family loves Tony. And he's so good to Scotty. Scotty is crazy about Tony even though they don't see each other often."

"I can't imagine Tony wanting to marry me and I don't want to marry Tony. I don't want to marry any rancher. Until Tony, I've never even dated one. Marriage to one would be a perpetual clash because I want to run my ranch my own way and I don't want some other rancher telling me to change the way I do things. And Tony is a take-charge person."

"Oh, dear." Savannah frowned. "You might have a problem."

"I have a big problem."

"Are you sure you're pregnant?"

"About ninety-nine percent, but that's why I want your doctor's name. I should see a doctor before I get Tony all stirred up. Other than you and Mike, I don't want anyone else to know I even suspect I'm pregnant until I verify it. Then I can tell Tony. I haven't even tried a home pregnancy test yet because I'll have to drive so far to get away from everyone I know, but I'm going today." She shook her head. "Even though I know what the outcome will be."

"Let me call my doctor's office and introduce you, then you can get on and make an appointment. Until you have a home test and the lab tests and have a doctor confirm your condition, you don't know for sure. You may not even be pregnant and may be worrying for nothing."

"Hopefully not, but if I had to bet, I'd bet the ranch that I am."

Savannah's eyes widened. "You mean that?"

Lindsay shrugged. "You get a feeling for things, you know?"

"Mike says you have a knack for knowing things and a touch that's just right. He's impressed by your abilities."

"That's nice. He hasn't mentioned that to me."

Savannah laughed. "You're his little sister. He probably doesn't realize he hasn't told you." She stood up. "Let me make that call before Scotty is up or Mike comes home. This doctor is so good about working people into his schedule."

Within the next thirty minutes Lindsay had an appointment in Little Rock on Thursday.

She sat again to face Savannah. "I really thank you for this. That was very nice."

"I'm glad to help. I only hope Mike doesn't suspect anything."

"Savannah, I don't want you to have to keep secrets from Mike. Just make it clear that you two are the only ones I'm telling at this point."

"I can wait a bit to tell Mike. He'll understand."

"You really don't need to, but thanks. I better go."

They walked to the door. "Take care of yourself," Savannah said. "Call me after you see the doctor. I'm your sister-in-law, and I'm also your friend. I can give you my doctor's name in Dallas, too." They gazed at each other and Savannah reached out to hug Lindsay.

"Thanks, Savannah. You're really good for Mike and good for our family."

"He and Scotty and the Calhouns are wonderful for me, too. Take care of yourself."

"I will," Lindsay said, and hurried to her pickup to drive home.

Thursday she drove to Dallas and flew to Little Rock to go to the doctor's office. She was thankful no one would know or question what she was doing or where she was going. The only person who came close was Abe, who had worked for her family since he was seventeen. She saw the questions in his eyes, but he didn't voice them.

The only thing that indicated his feelings was when she told him goodbye.

"Lindsay, if you want me to do anything, let me know," he said, looking intently at her, and she was certain he knew she had something she was hiding.

"Thanks. I will. I'm all right," she answered, looking into his light brown eyes. "I have my phone and if I need anything, I'll call. I'll be back tomorrow about noon."

"Sure," he said. He settled his brown hat on his head, nodded and headed back to the barn as she climbed into her pickup to drive to Dallas.

Now as she got out of the cab in front of the obstetrician's office, she felt her heart start to pound and her palms sweat.

But that anxiety was nothing to what she felt when she came out.

She felt so stressed she had to stop on the sidewalk. She stood staring and not seeing anything in front of her. Hot September sunshine blazed overhead, but chills skidded up her spine. She had known for the past two weeks that she was pregnant, but to have it confirmed by a home pregnancy test and now, to hear it officially announced by a physician after a lab test made it real.

How was she ever going to tell Tony?

Seven

Tony threw himself into work, coming home nights to an empty house that he had never felt alone in before. Constantly, he remembered Lindsay in his arms, and he wanted to talk to her or see her again. Every time he reached for the phone, he stopped, reminding himself she wanted them to break off seeing each other and he should, too, because it was inevitable.

In spite of logic, he missed seeing her. He knew from one of the men who worked for him that she had gone to Dallas and he wondered why and what she was doing there. He would get over her soon because he knew as well as she did, in spite of their truce, they were still the same people and she remained stubborn as ever. It was just a matter of time before there was another conflict between them, something she seemed to thrive on. Though common sense told him that he was better off without her, he missed her in a way he wouldn't have thought possible.

He woke up on Friday morning and she was still on his mind. He knew time would take care of this longing for her, but right now memories of her wouldn't stop coming.

He rose and got ready for a first-thing-in-the-morning meeting with Keane, who had problems with one of their trucks.

Tony stood on his porch with his foreman, who had his hat pushed far enough back on his head to reveal a pale strip on his forehead where his hat always shaded him. His tangled, curly brown hair framed his face. He was shorter than Tony, slightly stocky and the most capable ranch hand Tony had ever had.

"Keane, I heard an animal howling last night. I've seen it before on Lindsay's ranch," he said, remembering the eerie howls that had been so forlorn and sounded like an injured animal. As he had listened, he understood why the howls had unnerved Lindsay and caused her to call. They'd been jarring in the night, even to him. He'd finally got up and retrieved a rifle, switching off yard lights and stepping out on his dark porch. He'd seen it plainly in the moonlight, but he'd paused as he lifted his rifle, remembering Lindsay's request that the animal not be put down. He'd lowered his rifle and walked back inside to lock up, put away his rifle and go back to bed.

"It might be a dog," he told Keane now. "Might be a coyote. Lindsay thinks it's a wolf and she doesn't want it put down unless it starts killing livestock. Pass the word to leave it alone unless it kills something and until we know it isn't a big dog."

"Sure. Have you seen it?"

"Yes. It's big, has black and gray shaggy fur and, frankly, it does resemble a wolf, but I can't imagine it is."

Keane had a faint smile. "You know that old legend."

"If I thought that were possible, which I don't, I'd try to catch and tame the critter and I'd wish for rain."

"Amen to that one," Keane said, glancing at the sky. "Still none in the forecast. No break in the heat, either—over a hundred today. When it does rain, the ground will soak up water like a sponge. It'll just disappear. We need a month of rains."

"Right. Well, I'll see about replacing that truck," Tony said, and turned to go.

While Tony worked all day alongside the men, keeping his hands busy, he couldn't keep his mind from returning to Lindsay.

On second thought, he told himself, maybe he should tame that wolf and wish for amnesia. That might be the only way he'd forget her.

Feeling torn, miserable and caught in an uncustomary inability to make a decision, Lindsay stared at her dinner. She didn't want to eat but knew she should. Her thoughts were constantly on Tony. It seemed with each day she dreaded telling him about the baby more and more. She had to before she began to show and word got back to him. But when?

First she needed to go see Scotty, to hold him and think about having her own little baby, and then she needed to talk to Mike who would probably be a bulwark in the storm that would eventually rage around her. She didn't want to hide behind her brother from Tony, but Mike would take a levelheaded view of the situation and he and Savannah would support her in what she wanted to do.

Maybe she just needed to take Tony's call, go out with him and tell him the news. Get it over with and move on with her life and planning for her baby. Maybe Tony would back off and leave her alone.

She knew better than to expect that to happen. Mr. Take-Charge would dominate her life when she told him. Each time she thought of that happening, she was filled with dread.

She played with different scenarios in her mind: telling him soon, waiting four or five months to tell him or not saying a word until she had to. Like maybe when the baby was born.

As she headed to her house Friday afternoon, she was wrapped in worries and indecision and through it all, though she hated to admit it to herself, she missed Tony. She was so tired she paid little attention to her familiar surroundings until she steered her pickup toward the back of her house and saw a truck near the back gate. Frowning, she glanced at the house and saw Mike seated on the porch with his feet propped on the rail while he whittled.

She didn't know whether to be happy or annoyed with him and wondered whether Savannah had made him come.

As Lindsay parked behind his pickup and stepped out, Mike rose to his feet and put his knife away, along with whatever he had been whittling while he waited at the top of the steps. "What are you doing here?" she asked as she walked up the steps.

"Waiting to see if you need a big brother's hug," he said.

His kindness shook her and she walked into his arms. "I do," she whispered.

He hugged her, then stepped away to smile. "Let's go inside where we can talk and it's not a hundred degrees in the shade."

She tried to smile. "You mean where I can cry without

someone seeing me," she said, unlocking the door and leading the way. "Want a beer?"

"I'd like one, but not if it's going to make you want one."

"No. No problem there. I'll drink ice water." When they had drinks and were seated in the cool family room that overlooked the porch, patio and swimming pool, she sat facing him.

He had hung his hat on a hook in the entry hall and he raked his fingers through his hair. "Savannah said that you gave her permission to tell me." Mike leaned forward to place his elbows on his knees. "Here comes some brotherly advice and words of infinite wisdom."

She smiled. "There are moments I'm truly glad you're my big brother."

"I'm happy to hear that," he said. "There are moments I'm truly glad you're my little sis," he said, smiling at her. "Lindsay, don't forget for one minute that you have three brothers and three sisters-in-law who will support you in every way we can."

Tears threatened and she wiped her eyes. "Look at me, Mike. Do you know how few times in my life I've cried?"

"Chalk it up to hormone changes," he said. "I just want you to always remember you have our support and you can call me or Savannah anytime you want."

"Thanks. That means a lot," she said, meaning it with all her heart.

"Next thing—if being pregnant gets you down, just think of Scotty. You shower him with love and he seems to be a huge joy to you. He loves you and I know you love him. A baby in your life will be great."

"I know that and I do love Scotty beyond measure. He's adorable and I feel so close to him."

"He's a good kid. And he's going to love your baby. I

can promise you that. I'll let you tell Scotty when you're ready because he is very excited over Savannah's baby. He'll go into orbit over yours."

She smiled. "Maybe not so much if I have a girl."

"Oh, yes, he will. You wait and see. So now the next thing I want to mention, even if you don't want to hear it, is Tony. He's a good guy. I like Tony, and all the guys who work for him like him. All your brothers and sisters-in-law like him."

"I know that."

"Obviously, the two of you can get along. You were seeing each other after the auction."

"Does everyone in the state know we were going out together?"

"C'mon, Lindsay. All the Calhoun ranches and Milan ranches and the people that work on them—cleaning staff, cooks, cowboys—you think they don't get around and see who is leaving a ranch and who is entering one? Or talk about who they saw when they're out? The grapevine is alive and well in these parts. You and Tony were discreet about it, but your whole family probably knows you dated. Anyway, cut him some slack. He'll be shocked, but he's going to welcome this baby like I would, and you know it."

"Maybe that's what worries me. Tony is a take-charge guy."

Mike grinned. "I'm considering the source of that statement. Now, one last thing—would you like me to tell Mom and Dad before you talk to them?"

She thought about her parents and closed her eyes. She rubbed her hands together and looked at Mike. "Will Dad threaten Tony if he doesn't marry me? I haven't even wanted to think about dealing with our parents and, thank heavens, they're in California and have their own lives."

"Get some plans made before you tackle telling them. Tony's the one who has the difficult parents. Listen, all the rest of us will stand by you and between you and our folks. Mom will just have hysterics and faint."

Lindsay smiled and relaxed slightly. "Sounds ridiculous, but I think that might be exactly what she'll do. I've resisted her tears and hysterics plenty of times."

"The rest of us just hide from her. You're the brave one," he said, grinning. "Frankly, I don't think you'll have any pressure from our parents. They have their own lives, and I think when we grew up they let us go."

"I'm grateful for that. Tony is the person who worries me."

"You two will work it out." Mike squeezed her shoulder gently. He finished his beer and stood. "I've said what I wanted to say. I'll go home now. We're there for you—call in the middle of the night if you need us. You and Tony will work this out because you both love your families and you each will love this baby with all your hearts. You'll see."

"So when did you get to be such a counselor?" she said. Mike hadn't mentioned it, but she wondered if he or her other brothers would pressure her to marry Tony. "You know, even if we can be civil, Tony may not propose."

"There will probably be more than one pot for bets on that one," Mike remarked drily as they walked to the back door. Before they stepped outside, she closed her hand around his wrist.

"Thanks. Your advice might be a bit misguided, but your intentions are wonderful. You have cheered me up and I don't feel quite so alone."

"Lindsay, you should know your family well enough to know how very un-alone you are. Jake would be right here if you need him, or Josh. Tony's family will be the same." He stepped out on the porch, then resumed his talk. "There'll be plenty of kids on both sides of the family for your little one to bond with and to grow up with. Tony's sister, Madison, is pregnant. His brother Nick has a son, Cody, who is Scotty's age. I'll have another baby before yours is born. It'll be great." He reached out and gave her another hug.

"If only the father wasn't so take-charge and so stubborn."

"Said the kettle about the pot. You two are exactly alike in some ways and you're a strong enough woman to deal with most any man." He put his hat back on and made for the steps, then turned to her again. "Jake and Josh and I can go beat him up for you if you want."

"Mike, don't you dare!" He grinned and she saw he was teasing her. "Mike, shame on you, and I fell for it when I should know better."

"I made you smile," he said, sounding satisfied. "I gotta run, sis."

Lindsay followed him to his pickup. "Thanks for coming. I'll call Savannah and thank her. I liked her doctor—he was very nice, cheerful and kind. Now that I know for certain I'm pregnant, I'll have to find one around here. Savannah has one in Dallas she likes, so I'll probably get that name from her."

"When the time comes, you can stay at my house in Dallas if you want. If you stay on the ranch, you'll be a long way from your doctor and hospital."

"Thanks. We'll see."

"If you stay here, I guess it's a consolation that everyone on the place can probably deliver a baby."

"That's definitely not what I have in mind," she said

while she stood in the hot sun with her hands on her hips and stared at him.

"Call me and I'll do it." Grinning, he jumped into the truck and revved the engine.

"You're a wonderful brother, but you're not delivering my baby."

"For that matter, Tony can. He's good at delivering calves."

"Enough of you planning my life. How did I get tangled up with so many bossy men?"

"I think we're called alpha males," Mike corrected.

"Not in my view. I'll see you soon. Thanks for coming over."

"Sure." He smiled at her. "See you soon," he said, pulling along the driveway to head back to his ranch.

Smiling, she waved, but as the pickup drove out of sight leaving a plume of dust behind, her smile faded. None of Mike's cheerful advice or reminders of what a good guy Tony was changed the fact that Tony ran everything he could in his daily life. He was commanding, decisive, a Mr. Do-It-My-Way. Even as she enumerated those attributes, she felt a pain in her chest because she missed him. She ignored the feeling, certain it soon would stop haunting her and disappear forever.

She could tell him now, or she could tell him later. She was in for a fight and she felt it coming any which way she looked at her future.

Eight

Lost in thought, she walked into the house, mulling over how and when she would tell Tony.

By midnight she wasn't any closer to a solution. She sat in her darkened bedroom, looking out over her ranch and wondering what course of action she should follow. When the baby came, she would face more decisions. Stay home and take care of her baby all day or hire a nanny and go back to ranch work?

Eventually, she figured, that's probably what she would do, but she wanted to be home with her baby those first few months no matter what she decided to do later. Would she have to buy a house in Verity to secure a nanny or would she be able to find someone to live on the ranch? But maybe she was jumping the gun. First, she needed to find a doctor and have the baby.

She rubbed her forehead and thought about Mike's offer of his Dallas house in her ninth month. Tony might have some issue with that, being that he had a place in Dallas, too.

Tony. Mentioning his name made her remember he hadn't called her the past few days. Did he know she had been away from the ranch? She guessed he probably did, but he also knew she always had her phone. Had she heard the last from him until she contacted him?

On top of her worries and her woes, she missed Tony. He was too many wonderful things to suddenly have him disappear from her life and not feel his absence. She missed his energy, his optimism, his charm, his sexy ways. She didn't want to admit it, but a considerable amount of joy and excitement had gone out of her life. She dreamed about him at night, thought about him constantly during the day. Did Tony miss her at all?

The following Friday Tony climbed from his pickup after a long day. He'd helped some of his men clear a field. He was hot and dirty. He wanted a shower and a steak and he wanted to spend the evening with Lindsay. Since she hadn't taken his calls or answered his texts, he'd interpreted that as a sign she wanted to be left alone and he'd stopped calling. But that didn't stop him from wanting her.

He changed and went to his gym to work off the pent-up anxiety he felt from thinking about her. Exercising helped, as did swimming laps in his pool. But when he lay back in the pool, Lindsay invaded his thoughts once again. It was ridiculous, he told himself. If he didn't hear from her by next week, he promised himself he'd go out and forget all about her.

He swam laps until he couldn't stand to swim one more. Climbing out, he went in to shower and change, then work on taxes and his records. Later, he lay in the darkness, wanting sleep to come, hoping it was not another night of dreams filled with Lindsay.

During the night, he woke to hear a long, piercing howl. Stepping out of bed, he walked onto his balcony and gazed into the night. After a few minutes, another howl cut through the night. This one seemed to come from somewhere close to the barn nearest to his house.

Returning to his room, he pulled on his clothes and got a rifle. He went outside again to sit and wait, but the howls had stopped. He sat thinking about Lindsay, remembering times together, until he noticed the sky was getting lighter. It was dawn, so he went inside to shower and dress for the day.

After he had breakfast, he headed to the barn. Curious to see if he could find any signs of an animal, he knelt down and searched. But it was unlikely he'd find tracks in the hard, baked earth, so he rose and walked along slowly, studying the ground and turning a corner where thick bushes grew. He heard the faintest whine and froze for a minute. Then he moved slowly and cautiously toward the bushes, stopping instantly when he looked into a pair of brown eyes.

For a startled moment he thought it was a wolf, but then his gaze ran over the animal and he realized it was a big, furry gray-and-black male dog and it was hurt.

As the dog whimpered, Tony moved slowly, holding out his hand, wishing he had brought a piece of meat or something to offer. He spoke softly to the animal and knelt beside him. The dog tried to raise its head but lay back, watching him and giving one thump of its tail.

"Hey, boy," Tony said, speaking softly. "You're hurt." He saw the coat, tangled and matted with blood. One front leg and one hind leg each had bloody gashes. Tony pulled out his phone to call Keane.

* * *

Two hours later the dog was awake again, sedatives wearing off. Cleaned and bandaged, he lay in a stall in the barn on a blanket that had been tossed over hay spread on the floor. The barn was air-conditioned and comfortable.

Keane had helped Tony with the dog and, later, Doc Williams had stopped by. Now Tony was alone, sitting on the blanket by the dog and scratching its ears. He pulled out his phone and called Lindsay.

Warmth heated him at the sound of her voice. "I'm glad you answered."

"I've been in Dallas," she said, a cautious note in her voice that he'd never heard before.

He let her answer go without comment even though her phone had also been in Dallas. "Remember the howls and the coyote/wolf/dog?"

"Yes," she said, curiosity filling her voice so she sounded more like herself.

"He's in my barn. He was hurt, with lots of cuts. He may resemble a wolf, but he's actually just a big, furry gray dog that has been hurt. I thought you'd want to know."

"Oh, Tony, will he be all right?"

"Yes. Doc Williams has taken care of him. When the sedative completely wears off, he'll get a little steak. He's had some water. I held his head and sort of spoon-fed it to him. Want to come visit my patient?"

There was a pause. "Yes, I'll be there soon. Thanks for calling me. I'm headed to my pickup. By the way, how did you catch him?"

"I didn't catch him. He woke me in the night and when dawn came, I found him by the barn lying in the bushes where it was shady."

"I never thought about going to look for him. His

howling just gave me the creeps. But I'm so glad you rescued him. And it's a dog, huh?"

"Definitely. Mixed breed and looks like a wolf, but it's domesticated."

"It's wonderful that you saved him." He picked up the emotion in her voice.

"Well, well, Miss Tough Rancher is a real softie for dogs? How about men? Men named Tony?"

She laughed. "Maybe dogs."

He didn't press the point. He needed to slow down and just be happy that she'd taken his call. He brought the conversation back to the dog at his side. "Well, our patient already looks much better. Keane has a nice touch, and Doc said we did a good job. He said the dog has wounds from a fight. He's not sick, but Doc said he would stop by again and check on him."

"You're a good guy, Tony."

"I'm glad I can impress you," he said, brushing the dog's head as he talked. Despite his resolve, his eagerness to see Lindsay grew by the second. "We'll let you name him, Lindsay. Doc said no one had inquired about a lost dog that fit this one's description, and I've checked some ads and I don't see anything. I think he's homeless."

"I hope not any longer," she said breathlessly. "I hope you give him a home."

"We'll see how he fits in with the other dogs the guys keep on the ranch. I don't know what he's been fighting, but if he fights my dogs, I can't keep him."

"If you don't keep him, let me know." He heard her fumbling on the other end of the line, then she said, "I gotta go so I can drive."

"I'm in the first barn. Come on in."

"See you soon," she said and ended the call.

Putting away his phone, Tony smiled at the dog. He

was happy because Lindsay would soon be at his ranch. "Lindsay is coming to see you," he told the animal. "I hope she loves you and keeps coming to see you. Don't look too well too soon, okay, boy?"

The dog thumped its tail a few times. "I'll feed you in a while. Doc said to wait. Lindsay's going to love you and you're going to love her. Maybe you'll end up at her house and then I can come see you. Just be nice to all the ranch dogs. That's all that's required."

Big brown eyes looked up at him as the dog thumped his tail. Tony petted the dog's head gently, talking to it softly until he heard a motor. "Here she comes. Be a very nice dog now."

A pickup door slammed and Lindsay rushed in to stop in front of the stall. She had her hair in her usual braid and was in jeans and a blue T-shirt. She looked wonderful, and he fought the urge to get up, put his arms around her and kiss her.

"Hi, Tony. Oh, my, look at this beautiful dog," she said, coming into the stall to sit on the floor by Tony and reach out slowly to hold her hand in front of the dog, a treat in her palm.

He thumped his tail and raised his head slightly. His tongue licked out to take the treat.

"Oh, Tony, I'm so glad you didn't put him down. But he's all bandaged. Is he hurt badly?"

"Doc said he may limp. Other than that, he should heal just fine," Tony said, watching Lindsay instead of the dog. She smelled wonderful and she looked great. He still wanted to pull her into his arms and kiss her, but he knew that wasn't what she would want.

She placed her hand on the dog's head to pet him and he slowly thumped his tail.

"He has to get well. Thank you for calling me and

thanks for taking care of him. I think he's wonderful. Look at him. He's so sweet."

"You don't know if he's sweet yet. Remember, he still has the lingering effects of sedatives."

"He's sweet. You'll see. Look at those beautiful eyes."

"I am," Tony said, and she turned to look at him as he met her gaze.

She shook her head. "That's what I thought. You're not thinking about the dog."

"No, I'm not. It's good to see you."

She didn't respond to his statement. Instead, she teased him. "You know, if he had been a gray wolf, you could have had a wish granted, according to legend. As it is, you just became the owner of a stray dog."

"If I could have a wish, I'd wish that you'd go out with me tonight. But I guess, for the good of all, I would wish for rain this week."

"Doesn't matter. That was just a legend and he is just a dog." She petted him and Tony watched her. He couldn't help wishing those gentle hands were on his body, caressing him. But while her touch stilled the dog, it had aroused him.

"So," he prodded, "will you go out with me tonight?"

She turned to look at him solemnly, a slight frown on her brow, and he feared her answer. Then the frown disappeared and she nodded. "Tony, we need to talk," she said, suddenly sounding serious, as if she had something difficult to discuss. After her hesitation, she nodded again. "Yes. Tonight will be a big thank-you for rescuing this dog and giving him a home."

"Great. Let's go someplace fancy in Fort Worth. Someplace to dance, to talk and have a good time and super food, and then you can come back here and we'll see how our patient is doing."

Again he received a solemn look that puzzled him. "I don't know about coming back here, but we'll go out." Then, as if a thought just struck her, she asked, "But what about the dog? When you leave, he won't leave, will he?"

"I'll shut him in here where it's air-conditioned and he can be comfortable. In his condition, he can't get out. He'll have water and by that time I will have fed him something, so he should be all right."

"Do you want me to stay with him today?"

"Lindsay, I'm guessing you have a lot of things to do today."

She shrugged. "I suppose so, but I just don't want him to get up and go."

"He won't. I promise you."

She leaned down to croon to the dog and scratch behind his ears, and Tony took the opportunity to run his gaze over her. He didn't know if it was his imagination or just knowing what was beneath the clothes she wore, but she looked better than she used to with her braid, her old hat and jeans. Or was it because he hadn't seen her for a while and it was good to be with her again?

After a short time, she leaned back. "I need to get home, but I had to come see him."

They both stood and left the stall. While the dog raised its head, Tony closed the stall door and walked with Lindsay outside. "I'm glad you're going with me tonight. How about six so we have time to get to Fort Worth? I'll be glad to see you."

She smiled, but despite her acceptance of his dinner date, he sensed something off about her. Something had changed. There was a reluctance about her.

He tried to tease her out of her funk. "Still no fights between us, darlin'," he said quietly. "I'd say we've done well."

"Yes, we have, Tony. I hope it lasts," she said, and he had an even stronger feeling that something bothered her.

"Lindsay, come back into the barn for a minute."

She walked with him into the cool barn and turned to look at him with curiosity in her expression. "What's on your mind?"

"I wanted some privacy for us. Is anything wrong?"

Something flickered in her eyes and her cheeks became pink. "Not really. I just want to talk tonight."

He gazed into her eyes and wondered if he should probe more deeply. Then he figured they could talk tonight. But he couldn't let her go without doing one thing. When he stepped closer to place his hands on her shoulders, he felt her stiffen slightly. He studied her and then slipped his arm around her waist to kiss her.

"Tony, I should—" His lips on hers ended her talk.

For a moment she was resistant. Then all her stiffness vanished as she put her arms around his neck and returned his kiss passionately, a blazing kiss that meant whatever her problem was, she still couldn't cool the blazing sexual attraction between them.

When she stepped away, he let her go. She was breathing as hard as he was and they looked at each other a moment. Her blue eyes seemed clouded with worry. Turning away, she rushed out to her pickup.

"I need to get home, Tony. See you tonight," she called over her shoulder.

He hurried to watch her while she started the pickup. Gravely, she glanced at him and then drove away.

He stared after her. Something had definitely changed since the last time they were together. He didn't know what it was, unless she was trying not to tell him that she didn't care to go out with him again or receive phone calls from him. But knowing her as he did, he was certain she would have just said it.

That day was inevitable and he probably shouldn't have called her, but he knew she would want to see the dog. Oh, who was he kidding? He'd called because he wanted to see her. The dog was just an excuse. As much as he told himself to leave her alone and forget her, he couldn't stay away. His body seemed to crave her, the way a starving man craves food. Maybe tonight would be different, he told himself. Maybe tonight the reluctance and resistance he'd sensed in her would disappear. He could only hope.

He retrieved his hat and headed to his pickup to catch up with Keane and see how they were coming on clearing the land for the new pond.

But as he drove, he couldn't stop the niggling feeling that something big was going to happen tonight. Something sure as hell was wrong with Lindsay and he could only wonder what.

Lindsay spent the rest of the day at her house. Part of the time she helped her cook, Rosalee. Part of the time she was shut in her room deciding what to wear and how to tell Tony about her pregnancy.

She had wanted to wait, make her own decisions, but she couldn't go back to the carefree, happy times when she was with him after the auction. She had decided to tell him immediately and face dealing with him. It would come sooner or later and she wanted the battle over and done.

She wanted to look her best when she told him. When he was dazzled by her, Tony was much more cooperative. Take the night of the auction, for example. But then, that night she'd had surprise on her side. Oh, she had a surprise this time, all right. One that might make him faint.

Rummaging in her closet, she selected a black dress she had bought on impulse when she had been shopping in Dallas. She had never worn it, just because no occasion had arisen, but tonight should be one.

She yanked off her jeans to try on the dress. Before she pulled it on, she stopped to look at herself in the mirror. Even though it was too soon for physical changes, she couldn't keep from looking for them. It was satisfying to see she looked as slim as ever. Change was inevitable, but she hoped it didn't show really early. She wanted to keep working on the ranch, and if any of the guys noticed and realized, word would get to Abe. He would insist she stop and if she didn't, he'd probably talk to her brothers about it.

By five in the afternoon Rosalee had finished and left for the weekend. Lindsay had bathed and still worked to fix her hair, planning to leave it down in long spiral curls around her face.

As the time drew closer for Tony to arrive, her nerves became more raw. She dreaded talking to him, knowing all the peace between them would go up in flames tonight and they would each have to make a big effort to be civil and work out how they would deal with their new situation. Most of the changes would be in her life, but Tony would have adjustments and decisions, too. And their dates, their lovemaking, the fun they'd had—all that was over. It wasn't something she expected to get back in her life.

Feeling she had reached a point where her appearance was the best she could do, she went to the front window to watch for him coming up the drive. After a moment she stepped out on her porch to sit in a wooden rocker. In spite of the hot weather, she was chilled. Mounting dread about revealing her pregnancy to Tony enveloped her. She could anticipate his reactions and she suspected battles with him would fill the coming weeks. Underneath that dread was an undercurrent of anticipation, because she would finally be with him again.

When his sports car came into view, her pulse jumped. He might be bossy, but he still was the most charming, exciting, sexy man she had ever known. She went inside to take one more look at herself in the mirror, then stood waiting for the doorbell. Was she about to face her biggest struggle ever with Tony?

As Tony drove up the driveway to Lindsay's ranch house, his eagerness to see her grew. He'd been nervous all day to find out what disturbed her but, right now, knowing he'd see her in minutes, he couldn't help hoping for another hot, sexy night of lovemaking.

Never in his life had he been deeply involved in a serious relationship and he knew he wouldn't start now with Lindsay. They were just too different. Even so, at the moment he wanted to be with her; he missed talking to her and seeing her. He feared their tenuous relationship might be close to termination right now, but he intended to enjoy tonight to the fullest.

When the door swung open, his heart thudded and for seconds all he did was stare.

Lindsay wore another pair of stiletto heels with thin sexy straps crossing her slender feet, which matched her black sleeveless dress. Her plunging vee neckline revved his pulse another notch. Her straight, short skirt revealed her legs for him to view. Had she left her hair falling freely around her face to please him? Probably not, but he'd enjoy it anyway.

"You look gorgeous, Lindsay," he said. He was breathless, his voice deeper. "That black dress is killer on you."

She smiled at him, but it wasn't the wholehearted smile he had received before. "You've never been in my house. Come on in and look around."

He stepped in and the second he inhaled her perfume, he wanted to hold her and kiss her and forget about going out to dinner or eating anything for hours. He could cancel the reservations in Fort Worth and stay right here beside her.

He walked alongside her through a short hallway that opened out into a wide hall with a spiral staircase to the next floor. Above, a beamed ceiling was three stories high with skylights that let light pour into the house.

On either side of the stairs, the house opened up into spacious areas defined only by columns, furniture groupings and area rugs. The open rooms, high ceilings and lots of glass made the already large house seem twice as big.

"Like many other things about you, your house surprises me," he said. "It's beautiful, but not what I ever expected. I pictured you in a house more Western, but not the way you pictured mine would be. Just leather furniture and Western scenes in the paintings and traditional Western decor." He strolled into a living area he'd glimpsed from the hall and noticed a second-floor balcony extending over the length of one side of the room and the French period pieces upholstered in elegant silks and antique satins.

"Now I can picture you in your house," he said. "At least in part of it."

He turned to find her staring at him intently with a slight frown. Her expression jolted him. Just as he'd feared, something was very wrong and he didn't have a clue what it was.

"Lindsay, what's the problem?" he asked, unfastening the one button on his jacket and slipping out of it. He placed it on a chair. "Looks as if we need to talk."

As she wound her fingers together, her knuckles whitened. He took her hands in his.

"The weight of the world might as well be on your shoulders. Whatever is bothering you can't be that bad." He bent his knees so he could look directly into her eyes. Silently, he studied her.

"Before we talk, I think it would be wise to cancel our dinner reservation. I debated just telling you to come over for dinner, but I thought I might not have the courage to talk to you tonight—"

"Damn, Lindsay, what the hell? Is it—"

"Don't start guessing. Cancel the dinner reservation. My cook was here today and I had her leave us a casserole if either of us feels like eating later."

Watching her, he pulled out his phone, looked down and sent a short text. He put away his phone.

"I think you might like a drink. I'll get you a beer," she said.

Mystified, he stared after her. Whatever this was, the problem disturbed her a hell of a lot more than any other she'd encountered while he'd known her. From the way she was acting, it seemed even catastrophic.

Was it the ranch? Did she have to sell it? If she did, she wouldn't have any trouble telling him. Nor could it involve anyone in her family; he didn't think she would hesitate letting him know that.

He knew she had gone to Dallas recently. He also realized she had another life away from her ranch. Was it someone else? Did she have a lover in Dallas? No, she wouldn't have stayed with Tony if there'd been anyone else.

So why did she go to Dallas? Did she have some illness and need a big-city doctor?

She looked as healthy as anyone could hope to be, even though that was no indication of how she might feel or why she would have to see a doctor. The thought that Lindsay was sick was like a punch to his middle. What was wrong and how serious was it? Was it incurable? That question almost buckled his knees.

He watched her behind the bar fixing their drinks and went to join her. The more he thought about it, the more convinced he was that she had gone to Dallas because of a medical problem. She knew when she told him he'd need a drink.

What the hell could be so wrong that she knew ahead of time and it involved him enough for her to expect him to be upset?

His knees did almost cave on that one. He sat on the nearest bar stool while he stared without seeing anything and his head spun.

One possibility occurred to him and he knew in every inch of his being that he guessed correctly. Taking deep breaths, he looked up to see her coming around the bar with a glass of ice water for herself and a whiskey on the rocks for him.

"I thought you might prefer this," she said, handing him his drink. She frowned. "Tony, you look white as a sheet."

"You're pregnant, aren't you? You're carrying my baby."

Nine

"How did you find out?"

He closed his eyes. "Wow," he whispered. "I just figured it out. I tried to think of reasons for you to go to Dallas. And reasons for the big change in you since the way you were with me before you went to Dallas. And when you offered to get a drink for me, I realized it had to involve me, too. There was only one thing I could think of." He reached for the drink she held out. "I think I need that whiskey now."

He downed it in one swallow and set down an empty glass. "I'm in shock. You're going to have to give me a minute to digest this bit of news," he said. "You've had time to think about it a little."

He sat there staring at the floor but not seeing anything, just thinking about the changes coming in his life—changes that would be monumental.

He would be a father. Lindsay would have his child.

He was so dazed he knew he couldn't even fathom the changes that would downright transform his life. He couldn't even try.

There would be no financial worries for either one of them, so he could cross that concern off his list. But there was one giant problem—and only one solution.

He pulled himself together as best he could and stood up to take her hand.

"Lindsay, marry me."

His words didn't have the desired effect. Instead, he watched a transformation come over her and he had a sinking feeling a proposal wasn't what she wanted. Once again her stubbornness surfaced. He could see that in the set to her jaw and the fire in her eyes. Annoyance filled him as it always had. From the start he had known she always stirred up conflict, and this was no exception.

"Tony, that's a knee-jerk reaction. You take some time and think this through. I'm financially well-fixed, so that's not a consideration. I have a big, supportive family, so I'll have all the help I need. The biggest reason I can't marry you is that we are basically not compatible." Before he could make a point, she added, "You're bossy and arrogant and you want to take charge of every situation—which is exactly what you're doing right now. I don't want you telling me what to do."

Impatience stabbed him. Every issue was a conflict with her. Why did he think for one second this wouldn't be? She was, as always, her usual stubborn self. But then his gaze roamed over her and for an instant he forgot everything. She was stunning. Even steeped in worry, when he looked at her, she took his breath away.

"Lindsay, stop and think and consider my proposal. Don't answer now. It's the logical solution for a lot of reasons, plus we get along great in some ways."

With a slight frown, she started to answer, and he placed his finger on her soft lips. "Shh. Don't answer me now—give my proposal time and think of all the positive reasons to do this. We can be compatible, we have these big families that have drawn close and we'll be thrown together constantly. All you're thinking about right now is that I'm a rancher and how I run my ranch. Just think of all the things in our lives and give my offer consideration." He walked behind the bar to pour another drink. He stood there, not saying a word, sipping the whiskey while she was quiet. He suspected she was getting her argument lined up.

Shock still reverberated in him. Of all people—Lindsay would have his baby.

Everything fell into place—why she didn't want to see him, why she was so somber. He walked to the window with his back to Lindsay and the room and stared outside. His entire life was about to change drastically. After a few moments he turned around to find her still standing where he had left her. She looked at him but said nothing.

His mind reeled with questions. He gave one voice. "When did you find out?"

She told him. "As soon as I realized I was late, I had a feeling. I went to a doctor and had the lab work done. I wanted to confirm it before I told you."

He nodded. "This is something I thought would never happen—an unplanned pregnancy. I know you thought the same thing."

They lapsed into silence again as he contemplated the changes coming in his life. Fatherhood. Coming fast and unexpected.

"Did you get a doctor in Dallas? I assume that's why you went."

"No. I know too many people there. I called Savannah

and got an appointment with her doctor in Little Rock. I didn't want word to get back to you until I could tell you myself. I didn't think about you guessing correctly."

"Well, you'll have to find a doc closer than Little Rock," he remarked drily. "Damn."

"I will. I just couldn't take a chance going to any big Texas city where I could have run into someone I know."

Another silence fell and he was thankful again that she was giving him a chance to adjust to his new status before they talked very much.

"There are a few things I think we can decide tonight."

As he stared at her, he thought, *Here we go.* She sat at the edge of a pale antique satin sofa and crossed her legs. Long, beautiful legs—the best pair of legs he had ever seen. As he looked at her, he noted that her blond hair was like a halo around her head. In almost every respect, he knew this woman would be the best mother possible for his child. He just hadn't planned on fatherhood so soon. And he and Lindsay were not in love. She didn't like ranchers. He didn't like her stubborn streak, her knack for constantly living in conflict.

"We should keep this between us for a little longer, if possible," he said, "until we make some major decisions about the future."

She nodded. "When people hear I'm expecting a baby, I'm going to get questions."

"That's fine with me. Whatever you want. You said Savannah knows and, I'm assuming, Mike. Who else?"

"Besides you, no one else. Believe me, Mike and Savannah know how to keep quiet."

"Good. It's better for both of us to keep it quiet for now," he repeated. "You don't show at all and I doubt if you will for another month. That gives us time." He became silent, his thoughts swirling in his head. Like a mantra, one statement kept reverberating in his mind. Lindsay was pregnant with his baby.

His gaze swept over her again. She was the most beautiful woman he had ever known. And the sexiest. He remembered their lovemaking, which was never out of his thoughts long. Marriage to her would have big pluses, if her stubbornness didn't overshadow the rest.

She'd had a bit of time to think about this and adjust to the prospect of being pregnant, so she might have already made decisions about the future. He'd better come out of shock and plan what they should do.

Minutes ticked past while he tried to sort through the jumble of thoughts, possibilities and outcomes. Finally, her voice broke the silence.

"I never thought this would be a problem I'd have," she said, gazing up at him. Her blue eyes were wide and clear.

"There's a simple solution I've already given you." She directed a steady look at him and he could feel the battles looming between them. "Lindsay, we're going to have a baby," he said. "You know I'll love this baby with all my heart."

"I know you will," she replied.

"Did the doctor tell you an approximate due date?"

"Next May."

"Then we should have that wedding soon," he said, and her eyes flared.

"I'll do what I feel I have to do," she said, the old tension coming between them again. He could feel the first stir of his own anger over her answer. Trying to curb it, reminding himself of the huge upheaval this would cause in her life, he crossed the space between them to draw her to her feet and place his hands on her shoulders. She stiffened.

He could feel barriers coming up between them. Anger

plagued him over her stubborn refusal to cooperate, which showed in her body language as well as her facial expression.

But who was he kidding? In spite of the problems and differences between them, he still wanted her—in his arms, in his bed. The minute he touched her, that familiar desire flared up in every part of him, and if he wasn't mistaken, he caught the same response in her.

Unable to resist any longer, he pulled her into his arms to kiss her hard and passionately. For an instant she pushed against him, but he couldn't step away if he wanted to, and in seconds, her arm went around his neck and she surrendered to his kiss. It was all the invitation he needed.

In one motion he peeled away her black dress while he continued to kiss her. When her bra was gone, he caressed her breasts, kissing first one and then the other. Her moans and soft breaths encouraged him to take her. He paused only long enough to strip off his clothes. Then, naked and hard, he picked her up and lowered her onto the sofa. Without a second's hesitation he entered her in one smooth thrust. She was ready for him. Hard and fast, they moved together. Quickly, desperately, she clutched him to her as she climaxed with him, her cries muted by his frantic kisses. They both gasped for breath as wave after wave of ecstasy washed over them.

For Tony, though it was fast and furious, this was the best lovemaking he'd ever had. He leaned back to tell her as much till he saw the look in her eyes. He'd expected a contented haze; instead, he found a storm brewing in their blue depths.

She stared at him and he could feel her anger rising again.

Instead of lashing out, she simply pushed him off her.

"I'm going to shower, Tony. I'll be back shortly," she said, still breathless. She yanked up her clothes and left.

He watched her walk away and wondered if he could ever get her to listen and cooperate or if they were at an impasse. Gathering his clothes, he went to find a bathroom and dress. As he did, his thoughts were on Lindsay. Would she even talk to him when she came back?

He returned to wait and soon she entered the room. As always, she made his heart beat faster. "You look gorgeous."

She had changed from her dress and wore a white linen blouse and white slacks with white high-heeled sandals and she still looked good enough to model.

"Thank you," she said in a dismissive manner, as if she barely heard what he had said. "Tony, I think our evening is over. I don't feel like dinner together."

He tried to curb the flash of anger that returned. Stubborn, stubborn woman who wanted life her way and her way only.

He wouldn't leave, not without reiterating his proposal. "Lindsay, the logical thing is for us to get married. Think about it tonight."

"I will," she said, but from the way she replied, with anger in her voice, he suspected the next time he saw her, he would get only arguments about marrying.

She raised her chin. "Do you really think we can get along in day-to-day living?"

They stared at each other and he felt the palpable clash of wills.

"See. I proved my point," she said. "Frankly, Tony, I'm trying to hang on to my temper. I really would like to scream at you for getting me pregnant, except I know full well that I had as much part in that happening as you did."

"Thank you for that one." At least she was rational. "Lindsay, I just see one solution and I hope you'll come to the same conclusion."

"We irritate each other."

"Sometimes, but we can get past the problems. I know now that beneath the tough rancher is a stunning, sexy woman who can simply melt me."

"Tony," she said impatiently, "whatever we found compatible in the past few weeks since the night of the auction… it's gone. That's over."

"Not altogether," he remarked drily. "We found it again less than an hour ago."

Anger flashed in her expression. She closed her mouth tightly while she glared at him.

"I know we need to work this out," she said after a few minutes of silence. "I just can't be the same person with you that I was."

"Don't stop communicating. I won't be cut off from my child. I want this baby in my life and I feel strongly that, if possible, a baby needs both a mom and a dad. That isn't always feasible, but in this case, it damn sure is, Lindsay," he said, trying to keep his temper.

Again, he got a glacial stare. "I know it, Tony. We both caused this and I agree that we both need to be in our baby's life. But don't pressure me," she snapped.

"Dammit, Lindsay. Before you make any decisions, stop and think about our baby. I'll talk to you later." He walked out before he lost it with her.

He slammed the door and hurried to his car, then drove away. Had she already closed her mind to his proposal?

Lindsay felt as if all the frustration and anger building in her since realizing she was pregnant had finally burst and she couldn't act as if nothing had changed between them.

His controlling personality had surfaced in a big way tonight—a glimpse of what she would live with if she even considered his proposal. She couldn't imagine being married to him and taking orders from him every day.

She hadn't been able to resist his kisses, succumbing to sex, but afterward she regretted the intimacy. Sure, there was no doubt they were sexually compatible but, as she'd said many times, sex wasn't everything. Outside the bedroom, she couldn't live with him.

She had wanted him to leave. She wanted to tell him goodbye and not see him again until she worked things out for her future.

One thing her feelings were certain about was that she was not going to marry Tony. That would be disastrous for both of them.

Just as she'd expected, he had tried to take over her life tonight. In marriage he would take over her ranch, tell her what to do on a daily basis. Besides, they weren't in love.

She could imagine Tony wanting to put both ranches together with him running everything while she stayed home to raise their child. That wasn't going to happen.

In spite of her irritation with him, when she looked at the sofa, she saw Tony there, his marvelous, strong body, his vitality, his sexy lovemaking that still now made a tremor run through her. But it was over.

Though she was too upset to sleep, she got ready for bed and sat in a chair in the dark, her eyes adjusting to the moonlight that spilled into her bedroom.

Knowing she should go to bed but certain she would just stare into the darkness and sleep would still escape her, she sat where she was until she finally fell asleep in her chair.

When she crawled into bed, it was almost four in the morning. As soon as her head touched the pillow, memories of better moments with Tony bombarded her. Then she thought about tonight with him and felt her anger return.

The next day she sent a text to Abe that she couldn't work. She needed to tell him about her pregnancy, but she had to get a grip on her emotions. When she talked to Abe, she had to be able to tell him that she had decided to turn the daily running of the ranch over to him, and she had to be able to say it without tears. She loved her ranch, working on it, raising her horses, dealing with livestock and making decisions. Her land was beautiful to her, spreading endlessly to a blue horizon with gorgeous sunrises and sunsets. Tony wasn't going to marry and take that away from her.

She had been nauseated after breakfast this morning and she wondered if that was something she would have every morning. She needed to find a Dallas doctor, as well as decide where she would live in her ninth month.

Three days later she still hadn't told Abe anything except that she couldn't work. Soon he would come to see about her, but she dreaded telling him. He could keep it quiet, that she could count on. But him knowing just made it more real.

She tried to do some of her paperwork, but she couldn't keep her mind on it. There was no call from Tony, but that didn't surprise her. What did surprise her was how much she missed him.

She sat staring into space and thinking about Tony. If she wouldn't marry him, would it hurt when he married later? Would she be able to watch him go out of her life except when it was necessary to see him because of their child?

She hadn't considered that before and it hurt to think of Tony marrying someone else. If the thought of Tony marrying hurt, how much did she really care for him? Could she be in love with him?

No way she could be in love with him. He was too authoritative, too opinionated, so certain he was always right. There was a point where all her affection and his appeal came to a stop.

They would have their lives tied together for years to come, but going out with each other the way they had been had ended. She saw that clearly and felt it was for the best. Just as swiftly, she felt a pang at the thought of not going out with him, of not making love to him. Startled, she shook her head. Life with Tony was over and that was the way she wanted it. She would stop missing him soon.

And what about Tony? He might want out of seeing her just as much. He had been in shock last night. The proposal had been a knee-jerk reaction. Now that he was home to think things through alone, his conclusions about the future might have changed.

The idea made her feel even more forlorn, as if she were losing someone important. As the day passed, she tried unsuccessfully to shake the feeling of loss. How long would it be before she stopped missing him?

Ten

As each day passed, Tony tried to adjust to the situation. Without thinking, too often he reached for his phone to call Lindsay only to stop himself. He'd reminded himself how mulish she could be. But that didn't stop him from missing her.

Friday afternoon, the second of October, when he returned from work he saw Lindsay's pickup on his drive.

His heart jumped and he sped up his steps, all tiredness leaving him instantly. Lindsay stepped out of her pickup and his breath caught in his throat. She wore tight jeans, a clinging red T-shirt with a vee neckline. Her hair was in the usual braid and she had a wide-brimmed brown hat on her head. She looked great to him and his pulse raced as eagerness to talk to her made him walk even faster.

"Hi," he said as he approached, smiling.

She gave him a fleeting smile and he drew a deep

breath because she kept a wall between them. He could feel her coolness toward him and knew there was a specific reason for her visit.

"Come in, Lindsay."

"No, I just thought I'd stop in and talk in person instead of on the phone, but this won't take long. Now that my waist is getting a bit bigger—"

He looked down at her and wondered if she could even be one inch larger. "You don't look it."

"I feel it. Anyway, as I was saying, now that I'm getting bigger, I want to tell my family that I'm pregnant and I want to tell Abe and the guys."

"Lindsay, have you even thought about our baby?"

Her eyes narrowed and her cheeks flushed. He was certain she would start yelling at him any minute. He struggled to keep his temper.

"Yes, I have," she said. "I still don't want to marry you. You would want to take charge of every detail of my life and of our child's upbringing. Hell, no, I'm not marrying you."

"You're so damn stubborn, you'd mess up your own life."

"It still is my 'own life.' Are you okay with telling our families? I'll just tell them that we're working out our plans. They'll accept what I tell them."

"That's probably a good idea, because you need to get a doctor and word has a way of spreading, especially when it's about babies. I'll tell my family, too. And Keane and the guys. And I'll tell all of them I asked you to marry me and you said no—but that opens you up to some pressure."

"No more than I'll get anyway." She opened the door to her pickup. "Thanks, Tony. We got that settled."

He put his hand on her door and blocked her way from climbing in.

"It doesn't have to be this way."

"I don't see how things can be any other way," she said. He dropped his hand and held the door for her while she climbed in.

"Bye," he said as he closed the door, feeling as if this was a real and lasting farewell. That any intimacy or closeness they'd shared—the laughter and joy and steamy sex—all of it was over. Stepping away, he rested his hands on his hips as he watched her drive away, heading back to the county road to go home to her ranch. As her pickup widened the distance between them, he knew he would always remember the day she drove out of his life. He didn't think they would ever be close again. A cloud of gloom, along with his anger, settled on him as he entered the house.

The following week, Tony saw he had a text from his sister, Madison; she wanted to come see him. With a sigh he sent her a text in return.

Yes, you can come see me. Tonight's fine. Tomorrow morning is fine. Take your pick or suggest a time.

They had finally settled on early Saturday. He waited on the porch because it was a cool, sunny morning.

He watched Madison come up the walk. Her brown hair was in a ponytail. She wore jeans and a tan cotton shirt that was not tucked into her jeans. In spite of hiding her waist, it was obvious she was months along in her pregnancy. He placed his arm around her shoulders to give her a brief hug, then led her inside the house. "Haven't seen you in a while. I have breakfast ready. Or anything else you'd like."

"I've had breakfast. I'll just have a glass of ice water. It's a beautiful morning and what is even more wonderful is that rain is predicted next week—they give it a twenty-percent chance."

"If it actually happens, I'm going out to just stand in it. Might take a picture of it since it's been so long since I've seen any."

She smiled. "Is Gwynne here?"

"Not on Saturday. How are you feeling?"

"Fine. Just bigger by the day." She faced him, her green eyes sparkling. "Tony, congratulations. I've talked to you on the phone, but I wanted to tell you in person. I'm so happy for you and Lindsay. I know you have things to work out, but you will. A baby is so wonderful."

"Thanks, Madison. It's sort of a mixed blessing at this point in my life."

"It's an enormous blessing. And our babies will not be so far apart in age," she said, rubbing her stomach lightly.

"I can't think that far ahead," he remarked drily. "I'm just getting accustomed to this becoming-a-dad business."

She laughed and accepted the glass of water as he handed it to her. "I'll carry your coffee, Tony," she said as he helped himself to scrambled eggs from a pan on his stove. He added a piece of ham and picked up a slice of toast.

"I'm set. It's beautiful outside. Let's sit on the porch."

As soon as they were seated at a glass-topped iron table, he sipped his coffee and sat in silence, certain she had a mission.

"Tony, any chance you want some sisterly advice?"

"Actually, no," he said, smiling at her, "but since this drive to visit me was unprecedented and a little difficult for you under the circumstances, I'm sure I'm going to get some."

"I'm just concerned. And Jake is concerned about his sister. She's hurting, and I came to see for myself how you're faring."

"I'm faring fine," he said, startled to hear about Lindsay. He'd figured she had gotten on with her life and wasn't giving much thought to him. He knew she had stopped working with the men.

"Mike Calhoun's wife is expecting her baby this month, which is exciting. We'll have the three new babies, plus Cody and Scotty. Our families are growing and I think it's exciting and wonderful."

He smiled at her. "At the moment, you're in love with Jake, having his baby, and the whole world looks rosy to you," he said, studying her and realizing she looked happier and prettier than ever before.

"You're right," she agreed. "Are you okay?"

"I'm absolutely fine. And you're looking good yourself. I think marriage and motherhood really suit you."

"I'm happy, Tony. So happy with Jake," she said.

"Our dad should have stayed out of your lives and not deceived you about Jake, as well as driving him away," Tony said quietly. "I don't know how you can ever forgive him. Dad and I have butted heads since I was able to talk back to him. I paid for it, but I never got along with him the way Wyatt and Nick did."

"Wyatt is quiet and peaceful. Nick's the politician who's going to please the world and he started by pleasing Dad. And I always, well, until high school, did what he wanted. I never dreamed he would interfere in my life the way he did." Her frown disappeared and she smiled. "That's over. Jake and I are married, having a baby and I'm happier than I ever dreamed possible." Impulsively, she reached out to squeeze her brother's hand. "I hope you find that with Lindsay, Tony. You can't imagine how wonderful marriage can be."

He laughed. "I do believe you're in love, sis. That's good. You and Jake deserve all the happiness in the world. I'm amazed Jake hasn't punched Dad out."

"Jake isn't going to hit an elderly man, much less hit my father."

"He has a right to."

"Whatever," she said, flipping back her hair. "Anyway, I'm glad to hear you're okay. I just wanted to see for myself. I'm excited our babies will be fairly close in age. December and May aren't really far apart after the first year or two."

"Madison, you didn't drive out here to tell me how thrilled you are about our babies being close in age. You could have done that on the phone."

"Well, I more or less did. And to see if you're okay."

"I'm quite okay. But what's wrong with Lindsay?"

"I think she's just unhappy."

"Well, Jake should realize that being pregnant has put a big crimp in her lifestyle. For corn's sake, look how she's always lived—like one of the guys. Suddenly, she's a woman and her body has limitations because of her pregnancy. She's not accustomed to that, didn't expect it and evidently is having difficulty adjusting to it."

"Just be nice to her, Tony. It's a big change and for Lindsay, without a husband, without planning for a baby, changing her entire life and future is an enormous upheaval."

"She'll adjust. And she could have a husband if she wanted," he said, unable to keep the bitterness out of his voice. "She turned me down absolutely. Lindsay will handle this just like she handles everything else—in full control."

"You think a lot of her, don't you?" Madison asked.

"Sure, I do. Every rancher in the area does. She's capable and intelligent."

"You didn't take her out because she's capable and intelligent."

He laughed. "No, she can be fun and pretty."

"Lindsay has the looks of a model when she wants to. I saw her at the auction. Anyway, you be nice to her. She needs you now."

"I'll be nice to Lindsay," he said with amusement. "Though I don't think she needs me or wants to see me or talk to me."

Madison sat quietly so long that he turned to look at her. "What?" he asked.

She stood. "I've seen that you're doing fine. I don't want to pry into your life with Lindsay. I just want you to know that I'm excited about your baby. I should go home now."

"That was a short visit, but I'm glad you came. Madison, let me know when Mike's baby is born. I might not hear about it."

"Lindsay will tell you," she said.

"Lindsay isn't going to tell me one damn thing."

Madison looked startled and stared at him intently.

"We don't speak, we don't see each other. It'll have to change later, but that's the way she wants it now."

"Sorry to hear that. I'll tell you about Mike and Savannah." She gave him a hug, then leaned away to look intently at him again. "Be patient with Lindsay. This is a giant change for both of you."

"Sure," he answered, knowing his sister meant well. He stood on the porch and watched her drive away, his thoughts on Lindsay. Lindsay was unhappy? She did what she wanted to do.

And how unhappy was she? It had to be a lot to worry Jake enough to get Madison to drive out and talk to him. He wished Lindsay's unhappiness was because she missed him, but he knew better. She was probably unhappy with him and unhappy she had to change her lifestyle.

He carried his dishes into his empty house. As he passed his landline, he stared at the phone, tempted to pick it up and call Lindsay to just talk. He missed her and every time he realized that he missed her, it surprised him.

How important had she become to him?

He couldn't answer his own question.

The next week he threw himself into work, going to the corral to ride some of the unbroken horses at night with a few of the men who worked for him, just keeping busy. But none of it stopped the moments of longing for Lindsay.

Nights were long and unpleasant. He had always fallen into bed and been asleep instantly, sleeping soundly until early morning. Not anymore. His nights were filled with memories of Lindsay, dreams about her, moments of missing her.

The weekends were worse because he had no one he wanted to go out with. He missed her and the longing to see her intensified instead of diminished, until he finally sat up in bed one night, tossed back the covers and walked out on his porch.

The gray dog was still recovering, but better. The bandages were gone and his hair, where they'd had to shave it away to work on his cuts, was growing out again. He had gained weight and his coat was shiny now. Tony kept it brushed so it wasn't a tangle.

Tony let him stay at the house with him. The dog

seemed a faint tie to Lindsay, and Tony enjoyed having him around. When he went to the porch, the dog followed him, sitting with his head on Tony's knee while Tony scratched his ears. "Maybe I should invite her over to see you," he said to the dog, who wagged his bushy tail.

Tony sat quietly while he thought about Lindsay. He thought about her constantly each day. Was he in love with her and hadn't realized it when it happened?

If he was, he didn't know where it could lead. She was as stubborn as ever, refusing to give an inch, while she had accused him of being too take-charge and bossy. Plus, he was a rancher—the kind of man she said she would never marry.

He sat in the dark and mulled over his feelings for Lindsay and the problems between them.

Madison had said Lindsay was unhappy. Was their parting a cause of her unhappiness? Could he ever get past her stubborn nature? He had some of the time. His heartbeat quickened at the thought of getting past their problems. Could he think before he told her what she should do?

Could he live without her?

Was he in love with her?

Staring into the dark, he realized he was. He wanted her in his life. Lindsay would be a challenge, but if he loved her, he would cope with her. But could he get her to consider working with another rancher? That wasn't impossible. He worked with them all the time and for that matter, she did, too.

Suddenly feeling better, he wanted to call her and he wanted to be with her. One thing he knew for certain: he didn't want to lose her. Someone would come along and marry her and, at the thought, he felt as if he had been punched in his heart.

He needed to get her a ring and tell her how he felt and propose—for real this time. He had fallen in love with her and hadn't even recognized the depth of his own feelings.

He remembered her call at three in the morning when the dog was howling. It was about four o'clock now. What would happen if he called her, told her he had to see her? Could he get her to listen to him and go out with him?

Or was she out of his life no matter what he felt for her?

Lindsay sat up and shook her hair back away from her face. She stared into the dark bedroom as she clutched the phone. "Tony?" she asked, sounding more alert. "It's four in the morning. What's wrong?"

"Lindsay, I need to see you. Let me pick you up for dinner tonight."

She frowned at the phone. "You called at 4:00 a.m. to ask me to dinner?"

"You called at three to tell me a dog was howling. Will you have dinner with me? We need to talk."

She couldn't imagine what the urgency was, but her heartbeat quickened because she missed him and she wanted to be with him.

"Yes, I'll go to dinner with you. But you do know I'm pregnant and need my sleep, right?"

"I figured four is close enough to when you'll get up anyway. And can't you go back to sleep?"

"Yes," she said, but she wondered whether she would or not.

"Me, too, darling'," he said, and a warm fuzziness filled her. She hadn't heard that endearment in too long and it made it worth the wake-up call. "How about I pick you up at six?" he asked.

"That's fine," she said, curious what was on his mind.

"See you then," he said, and was gone.

She settled in bed, turning toward the windows so she could look at the bright moonlight outside. White cumulus clouds drifted rapidly across the black sky. She missed Tony more than she would have believed possible. She missed him every day and thought about him constantly and got lost in memories too often each day.

When had Tony become so important to her? At first she'd thought she would forget him as the days passed. Instead, each day she missed him and thought of him more.

She hadn't faced the question that hovered in her mind. Was she in love with him? Had she fallen in love with a man who would always want to run her life, their child rearing and her ranch? All indications said she had. She didn't know his feelings for sure, but she knew he hadn't been in love with her when she last saw him.

Tony had been so many good things—energetic, sexy, positive and upbeat, full of fun and life. She knew he was a good rancher. And she knew he was a take-charge person. Could she cope with having him back in her life? And on a larger scale? She couldn't answer her own question. The only solid answer she could give was that she had been miserable without him. She didn't want to tell him goodbye and watch him marry another woman while she raised his child.

This time without Tony had been the unhappiest stretch in her life. Excitement coursed through her at the thought of seeing him again. What was so urgent that he had to see her tonight? She hoped it was to get back together. She didn't know how they could, but she was ready to try.

She climbed out of bed, moving restlessly to a chair to think about Tony. She was guessing he wanted to see her because he missed her, too. But what if he had another reason—like a permanent parting of the ways?

That possibility filled her with concern. It couldn't happen now, she told herself, not when she finally realized she wanted him back in her life with all her being.

He still might propose to her again, even if he didn't love her. If he did, was she willing to accept that and hope she could win his love over time?

She ran her hand across her flat stomach. Their baby needed them. Could they set aside their monumental differences and give love a chance?

There was love on her part. She was ready to admit it now. She was in love with Tony, alpha male or not. She had gotten herself into this situation by bidding on him at the auction, and now she was in deep, over her head.

Would she tell him that she was in love? Or keep it from him until he declared feelings of love for her? She didn't see how she could keep from revealing her love to him. At the thought of seeing him tonight, what she most wanted was to throw herself into his arms when she opened her door. Now that she knew she would see him and had finally admitted that she was deeply in love, she ached to be with him and hoped with all her heart he might have missed her or, better yet, be as in love as she was.

She glanced at her clock and saw it was almost five. In just over twelve hours she would be with him and get an answer to the question that plagued her. What did Tony feel for her?

Only time would tell.

By six that night she had even more questions. As she left her room, she turned for one more look in the mirror. She wore a deep blue sleeveless dress with a low-cut back, a hem that ended above her knees and high heels. She had left her hair falling freely because Tony liked that best.

Downstairs, promptly at six she watched him step out of his black sports car and come up her front drive, and her breath rushed from her lungs. He looked handsome, filled with vitality. He also looked like a Texas rancher in his white Stetson, his black boots, black Western-cut trousers and a pale blue, long-sleeved cotton shirt that was open at the throat. She longed to throw herself into his embrace, but she restrained herself, opening the front door and smiling.

His blue-green eyes filled with desire that revved up her heartbeat. "Darlin', you look gorgeous," he said, his gaze moving over her slowly, a tantalizing perusal that set her pulse pounding. "You look more fantastic than ever. I'd say that pregnancy becomes you."

"Thank you. I'd say prospective fatherhood becomes you, because you're a sexy hunk, Tony Milan." As she spoke she was unable to keep from letting her gaze skim over him, wanting more than ever to be in his arms and kiss him.

"Lindsay," he said.

She looked up to meet his hungry gaze and her heart thudded at the heat and desire she saw there. He stepped inside and closed the door. She didn't have to throw herself into Tony's arms. He drew her into them and kissed her.

Her heart slammed against her ribs and she clung to him to kiss him in return. "Tony, I've missed you," she whispered breathlessly between kisses.

"I'm not doing any of this the way I planned," he said, between showering her with kisses.

Looking into his eyes, she felt a physical impact that

heated her insides. It seemed months instead of weeks since she last saw him.

He kissed her and she closed her eyes again, holding him tightly while her heart pounded.

"I might not let you go this time," he whispered. He showered kisses on her and finally picked her up, carrying her as he kissed her. "We were going to my house, but I think that's temporarily on hold. This is far too urgent," he said. "Lindsay, I've really missed you."

Clutching his shoulders, she kissed him slowly and thoroughly. "I've missed you."

He took the stairs two at a time, hurrying to the big bed in her room.

It was covered with dresses, lacy underwear, bits and pieces of clothing that she had tried on earlier.

He yanked back the cover and all of the clothing flew off. He turned to kiss her, his fingers trembling as he drew the zipper of her dress down while she twisted free the buttons of his shirt. She couldn't wait to show him how much she loved him.

Over an hour later, she lay wrapped in his arms beside him in bed while he lightly combed her hair away from her face with his fingers and showered feathery kisses on her temple and cheeks.

"I think we were going to my place for dinner," he whispered, nuzzling her neck and kissing her throat so lightly.

"We still can if you want or I can find something here to feed you."

"I had plans and I wanted to show you the dog."

She sat up so fast he rolled away slightly. "The dog? You didn't tell me. Is he okay?"

"He's more than okay," Tony said, smiling as he pulled

her back against his shoulder and held her close. "Lindsay, I've missed you, darlin', more than I thought possible and I've thought about my feelings for you."

She focused on him, her heart beginning to drum, and she could barely catch her breath upon hearing his words. He gazed into her eyes and looked at her intently. "Lindsay, I love you."

"Oh, Tony," she gasped, wrapping her arms around his neck to kiss him and hold him tightly. "I'm in love with you. I didn't want to be in love with a rancher, absolutely not the controlling type, which you are. I tried not to be. We're misfits, you and I—two ranchers. I know you think I'm too stubborn and maybe I am. Am I babbling?" she asked. Without pausing for breath or for his answer, she continued. "I've been miserable without you in my life. You're too take-charge. We'll clash and it won't be any more peaceful in the future than it was in the past—"

"Damn, Lindsay," he said, and kissed her, stopping her chatter. She clung to him, kissing him, pouring out the love that she felt along with joy and relief over his declaration.

Suddenly, she leaned away to look at him, framing his face with her hands. "You really, really love me?"

"I really, really love you. Lindsay, will you marry me?" he asked, holding her close against him with one arm wrapped around her waist.

Her heart thudded. "Yes," she gasped. "Oh, yes, Tony. We'll fight, but we'll be in love."

"We might not fight," he whispered. "We may learn to negotiate." She heard the laughter in his voice. He wrapped his fingers in her hair and tugged lightly so she had to look at him. Startled, her eyes flew wide as she looked up at him.

"Will you marry me?" he repeated.

"Yes, I will," she answered.

"Then I'm the happiest man in the world tonight," he said. "I don't care about the differences and I can cope with you and you can cope with me. You'll get used to this rancher, darlin'. You may not get used to my take-charge ways, but we'll work things out because I promise to try to keep you happy. I promise to shower you with love so you won't ever regret marrying an alpha male cowboy."

"Shh, Tony. Stop making wild promises you can't keep," she said, laughing, trailing light kisses over his face. "I love you, cowboy. I love you with all my heart."

He kissed her, a kiss of joy and promise, a kiss that melted her heart and ignited desire again, and soon she was lost in passion.

It was almost ten when she sat with him in her tub while hot water swirled around them and he held her close between his legs as she leaned back against him.

"Hungry? I was going to cook steaks."

"I hadn't thought about it," she said. "I don't know about hunger, but I'm shriveling up from being in this hot water so long."

He chuckled, cupping her full breasts in his hands to caress her. "Not too shriveled," he said. "We'll get out, dry and go eat something. I know you have something in this house and if you don't, we'll head to my place." With big splashes, he stood, pulling her up with him and helping her step out of the tub. He picked up a towel and began slow, light strokes to dry her.

She caught the towel, wrapping it around herself and picking up another folded one to hand to him. "If you keep doing that, we'll end up in bed again. I'll dry my-self and you do the same, then get dressed and I'll meet you downstairs. I'm getting hungry and for some reason, I can't skip meals like I used to be able to."

Nodding, he grinned. "Not as much fun, but I'll co-operate."

When he met her downstairs in her kitchen, she already had a casserole heating and in minutes it was on the table. His fingers closed on her wrist and she looked up at him, startled.

"Darlin', I had this evening planned and it hasn't gone the way I expected from the moment you opened the door. But I came prepared for whatever happened." He reached into a pocket, pulled out a small folded bit of tissue paper tied with a tiny strip of blue ribbon. "This is for you, Lindsay."

Surprised, she looked up at him, giving him a searching look, and then she took it to tug free the bow and open the paper carefully, her heart drumming as she did. She looked at a dazzling ring. "Oh, Tony," she gasped, thrilled to look at the ring he had for her. It was a huge, emerald-cut diamond, surrounded by sapphires and diamonds with more diamonds scattered on the gold band.

He took it from her and held her hand. "One more time, the way I should have done it the first time. Lindsay Calhoun, will you marry me?"

"Oh, yes," she replied, laughing. "Yes." She threw her arms around him after he slipped the ring on her finger. Wrapping her arms around his neck, she kissed him and he held her tightly, kissing her in return.

When they finally stopped, he took her hand to walk to the table. "Lindsay, you need to eat. Let's sit and eat and talk about when we'll have a wedding. I hope we can agree on a date soon. Very, very soon."

He held her chair and then sat facing her. She could

barely think about eating because of the excitement and joy churning in her.

"Tony, I've missed you so and I realized I've been in love with you for a long time. I don't know how marriage will work with the two of us, but I can't wait to try."

"You'll be you and I'll still be me. We're in love, so we'll work it out." He grinned and picked up her hand to brush kisses over her knuckles. "I love you, darlin'. Back to the date. Lindsay, let's get married soon. Really soon.

She stared at him and then nodded. "In that, we're in agreement. The sooner the better for so many reasons, not the least of which is I love you with all my heart."

His eyes took on the greenish hue that she recognized from moments of intense emotion or passion. He held her hand and, without taking his gaze from hers, lifted it to his lips to brush more kisses lightly over it.

"Lindsay, I love you and I always will."

"Even if we fight?"

"Even if we fight. But I don't think we really will." He wagged his brows and grinned. "Well, maybe sometimes."

"Now, do you want a surprise?" she asked.

"I think my entire life will be filled with surprises. What's this one, darlin'?"

"It's early, and I'll have an ultrasound later this month, but my doctor thinks I may be having twins."

Stunned, he stared at her. "Twins?" He got up and walked around the table to reach down and draw her to her feet to kiss her hard. When he released her, he grinned. "Lindsay, why do I think my whole life will be like this night? One shock and one change after another."

"You know it won't be that way all the time."

"Get a calendar and let's have this wedding this month."

"Savannah's baby is due this month, but I'd like to

have the wedding soon, too. I've waited as long as I want to wait without you in my life. I don't ever want to go without you again," she said, holding him tightly.

He slipped his hand behind her head and leaned close to kiss her, a long kiss that made her want to be in his arms again and forget wedding plans.

"Tony," she whispered.

"Go get a calendar or I'll get my phone and we'll look at my calendar."

"I have one here." She turned to open a cabinet and came back with a calendar.

With it on the table between them, they discussed dates while they ate.

"After dinner we can call our parents and then start calling our siblings."

"Tony, I love you and I'm so happy."

"I'll show you how I feel in a little while," he said, smiling at her.

Her phone played a tune and she got up to answer it. "Sorry. Anyone calling at this hour has to have a good reason."

"Or a wrong number," he remarked, pulling the calendar close.

She picked up her phone and listened before turning to come back to the table. "That was Mike. Savannah went into labor and they didn't make it to Dallas. She delivered a little girl in the Verity hospital." She couldn't stop the smile that lit up her face. "Wyatt met him at the hospital to get Scotty. He said he texted me earlier, but he didn't hear back. He wants me to come to the hospital to see their baby. Mike sounds incredibly happy."

Tony pulled his chair close beside her. "Sit for a minute and let's pick a date so we can tell everyone and you can show them your ring."

"I don't want to detract from the baby," she said.

He gave her a look. "You're not going to. Babies are wonderful. We're probably not going to surprise anyone. We'll just announce it before we tell everyone goodbye. I didn't intend to walk in and say 'look at us,'" he said.

"You win," she said, smiling at him. "I can't keep it quiet anyway. Well, now we don't have to worry about our wedding interfering with Savannah having her baby."

Tony took her hand. "Lindsay, I want you to have a big wedding, the one you always dreamed of as a little girl. This is once in a lifetime. You won't do it again, I guarantee it."

She gazed at him and then turned to kiss him lightly. "Sometimes you're a very nice man even when you're bossy."

He smiled at her. "Don't sound so surprised." He tapped the calendar. "Pick a date so we can go see your new niece and the happy family."

Eleven

On the first Saturday in November, Lindsay stood in the foyer of the Dallas church watching Scotty walk down the aisle. Dressed in a black tux with black cowboy boots and his hair neatly combed, he was doing just as he had been told. He scattered rose petals along the aisle and took his place at the front by his dad.

Milans and Calhouns were present in abundance. Tony's best man was his older brother Wyatt. Tony had said they would kill the old feud between Calhouns and Milans, so along with his two brothers, he had asked her brothers to be groomsmen and all three accepted. Scotty stood in front of his dad and both of them looked pleased.

Lindsay had asked Savannah if she felt up to being matron of honor. After thanking her, Savannah had declined because of her new baby girl, Caitlin. Lindsay then asked Josh's new wife, Abby, and she accepted instantly, seeming grateful that Lindsay had thought of her. Madison had declined to be a bridesmaid because she was almost into the eighth month of her pregnancy.

"It's time," the wedding planner said, smoothing the train to Lindsay's white satin dress and checking her veil. She smiled at Lindsay as her dad took her arm.

"Lindsay, I wish you all the happiness possible," he said to her as they walked down the long aisle.

"Thanks, Dad," she replied. She looked at Tony in his black tux and best black boots and her heart beat faster with joy. She loved him with all her heart. It seemed like a miracle, something she once thought impossible.

When she joined him at the end of the aisle and met his gaze, she lost all awareness of their families and friends. The big Dallas church was filled, but she could see only Tony.

She repeated her vows, meaning every word, feeling as if there would be enough love between them to carry them through any kind of adversity, even the kind they stirred up themselves.

It seemed a long ceremony, but finally they were pronounced husband and wife. Above a fanfare of trumpets, an organ, and applause from the audience, thunder boomed as they rushed up the aisle.

"Wow," Tony said, glancing over his shoulder at double glass doors. "Is that really thunder?"

"Rain on our wedding day—"

"We had sunshine this morning and rain would be the best possible thing next to being alone with you within the hour."

"Rain is more likely to happen than that," she replied, laughing. "Look how dark it is outside," she said, turning to stare.

"Dare I hope?" Tony replied. "How long will this reception take?"

"Tony, you've asked me that half a dozen times. Hours. It will take hours for me to dance with all the Milan and Calhoun men who are going to ask me to dance because it's the courteous thing to do, much less all the guys who work for me that are here and will be polite and ask me to dance."

"They're not asking because they're polite. This is probably the first time they've seen you look like this and they're having the same kind of reaction I did the night of the auction," he remarked.

"I hope not." A bolt of lightning streaked in a brilliant flash, followed by thunder that rattled windows. Tony grabbed her hand. "C'mere," he said, stepping outside and drawing her beside him as he inhaled deeply.

"Smell that," he said. "And look at the trees. We have an east wind. It's going to rain. Hallelujah!" He yanked her to him to kiss her hard, and for a few minutes she forgot everything else until the first big drop hit her.

"Ki-yi-yippie-ki-ay!" Tony yelled, turning his face up to feel the rain.

"Celebrate inside." She grabbed his hand. "Let's go around where we're supposed to or everyone will be out here and we'll have a mob scene."

They rushed through an empty hall and Tony pulled her into an empty room and closed the door. "Just one more kiss," he said.

"Oh, no. You'll mess us both up for pictures. You have to wait. Come on, Tony," she said, wiggling away and stepping through the door into the hall, smiling and looking away.

"We're coming," she called. "Hurry, Tony."

He stepped out. "Yes, Miss Bossy." He looked down the hall. "Who were you talking to? I don't see a soul.

You made that up to get me out here," he accused, shaking his head but still smiling.

"Come on," she said, laughing and hurrying along the empty hall.

When they passed double glass doors, Tony pulled her to a stop. "Look at that," he said in awe, giving another whoop of joy while she clapped.

"Tony, rain! Finally."

"Just pray it lasts for a week," he said. "What a fantastic wedding gift—rain. Buckets and buckets of rain."

"Reception, remember?" she said, tugging on his hand.

Over an hour later, Tony took her into his arms for their first dance as husband and wife. "Lindsay, you're the most beautiful bride ever. You look even more stunning than the night of the auction," he said, meaning every word. He knew as long as he lived, he would never forget looking at her as she walked down the aisle to marry him.

"Tony, I'm so happy. I didn't think I could ever be this happy."

"Hang on to that as long as you can. I'll try to always make you happy, darlin'."

"Don't make wild promises."

"I'm not. I want you happy. I love you," he said, his arm tightening slightly around her waist as he held her. "Thanks again for agreeing to move into my house. My offer still stands—anytime you want me to build a new house for us, it's fine with me."

She smiled. "I think your house is wonderful," she said. "We'll see, but right now, it looks quite suitable. As long as you love me and you're in my bed at night, what more could I ask for?"

"I wish I could dance you out the door, through that pouring rain, into the limo and off to that bed right now."

"You can't do that. We have to stay and be sociable before we leave for New York."

"I hope you're still happy with going to New York for a few days."

"Very happy. After our babies are born, we can go to Paris and Italy, but I don't want that big a trip right now while I'm pregnant."

"It's your choice, darlin'." He held her close, inhaling the faint scent of her perfume. He just wanted to make her happy because she made him happier than he had ever been in his life.

"Lindsay, we still haven't told anyone we're expecting twins."

"It's just been confirmed and it's still early in my pregnancy. I want to wait a bit. We have time."

"We'll do it however you want," he said, and her blue eyes twinkled.

"I love it when you say that and I hope I hear it millions of times."

He grinned. "I'll try. That's the best I can do, just promise to try. Something I'm trying to resist doing is going out and standing in the rain. I may succumb to that one before we leave."

"Don't you dare. A soggy tux would be dreadful."

"Soggy from rainwater would be dreadful? I beg to differ."

She laughed. "Tony, life is a blast and I intend to enjoy being married to you."

"I'll keep reminding you of that. I'm going to wish I recorded it to play again."

"You still think we're going to fight. I don't think so. You're doing a great job so far of keeping me happy."

He laughed. "You can't imagine how badly I want to get you out of here and all to myself," he said.

"I'll see what I can do about that. Maybe I can hurry things up a bit."

"Darlin', you do know how to please a man."

She felt as if she'd danced with every cowboy in Texas when Mike stepped up to ask her to dance. She smiled at her brother as they danced away.

"Caitlin is a beautiful baby, Mike,"

He grinned. "Thank you. I agree. You look beautiful, too, Lindsay."

"Thank you."

"And happy. I'm glad. Tony's a good guy."

"I agree with you on that one. Savannah said Caitlin is a quiet baby."

"She is and she's a little doll. Someone's holding her constantly. When Mom and Dad arrived, they stayed with us last weekend instead of their usual hotel stay."

"Our mother?"

"Yes, she did. She thinks Caitlin is adorable."

"I'm so glad. She looks like Savannah, even as tiny as she is."

"I agree. I see Jake watching us, so I'm sure he's going to want to dance with you next. I talked to Abe. He's happy for you and he'll run the place just fine while you're gone. I told him if he needs me, call."

"That was nice, thanks," she said. "I've never been away like this."

"It's time you did, Lindsay, and time you got a life of your own. You don't have to get out there and work like one of the boys."

She laughed. "I think those days may be over. Being a mama sounds like a big responsibility."

He smiled at her and danced her toward the sideline. "I'll give you to Jake. You have so many guys who will want to dance with you that you and Tony will never get away."

"Thanks, Mike," she said, planting a kiss on his cheek as they halted and Jake stepped up to take her hand.

Mike was almost right. By the time she'd danced with all the Milans and Calhouns and talked to each of their guests, it was hours later. Finally they made it out of their reception hall.

For just a moment Tony stopped, standing in a downpour and laughing, dancing a jig until she grabbed his wrist and tugged.

They rushed to the waiting limo and fell laughing onto the seat as their chauffeur closed the door.

"The drought will lessen now and your brother told me rain is predicted for the next three days," Tony said, pulling her to him to kiss her before she could answer.

When she pushed him away she laughed as she shook her head. "You're incredibly sexy and appealing, but that wet tux is going to ruin my wedding dress."

"It's rainwater. Do you really care?"

As she shook her head, she laughed until he drew her close to kiss her again.

Tony had a private plane waiting at the airport, but it was the wee hours of the morning when he finally carried her over the threshold into the New York penthouse suite he had reserved for their honeymoon. Standing her on her feet, he pushed away her short charcoal jacket and wrapped his arms around her.

"I love you, Lindsay. I don't think I can ever tell you enough. All I can do is try to show you. I've waited all day for this moment when we would be alone together."

Wrapping her arms around his neck, she smiled at him.

"Mrs. Anthony Milan! It's a whole new life for me. Tony, once again, I am happier than I ever dreamed possible."

His smile vanished as he held her and began to unfasten the buttons down the back of her navy dress. "I hope so and I want to always make you happy, Lindsay. You've filled a huge void in my life. I want to be with you, to love you, to have a family with you. I need you, darlin'."

She tightened her arms around his neck to pull his head down and kiss him. He held her close against him, their hearts beating together.

Joy filled her. She had never known as much contentment as she had found with Tony, and so much excitement as they looked forward to their babies. She couldn't wait to start her new life, a life shared with the man she loved with all her heart—the one rancher in the whole world she could love.

* * * * *

BIDDING ON
HER BOSS

RACHEL BAILEY

This book is dedicated to Sharon Archer, who is not only an amazing author, but is also a brilliant critique partner and very dear friend. Sharon, thank you for being on this journey with me.

One

Dylan Hawke had done a few things he regretted in his life, but he had a feeling this one might top the list.

The spotlight shone in his eyes, but he smiled as he'd been instructed and gave a sweeping bow before making his way down the stairs and onto the stage. Applause—and a few cheers that he suspected were from his family—greeted him.

"We'll start the bidding at two hundred dollars," the emcee said from the front of the stage.

Dylan sucked in a breath. *And so it begins.* Step one of rehabilitating his image—donate his time to charity. Now that his brother was marrying a princess, Dylan's own mentions in the media had skyrocketed, and he'd quickly realized his playboy reputation could be a disadvantage for his future sister-in-law and the things she wanted to achieve for homeless children in LA.

"What do I hear for Dylan?" the emcee, a sitcom actor, called out. "Dylan Hawke is the man behind the chain of Hawke's Blooms florists, so we can guarantee he knows about romancing his dates."

A murmur went around the crowded room as several white paddles with black numbers shot into the air. He couldn't see too much detail past the spotlight that shone down on him, but it seemed that the place was full, and that the waiters were keeping the guests' drinks topped off as they moved through the crowd.

"Two fifty, three hundred," the emcee called.

Dylan spotted his brother Liam sitting with his fiancée, Princess Jensine of Larsland. Jenna—who had been hiding incognito as Dylan's housekeeper before she met Liam—gave him a thumbs-up. This was the first fundraising event of the new charity, the Hawke Brothers Trust, which Jenna had established to raise money for homeless children. Now that she and Liam were to be married, they planned to split their family's time between her homeland and LA, and the trust would utilize the skills she'd gained growing up in a royal family. It would be the perfect project for her—she'd said it was something she could sink her teeth into.

Dylan believed in the cause and believed in Jenna, so his job tonight was to help raise as much money as he could. He just wished he'd been able to do it in a less humiliating way. Like, say, writing a check.

But that method wouldn't help rehabilitate his image.

Which had led him to this moment. On stage in front of hundreds of people. Being sold.

"Five hundred and fifty," the emcee said, pointing at a redhead near the side of the room, whose paddle said sixty-three.

Dylan threw Sixty-Three a wink, and then crossed to where a blonde woman held up her paddle. The emcee called, "Six hundred."

Dylan squinted against the lights. There was something familiar about the blonde... Then it hit him and his gut clenched tight. It was Brittany Oliver, a local network weather girl. They'd been out two or three times a few years ago, but she'd been cloying. When he found out that she was already planning a future and children for them, he'd broken it off. He swallowed hard and sent up a prayer that someone outbid her. Maybe the cute redhead with paddle sixty-three.

He dug one hand in his pocket and flashed a charming smile at the audience—a smile he'd been using to effect since he was fourteen. He was rewarded when a stunning woman with long dark hair and coffee-colored skin raised her paddle. He was starting not to mind being on stage after all.

"Six fifty," the emcee called. "Seven hundred dollars. Seven fifty."

He knew Jenna was hoping for a big amount from this auction to get their charity started with a bang, so he took the rosebud from his buttonhole and threw it into the crowd. It was a cheesy move, but then the bidding happened so quickly that all of a sudden it hit two thousand.

Dylan steeled himself and looked over at Brittany, and sure enough, she was still in the running. He had no idea whether she'd want to chew his ear off for breaking things off or try to convince him they should get back together. Either way, it would be an uncomfortable evening. He should have had a backup plan—a signal to tell Jenna to bid whatever it took if things went awry. He could have reimbursed her later.

"Three thousand four hundred."

It was the redhead. Dylan looked her over. Bright copper hair scraped into a curly ponytail on top of her head, cobalt blue halter top, dark eyes that were wide as she watched the other bidders, and a bottom lip caught between her teeth in concentration. She looked adorable. In his pocket where the audience couldn't see, he crossed his fingers that she won. He could spend an enjoyable evening with her, a nice meal, maybe a drive to a moonlit lookout, maybe a movie.

"Four thousand six hundred."

A flash bulb went off and he smiled, but he needed to get the bidding higher for the trust. He ambled over to the emcee and indicated with a tilt of his head that he had something to say. She covered the mic with her hand and lowered it.

"Make it three dates," he said, his voice low.

Her eyebrows shot up, and then she nodded and raised the mic again. "I've just received information that the package up for auction now consists of three dates."

Over the next few minutes, there was another flurry of raised paddles before the emcee finally said, "Going once, going twice, sold for eight thousand two hundred dollars."

Dylan realized he'd stopped following the bidding and had no idea who'd won.

"Number sixty-three, you can meet Mr. Hawke at the side of the stage to make arrangements. Next we have a sports star who will need no introduction." The emcee's voice faded into the background as Dylan realized the cute redhead had made the top bid. He grinned.

Maybe turning his reputation around and doing his bit for charity wouldn't be so bad after all.

Faith Crawford stood, adjusted the hem of her halter top over her black pants and slipped between the tables to where Dylan Hawke was waiting for her by the side of the stage.

Her belly fluttered like crazy but she steeled herself and, when she reached him, stuck out her hand.

"Hi, I'm Faith," she said.

Dylan took her hand, but instead of shaking it, he lifted it to his lips and pressed a kiss on the back. "I'm Dylan, and, on behalf of my family, I appreciate your donation to the Hawke Brothers Trust."

He gave her a slow smile and her insides melted, but she tried to ignore her body's reaction. Her body didn't realize that Dylan Hawke was a notorious charmer who had probably used that exact smile on countless women. Which was why her brain was in charge. *Well*, she thought as she looked into his twinkling green eyes, *mostly in charge*.

Dylan released her hand and straightened. "I have a few ideas about places we could go on our first date—"

Faith shook her head. "I know where I want to go."

He arched an eyebrow. "Okay, then. I like a woman who knows what she wants."

Oh, she knew exactly what she wanted. And it wasn't Dylan Hawke, despite how good he looked in that tuxedo. It was what he could do for her career. She'd just made a large investment in her future—having bid most of her savings—and she wouldn't let it go to waste.

He slid a pen out of an inside pocket of his jacket and grabbed a napkin from a nearby table. "Write down your address and I'll pick you up. How does tomorrow night sound?"

The sooner the better. "Tomorrow is good. But instead of picking me up, I'd rather meet you. Let's say in front of your Santa Monica store at seven?"

He grinned, but this time it wasn't a charmer's smile. It was genuine. She liked this one more—she could imagine getting into all sorts of mischief with the man wearing that grin.

"A woman of mystery," he said, rocking back on his heels. "Nice. Okay, Faith Sixty-Three, I'll meet you in front of the Santa Monica Hawke's Blooms store at seven o'clock tomorrow night."

"I'll be there," she said and then turned and walked along the edge of the room to the door, aware that several curious gazes followed her exit. Including Dylan Hawke's. Which was just how she needed him—with his full attention focused on her.

Now all she had to do was keep her own attention soundly focused on her career, and not on getting into mischief with her date and his grin.

Dylan pulled his Porsche into the small parking lot in front of his Santa Monica store. He tried to get around to all thirty-two stores fairly regularly, but given that they were spread from San Francisco to San Diego, it didn't happen as often as it used to, and he couldn't remember exactly when he was last at this one. It looked good, though, and he knew the sales figures were in the top quarter of all the Hawke's Blooms stores.

Movement near the door caught his attention. It was Faith. Her red hair gleamed in the window lights and bounced about her shoulders. She wore a halter-neck summer dress that was fitted in all the right places and flared out over her hips, down to her knees, showing shapely calves atop stylish heels. His pulse picked up speed as he stepped out of his car.

All he knew about this woman was that she liked halter tops, her hair could stop traffic, she was wealthy enough to have spare cash lying around to help out a new charity and her lips could set his blood humming. But damn if he didn't want to know more.

"Evening, Faith," he said, walking around and opening his passenger side door.

She didn't take a step closer, just stood at the shop door looking adorable and said, "We won't be needing your car tonight."

He glanced around—the parking lot was empty. "You have a magic carpet tucked away somewhere?"

"No need," she said brightly. "We're already here."

She dug into her bag and came out with a handful of keys looped together on what looked like plaited ribbons. As he watched in surprise, she stuck a key into the front door, and he heard a click. She stepped in, efficiently disabled the alarm and turned back to him. "Come on in."

Dylan narrowed his eyes, half expecting one of his brothers to jump out and yell "gotcha" because he'd fallen for the prank. But Faith was busy putting her bag behind the counter and switching on lights. Shaking his head, he set the keyless lock on his car, followed her into the store and closed the door behind them. He had no idea what she had planned or what she really wanted out of this date, but for some reason that didn't bother him. This woman was piquing his interest on more than one level—something he hadn't experienced in a long while—and he realized he was enjoying the sensation.

"Who *are* you, Faith Sixty-Three?" he asked, leaning back against the counter and appreciating the way her dress hugged her lush curves.

She faced him then, her cheeks flushed and her warm brown eyes sparkling. "I'm a florist. My name is Faith Crawford and I work for you in this store."

Faith Crawford? That name rang a bell, but he couldn't remember any specifics. He narrowed his eyes. "Mary O'Donnell is the manager here, isn't she?"

"Yep, she's my manager," Faith said over her shoulder as she turned the light on in the storeroom in the back of the shop.

He wrapped a hand around the back of his neck. This had gone past Woman of Mystery and was fast becoming ridiculous. Why would an employee want to spend a purseful of money on a night or three with the boss? Could she have an axe to grind? Was she hoping to sleep her way to a promotion?

He blew out a breath. "How long have you worked for me?"

She turned to face him, standing a little taller. "Six months, Mr. Hawke."

"So you know Hawke's Blooms has a no fraternization policy." A policy he wholeheartedly believed in. "Managers can't be involved with anyone who works for them."

She didn't seem fazed. "I'm aware of that, yes."

"Yet," he pressed, taking a step closer and catching a whiff of her exotic perfume, "you still paid good money for a date—well, three dates—with me."

A small frown line appeared between her brows.

"Nowhere was it specified that they were supposed to be romantic *dates* with the bachelors."

Dylan was about to reply, then realized he was losing control of the conversation. "Then what do you want from me?" he asked warily.

She grabbed a clip from her handbag and pulled her hair back. "I want you to spend the evening here with me."

"Doing what, exactly?" he asked as he watched her clip her red curls, which burst out the top of the clasp in copper-colored chaos.

"Watching."

He felt his eyebrows lift. "I have to warn you, kinky propositions still fall under the no fraternization policy."

Faith rolled her eyes, but he saw the corners of her mouth twitch. "I'll be making a floral arrangement."

Right. As if he didn't get enough of that in his average day. And yet, he thought, glancing at her pale, long fingers, there was something appealing about the idea of watching Faith at work. Her fingers looked as if they'd be gentle yet firm. He could almost feel them on his jaw, then stroking across his shoulders. His skin tingled…and he realized he was getting carried away. This was not a path he could take with an employee—which he'd only just explained to her.

Besides, his attraction was probably a result of being in the store at night, alone, cocooned in the area illuminated by the lights. It couldn't be more.

He rubbed a hand down his face. "Let me get this straight. I know what you're earning, so unless you have a trust fund, your bid was a decent amount of money to you. Yet you paid it to have me sit and watch you do the job that we normally pay you to do."

She beamed at him. "That's it."

"I've missed something," he said, tilting his head to the side. She was becoming more intriguing by the minute.

She opened the fridge door and pulled out buckets of peonies, lilacs and magnolias. "Have you ever had a dream, Mr. Hawke? Something that was all yours and made you smile when you thought about it?"

Dylan frowned. His career dreams had always been for Hawke's Blooms, but they were dreams he shared with his family. Had he ever had one that was his alone?

"Sure," he said casually, knowing it was probably a lie and unsure how he felt about that.

While looking at him, she began to strip the leaves from the flower stems. "Then you know how it is."

As he took in the glow on her face, his pulse picked up speed. "What's your dream, Faith?"

She smiled mysteriously. "I have many dreams, but there's one in particular I'm trying to achieve now."

He met her gaze and the room faded away. He could have looked at her all night. Then her eyes darkened. Her breathing became irregular. Dylan wanted to groan. She felt the chemistry between them as well. His body responded to the knowledge, tightening, heating. But he couldn't let that happen. This was dangerous. He frowned and swung away.

"Tell me about the dream," he said when he turned back around, this time more in control of himself.

After a beat, Faith gave a small nod. "To open the Hawke's Blooms catalog and see one of my designs there on the page."

This was all about the catalog? He leaned back against the bench opposite the one Faith was working on and crossed his ankles. "We have a procedure in place for that."

"I know it by heart," she said, taking foam and a white tray down from the shelf. "'Any Hawke's Blooms florist may submit an original floral design to his or her manager, accompanied by a completed, signed application form. If the manager believes the design has merit, she or he will pass it to the head office to be considered for inclusion in the catalog of standard floral designs used for customer orders.'"

Dylan smiled. She'd recited the procedure word for word. "And," he added, "that process doesn't cost a single penny. Why didn't you go that route?"

"I did." She clipped the bottoms from a bunch of peony stems. "About twenty times, in fact. After my manager rejected number sixteen, I began to think that way might not work for me." She smiled and her dimples showed.

He thought about her manager, Mary O'Donnell. Mary was simpering to management, which was annoying, but he knew she ran a tight ship. Was it possible she was blocking her own staff from advancement? "Are you making a complaint about your manager?" he asked, serious.

She shook her head, and her hands slowed to a stop as she met his gaze. "I'm a good florist, Mr. Hawke. I take pride in my work, and take direction from my manager. I do my best by our customers and have a good group of regulars who ask for me by name. So I don't think it's too much to ask to have just one of my designs considered so I can move my career forward."

Dylan knew he was lucky—he'd grown up in the family business, where his input had been not only lis-

tened to but also encouraged. But what if he'd been in
Faith's shoes? An employee of a large company who
was struggling to have her voice heard. He watched her
place flowers in the foam, turning the arrangement with
the other hand as she went. He'd like to think he'd have
gone the extra mile, the way Faith was doing tonight.

"So you decided to get creative," he said, hearing the
trace of admiration in his own voice.

"Seeing you were auctioning off a night of your time
seemed like a sign." She glanced up at him, her long-
lashed eyes earnest. "Do you believe in destiny, Mr.
Hawke?"

"Can't say it's something I've ever paid much attention to," he said. Unlike, say, the way the side of her
jaw sloped down to her neck, or the sprinkling of pale
ginger freckles across her nose.

"Well, I do, and I'd just been thinking 'If only I could
speak to someone in the head office myself' when the
posters for the auction went up in the window. The
very window where I work." She paused, moistening
her lips. "You can see it was too strong a sign to ignore, can't you?"

He wasn't sure if he wanted to chuckle or to kiss
those full lips her tongue had darted over. Instead, he
murmured, "I suppose so."

"So I attended the auction, used a good portion of my
savings, and here we are." She splayed her free hand to
emphasize her point, and then picked up a roll of ribbon
and went back to what she was doing.

Dylan shifted his weight. Something about this
situation and her confidence was beginning to make
him uncomfortable. After she'd spent that amount of
money—which he'd reimburse now that he knew she

was an employee trying to get a meeting with him—
and she'd gone to this much effort, how would she react
if he agreed with her manager?

"Tell me, Faith," he said carefully. "What happens
if, after all this effort and expense, I don't like your design enough to put it in the catalog?"

She looked him in the eye again. There was no arti-
fice, no game playing in her deep brown gaze. "Then
I'll know I've given it my best shot, and I'll work harder
to create an even better design."

Dylan nodded. She believed in herself but didn't have
a sense of entitlement and was prepared to put in the
work to improve her situation. He liked her attitude.
In fact, there were a number of things he liked about
Faith Crawford—including things he shouldn't allow
himself to like now that he knew she worked for him.
Such as the crazy hair that his fingers were itching to
explore, and the way her sweet-shaped mouth moved
as she spoke.

There was also a vibrancy about her that dragged
his gaze back every time he looked away. How would
it feel to hold all that vibrancy in his arms? Her kisses
would be filled with passion, he just knew it, and in his
bed… Dylan held back a groan and determinedly refo-
cused on Faith's floristry skills.

Her movements were quick and economical but still
flowed, almost as if her hands were dancing. He'd had a
stab at displaying flowers in the past but hadn't pulled
off more than rudimentary arrangements. It had been
enough for the roadside stall his family had started the
business with but hadn't come close to what a florist
with training and flair could create. Yet having been

around professional florists for his entire adult life, he was good at spotting skill in someone else.

He could already tell that Faith didn't just have the training all florists employed by Hawke's Blooms stores required. She also had that indefinable, creative *something* that differentiated the great from the good. Whether she'd harnessed that talent, and was able to use it to create designs of the standard needed to be included in the catalog, was yet to be seen.

But if nothing else, tonight Faith Crawford had achieved one thing she'd set out to achieve—she definitely had his full attention.

In fact, he was having trouble looking anywhere but at her.

Faith added another peony to the arrangement and tried to ignore the prickles on the back of her neck that told her Dylan was watching her again. Of course, that's what the whole night had been engineered to achieve, but he was only sometimes following what her hands were doing. At other times…

Heat rose in her belly as she thought about the way he'd been staring at her mouth a few minutes ago. She couldn't remember the last time a man had looked at her with that much hunger. Especially a man she'd been wanting to wrap herself around and kiss as if there was no tomorrow ever since he'd stepped out of his sex-on-wheels car.

And that it had to be Dylan Hawke, the CEO of the company? Well, that was fate playing a cruel joke on her. So she pretended that she wasn't wildly attracted to the man in front of her and that he wasn't sending her the same signals. She focused on the flowers. Which was working out fairly well, except for the prickles on the back of her neck.

But she needed to concentrate, to stop letting herself be distracted. Ruthlessly she reminded herself of what was at stake: getting this right could mean a fantastic boost to her career. She turned the arrangement with quick flicks of her wrist, checking for symmetry. Just a few stray leaves to trim. She snipped them away carefully. It looked good, balanced in color and form… but was it special enough to go into the catalog? She'd controlled her wilder artistic urges and gone for a safer conservative arrangement to impress. Butterflies fluttered mercilessly in her stomach. For the first time, she realized how much Mary's criticism had dented her confidence in her creativity.

She reached out to touch a crisp green leaf. This arrangement was finished—but still she hesitated.

"All done?"

She jolted at the sound of Dylan's voice so close to her ear. Last time she'd been aware of him, he'd been on the other side of the bench. She tried to move to the side. Her foot caught on something and she felt herself begin to fall. A hand closed around her arm, and her almost certain tumble was averted. She closed her eyes, and then opened them to find Dylan staring at her. The picture of him on the company website was nothing like the living, breathing man before her.

With him so close, no more than a hand span away, his scent surrounded her. It was dark and mysterious, surprising. She'd have expected something lighter, more recognizable, perhaps one of the expensive name-brand colognes. Yet this had undertones of a night in the forest—earthy, secretive and alluring. A shiver ran down her body to her toes. Dylan stilled.

Her breath caught in her throat. She could feel the heat from his body reaching out to envelop her. The world receded around her and all she could see, all she could feel, was Dylan. His eyes darkened and she swallowed hard. She should step away, not let her body lead her into temptation. But, oh, what temptation this man was. She could feel her pulse thundering at the base of her throat and saw Dylan's gaze drop to observe the same thing.

"Faith," he murmured, his breathing uneven.

She closed her eyes, fighting the effect of hearing her name on his lips, and when she opened them again, he was closer than before, his breath fanning over her face. Her hands found their way to his chest, so solid and warm.

A shudder ran down his body at her touch.

"Please—" she said, and before she could finish the thought his mouth was on hers. A small part of her mind told her to pull away, but instead, her hands fisted in his shirt, not letting him go.

He groaned as she opened her mouth to him, and his arms wrapped around her, holding her close while pushing her back against the workbench. His tongue was like nothing else as it stroked along the side of hers, leaving her wanting more. To be closer. So much closer.

She was lost.

Two

As Dylan drew away, Faith tried to catch her breath. It seemed as if he was doing the same. Except she wasn't sure she'd ever get her breath back again—that kiss was unlike anything she'd experienced before. In fact, if she just leaned forward a little, she could experience it again…

And then the enormity of the situation hit her, sending her knees wobbling.

She'd just kissed her boss.

No, not *her* boss—the *big* boss. She'd just kissed the man with ultimate responsibility for every single Hawke's Blooms store.

Or he'd kissed her—she wasn't sure about the details of what had just happened. All she knew was she'd never been kissed with that much hunger. That much passion. That much mind-numbing skill. That it had been her employer, someone she shouldn't have been kissing in the first place, was a cruel twist of irony. If she'd screwed up her well-ordered plan or caused him to not take her seriously, she'd never forgive herself.

"Faith," he said, his voice a rasp. "I'm sorry. That was completely out of line."

Honesty compelled her to point out the truth. "You weren't there alone."

"But I'm the one who's the boss." He winced. "It's my responsibility not to cross the damn line. You shouldn't feel pressured or uncomfortable in your workplace, and I apologize."

"I don't feel uncomfortable. Well," she amended, looking down at her hands, "I didn't feel uncomfortable or pressured *then*. I guess I'm uncomfortable now." She glanced back up, meeting his wary gaze. "But you should know, I wanted to kiss you. Then."

His head tilted to the side. "But not now?"

"No." Which was a lie. She definitely wanted to kiss him again. Wanted it more than almost anything. The key was the *almost*. She wanted a flourishing career more than she wanted to kiss Dylan Hawke again.

He blew out a breath. "That's a relief, but it's not enough. It was selfish of me to kiss you when you wanted me here for a completely different purpose. I give you my word it won't happen again."

"I appreciate that," she said, trying to conjure a professional facade.

He was silent for a couple of beats, his gaze assessing. "You seem quite certain, considering you just said you'd wanted me to kiss you only a few minutes ago."

She wasn't sure where he was coming from—it didn't look like flirting, but she couldn't read him well enough to know. Maybe he was testing her, wanting to ensure she wasn't going to change her mind and make waves in the company. Whatever it was about, she had to be absolutely clear so he understood her position.

She drew in a breath and lifted her chin. "Boyfriends and lovers aren't hard to come by, Mr. Hawke. What I need more than a man is someone to appreciate my talent. I hope this isn't offensive, but I want you professionally more than personally."

He flashed her a self-deprecating smile. "Understood. Which means I'd better have a look at this arrangement."

She stood back to give him some room. Everything she'd done recently, from making the plan to attending the auction to spending most of her savings to meeting Dylan here tonight, had led to this moment. It was the do-or-die moment, and all she could do was step back, cross her fingers and hope he'd still give an honest assessment after he'd kissed her.

Dylan dug his hands in his pockets as he faced her arrangement. He moved around, looking at it from several angles before straightening with a grimace.

"That bad?" she asked, her stomach in free fall. "You're grimacing."

"No, it's not bad." He leaned back against the bench and crossed his arms over his chest. "If I'm not smiling it's because I really wanted to put your arrangement in the catalog."

She felt the words like a slap. Tears pressed against the backs of her eyes, but she wouldn't let them form. "But you're not going to."

"I'm sorry, Faith," he said, his voice gentle. "Especially after…" He gestured toward the other end of the bench, where they'd been when he'd kissed her.

She bit down on her lip. She might feel bad, but she didn't want him to feel bad as well. He was only doing his job. "Don't apologize. If it's not good enough, that's my problem, not yours."

"The thing is, it's good, really good, but it looks a lot like the arrangements that are already in the book. If we add something new, then it needs to be unique. It has to offer our customers a genuine alternative to the options already there, and this arrangement, though beautiful, is—"

"Too much like what they can already choose," she finished for him, understanding his point, but still deflated.

He moved closer and laid a hand on her shoulder, his eyes kind. "But I'll reimburse the money you paid at the auction. You shouldn't have to pay to have an appointment with someone at the head office."

Her back stiffened. He wasn't going to wriggle out of this that easily. "I won't take the money back. I have two more *dates* left and I plan to use them."

There was no way she was giving up this direct line to the head of the Hawke's Blooms stores. It had been a good plan when she'd made it, and it was still a good plan…as long as she hadn't blown her chances by kissing him.

Sure, tonight hadn't been the raging success she'd hoped for, but there were two more dates yet. When she set her mind to something, she didn't give up until she'd achieved it. She'd impress him yet and get one of her arrangements in the catalog.

He dropped his hand and sighed. "The thing is, Faith,

I can't force you to take the money back, but it would be easier for me if you did."

"Perhaps," she said and smiled sweetly. "But it wouldn't be easier for me."

"Look, can I be honest?"

He thrust the fingers of both hands through his hair and left them there, linking them behind his head. This wasn't the same man who'd kissed her moments before, or the man who ran an entire chain of retail stores, or even the man who'd confidently strutted the stage at the auction. This one seemed more real.

She nodded. "Please."

"I'm in the process of trying to rehabilitate my image." He gave her half a smile, and she tried not to laugh at how adorable he looked now.

"From playboy to the future brother-in-law of a princess?"

He shifted his weight to his other leg. "Yeah, something like that."

"So to stop people seeing you as a playboy, you auctioned yourself off to the highest bidder?" She jumped up to sit on the bench, enjoying his discomfort more than she would have expected, but also enjoying seeing this private side of him.

He coughed out a laugh. "Yeah, when you put it like that, it sounds crazy."

Suddenly she was more than intrigued. This man was a mass of contradictions and she wanted to know more. To understand him. "Then how would you put it?"

"I'm throwing myself into our new charity. The auction was only the first step, but I'll be involved every step of the way."

"A respectable, upstanding member of the community." She could see him pulling it off, too. Going from a playboy to a pillar of the community.

"So you can see that the very last thing I need is a scandal involving a staff member, especially given that we have a policy about management being involved with staff."

A scandal? She frowned. What, exactly, did he think she wanted from those other two dates? "Dylan, I'm not expecting romance on the other dates any more than I expected it on this one."

He shrugged one shoulder. "But image is everything."

That was true. She cast her mind around for a solution. There was no way she was giving up her remaining dates without a fight. "What if no one knows? We could do them in secret."

"That boat pretty much sailed when the auction was covered by the media," he said and chuckled. Then he sobered and let out a long breath. "But it's more than that."

Understanding dawned. "Our kiss changed things." She said the words softly, as if acknowledging the truth too loudly would make a difference.

He nodded, his gaze not wavering from her eyes. "And it's very important that I see you only as an employee, and you see me only as a boss."

"I won't have any trouble with that. Are you saying you will?" She arched her eyebrow in challenge, guessing Dylan Hawke was a man who didn't shrink from a challenge.

One corner of his mouth kicked up. "If you can do it, I can."

"Then it looks like we don't have a problem, do we?"

Knowing he was trapped in the logic of it, she jumped down from the bench and grabbed the trash.

She felt him behind her, not moving, probably assessing his options. Then finally he took the trash can from her and began to sweep stem cuttings together with his free hand.

"It appears you've won this round, Faith Sixty-Three," he said from beside her.

She flashed him a wry smile. "Dylan, if I'd won this round, my design would soon be featured in the catalog. All I've done is kept the door open for another round."

"You know what?" he said, his voice amused. "Even though I know I shouldn't be, I'm already looking forward to the next round."

She turned and caught his gaze, finding a potent mix of humor and heat there—something closer to the real man she'd glimpsed earlier. Quickly she turned away. This was going to be hard enough without seeing him as anything more than the head of the Hawke's Blooms stores. And she had a sinking feeling it might already be too late for that anyway...

Two days later, Dylan pulled into the parking lot of the Santa Monica store. He hadn't done an all-day inspection for a while. It used to be part of his management style—show up in the morning unannounced, hang around in the background and help out where he could. Nothing beat it for getting a good feel for how a store was working and what needed improvement.

He'd been meaning to start doing a couple of these a month, so his office staff hadn't thought there was anything strange when he'd told them to clear his schedule for today. Of course, they weren't to know what he was trying to deny to himself—that he hadn't stopped thinking about one of the Santa Monica store's employees since the moment he'd dropped her home that first night.

Under different circumstances, there was no question he'd ask her out. That kiss had been beyond amazing and had been on an automatic replay loop in his mind ever since, but he'd also enjoyed her company. He never knew what she was going to say or do next, and that made her fun to be around.

He sighed and stepped from his car. No use wasting energy wanting what he couldn't have. She worked for him. End of story.

But that didn't stop him from wondering how this particular store was doing. Despite rejecting Faith's arrangement himself, he'd been left wondering if her manager was doing all she could for the advancement of her staff if Faith had put in twenty applications to the catalog of standard arrangements and not one had made it through to the head office.

Sure, he'd rejected the one he'd seen last night, but given Faith's enthusiasm and skill, a good, supportive manager should have found a way to guide her toward a more appropriate arrangement by now. Perhaps even submitted one or two just to encourage her. Yes, it was definitely time he had a closer look at how this store— and the other stores—were doing.

As he stepped through the front door and removed his aviator sunglasses, the manager, Mary O'Donnell, looked up and waved enthusiastically.

"Mr. Hawke!" she called, her voice obsequious. "So good to see you. Here, Faith, take over this arrangement. I need to talk to Mr. Hawke."

At the mention of his name, Faith froze, then looked

up like a deer caught in headlights. Her tongue darted out to moisten her lips, and he was assailed by memories of her mouth. Of how incredible it had felt under his. Of how it had opened to allow his tongue entry. Before he could forget all the reasons not to kiss her again, he determinedly drew his gaze to Mary O'Donnell.

"No need," he said. "I'm here for the day. Don't stop what you're doing—I just want to get a feel for the store."

"You haven't done an all-day inspection for quite a while." Mary shot a suspicious glance around the room. "Is there a problem?"

"Just continuing a procedure that worked well for us in the past. I've let it slip a bit as we've grown, but I'll be working my way around to all the stores in the coming months."

"And we're first?" she asked, pride beaming from her features.

"Yes, you are." He'd let her think it was a compliment. Plus, it was a much more professional reason than the fact that he hadn't been able to stop thinking about one of her employees.

"Well, in that case, let me introduce you to the team." She grabbed a middle-aged blonde woman by the wrist and dragged her over. "This is Courtney. She's our senior florist. If you want any bouquets made to take home at the end of the day, Courtney's your woman."

"Good to meet you, Courtney," he said, shaking her hand.

Courtney smiled openly. "Nice to meet you, too, Mr. Hawke. Though, if you don't mind, I need to finish this order before the courier arrives in a few minutes?"

"Of course," he said and watched her go back to

work on one of the long benches. She seemed efficient
and nice enough, and the arrangement she was working on was good.

"And this is our other florist, Faith Crawford," the
manager said, pointing in Faith's direction. He watched
the reactions of the other two women closely, checking to see if they knew Faith was the person who'd won
the bid at the auction, but neither gave anything away.
Interesting. Faith obviously hadn't told them, and the
company grapevine hadn't caught up with the news
yet. Most of the staff from the head office had been at
the auction the other night, but even if they'd managed
to get a good look at Faith in the dim light, it seemed
none had recognized her.

He glanced over at her now. She had a bright yellow Hawke's Blooms apron covering the halter top he
could see peeking out from underneath. Her curly red
hair was caught up in a clip on the top of her head. She
looked up and he paused, waiting to see her reaction.
Her eyes flicked to her manager, then back to him. He
wasn't comfortable with an outright lie to his employees—it was probable that the information would circu-
late around the company at some point, and he didn't
want to be caught in a lie—but that didn't mean he had
to share all the details of their short history.

"Ms. Crawford and I have met before," he said as a
compromise.

The manager's eyes darted between them, looking
for snippets of information, so he cut her off at the pass.
"Do you have an apprentice in this store?"

"Oh, yes. Sharon. But she's not in until lunchtime
on Mondays."

He nodded and took off his sport coat. Instead of his

usual work attire of a business suit, today he'd worn a polo shirt and casual trousers—closer to the clothes the staff in-store wore. "Before she gets here, I'll do the sweeping and answering the phone. Wherever you need an extra pair of hands."

Unbidden, his gaze tracked to where Faith worked at her bench, and he found that she'd looked up at him at the same time. *Wherever you need an extra pair of hands...* He could still feel his hands in her hair, cupping her cheek, under her chin.

A pink flush crept up Faith's neck to her cheeks, and he knew she was remembering the same thing. He cleared his throat and looked away.

If he was going to make it through the day without letting everyone know he'd kissed his employee, he would have to do better at keeping his thoughts firmly under control.

It had been two hours since Dylan had appeared in the doorway, looking as if he'd just stepped off a photo shoot for a story entitled "What the Suave CEOs Are Wearing This Season." She'd spent those two hours trying to pretend he wasn't in the room, just so she could get her work done.

But every time he swept up the clippings from where she was working, or he handed her a slip of paper with an order that had come in over the phone, she lost the battle and was plunged back into those moments when they'd been in this very spot, at night, alone.

And occasionally, when their eyes met, she thought she saw the same memory lurking in his.

But she couldn't let herself be sidetracked. She needed to impress the businessman, Mr. Hawke, not the red-blooded Dylan who'd kissed her senseless. Men came and went, but this particular man could help her career. It was Mr. Hawke she needed to impress with what she could do.

They'd had a steady stream of orders in person, over the phone and on their website, and she was glad. It gave her an excuse not to talk to Dylan—no, Mr. Hawke— just yet. He'd sat with Courtney earlier and had a cup of coffee, asking her about her job and ideas for the store, and said he'd be doing the same with all the staff members.

The bell above the door dinged, and she looked up, smiling to see one of her favorite customers.

"Hi, Tom," she said, heading for the fridge. "How was your weekend?"

"Not long enough," he said ruefully. "Yours?"

Her eyes flicked to Dylan, who was thumbing through their order book, his dark reddish-brown hair rumpled, his sport coat gone and his tie loosened. His hand hesitated and his chest expanded as if he'd taken a deep breath.

"How about I go with *interesting*," she said, turning back to her customer.

Tom laughed. "Sounds as if there's a story there."

"My life is never dull." She reached into the fridge and drew out the assorted foliage she'd put to the side earlier. "I found some fresh mint at the markets this morning, as well as these cute little branches of crab apples. How does that sound?"

"Like a winner. Emmie loved the daisy and rosemary bouquet last week."

Out of the corner of her eye, she saw Dylan watching the conversation and then moving to her elbow. He put his hand out to Tom. "Hi, I'm Dylan Hawke, CEO of the Hawke's Blooms retail chain."

"Wow, the big boss," Tom said, winking at Faith.

Dylan turned to her. "You bought crab apples and mint yourself for this bouquet?" His tone was mild, but his focus had narrowed in on her like a laser pointer. "This sounds interesting. Can you talk me through the thinking behind your plan?"

Her stomach clenched tight. She'd wanted the attention of the businessman side of him, and now she had it, which was great. But if he thought what she was doing was too bizarre, then she might have lost her chance to win his approval. A second strike against her in a row might be too much to overcome.

All she could do was paste on a smile and do her job.

"Tom comes in each Monday to pick up some flowers for his wife," she said, her gaze on the work her hands were doing. "Emmie is blind, so I always put some thought into combinations that she can enjoy."

"You picked up the mint on your way in?" Dylan asked, his tone not giving anything away.

She nodded. "Monday mornings I leave home a bit earlier and drop in at the flower markets, looking for some inspiration. We usually go outside the standard range of flowers that the store stocks to get the right elements for Emmie's bouquet. I like something fragrant—" she picked up the mint "—and something tactile—" she pointed to the crab apple branch "—along with the usual assortment of flowers."

She cast a glance at the buckets bursting with bright blooms around them, looking for inspiration. *Something white, perhaps?*

Dylan raised an eyebrow and she hesitated. Maybe

he didn't like florists going this far off the beaten track? Her manager hadn't been particularly supportive and always complained if she tried to get reimbursement for the extras from petty cash, but Faith loved the challenge of something new each week, and the fact that Tom wanted to do this for his wife always melted her heart. Were there other men like Tom in the world? Men who were so dedicated to bringing a smile to the faces of the women they loved that they'd go the extra mile every single week? That sort of constancy was a beautiful thing to be a part of.

Perhaps Dylan Hawke didn't see the situation the same way. She held a sprig of mint out to him. "If that's okay, Mr. Hawke?"

"More than okay," he said, taking the mint and lifting it to his nose. "I think it's a great example of customer service."

Dylan's approving gaze rested on her, and her shoulders relaxed as relief flowed through her veins. But she was also aware that his approval was having more of an effect than it should...

As she worked, he blended into the background, but she felt his eyes on her the entire time she was making the crab apple, mint and white carnation arrangement. After Tom left, pleased with the results, Dylan cornered her near the cash register.

"Please tell me you get reimbursed for those extras you purchase on Monday mornings," he said, his voice low.

She maintained a poker face. Getting her manager into trouble was a quick route to reduced hours, but she couldn't lie, either. He could check the store's accounting books and find that she hadn't asked for reimbursement after the first few times, not since Mary had finally put her foot down and said she should use stock that was already in the store. And being caught in a lie by the CEO would be even less healthy for her career than not covering for her immediate manager.

"Sure, but sometimes I forget to hand the receipts in," she said in what she hoped was a casual, believable tone.

"I see," he said, and she had a feeling he really did see.

"I don't mind paying for those extras," she said quickly. "I know I should only use what we have in stock, but I get such a kick out of Tom's expression when he knows he's taking home something Emmie will love. It's like a present I can give them."

"It's your job, Faith. You shouldn't have to pay money to do your job." He crossed his arms over his chest. "Do you have the receipt from this morning?"

She picked up her handbag from under the counter and dug around until she found the crumpled bit of paper. "Here," she said, passing it to him.

Their hands brushed, and she couldn't help the slight gasp that escaped at the contact. Tingles radiated from the place they'd touched, and she yearned to reach out and touch him again. On his hand, or his forearm. Or— she looked up to his face—the cheek she'd stroked with her fingertips when they'd kissed. His eyes darkened.

"Faith," he said, his voice a rasp, "we can't."

"I know," she whispered.

"Then don't—"

"Anything I can help you with, Mr. Hawke?" Mary asked from behind them.

Without missing a beat, Dylan turned, his charming

smile firmly in place, where only seconds before she'd seen something real, something raw.

"I was just chastising your florist about not submitting her receipts for the extras she's been buying for that customer's weekly order." He handed over the receipt. "Ms. Crawford has promised she'll turn them in to you from now on, haven't you, Ms. Crawford?"

"Ah, yes," Faith said, not meeting her manager's eyes. "If you'll excuse me, I have another order to make up."

She slipped away and left them to their discussion, finally able to take a full breath again only when she was immersed in her next arrangement. This day couldn't end soon enough. He was too close here. In her space. Making her want him.

Yet even if he weren't the owner of the company, the last man she could give her heart to was a man whose love life had no stability. She'd heard the rumors about Dylan, that he changed female companions regularly, never seeming to form attachments. She couldn't fall for someone like that—she wouldn't do it to herself. She'd spend the entire time waiting for the moment he'd move on. Better to stay independent and create stability by relying on herself.

She repeated the words to herself over and over while she worked, the whole time trying to ignore her body's awareness of where he was in the room. And resisting the urge to walk over and touch him again.

Three

By late afternoon, Dylan was back in his office, staring out the window at the LA skyline. He had achieved what he'd set out to that morning—a detailed understanding of how the Santa Monica store was operating. He'd managed to sit down with all four employees during the day and chat about their perceptions and ideas, and had seen for himself that the customers were pleased with the floral arrangements being produced.

He'd also discovered one other thing—this fledgling attraction for Faith Crawford wasn't going to fade away. From the moment he arrived, he'd fought to stop his gaze traveling to her. Wherever she was in the store, he could feel her. And occasionally he'd caught her watching him with more than an employee's interest. His heart picked up speed now just thinking about it.

He'd cursed the Fates that he'd had to meet her while she worked for him.

He'd also noticed she was far from an average employee. He'd been taking orders over the phone and in person all day from people who wanted only an arrangement made by Faith. When he'd tried to suggest that another florist serve them, they'd said they'd wait. And he could see why. Her arrangements were spectacular. Why had she made such a conservative design the night she'd tried to impress him? When she was in her element, her work was original and beautiful. They were designs he wanted in the catalog so florists in the other stores were reproducing them.

And the bouquet she'd made using mint and crab apples for the man to give his blind wife had been the most cutting-edge design Dylan had seen in a long time. He liked it when staff went the extra mile for customers, adding that personal touch, and her customers seemed to appreciate it. In fact, just about everything about Faith impressed him. On every level, from the professional to the personal to the physical...

His skin heated.

Shaking his head, he focused back on the professional.

Faith Crawford was someone with a lot of potential. And he wanted to help her reach that potential for the benefit of Hawke's Blooms, and because he really wanted to see Faith get her just rewards. That manager of hers wasn't going to recognize her talents anytime soon, despite the overwhelming evidence under her nose.

He grabbed the phone on his desk and dialed Human Resources. "Anne, do you have a minute?" he asked when the head of HR picked up.

"Sure. What do you need, Dylan?"

"I did an impromptu inspection at the Santa Monica store today."

"Great," she said brightly. "You always bring back good feedback when you do one of those. What do you have for me?"

He dug one hand in his trouser pocket and looked out over the skyline. "One of the florists there has a lot of potential, and I want to do something about that."

"What was her name?"

"Faith Crawford," he said, ensuring his voice was even and didn't give away his reaction to her.

There was a pause, and he could hear fingers tapping on a keyboard as Anne brought up Faith's file. "What do you have in mind?"

"Her work is good. Really good. Original and creative. But in the interest of full disclosure, I should let you know that Faith is the person who bought the dates with me at the trust's bachelor auction."

"I was sorry to miss that night, it sounded like a lot of fun," Anne said, chuckling. "So how do you want to handle this from here?"

He rubbed a hand through his hair. "She's got a lot of potential, and I want to see Hawke's Blooms benefit from that, but I don't want any suggestion that she bought her way into a promotion. How about you get someone else to go out and assess her? Don't tell them that the idea came from me, just let them go to the Santa Monica store without any preconceptions and see her work."

"I'll see what I can arrange and let you know."

"Thanks, Anne."

He hung up the phone, feeling very satisfied with his day's work. The only thing that could make it better was to be the one who actually gave Faith the promotion, so he could be there when she found out about it. But he didn't want her to think this had anything to do with their kiss, so it was better that she had a fair and independent assessment first. He had no doubt that whoever did that would see what he'd seen and recommend her for something more senior.

But still, a good day's work indeed. He smiled, thinking about Faith's reaction. She was going to be over the moon.

As Faith picked out a long-stemmed apricot rose from the bucket at her feet, Mary appeared across the bench from her with a folded piece of paper in her hand.

"I've just had a call from head office about you," she said, her voice accusing.

Faith stopped what she was doing and looked up. "About me personally?"

Besides the initial paperwork when she'd started at the store, she hadn't had any direct dealings with the head office other than the impersonal pay slips. She wiped her hands on her apron and waited.

Mary planted her hands on her hips. "Have you been talking to the head office without my knowledge?"

"Of course not," Faith said, and then realized she'd been talking to Dylan on the weekend without her manager knowing. And would be talking to him again about their next two dates. But he had her phone number—he wouldn't be contacting her via her manager.

Hands still on her hips, Mary lifted her chin as she spoke. "It was Anne in Human Resources. They're offering you a promotion."

Faith's breath caught. *Hang on...*

"A promotion?" she repeated, trying to make sense of it.

"To the head office." Mary thrust the piece of paper at her. "They emailed the details."

Faith took the paper but didn't want to open it in front of the entire store. "I'll be back in a few minutes," she said and went out the back door to the lane. Then she opened the folded email printout.

It was a formal letter of promotion to the head office. To a desk job. She scanned the list of duties and found they were all things that didn't involve customers. Or flowers.

Frustration started simmering in her belly. She'd spent most of her life being told what would happen to her. Announcements would come that she'd be moving to another family member's house the next week, that she'd have to change schools, that her father would be visiting and taking her to a theme park, that he would be returning her to yet another relative afterward. The best thing about being an adult was that she was in charge of her own life.

So getting notice out of the blue saying she was being moved to a desk job that she hadn't applied for and certainly didn't want was particularly unwelcome.

She was ambitious, yes, but not for just any promotion. She had a very clear vision of what she wanted in her career, and this job—being stuck in a boring office, away from customers and the daily joy of working with flowers—wasn't it.

Besides, was this really out of the blue?

She'd kissed the CEO, and in less than a week he'd come to the store for a full-day inspection—something the others said he used to do, but hadn't done since she'd been working there. And now a promotion.

What was Dylan Hawke really up to?

The thought made her uneasy, so she went back through the door and told Mary that she was declining the offer.

Dylan drove into the parking lot of the Santa Monica store for the third time in a week, still not sure what to make of the call he'd had from Anne telling him Faith had turned down the promotion. With all her ambition, he'd expected her to leap at the opportunity. So, surprised and intrigued, he'd jumped into his car to talk to her face-to-face.

As he walked through the door, Mary dropped what she was doing and headed for him, her face covered in a fawning smile. Faith wasn't in sight, and he was more disappointed than he should have been at not seeing an employee.

Then she walked in from the cold room, carrying a bucket full of flowers. She was wearing black biker boots that almost reached her knees and a bright purple dress that peeked out around the yellow Hawke's Blooms apron. Her wild hair was caught up on top of her head and sprang out in all directions. He only barely resisted a smile—this woman was a force of nature.

Her step faltered when she saw him.

"Mr. Hawke!" Mary said when she reached him, darting suspicious glances at Faith. "Twice in one week. We're honored."

He paused before answering. He hadn't planned what he should say here—how had the offer of the promotion gone down at the store level? Should he mention it now, or play it cool for the moment? He glanced across at her as she pulled stems one by one from the bucket. His gut was telling him not to mention it until he'd at least spoken to Faith.

He smiled at Mary. "I just have a few follow-up questions from the other day."

"Well, I'm at your service," she said, untying the apron strings at her back. "Would you like to talk here, or perhaps at the café next door?"

"Actually, I'd like to talk to Faith if she has a few minutes."

Faith's hands stilled and her face grew pale. He was torn between wanting to reassure her and wanting to demand an explanation. Instead, he turned an expectant expression to Mary.

"Of course, Mr. Hawke. If that's what you want." But her face was sour. She really didn't like Faith getting more attention than her.

"Excellent." He smiled and rocked back on his heels. "You mentioned a café next door?"

Mary's mouth opened and closed again. "Er, yes. Courtney can finish that order. Faith. Can you come and talk to Mr. Hawke, please?"

"Certainly," Faith said, wiping her hands on her apron and removing it. The entire time, she kept her gaze down.

"Thank you," he said to Mary, and then opened the door for Faith and followed her out onto the pavement.

"Have I just made things difficult for you in there?" he asked.

She lifted her chin. "Nothing I can't deal with."

He was beginning to see how true that was. Faith Crawford was most definitely her own woman. From bidding on the CEO of her company at a charity auction to get his attention for her work, to turning down a promotion most of his staff would jump at and not bowing to the head office... The more he got to know this woman, the more he liked her.

They found a secluded booth at the café and ordered coffees.

"I heard you were offered a promotion." He leaned back and rested his arm along the top of the padded vinyl booth. "You turned it down."

The corners of her mouth twitched. "You *heard* I was offered the job? Are you sure you don't mean you *arranged* for me to be offered the job?"

He grinned. The fact that she spoke her mind was a very attractive feature. "Okay, I might have had a hand in it. After watching you in the store for a day, I realized your potential was being underutilized, and I implemented a plan to rectify that."

"Is that all it was?" She arched an eyebrow and waited.

"You think it's about more?" His gaze dropped to her mouth, and his pulse picked up speed. "You think you were being promoted because I'd kissed you?"

"Maybe it wasn't that straightforward, but we kissed, and suddenly the store has an all-day inspection and I get offered a job in the head office. Tell me that's not a coincidence." Her gaze didn't waver, challenging him to be honest.

"It's not a coincidence, but it's not direct cause and effect, either—there were steps in between. When you talked about your store and your designs not being submitted for the catalog, it made me wonder what was going on here, and I came to check it out. That's when I realized your potential."

She tapped her nails on the table, but the rest of her barely moved. "So it wasn't payback of some kind? Or a way to assuage your guilt about kissing an employee?"

"I don't work that way." He tried not to be insulted, given that she didn't know him very well, but it was good at least to have her concerns addressed now, before they had their other two dates. "I passed your name to HR with a suggestion that they check you out. They arranged a couple of people to come in as customers and ask for you so they could see your skills and how you interact with customers, and then one of the staff from the head office dropped in to see Mary and watched you while she was there. Her name was Alison—she chatted to you for a while on your break, apparently. You earned this completely on your own merits."

She looked into his eyes for a long moment and then nodded. "I believe you."

Their coffees arrived, and she tipped a packet of sugar into her cappuccino. He watched her hands as they worked—as efficient and graceful with a sugar packet as they were with flowers. What would they be like on his body? Fluttering over his neck and collarbone. Trailing a path down his chest, his abdomen.

He tore his gaze away and stirred cream into his own coffee. "Did you turn the job down because you thought you hadn't earned it?"

That fitted the emerging profile of this woman, but she shook her head.

"I don't want a desk job."

"But you want your career to go places," he pointed out.

"The places I want to go are filled with flowers and customers."

He took a sip of his coffee and replaced the cup on its saucer, giving himself a moment to think the situation through. "I honestly thought you'd want this job."

She frowned, her head tilted to the side. "If you'd wanted to do something nice for me, instead of doing something you thought I'd like, you could have done what I asked for in the first place."

"Put one of your designs in the catalog of standard arrangements." It seemed obvious now, but hindsight was twenty-twenty.

"Bingo." She lifted her coffee cup to her lips, smiling over the rim, her dimples peeking out.

He regarded her as she took a sip and then ran her tongue over her bottom lip to catch a droplet. In her vivid purple dress and with the smattering of pale freckles over her nose, she was the brightest thing in the whole café, as if her own personal beam of sunshine followed her around and shone down on her wherever she was. Yet the arrangement she'd made for him to consider had been as conservative as they came. It was a contradiction he wanted to understand.

He leaned back in the booth and interlaced his fingers on the table. "Why did you show me such a conservative design that night? It's not who you are."

For a brief second, her eyes widened. "Who am I?"

He thought back to the first time he'd met her, near the stage at the auction, to the night he'd kissed her, to the day he'd watched her work in his store. "You're crab apple, carnation and mint bouquets. You're mixing wild colors with flair that's uncommon. You're edgy and fresh." And so much more. "Why didn't you show me any of that?"

Her eyes lit from within. "I didn't think you'd want to see that. I thought you'd prefer more conservative designs, like the ones already in the catalog."

"But that's the point." He leaned forward, wanting her to understand this if nothing else. "We already have designs like that. We don't have *your* designs. Hawke's Blooms needs your vision."

An adorable pink flush stole over her face, from her neck up to her cheekbones. "So, you're not mad I turned the job down?"

"Mad? No." He rubbed two fingers across his forehead. "It was my fault—I leapt ahead without talking to you. With any other employee, I would have researched first, found out what they wanted before making a decision."

"So, why didn't you?" she asked, her voice soft.

Good question—one he'd been asking himself. And she deserved the real answer. "To be honest, you've had me off center from the start."

She gave him a rueful smile. "I know how that feels."

He smiled back, and their gazes held for one heartbeat, two. Part of him was glad he wasn't the only one off kilter—that it was the result of some inconvenient mutual chemistry—but another part of him wished it had been more one-sided. That he could justify to himself that reaching across the table for her now would be an unwelcome advance, and reinforce that he had to keep his hands to himself.

What they needed was a new start. He drew in a deep breath and pushed his cup to the side. "How about we forget the promotion and you continue working in this store for now. I know the customers here will be glad to keep you."

"I'd like that," she said with a quick nod.

She glanced in the direction of her store, and a thought suddenly occurred to him. This wouldn't be a new start for her—he already suspected Faith's manager might resent her, and now she'd be heading back into that same environment after turning down a promotion. That could get awkward fast. He'd made a complete mess of this from start to finish.

"You know," he said, thinking on his feet, "another option is to move to a different store. I can think of a few managers who'd welcome someone with your skills and ability to form rapport with customers."

"Thank you, I appreciate the offer but I'm happy here." She turned her wrist over and checked her watch. "Speaking of which, I'd better get back."

He resisted a chuckle. Many of his employees would try to drag out their one-on-one time with him, especially if they'd already spent money on an opportunity to impress him. Not Faith. "You realize you're out with the person in charge of the entire chain of stores, right? You're not playing hooky."

She shook her head, unmoved by his reasoning. "We have a lot of orders to fill before I clock off."

"What time do you finish today?" he asked, an idea forming in his head as he said the words.

"Three o'clock."

"That's in two hours. How about I pick you up then and we go on our second date?" Since she wouldn't let him buy the dates back from her, it was probably better to get them out of the way as soon as was practical.

"Sure," she said as she stood. "But do me a favor and

don't come back to the store. It won't help my popularity in there."

It was a reasonable point. He liked that she thought that way. She could have used the opportunity to gain points against her manager, perhaps engage in a game of one-upmanship, but he'd come to see that wasn't the way Faith operated.

He pushed a paper napkin across the table and took a pen from the inside pocket of his jacket. "Give me your address and I'll drop by your place at about three-thirty."

She leaned over and wrote her address on the napkin before pushing it back to him and leaving.

He watched her walk out, taking in the sway of her hips as she moved, and then looked down at the napkin in his hand. After her address, she'd written four words. *I like the beach.*

A grin spread across his face. He was already looking forward to this afternoon way too much.

Four

By three-twenty, Faith was waiting at her front door. She wanted to be ready to dash down the front steps when Dylan arrived because the last thing she needed was him knocking on her door. Being alone with him would lead to the possibility of her dragging him inside and repeating that kiss. And knowing there was a bed in the next room couldn't be good in that situation...

The beach suggestion had come from the same train of thought—she knew they had to go somewhere public. Though she'd also wanted it to be informal so she had a chance to question him casually and get more insight into what he was looking for with the catalog, to make her next attempt more likely to succeed. She had high hopes of getting the information while sitting next to him on the sand and not having to look him in the eye.

At three twenty-seven, his Porsche convertible drew

up, and she pulled her front door shut behind her, hiked her beach bag higher on her shoulder and jogged down the concrete stairs to the road. She loved the idea of owning a convertible, of having the wind in her hair as she drove, but the sheer expense of the model Dylan owned simply served to reinforce the differences between them.

"Have you got your swimsuit in that bag?" he asked as she slid into the passenger seat.

Was he kidding? Being half-naked in his presence could be disastrous. And seeing him in board shorts, his bare chest dripping with water…? Yeah, that was only going to lead to trouble. Whether they'd be in public or not, her willpower had its limits.

Though, she thought as she glanced over and took in the red-and-white-striped T-shirt that bunched around his biceps and stretched across his shoulders, perhaps his covered chest wasn't going to be much easier to cope with.

She faced the windshield and shrugged. "I was thinking more along the lines of sitting on a towel with the sand between my toes."

"That sounds safer," he said as he pulled away from the curb.

So he was still having trouble, too. Interesting. They talked about the weather and made other small talk until he found a park and they stepped out into the sunshine.

He looked down at her Hawaiian print bag. "Did you bring a towel, or should I get the picnic blanket?"

"You keep a picnic blanket in your car?" She couldn't help the smile—it seemed such a sweet thing for a playboy like Dylan to do. Although maybe he used it to seduce women under the stars…? Her smile faded.

"My brother Liam and I took his daughters, Bonnie and Meg, for a picnic a couple of weeks ago. The blanket is still in the back."

Her smile returned. She'd read the newspaper stories about Liam Hawke's engagement to Princess Jensine of Larsland—everybody had—and seen the photos of Liam's tiny baby, Bonnie, and Jenna's daughter, Meg, who was only a few months older than Bonnie. She just hadn't quite imagined Dylan actually interacting with the little girls. Which was probably unfair—by all accounts, the three brothers were close.

She hitched the bag over her shoulder. "No, I have a towel."

He nodded and set the keyless lock. They found a spot on the white sand to spread out her towel. The beach was fairly quiet, so there was no one else close enough to hear them, but there were still people around—people swimming in the sparkling blue Pacific, a couple of guys throwing a Frisbee back and forth, couples on towels farther away, occasional joggers.

Dylan slipped off his shoes and rolled up his chinos before sitting at the other end of the towel, leaving plenty of space between them. She wasn't facing him, which was supposed to be safe, yet her attention seemed to be located on his bare ankles, which she could see out of the corner of her eye. Why had she never noticed how attractive men's ankles were before? Or was it something special about this man's?

She swallowed hard and brought her focus back to her career. These dates were for her career.

"Mr. Hawke, you—"

"Dylan," he said, interrupting her. "'Dylan' is fine when we're alone."

"Are you sure?" A light breeze toyed with the hair that had escaped her clip, so she tucked it behind her ear. "If we become personal, won't we risk...?" She didn't know how to end that sentence, so she left it hanging.

He pulled his legs up and rested his forearms on his bent knees. "I hardly think using my first name will lead to me leaping on top of you here on the towel. Besides, 'Mr. Hawke' is too formal for the beach."

As soon as he'd said the words *me leaping on top of you*, she had trouble drawing breath. For a long moment, she couldn't get past the image of him above her, feeling his weight pushing her into the sand. She bit down on her bottom lip, hard. It seemed that he was right—using his first name wasn't the problem since she hadn't said it yet.

"Okay. Dylan." She gathered a handful of towel and the sand beneath it and gripped tight, as if she could draw strength from the beach itself. "You mentioned that the catalog didn't have anything like the designs you saw me do when you were at the store."

"That's true," he said, his voice deep and smooth. "We don't have anything like them."

She twisted around a little so she could see his eyes, but more importantly, so he could see hers and know she was serious about this. "Will you give me another chance to submit a design? One that's more...*me*?"

A slow smile spread across his face, and he nodded once. "I was hoping you'd still want to submit. Hawke's Blooms needs at least one Faith Crawford design between the covers of its catalog."

"Thank you," she said, excitement building inside. She'd been pretty sure he'd be open to looking at another arrangement, but even so, she hadn't wanted to count her chickens before they hatched. This time she'd blow his socks off.

"But," he said, "explain this to me, because I still don't understand. You're ambitious enough to use your savings to get access to me, yet you don't want a promotion." His expression was curious. It didn't feel as if the man who'd offered her the promotion was asking this time—it was more like a friend asking.

She looked out over the blue Pacific Ocean, the sound of the waves crashing on the shore lulling her into feeling at ease. "I like working with flowers. Flowers make people happy. They make *me* happy."

"So, what do you want out of your career, Faith?" His voice was soft near her ear, but she didn't turn, just watched the rhythmic pounding of the waves.

"I want to keep growing as a florist, to move on to new experiences and places, to be doing bigger and better arrangements all the time." She risked a glance at him, wondering if she dared tell him the size of her dreams. She'd never told a soul—had always been scared people would laugh at her.

"There's more, isn't there?" he asked, his gaze encouraging.

There was something about him looking at her like that. He could ask her anything and she'd probably tell him. She nodded. "One day, my arrangements will grace important places, large-scale events—they'll reach hundreds, maybe hundreds of thousands of people and bring them happiness."

One side of his mouth pulled into a lopsided grin. She looked back at the waves crashing on the shore and the children building sand castles. "You probably think that's silly."

From her peripheral vision she saw him reach out as if to run a hand down her arm, but he let it drop a moment before he touched her. She felt his gaze, however, remain trained on her. "I think it's amazing."

"You're not teasing?" she asked, turning to him, hardly daring to breathe. She wanted so badly for him to be telling the truth.

"I've heard a lot of reasons that people have chosen floristry before, and most of them were really good. But I think yours is my favorite." His voice was soft, intimate. Despite sharing the beach with countless other people, it was as if they were completely alone on the towel. From a distance, they might look like any couple together for an afternoon, and the idea was exhilarating.

"Thank you," she whispered.

There was silence for a long moment when all she could hear was her own breath. Then Dylan rubbed a hand down his face and sat a little straighter. "So is there a destination for your life's plan? Somewhere in particular you're headed?"

She picked up a handful of sand and let it fall through her fingers. "Not really." In fact, the idea of reaching a destination made her uneasy. "I guess I'm more comfortable staying on the move."

"Hmm… There's more to that answer, isn't there?"

She looked up, startled that he'd seen through her. Again. Then she nodded. "I've moved so much in my life, changing everything each time, that I've become something of a rolling stone."

"That makes me wonder, Faith Sixty-Three." He raised an eyebrow. "Are you moving all the time because you want to, or are you worried that if you stop, you'll sink?"

She laughed softly. "That's ridiculous. I move because I want to. I like my life this way."

But was that true? Something inside her tensed at the thought. Perhaps she was more comfortable choosing to move on, being a step ahead of anyone who might make her leave. That little girl who was always waiting for the axe to fall was still inside her. A cold shiver ran down her spine. Honestly, she was only comfortable if she decided to move on her own terms—jumping before she was pushed. If she jumped, she was in control of the situation, so since she'd become an adult, she'd been jumping from place to place. So far she'd avoided being pushed away.

Not that she'd ever admit that to Dylan Hawke—she'd pretty much reached her limit on sharing. Yet this was still the most open she'd been with anyone, and it didn't scare her the way it usually did. Why was that, exactly?

She took in his strong profile, his dark hair that was moving in the gentle breeze, the day-old stubble that covered his jaw. She felt safe with him.

"You know," she said, feeling this was something that he *should* know. "I haven't told anyone this before. About being a rolling stone."

His green eyes softened. "Thank you for sharing it with me." His forehead crumpled into lines and he swallowed. "And it seems only fair that I repay your honesty in kind."

"Yes?" she said and held her breath.

"The night we met, you asked if I'd ever had a dream of my own." His voice was stilted, as if he hadn't put these thoughts into words before. "I didn't answer you, but the truth is, no. The only dreams I can remember having are the dreams I have in common with my family for our business." His gaze was piercing, looking deep within her. "Are you shocked?"

She swallowed hard to get her voice to work. "I'm honored you shared that with me."

"And if we're being completely honest," he said, his chest rising and falling faster than it had only minutes ago, "I have to tell you that I've never wanted to kiss a woman more than I do in this moment. But I can't let myself."

She squeezed her eyes shut against the truth, but he deserved to know he wasn't alone. Deliberately she opened her eyes again and met his gaze. "I've never wanted to kiss a man this much, either. Ever since the moment our lips first touched, I've been thinking about doing it again."

He groaned and let his head fall into his hands. "I'm not sure if I prefer knowing that, or if it was easier not thinking you felt the same."

She sighed, understanding how he felt. "You're not the only one feeling the chemistry. But I don't want to act on it, either."

Without looking up, he reached across the towel and intertwined their hands. The slide of his skin against her fingers made her breath hitch. Holding his hand was such a poor substitute for what she really wanted, but it would have to be enough.

Dylan refused to look down at where his fingers were wrapped around Faith's. If he acknowledged it, he'd have to break the contact.

What were they doing at the beach, anyway? She'd been clear from the start that she'd bought the time with him to help her career. Since this was their second date, he should be doing something for her career now.

Reaching a decision, he released her hand and jumped to his feet. "Come on. There's somewhere I want to take you."

She looked up at him warily. "Where?"

Her meaning hit him—he'd said he wanted to kiss her and then held her hand. It was natural she would think that next he might push the boundaries further. "It's job-related, I promise."

He held out his hand again, but this time it was to help her up. She took it and he pulled her up to stand in front of him. She was so close he could feel her body heat. She smelled of flowers, which was no surprise given that she'd been handling them all day, but also of strawberries. His gaze dropped to her lips, which had a slick of red gloss coating them. She was wearing strawberry lip gloss. His pulse spiked, imagining the flavor when he kissed her.

Abruptly she released his hand and stepped back. "You said we were going somewhere job-related?"

He picked up the towel and shook it with more force than was necessary before answering. "I want you to see the Hawke's Blooms flower farm."

Her eyes lit with the same passion she'd shown when she talked about her future. "I'd love that!"

As they walked back to the car, then drove out of LA to San Juan Capistrano, where the farm was located, she peppered him with questions about the farm's capacity and stock.

"Have you always had it out here?" she asked once they drew close.

He nodded. "We moved here when I was a kid. My

parents had been farmers, so when they came out to California, they tried their hand at growing flowers. They wanted something that would give their three sons opportunities and thought this was the way to do it."

"From your success, I'd say they were right." Her voice held no trace of flattery. It was an honest observation, and it had more weight for it.

"Yeah," he said, allowing satisfaction about the business he'd built with his family to fill his chest. He owed his parents more than he could ever repay. Not that they wanted anything other than to see their sons happy and thriving, but he'd find a way to show them how grateful he was one day.

"So, whose idea was it to sell the flowers as well as grow them?" Faith asked.

"We had a roadside stall when we started." He smiled at the memory. "Dad would sell to the flower markets, but every weekend, Adam and I would go with Mom and sell whatever we had left."

"What about your other brother?"

He chuckled. "Liam prefers plants to people, so he'd stay home with Dad. And it's a good thing he did—it was Liam's breakthroughs with new flowers that put us on the map."

"I was really impressed with his Midnight Lily. The customers have been loving it."

"It's a great flower," Dylan said, feeling a surge of pride. The new blue lily had been launched a couple of months earlier and had been selling like crazy ever since.

She lifted one foot up, rested it on the seat and wrapped an arm around her knee. "So you and your other brother were stuck selling by the roadside?"

"There were three of us there, but the sales came down to our mom and me. Adam always saw himself in a more...managerial role." Adam had set himself up behind the stall in what Dylan and his mother had called "Adam's office."

Out of the corner of his eye, he saw her cock her head to the side. "How much management does a roadside stall need?"

"Even though I teased him about trying to get out of work, he probably worked harder than any of us. He made posters and put them on stakes by the road, experimented with price points and kept a chart of the sales so he could work out what to stock. During the week, he was always doing something to our stall, too. Either painting it a different color to see if that attracted more people, or constructing new benches for the flower buckets from wood he salvaged."

"Sounds like quite the entrepreneur." There was a smile in her voice.

"He is," Dylan said with no small measure of affection. "That's why Liam and I let Adam run the overall company. Liam's happier with his plants, anyway."

"And you?" Her voice grew soft. "What do you prefer?"

He shrugged one shoulder. "I'm more of a people person. I like the buzz of retail. The colors of it. I like talking to staff and customers—interacting."

"I can see that about you," she said, her tone pensive.

"When we opened our first store, my mother and I staffed it." They'd been amazing times, full of energy and excitement. "Liam and Dad were back home growing the plants and drawing scientific charts of plant breeding, and Adam was in his room, making spreadsheets and plans. My job was more fun."

"To you. But I'll bet to them, your job sounded like hell."

He grinned. "Actually, yes. Being in a room full of people has been known to make them both yearn for their charts and spreadsheets."

He pulled into the drive to Liam's place and went through security. It had been tightened now that Liam was engaged to a princess, and Dylan was glad for the little girls' sakes.

"This looks more like a private residence," Faith said warily.

"Liam still lives on-site. It's the same house we grew up in, actually, though he's had so much work done to it, you'd never know."

"But there was a specific farm entrance before this driveway," she said, pointing.

"If I came all the way out here and didn't tell him, he'd kill me. Well," he amended as he thought about what he'd said, "he probably wouldn't notice, but his fiancée definitely would kill me. We'll only be there a minute or two—just passing through."

"Hang on—" she put her hands on the dashboard as if she could slow their approach "—you're taking me to meet his fiancée?"

"If that's okay with you," Dylan said, glancing over at her. He hadn't thought she might be uncomfortable—Faith always seemed as if she was ready for any adventure life threw at her.

Her mouth opened and closed again before she replied. "She's a princess!"

"As it turns out, yes." He wanted to smile at the awe

in her voice, but he restrained himself. He'd known Jenna before he'd found out she was a princess, so he hadn't had a chance to be overwhelmed by her royal status. However, he understood that this was probably an intimidating situation for Faith to be thrown into with no warning. He had confidence that she'd cope—he couldn't imagine anything overwhelming Faith for long.

Her expression was still uncertain as he pulled up in front of the house. But he wasn't driving out here without at least saying hello to little Bonnie and Meg.

He walked around to open her door. "Are you coming?"

"Are there protocols about what I should say?" she asked as she climbed out.

He shrugged one shoulder casually. "I'd go with complimenting their daughters and being particularly nice to me."

"You?"

"What can I say? The princess is fond of me."

She narrowed her eyes at him as she realized he was teasing, but she'd lost the slightly awed look, which was what he'd been aiming for.

Jenna met them at the door, twelve-month-old Meg on her hip. "Dylan," she said in her lilting Scandinavian accent, "what a nice surprise."

He kissed her cheek, took Meg from her and held her up in the air until he elicited a giggle, and then kissed her cheek as well. "I'm not here long. We're on our way down to see Liam and stopped by to say hello first."

"Liam's in his office, working on his latest project. In the meantime," she said, taking Meg back, "why don't you introduce me to your friend?"

"Jenna, this is Faith. She's a florist at our Santa Monica store." He didn't need to emphasize the point. Jenna knew as well as any of them that he couldn't get involved with one of their florists. "Faith, this is my future sister-in-law, Jenna."

Jenna held out her hand. To Faith's credit, she hesitated only a moment before accepting it. "Lovely to meet you," Faith said.

Jenna smiled, and he could see her brain working overtime, trying to work out if there was something going on between them. She was far too insightful. "Would you like a drink before you set out?"

Faith shook her head, and he wanted to get moving and focused on work again before Jenna could corner him with awkward questions. "We're fine."

"Do you mind if we come with you? Bonnie is still napping, and our housekeeper can keep an ear out for her. I haven't been outside the house all day, and I'd like Meg to get some fresh air and see something other than me."

"That would be great." And it would keep him on his best behavior. None of those intimate moments they'd accidentally had at the beach.

Five minutes later, they were walking out the back door.

"It's huge," Faith said, looking out across the fields of brightly colored blooms. "Do you use them all?"

"The main purpose is to stock our own shops," he said as he opened the small gate that marked the edge of Liam's yard, "but we sell the excess to other stores at the flower markets."

They followed a paved path to a building off to the side—Liam's pride and joy. The Hawke's Blooms research facility.

When they went through the sliding doors, Jenna lifted Meg from the stroller and carried her in her arms, and Dylan spoke to a woman at the front desk. "Can you let Liam know that I'm here to see him, please?"

She put a call through, and then looked back to him. "He's on his way down."

Dylan dug his hands into his pockets and glanced over at Faith as she made baby talk with Meg. He had another plan in mind to help her career, and this time he'd be sure to take it slow and check that she was on board first. But despite his caution, he had a very good feeling about this particular plan. And that made him happier than he should have been comfortable with.

Five

Faith was aware that Princess Jensine of Larsland was studying her, and she had to resist squirming. It seemed almost surreal that a small-town girl who'd spent her entire childhood being shunted from one relative to another should find herself face-to-face with a member of royalty.

"You look familiar," Jenna eventually said. "Have we met before?"

Dylan cleared his throat. "You might have seen her at the auction," he admitted. "Faith had the winning bid on a date with me."

Jenna's eyes widened. "This is a date? You brought a *date* to a research lab?"

"It's not like that," Faith said quickly. "Besides, even if we wanted to, we couldn't have a real date because of company policy."

She covered her mouth with two fingers. Had she just admitted she would have liked to date Dylan if the situation had been different? No one else seemed to have taken it that way. But she needed to stay on her guard because, deep down, there wasn't much in the world she would want more than for Dylan to kiss her again, and she didn't want anyone—especially Dylan—guessing that.

"Ah, yes," Jenna said. One corner of her mouth turned up. "That old fraternization policy. I know it well."

Liam pushed through the door into the waiting room and beamed when he saw his fiancée. He took Meg from her, swung her around onto his hip and kissed Jenna softly. "Hi," he said.

"Hi, yourself," she said back and kissed him again.

Dylan coughed loudly. "Hey, other people present."

Liam looked up but pulled Jenna under his arm. It was only then that he seemed to register there was a stranger in the room. He released Jenna and stuck out a hand. "I'm Liam Hawke, since it seems my brother isn't going to introduce us."

"I'm Faith Crawford," she said, straightening her spine as she shook his hand. "I work for you."

"You do?" Liam asked, his head cocked to the side.

Dylan took a step closer to her elbow. She could feel his body heat. "Faith is a florist at the Santa Monica store."

"Okay, good to meet you," Liam said.

Jenna looked up at her man, her eyes full of mischief. "Faith won Dylan at the auction."

Dylan held up a hand. "She didn't win me." His gaze darted to Faith before turning back to his brother. "She had the winning bid on some *time* with me."

"Three dates," Jenna supplied helpfully.

"They're not dates, just time," Dylan clarified. "In fact, this is some of that time now. Faith has a lot of creativity in her designs, and we've identified her as someone with potential. So I wanted to show her around the building."

"Sure," Liam said casually, holding Dylan's gaze. "The public areas?"

"Up to you," Dylan said just as casually.

Faith looked from one to the other, trying to work out what they were really saying. It was obvious something else was being discussed, but what?

"You'll vouch for her discretion?" Liam asked.

Dylan nodded. "I'm willing to bet on it."

"Then you're about to." Liam looked up at Faith and smiled. "Welcome to my world. Let me show you around."

It seemed she'd passed some kind of test on Dylan's say-so, but she had no idea what it had been for. They spent the next twenty minutes walking through the research rooms, and Faith was enthralled with all the projects they had going on. Crossbreeding for stronger scent or bigger flowers, rooms full of benches with lines of pots containing grafted plants. Excitement buzzed through her blood at seeing the powerhouse behind the business.

Then they reached a locked door. Liam caught her gaze. "Past this door is my personal project. Very few people know what's in here, and even fewer have seen it. If we go inside, I need your word that you won't leak the information."

"You have my word," she said without hesitation.

Liam looked to Dylan, who nodded, and opened the door.

The room was like many of the others in that it had

benches with rows of pots, each containing plants at different stages of growth. But the flower that many of the pots had was like nothing in the other rooms. Or anything she'd seen before. Faith knew flowers. She knew the conditions they preferred and their shelf lives. She knew which flowers were in season at any given time in which area of the country. She knew what colors each variety came in. But she'd never seen anything like the flower in those pots.

She stepped closer. It was an iris, but it was a rich red. She wanted to touch it but was unsure, so she looked up at Liam. "May I?"

He nodded his permission. With her fingertip, she touched the petal of one of the more advanced flowers. "It's beautiful," she breathed.

"Thank you," Liam said.

Dylan moved to her elbow. "How do you think it will go with the customers?"

She lifted her head and found his deep green gaze. "I think we'll be stampeded." She meant it. There was nothing like this flower on the market, and it was stunning. Already she could imagine how perfect it would look in a bridal bouquet or dramatic table decoration. Its crimson bloom would be the center of attention.

"Tell me, Faith," Dylan said, crossing his arms over his broad chest, "what would you put with it to showcase it?"

"The design would need to be simple. It's so beautiful, it doesn't need much adornment. Perhaps something with soft white petals, like old-fashioned roses. Maybe a touch of silver foliage."

Dylan gave her an indulgent smile and dug his hands in his pockets. "Do you want a chance to try?"

"Make an arrangement with one of these?" she asked, her heart racing with excitement. "Now?"

Dylan lifted an eyebrow at Liam, who nodded. "Yep, now. We'll wait here while you go out to the farm. Collect whatever you want. Then come back and make us an arrangement."

Chest almost bursting, Faith nodded and threaded her way back to the door.

As soon as Faith was gone, Dylan looked to his brother. "Thanks."

"If you believe in her, then that's enough for me. But," he said, his voice becoming serious, "do you know what you're doing? She's an employee."

Dylan arched an eyebrow. "That didn't stop the two of you."

"It did for a little while," Jenna said, grinning up at Liam.

Liam returned the grin and then said, "It was different for us. Jenna was working for me personally, not the company."

Dylan leaned back on the bench. He'd had enough of this topic of conversation. The last thing he needed was for them to discover he'd crossed the line in a spectacular fashion on the very first night by kissing her.

He shook his head once. "There's nothing to worry about. I'm just being a good boss and giving opportunities to someone with potential."

"Sure you are," Jenna said and winked.

"How are Bonnie and Meg?" Dylan asked, hoping the new topic would sidetrack them both for the short while it took Faith to return.

"They're just perfect," Jenna said, a dreamy look of contentment on her face.

Dylan asked Jenna a few more questions about the girls and suggested Liam find some floral tools for Faith to keep them occupied. Finally there was a call from the front desk, and Liam told them to let Faith back through.

She entered with her arms full of flowers, her bright red hair falling from the clip she'd used to try to tame her curls. Dylan jumped up to help, taking some of the blooms and spreading them across a vacant bench.

"Here, you might need these," he said, passing her the box of tools. As their fingers brushed, he felt a tingle of electricity shoot up his arm, but he did his best to ignore it. This was a professional situation, and even if it weren't, she was still an employee, as Liam had just pointed out.

After recapturing her hair in the clip, Faith began to work with the flowers, trimming the thorns and leaves from the white roses, using floral wire on the blush-pink gerbera daisies and arranging them together. Liam cut three of his red irises and handed them to her.

The expression in Faith's eyes, of awe and honor, made Dylan's heart swell in his chest. Her passion was contagious—he felt alive, as if every cell in his body was waking up.

"Thank you," she said as she took the flowers from Liam, her voice breathless. Then she wove the other flowers around them, creating a design that was elegant in its simplicity, yet stunning.

When she was finished, she held the bouquet out to Dylan. He smiled as he took it and then showed it to Jenna and Liam.

"What do you think?" he asked his brother and soon-to-be sister-in-law. They knew what he was really asking—they'd begun talks already about launching the new flower on the market with an event, in the same way they'd launched the Midnight Lily a few months ago. Jenna had been the brains behind that and it had been a roaring success. They'd already started on preliminary plans for the second launch, and Jenna had asked him to supply a florist from his staff to work on it part-time.

Jenna turned to Liam, one eyebrow raised, and he nodded. Then she turned to Faith.

"Faith," she said, her musical voice soft. "What would you say to working part-time with me on the launch of the new iris? I need a florist to handle the arrangements and a few other duties, and we think you'd be perfect."

Faith looked from Jenna to Dylan, eyes wide. Wary about pushing her into a job she didn't want again, he explained further. "If you want to do it, we'll work your hours at the store around this. You could do part-time at each until the launch, then go back to full-time at the store."

"Then I'd love to," she said, her warm brown eyes sparkling, and Dylan felt the satisfaction of a good plan coming together.

Jenna grinned. "Great. I have to take Meg back up to the house, but I'll be in touch about the details."

As they drove away a short while later, Dylan glanced over at Faith. He wanted to make sure this was really what she wanted, especially after he'd botched things the last time he'd tried to help her career.

"Faith, I want you to know that this is totally up to you. If you'd enjoy the work, we'd love to have you on the project. But you can still change your mind, and it won't affect your job at the Santa Monica store."

She gave him a beaming smile. "Honestly, I can't thank you enough. The opportunity of doing large arrangements that will be seen by hundreds of people is a dream come true. And Jenna seems lovely—I think I'll enjoy working with her."

As he stopped at a red light, he glanced over and found Faith looking at him as if he'd hung the moon. His heart clenched tight. He had a bad feeling that, despite everything, he'd do whatever it took to keep that look on her face. The light turned green, and he trained his gaze on the road ahead, shoring up the strength to do the right thing.

One week into her new working life, Faith looked up from the arrangement she was making to find Dylan letting himself in through the door of the secure room where they were keeping the new flower a secret from the world.

As he crossed over to her, she bit down on a smile, unwilling to let it escape. He was earlier than expected, and that made her happier than it should have. Of course, every time she saw him—no, every time she even thought about him—it made her happier than it should. And yet it also made her sadder, since this was one man she shouldn't be thinking about, or daydreaming about, in the first place. Her reactions to him were stronger than they should have been to a boss, and somehow she had to find a way to contain that.

This week she'd been designing arrangements with the new iris for the Hawke's Blooms promotions team to use for posters and media releases after the official launch. To give them enough lead time for their own design work, she'd agreed this would be her first priority. It hadn't been a problem to work quickly—she was bursting with ideas. She'd even suggested they call the new flower the Ruby Iris, and everyone had liked the name. She loved that this flower would permanently have a little piece of her attached to it.

And this afternoon, a panel of the three Hawke brothers and Jenna would choose the two arrangements to send the publicity team from six Faith had made. Her stomach had been filled with butterflies all day.

"Hey, Dylan," she said when he reached her. "I didn't expect you for another hour, when the rest of the panel is coming."

He dug his hands into his trouser pockets. "I had a bit of time on my hands and thought I'd stop by in case you needed any last-minute help."

"You've already been a huge help."

He'd dropped in a couple of times already this week. She'd taken advantage of that time, peppering him with questions about the launch of the Midnight Lily, looking for details that would give her clues about what they'd be looking for this time. Dylan had answered all her questions. She wondered, though, if he was also keeping an eye on her—he'd suggested her for this job, so if she messed it up, it would reflect badly on him.

He made himself busy clearing the bench where she'd been working.

"You don't have to do that," she said, her gaze on the white iris in her hand. "I've left enough time to clean up before the others arrive."

He flashed her a smile. "But I'm here. I may as well do something to help."

She paused, watching him clearing the bench with bold, sweeping movements, fixing things. Making things better for her. Dylan Hawke was a mystery in many ways. She'd worked for several florists and had quite a few bosses over the years, but never had she found any who were happy to roll up their sleeves and get their hands dirty. They usually preferred to have their underlings do the menial tasks.

She popped the flower back into the jug of water and turned so she could see him more clearly. "Why is it that you're the only boss I've ever had who was willing to do this?"

His broad shoulders lifted, then dropped, as if it were no big deal. "Someone's got to do it. Don't see why it shouldn't be me."

"Because your time is more valuable." He opened his mouth, and she could tell there was a denial on his tongue, so she held up a hand. "Seriously, your hourly rate must dwarf mine."

"I might get paid more, but I can't create something like that," he said, gesturing to the design she had almost finished. But there was something else in his eyes, something he wasn't admitting to.

She crossed her arms under her breasts. "Tell me what the rest of that story is."

"Don't you have work to do?" He tried to frown, but the corners of his mouth were twitching.

"Conveniently, someone just cleaned up my work area, so now I have a few extra minutes to play with. And I'd like to spend them hearing the real story behind the line you just tried to feed me."

"A line?" His hand went to his heart. "You wound me."

"Wow," she said, hoisting herself up to sit on the

bench. "You really don't want to talk about this, do you?"

He arched an eyebrow, leaning on the bench only a hand span away. "You really want to know the truth?"

"Yeah, I really do."

Something changed in his face, his demeanor. She couldn't quite put her finger on it, but she knew without a doubt that he was baring himself to her. Trusting her. The knowledge squeezed her heart tight.

"Truth is," he said, his voice deep, "lately I've been thinking about the buzz I used to get, setting up the original stores. Working with customers and having a new challenge were what got me out of bed in the mornings."

"Your job now must have challenges." Being the head of the Hawke's Blooms stores sounded as if it would be pretty much all challenge.

"Sure. But there was a joy back then that doesn't exist now." He ran his hands through his already rumpled hair. "I'm not sure how to explain it exactly, but in the old days, when my family was first starting the company, we never knew what each day would bring. I can glimpse that excitement again when I watch you work."

Dylan looked into Faith's trusting brown eyes. There was another part to the answer that he dared not say aloud—he found that excitement again not only by watching her work but also by being around her. He never knew what she'd say or do next, and it was the most refreshing thing he'd experienced in a long time.

A knock on the door drew him out of his thoughts. He looked up to see his oldest brother, Adam, poking his head around the door. He suddenly realized how close he was standing to Faith and took a step to the side.

As Adam made his way over to them, his face was blank, but after a lifetime of knowing him, Dylan could read the question in his eyes.

"Liam and Jenna aren't here yet," Dylan said by way of a greeting—he'd spoken to Adam a couple of times today already, so a greeting seemed superfluous.

"That's okay," Adam replied. "It gives me a moment to meet our star florist."

Again, Adam's outward facade—politeness this time—didn't match what was going on underneath. He had sensed something and had every intention of getting to the bottom of it. Dylan squared his shoulders.

"Adam, this is Faith Crawford. Faith, this is Adam, the CEO of Hawke's Blooms Enterprises, which is the overall company that encompasses the stores, the farm and the markets."

Faith stuck out her hand, and Dylan didn't think his brother noticed the slight tremble as she shook his hand. "Good to meet you, Mr. Hawke."

"You'll have to call me Adam, or this meeting is going to get very confused with the three Mr. Hawkes together at once."

"Oh, of course." Her eyes darted to Dylan. "Thank you, Adam."

Dylan looked back at the bench and realized Faith wasn't quite finished with the last arrangement—he'd made her lose precious minutes. He swore under his breath.

He turned to his brother. "How about we give Faith a few minutes to make the last touches before the others arrive?"

"Sure. There are a few things I wanted to discuss with you, anyway."

As they headed for the door, Dylan threw Faith a smile over his shoulder, and she mouthed "thank you" back to him. Knowing her, even once she'd added the final couple of flowers, she'd want a few minutes on her own to get her head together without worrying about a new Hawke brother watching her.

Once the door closed behind them, Adam said, "Coffee?"

"Excellent plan."

The staff room was empty, and Dylan headed for the coffee machine, making an espresso each for himself and Adam.

"So, what's the deal with you and Faith?" Adam asked bluntly as he grabbed the sugar jar.

Dylan handed his brother a coffee. "Just helping an employee with potential to advance her career."

Adam sighed, but there was a smile lurking in his eyes. "Dylan, I've known you your entire life. I saw you when you had your first crush, and I drove you to the movies on your first date. Don't try to bullshit me. Your interest in that woman is more than an employer's."

Dylan leaned back on the counter. "It's really that obvious?"

"Maybe not to everyone, but to me? Yes." Adam moved closer and clapped him on the back. "What are you going to do?"

"I've got it under control."

"You call this under control?" Adam rolled his eyes to heaven as if appealing for help. "What happened when you kissed her?"

Caught off guard, Dylan felt as if he'd been sucker punched. "How do you know I kissed her?"

Adam's eyebrows shot up. "I didn't until you just confirmed it."

Realizing his mistake too late, Dylan groaned. "What you have to understand—"

"Oh, good. Stories that start this way are always juicy."

Ignoring him, Dylan started again. "What you have to understand is that we didn't meet at work. Well, not exactly."

Adam sipped his coffee. "You ran into an employee socially?"

"Remember that bachelor auction Jenna organized for our charity? The one you managed to wriggle out of being involved with?" he asked pointedly.

Uncharacteristically, Adam's gaze dropped to the floor. "I was, uh, busy that night."

"Sure you were," Dylan said, not believing it for a second. "Anyway, Faith placed the winning bid on me."

"You were bought by one of your florists?" Adam said, horrified.

"She bought some of my *time*," Dylan clarified.

Adam's expression didn't soften. "You've been out on a date with an employee?"

"No, she didn't want dates."

"What did she want?" he asked, his eyes narrowing.

"She asked me to meet her at the Santa Monica store and made a submission for the catalog."

"Did you accept it?"

"Nope."

"Her design wasn't even good enough for the book,

yet you have her here working on the most high-profile event in our history?"

"Her work is good. She deserves this spot, no question. The design she showed me that night was what she thought I wanted. When she does her own work, she's amazing."

"You said you wanted to rehabilitate your image. This won't help."

"It won't hurt, either, because nothing is going to happen."

"Sure. Let's get back to you kissing an employee."

"Yeah, I'd rather not. I'm trying to forget it."

"How's that working out for you?"

"Not as well as I'd like."

"Dylan," Adam said, shaking his head. "This is dangerous."

"I know."

"Do you? She seems nice, but if this goes badly for her, she can sue you. Hell, she can sue all of us because we have a policy that you've violated, but you're especially vulnerable."

"She's not like that. She wouldn't."

"You haven't known her long enough to be sure. You're the head of the chain of stores she works for, so she's been on her best behavior."

"I have no doubt that I've seen the real her."

"Now I'm even more worried. Is this woman really worth risking your career over? Exposing the entire company to legal action and a potential scandal?"

Liam poked his head around the door. "I thought I might find you two in here, stealing my coffee."

Dylan raised his mug. "You should have cookies in here, too."

Liam snorted a laugh. "Faith is ready if you are. Jenna's already in there."

Adam didn't move. "Come in here a minute and close the door."

Liam took the extra step inside the room and shut the door behind him. "What's up?"

Adam gestured in Dylan's direction. "Did you know about him kissing his florist?"

"Yes. Wait, no." He turned to Dylan. "You kissed her?"

"He kissed her," Adam confirmed, rocking back on his heels. "I'll brief the lawyers this afternoon in case we need to take preemptive action."

Dylan groaned. "Glad we're not overreacting."

Liam blew out a breath. "Look, I know things were different with me and Jenna, but I kissed her—heck, I made love to her—while she worked for me, and the world didn't end."

Dylan chuckled. "You sure acted as if it had ended there for a while. Remember that day we came over and—?"

Liam hit him upside the head. "I'm trying to help you, idiot."

"Uh, thanks?" Dylan said, rubbing his head.

Adam narrowed his eyes at them both. "You were lucky with Jenna. Most women in that situation would have reacted differently. Would have taken what they could get."

Dylan frowned at Liam. "Since when did he get so jaded about women?"

Liam shrugged a shoulder. "Many years ago. I always figured someone had broken his heart."

Adam threw up his hands. "I'm standing right here."

"Good point," Liam said. "So tell us who broke your heart? Was it Liz in college?"

"Nope," Dylan said. "He left her. I had to talk to her when she started calling the house, brokenhearted. Maybe it was—"

"Stop," Adam said in his oldest brother voice. "We're not discussing my dating history. We're talking about Dylan and the here and now."

"Actually," Liam said, "we're talking about which arrangements we want on the publicity materials. And two people are waiting for us." He opened the door and indicated the hallway with a hand. "Shall we?"

Adam straightened his tie, gave a last pointed look to Dylan and headed out.

"Thanks," Dylan said to Liam.

Liam nodded. "Just don't mess this up and get us into legal problems."

"I'll be careful," Dylan said and followed his brothers out the door, hoping like all hell he *was* capable of being careful around Faith Crawford.

Six

From the corner of Liam's research lab, Faith watched the three Hawke brothers and Jenna as they walked around the designs she'd been working on all week. She'd been nervous the night she'd made the first arrangement for Dylan, but this was more intense. There was so much more riding on this verdict.

Finally Adam looked up and said, "Is everybody ready to make a decision?" The others nodded, so he continued. "I like number three. It's simple enough to work well in publicity, it keeps the focus on the iris and it's elegant, which will appeal to the public."

"Agreed," Liam said. "It's one of my top two choices as well."

They quickly settled on that arrangement and then had a robust discussion about the second choice, since the vote was split between two options.

As Faith watched the conversation, the excitement began to outweigh her nerves—the four of them were so animated about her designs. Her personal favorite hadn't been mentioned at all, and now that she'd heard the reasoning for their other choices, she could assume that her favorite was too cluttered to be effective in the posters. It was fascinating to hear the opinions of people more experienced than she was in this side of the flower business. In such a short time, she'd learned so much.

Once the decisions were made, all four of the panel members complimented Faith on her work, though it was Dylan's praise that made her heart swell. She tried not to watch him as the others spoke, tried to keep her reaction to him veiled, but there was a charisma that surrounded him, a magnetic force that drew her gaze back against her will.

Then Adam excused himself to rush off to a meeting, and Liam turned to Dylan. "Are you still okay to take them to the photographer's studio?"

"Sure," Dylan said. "I drove here in one of the refrigerated delivery vans. Faith, did you want to come to the photo shoot?"

Faith jerked her head up. She'd known they'd booked the photographer for this afternoon and that the chosen designs would be taken straight to the studio, but she'd been able to concentrate only on her part. She hadn't thought further than the panel arriving and assessing her work. Now, though, she could barely contain her enthusiasm about seeing the two successful designs photographed.

"I'd love to," she said, trying not to bounce on her toes. "If that's okay."

Jenna smiled. "Seems only fair that since you created them, you get to see it through."

"Then I'm in. I'll grab my bag."

While she gathered her things, Liam and Dylan
sealed the two chosen arrangements plus a few single
stems in boxes—since the new iris was still a secret—
and carried them out to the delivery truck.

"What about my car?" Faith asked once the flowers
were all loaded.

Dylan's green gaze flicked from her to her car.
"Since your place is near the studio, how about I drop
you home afterward, then bring you back out here in
the morning for work?"

Jenna nodded. "This parking lot is secure overnight—
the security gates will be shut and monitored."

"Okay, that sounds good then. Thank you."

"Not a problem," Dylan said as he opened her door
for her. Her arm brushed his hand as she climbed in,
sending a buzz of awareness through her body. He held
her gaze for an instant, showing that he'd felt it, too.
She pulled her seat belt over her shoulder and tried to
pretend the moment of connection hadn't happened.

Once they'd set off on the road, he flashed her a grin.
"So how did your nerves hold out? That must have been
trying for you."

She tucked her legs up underneath her on the seat.
"I have to admit, I was pretty tense while you were all
judging, but it was thrilling, too. Thank you again for
this opportunity."

"No, thank you," he said as he changed lanes to overtake a station wagon. "Even Adam liked your work, and
he's hard to impress."

Her thoughts drifted back to seeing the three brothers together. They all looked so alike—tall and broad-shouldered, with thick, wavy hair the color of polished mahogany—yet so different at the same time. There was something...*more* in Dylan. An energy down deep in his soul, a passion for life that shone through in everything he did. In every move he made.

"I found Adam difficult to get a read on."

"That's Adam for you. He's what our mother calls 'self-contained.' Doesn't like sharing parts of himself if he can avoid it."

Curiosity made her turn to face Dylan. "Even with you and Liam?"

"Liam and I have found ways over the years to nudge him until he cracks." Dylan's expression changed—there was a touch of devilish mischief in the way his mouth quirked. "Some less fair than others."

"Like what?" she asked, intrigued.

"Oh, we just know what buttons to push." He grinned. "But we try to use our powers for good instead of evil. Most of the time we succeed."

Faith laughed. "Your powers are truly scary. I think I should be more careful around you."

There was silence for several heartbeats, and she felt the mood in the car—no, between *them*—change. Deepen.

"Pushing buttons isn't the reason you should be careful around me, Faith," he said, his voice like gravel.

Her skin heated. Even though she knew she shouldn't, she asked, "Why is it, then?"

"Because I start to lose perspective around you." He didn't look at her; his gaze remained focused on the road ahead, but she felt as if he was whispering in her ear.

"Sometimes I think you could crook your finger at me and I'd forget the company rules."

The breath caught in her throat. She was on the edge of a precipice, desperately wanting to fall, to let go, but she knew she couldn't. She swallowed hard and tried to make light of his comment. "Don't worry, I've never been able to master whistling, skipping or crooking a finger."

He laughed, but it sounded tight and unnatural. "Then we won't have a problem."

They talked about less loaded topics for the rest of the trip back to LA until they finally pulled up at the studio. They carried the boxes of arrangements and single stems to the front door, where the photographer was waiting for them.

"Come on in," she said. "The others are already here."

Dylan leaned over to whisper to Faith, "A couple of the publicity team members from Adam's office are meeting us here."

Once they were inside, the shoot seemed to move forward like clockwork. Dylan introduced her to the women from Hawke's Blooms' publicity team. Then she found a chair a few feet behind the camera and tried to stay out of the way.

Dylan, however, seemed to be the center of everything. His people management skills were on display, and in a charming, relaxed way, he was in total control of the photo shoot. She couldn't take her eyes off him. He exuded confidence, charisma and power. He raised an arm and everyone turned to see what he was pointing at. He called for assistance with something and several people rushed to help. He looked at her with his simmering gaze, and she practically swooned.

One of the publicity staff members, Amanda, took a seat next to her. "I can't wait to see how the photos turn out. You did some great work with those arrangements."

Faith felt the blush moving its way up her neck and was grateful that Amanda was watching the work in front of them and wouldn't notice. "Thank you. I'm looking forward to the photos as well."

"You're so lucky, getting to work with Dylan. All the girls in our office have a bit of a crush on him."

Faith tensed. Did Amanda know? Was she fishing? But the other woman still hadn't spared her a glance— if she'd been fishing, she would have been watching for a reaction.

Faith drew in an unsteady breath. "You all work for Adam, don't you?"

"Yep, and don't get me wrong. We love Adam, too. He's a great boss. But Dylan? He could charm the pants off just about anyone if he put his mind to it."

Faith felt the blush deepen and creep up to her cheeks. She didn't doubt that assessment in the least. Fortunately, Amanda didn't seem to be waiting for a reply.

"There's something about the way that man moves," Faith's new friend said. "You can tell he'd be a great lover."

Faith's heart skipped a beat. Just at that moment, Dylan glanced their way. He must have seen her looking a little flustered because he mouthed, "You okay?"

Amanda's words replayed in Faith's head, and she imagined lying naked with Dylan Hawke. Touching him without reserve. Being touched. Her mouth dried. Dylan frowned, taking a step toward her, and she realized she hadn't replied to him yet.

Summoning all her willpower, she found a smile and nodded, and he went back to overseeing the shoot. Amanda was called away and Faith tried to focus on something, anything that wasn't Dylan. Luckily, several people stopped to comment on her arrangements, so that gave her a ready-made distraction.

By the time the photographer said she had enough shots and called a halt, Faith had successfully avoided looking at Dylan since he'd asked her if she was okay. So when he appeared in front of her, tall, dark and smiling, she lost her breath.

"You ready to go?" he asked.

She blinked. "Yeah. You sure you don't mind dropping me home? I can catch a cab."

"Actually, I was thinking we should do something to celebrate the success of your designs first."

"Like what?" she practically stammered. *Celebration* and *Dylan* were two words that could be dangerous when paired together.

He ran a hand over his jaw. "A fine champagne should do it."

She looked around. "Here?" Maybe it wouldn't be so dangerous if the others were involved as well.

"I need to drop these flowers off at my place so the delivery van can be picked up—the iris is still under wraps, so I can't let them go anywhere else. But there's a bar downstairs in my building. How about we drive over, I'll race the arrangements upstairs and then we can have a bottle of their best champagne in the bar before I drop you home?"

The plan sounded harmless—he hadn't suggested she go up to his apartment with him, so they'd be surrounded by people the whole time. They couldn't get carried away the way they had at the store on their first meeting. And truth was, she was too buzzed about the day's events to go home just yet. This would be the perfect way to end the day: a small celebration with the person who understood how much making those arrangements and having them photographed for the publicity posters meant to her.

"I'd love to," she said.

They set the flowers back in the boxes and carried them out to the delivery van, said their farewells and set off for Dylan's building. Once they got there and parked, he went around to the back of the van and opened the doors.

"How about you grab us a table while I take these up," he said as he drew out the boxes. "I'll only be a couple of minutes."

"Sure," she said. Part of her wanted to go with him and see his apartment, and the other part knew how dangerous that would be. Best to stay to public areas.

It was still fairly early, and the bar mainly had the after-work crowd, not the evening revelers yet, so she didn't have any trouble finding a booth. She was perusing the cocktail list on the wall behind her when she heard the sound of fabric moving over vinyl. Dylan slid onto the bench seat across from her. His sculpted cheekbones and sparkling green eyes seemed to make the whole world brighter.

"Would you prefer a cocktail?" he asked.

It wouldn't be very smart to drink stronger alcohol when she was alone with this man. "No, I think you're right. Champagne is perfect to celebrate."

"Good, because I just ordered a bottle." His grin just about had her melting on the spot. And over the course of a couple of glasses of champagne each, the effect of Dylan Hawke on her system only intensified.

His cell beeped and he fished it from his pocket. "That was quick," he said as he thumbed some buttons. "The photographer has sent some preliminary shots over."

Her pulse jumped. "Can I see?"

He turned the cell screen to her, but the images were small, so she couldn't see much detail on how the individual iris looked at the center of the shot. "I can't tell much," she said.

He turned the cell back to himself and rotated it as he swiped the screen, flicking through the photos. "We could run up to my apartment and look at them on my computer screen."

He'd made the suggestion almost absent-mindedly, not lifting his gaze from the photos on his phone, and she wondered if he realized the enormity of the possible consequences of his offer.

"Is that wise?" she asked and laced her hands together in her lap. "We agreed it was best to stick to public places."

He stilled. Then his gaze slowly lifted to meet hers. She was right—he hadn't thought it through. He blew out a breath and shrugged. "It'll be fine. It would only be a few minutes, and we'll be focused on the flowers. Then I'll bring you straight back down and drop you home."

She chewed on her bottom lip. She really did want to see those photos, and since the flower was a secret, she wouldn't ask him to forward them to her own email address, so this was the only chance she'd have to get a sneak peek before the posters were produced. Surely she could control her reaction to this man for a few minutes. In fact, when she thought of it that way, her caution seemed crazy—she wasn't ruled by her lusts. Of course she could keep her hands to herself.

Decision made, she nodded. "I'd appreciate that."

She followed him out of the bar, then down a short corridor to a bank of elevators. One was waiting and he ushered her inside, then punched in a code before hitting the *P* button, which she assumed stood for *penthouse*.

They were silent as they stood side by side in the small space, both watching the doors. Perhaps this had been a bad idea after all. Even these first few moments of being alone were filled with tension. A feeling of leashed anticipation.

She opened her mouth to suggest they skip this and he drop her home when the doors whooshed open. He held out a hand to let her precede him into another hallway, and she hesitated.

"Is something wrong?" he asked.

Her mouth was suddenly dry, so she swallowed before speaking. "I guess I'm having second thoughts."

"You know," he said, reaching out to hold the lift doors, "we've been alone quite a bit of time, if you think about it. In the car, the delivery van, the room where you've been working at Liam's. And not once in those times did I lose control and leap on you."

But each of those times there had been the threat of someone entering the room or people in other cars looking through the windows. This time they'd be utterly alone. She moistened her lips.

"If it helps," he said, one corner of his mouth turning up, "I swear to keep my hands to myself."

She believed him. In the time she'd known him, he'd proved to be a man of his word. So she nodded, but as he unlocked his door, she admitted to herself that it wasn't *his* control she was worried about…

Dylan pushed open his door and hoped like hell he could keep the promise he'd just made.

"Do you want anything? A drink? Water?"

She shook her head. He closed the door behind her, then led the way through his living room to a study off to the side. As he booted up the computer, he pulled a second chair over to the desk, but Faith was still in the doorway, standing at an angle, looking out into his living room. He moved to her side, curious to see what she was looking at. Following her line of vision, his gaze landed on the flower arrangements she'd made only hours before.

"You did a really good job," he said, his voice low. "They're beautiful."

She didn't move. "Mainly due to Liam's work creating the Ruby Iris."

"No, mainly due to you. You forget what line of work I'm in." With a gentle finger, he turned her chin to him so he could see her eyes. So she could see his and know he meant this. "I've seen beautiful flowers rendered awkward by a bad arrangement. You, however, have enhanced the Ruby Iris's beauty."

Her eyes darkened. He realized she was close enough that he could lean in and kiss her again. Hell, how he wanted to. But he'd made her a promise to keep his hands to himself. So he dropped his hand and stepped back.

He cleared his throat to get his voice to work again.

"Speaking of your skill, let's have a look at those photos."

He held a chair out for her, then sat in his and opened the email.

There was a tiny gasp from beside him, and he turned to watch her reaction. "What do you think?" he asked.

"I've taken snapshots of my arrangements before, but I've never seen professional photos of them." Her voice was soft, as if she wasn't even conscious she was speaking.

"The photographer has done a good job." He passed the mouse to her so she could flick through the photos at her own pace.

"The lighting is amazing," she said as she scrolled. "And the angles…"

He was sure the lighting and angles were out of this world, but he didn't even glimpse them. His attention was firmly focused on Faith. Her eyes shone with unshed tears—were they of pride? Or joy? As one of those tears broke away and made a track down her cheek, he brushed it away with his thumb.

She turned to him, eyes shocked, lips slightly parted.

"Dylan—"

He withdrew his hand and sat on it and his other hand for good measure. "I'm sorry. I promised not to touch you, and I won't."

Her chest rose and fell more quickly than it had only a few minutes before. "You cross your heart?"

"Yes. I give you my word."

She sucked her luscious bottom lip into her mouth, obviously considering something. Finally she released her lip and met his gaze again. "Then do you mind if I do something?"

"Whatever you want," he said and meant it.

She lifted her hand and cupped the side of his face, running her thumb along his skin, the roughness of his jaw. "I've been dreaming about doing this, but I knew if I did, it would start something neither of us wanted. But since you've promised, then I just wanted to see…"

His pulse had spiked at her touch, and now it raced even faster.

"Faith," he said, his voice ragged. "Have a little mercy."

"Just a moment more," she whispered as her other hand joined in the exploration of his face.

Dylan tensed the muscles in his arms, trying to retain control over them, but he kept sitting on his hands. He didn't dare move. Then her index finger brushed over his lips, and he couldn't stop his tongue darting out to meet it. She pressed a little harder into his bottom lip, and he caught the tip of her finger between his teeth. She moistened her own lips and watched his mouth as if there was nothing she wanted more than to kiss him. He knew exactly how that felt.

"Faith," he said as her fingers moved to his throat. "This is a dangerous game."

"I'll stop in a moment." But her fingers continued their path, moving from his throat up to thread through his hair. "I've been thinking, daydreaming about doing this, and I'll never get another chance."

He groaned. She'd been daydreaming about him? About touching him?

All the blood in his body headed south. He adjusted his position on the chair but didn't release his hands.

"It seems as if it's been forever since our kiss," she continued as her hands traced a path down his throat again, but this time not stopping, instead spreading over his chest. "And even though this can't go anywhere, I've sometimes thought I'd die if I never touched you again. So I just want to make a memory to keep."

"You'll be the death of me." His head dropped back—he couldn't handle her touch combined with the sight of her a moment longer. Though some devil inside him made him ask, "Tell me what else you daydreamed."

There was a pause and he thought she wasn't going to answer, until in a soft voice she said, "You were touching me as well."

"I've thought about that." A lot. And he was thinking about it now. There was something about this woman who made him feel more alive than he had in a long time. Being around her when she worked, laughing with her, having her hands on him.

"Dylan?" she whispered, her voice close to his ear.

Her breath was warm on his earlobe, and he could barely get enough brain cells working to answer. "Yes?"

"What would it take to get you to break that promise?"

A shudder raced through his body. "Faith," he warned.

"Would you touch me if I begged?" Her hands trailed down his arms to rest on his wrists—as far as she could go while he was still sitting on his hands.

His arms trembled but he didn't move, couldn't speak. Then her hands cupped either side of his face and brought his gaze down to land on her. The air from her lungs fanned across his face.

"Please," she whispered against his lips, and then leaned in the last inch and kissed him.

And his last thread of control snapped.

Seven

Faith knew she was being reckless, but the moment Dylan's mouth closed the tiny space to reach hers, she didn't care. She'd been craving this since the last time they'd kissed. Had been craving *him*.

As she gently landed in his lap, his tongue pushed between her parted lips. She couldn't have contained the sound of satisfaction that rose in her throat if she'd tried. And she definitely didn't want to try. She could talk for an hour about the reasons they shouldn't cross the line again, but this, *this* felt too right. She speared her hands through his hair, reveling in the slide of it over her sensitive fingers.

His arms closed around her, holding her close, but it wasn't close enough. She dug at his waistband until she worked his shirt free, then skimmed her hands underneath, over his abdomen and up as high as she could reach with the fabric restraining her hands. His light chest hair tickled, and she dug her nails in.

"Faith," he said as his head dropped back, but his arms didn't relax their grip an inch.

His arousal pressed against the underside of her thighs, and she wriggled against it. A groan seemed to be ripped from him, and he lifted his head to meet her eyes. "I knew you'd be the death of me."

She smiled and kissed him. He tasted of champagne and heat, and she'd never tasted anything so decadent. After minutes, or hours, her lungs screamed for air, so she pulled back, gasping, but he didn't miss a beat. He scraped his teeth across her earlobe, and electric shivers radiated out across her body. She'd never been this desperate for any man. There was something about Dylan Hawke that drove her to the brink of insanity.

"If we're doing this—" he said, gasping between words.

Before he could finish his sentence, she said, "Oh, we're doing this."

He grinned against her mouth. "Then let's move somewhere more comfortable."

He stood, taking her with him and setting her on her feet, and began to walk her backward, through the living room and down the hall, expertly guiding her so that she didn't hit anything, his mouth not leaving hers the entire time.

Once they reached his bedroom, she had no interest in looking around except to ensure there was a bed. Her gaze found a large one with a dark wood headboard and a navy blue comforter and pillows. Perfect. Dylan flicked on a lamp, and its soft yellow light joined the last rays of the sunset filtering through large windows that overlooked downtown LA. The sunset was stunning, but nothing compared with the man before her.

His hands explored her shape through her clothes, but she had less patience—she slid her hands under his cotton shirt so that she could feel his skin again. It had been only minutes since she'd touched his bare chest, but she missed the sensation. She worked up from the ridges of his abdomen, higher, until she found the crisp hair that covered his pecs. It still wasn't enough, so she unbuttoned the shirt and began the journey again, this time with more freedom.

He groaned and pulled her closer, trapping her hands between them, and with palms cupping her bottom, he lifted her until she was standing on her toes, pressed against him. The ridge of his arousal pressed at the juncture of her thighs, the pressure only teasing and nowhere near enough. There was an ache deep inside her and it was only intensifying.

With a hand flat on his chest, she pushed him back. She reached out and unbuckled his belt, pulling it through the loopholes until it came free in her hands, and then dropped it over her shoulder. It clattered on the polished wood floor, and Dylan let out a laugh.

"Seems like you have flair in more than one area of your life, Faith Sixty-Three."

"Seems like you're a smooth talker in more than one area of your life." She undid the button at the top of his trousers and slowly lowered the zipper. With thumbs tucked into the sides, he gave the trousers a nudge and they fell to his ankles, along with his underwear.

He continued to walk her backward to the bed, but she put her hands on his shoulders, stilling him. "Give me a moment to appreciate you."

Obligingly he nodded, but almost immediately he cradled her face and kissed her again. She moved in, closing the distance between them, feeling the heat of his naked body through his clothes. So much, but not enough.

When she didn't think she could take it another second, he stepped backward until he hit the side of the bed and then sank down, bringing her with him to straddle his lap. She pushed up on her knees to give herself a little extra height and took control of the kiss. He ran his hands along her exposed thighs, up underneath her skirt, and then wrapped them around her hips. Her heart beat so strongly, she could feel the resonant thud through her entire body.

"Dylan," she breathed between kisses. She'd never wanted a man this badly before. Couldn't imagine ever wanting someone this badly again.

One by one, he undid the buttons on her blouse, and then peeled the fabric back to reveal her blush-pink demicup bra. He traced a finger around its lacy edges and over the slope of her breasts just before they disappeared into the cups. "So beautiful," he breathed. "Every inch of you is just so beautiful, Faith."

He hooked a finger into one of the cups, pushing down, seeking, and ran the back of his nail over her nipple. She shuddered. The corner of his mouth quirked up, and he did it again, eliciting the same response. Then he pulled the lace down, exposing her breast, and her back arched.

His mouth closed over her nipple and she shuddered. He wrapped an arm around her back, holding her to him as his teeth scraped her skin, followed by his tongue licking her. Through the fog of desire, she was only barely aware of his free hand working deftly behind her to undo the catch on her bra. He finally pulled it down her arms and threw it to the side.

The knowledge that they wouldn't have to stop before they were carried away this time created an intimacy that stole her breath. After all the wanting, finally being together without the barriers between their skin was almost too much to comprehend.

She pushed his open shirt over his shoulders, kissing the skin she'd exposed. The muscles of his shoulders bunched and tensed as first her lips made contact, then her tongue. The scent of his skin was intoxicating.

He fell back against the covers, taking her with him. She was still straddling his hips but now leaning her weight against his torso. She had a semblance of control, but her options for touching him were limited because most of him was either covered by her or hidden against the comforter. He, however, had full access and was taking most delicious advantage, his hands exploring her back, her sides, wherever he could reach.

Her skin was scorching, everything inside her so hot she thought she might explode into flames. And if that happened, so be it—being with Dylan would be more than worth it.

Then he rolled them over so that she was beneath him, his glorious weight pushing her into the mattress. But before she'd had a chance to appreciate the sensation fully, he moved down the bed, lifting her knee as he went. He ran his lips along the inside of her calf, stopping to press a kiss and then to bite lightly at the sensitive back of her knee. Electricity shot along her veins. His hands moved higher, capturing her skirt as he went, taking the fabric with him as his fingers skimmed over her thighs, her hips, until it bunched at her waist.

His fingers hooked under the sides of her pale pink underwear, pulling it inch by inch down her legs. Once it was removed, he covered her with one hand, applying delicious pressure, moving in patterns that were designed to take her to the brink.

Without pausing his hand, he moved back up her body to find her gaze and placed a tender, lingering kiss on her lips. "I feel as if I've wanted you forever. I can't believe you're really here."

"I can barely believe I'm here, either." Her heart squeezed tight at his expression. "It's like a dream."

"It's no dream," he said with a wicked grin. "Let me show you how real this is."

Breaking contact, he disappeared for excruciating moments before reappearing with a foil packet. He ripped it open, but before he could put the condom on, she took it from him and rolled it down his length. When it was on, she circled him with her hand and, taking her time, let herself learn his shape, his secrets. Air hissed out from between his teeth.

Abruptly, and with a pained expression on his face, he grabbed her wrists, freed himself and knelt between her legs. As he lifted her hips, she held her breath. Then he guided himself to her and filled her bit by bit until she gasped.

"Okay?" he asked, his brow furrowed.

She smiled. "More than okay."

He returned the smile and then began to move. She met each stroke, wanting to make the most of every last sensation. But as the tension inside her climbed, she forgot to move, forgot everything but Dylan above her.

His rhythm was driving her slowly out of her mind. She gripped frantically at his back, trying to find purchase, but it felt as if the world was slipping away and all that remained was Dylan moving above her, within her.

Heated breaths near her ear drove her higher, his whispered words telling her she was beautiful, higher still.

His hand snaked down to where their bodies joined, and as he applied pressure with his thumb, she called out his name and exploded into a thousand little pieces, every single one of them filled with bright, shining light. He groaned, and a few strokes later he followed her over the edge before slumping his weight on top of her. She welcomed the heaviness as if it could keep her grounded here on Earth while her soul wanted to fly away.

Whispering her name, Dylan rolled to the side, taking her with him, holding her close. She nestled against his chest, feeling more safe and secure than she could ever remember.

Faith woke slowly and stretched, deep contentment filling her body, down to her bones. And before she was even fully awake, she was wary. It was the contentment that made her suspicious—she'd learned young not to trust the feeling.

The night before came back to her in snatches, then in its entirety. The sensation of Dylan's hand caressing her face, the taste of him in her mouth, the sound he'd made at the back of his throat when he'd found his release.

She'd made love with Dylan, and it had been glorious. And dangerous.

High moments had always preceded her lowest moments, and last night had been a huge high, meaning there was a low—just as huge—coming, whether she was ready or not.

She opened her groggy eyes to the early morning light and found Dylan lying a hand span away on the thick white sheets, watching her. No chance of sneaking away or not facing the consequences of what they'd done.

"Good morning," he said. His voice was sleep-roughened and his hair rumpled, but his expression was guarded. She couldn't get a read on him.

"Good morning," she replied and gathered the sheet a little higher to reach her neck, as if that could give her a buffer between what they'd shared last night and the reality of the morning after. They'd gone too far this time and crossed a line that couldn't be uncrossed. She'd slept with the boss.

He arched an eyebrow and looked pointedly at the sheet she was clutching. "It's a little late for that, don't you think?"

Memories assaulted her—of seducing him, of begging him to touch her. Even as her skin heated with desire, she recognized that this mess they were in was her fault, and she had to find a way to fix it.

"Dylan—" she began, gripping the sheet more firmly. Before she could say anything else, he interrupted with a false smile stretched across his face. "I'll make us some coffee."

He swung his legs out from the bed, the sheet dropping away to reveal six feet of toned perfection. Her breath caught high in her throat. Dylan in the early morning light was just as impressive as Dylan in the lamplight in the middle of the night. Her hand demanded a chance to touch, but that was what had gotten her into this situation in the first place, so she resisted. Barely.

He found a pair of jeans in his closet, slipped them on and then pulled a charcoal T-shirt over his head before turning back to her.

He indicated a door to the left that she remembered from last night was the bathroom. "Feel free to use the shower or whatever you need."

"Thanks," she said, not releasing the sheet even an inch. She would have loved a shower, but more than that, she wanted to be home, safe and cocooned. Away from temptation that could ruin everything and these messy feelings that Dylan seemed to evoke in her.

After he left the room, she jumped up and grabbed her clothes from the floor where he'd dropped them after he peeled them off her. Maybe once she was dressed she'd feel more in control, though she had a sneaking suspicion it wouldn't be enough.

She'd been becoming more concerned about her attachment to this man every time she saw him. But in her experience, attachments didn't last. Her family had shown her that no matter how sincere people appeared, they'd drop you like a hotcake when someone better came along. And Dylan had had a reputation as a playboy before they met.

Her aunt had promised that she loved her and would always be there for her, but as soon as she'd gotten pregnant, she'd shipped the eleven-year-old Faith off to her grandparents.

Her aunt had been apologetic, saying she just didn't think she could cope with a new baby as well as a child in the house, and Faith had understood that. She'd never blamed her aunt. Instead, she'd just felt stupid that she'd let herself believe this time it might be different. Had let herself hope.

Hope was dangerous.

After the way she'd felt in his arms last night, it was clear that if she let herself begin to hope with Dylan, it would end up devastating her when he left. She'd allowed herself to feel too much.

By reputation, Dylan Hawke was the last man whose commitment she could depend on. No matter how sweet he was being to her now, she'd never be able to hold his attention for long. Better they step back from each other now, before she was hurt by his straying attention later.

As she found her way down the hallway to the kitchen, the scent of freshly brewed coffee hit her senses, promising that everything would be better after she was caffeinated.

She rounded the corner and found Dylan leaning back against the counter, tapping his fingers in a rapid tattoo. He looked about as confused as she felt, and that gave her the confidence she needed.

"I think we need to talk," she said, hoping her voice didn't wobble.

Dylan nodded and handed her a mug of coffee. "I'm sorry about last night."

"If anyone's going to apologize, it should be me." She looked down into her steaming mug. "You held to your word longer than I did."

"Nevertheless, I shouldn't have given in at all." He rubbed a hand up and down his face, clearly annoyed at himself.

"Dylan, I don't want to get into the blame game. I'd rather we look at where we go from here." She leaned a hip on the counter across from him. "First, I think we crossed a line."

He coughed, almost choking on his coffee. "That's pretty safe to say."

At least they agreed on that. However, what to do about it was another matter entirely. She prayed for the strength to see this through. To avoid giving in and dragging him back to the bedroom now.

Interlacing her fingers in her lap, she focused on the cabinet over his shoulder as she spoke. "Crossing lines is becoming something of a habit for us."

"A habit?" He coughed out a laugh. "More like an addiction."

"And like all addictions, it's not healthy," she said reluctantly. "But clearly, I don't know how to stop."

He gave her a wry smile. "I guess that's the exact reason why people struggle with addictions. The how to stop part is hard."

Taking a deep breath, she met his gaze squarely. "So what do you think we should do?"

"There's only one solution. Cold turkey." There was a slight wince in his features as he said the words.

"That sounds final." And severe. Her body tensed just thinking about it. She imagined her reaction the next time she saw him, having to lock down her need as if they hadn't shared the deepest of connections. "How would cold turkey work?"

He put his empty mug in the sink and was silent for a long moment, his gaze trained on the view out the window. When he spoke again, he didn't turn back. "You're still working on the project, so we'll be seeing each other at meetings and at Liam's lab. But in general, we give up spending time alone."

"We haven't gone out of our way to spend time alone up until now. It's just kind of happened." When said aloud, it sounded feeble, but since that first night, when she'd realized they had a problem, they'd both tried to be careful. Yet they'd still ended up in his bed.

He turned back to her, crossing his arms over his chest, a tiny frown line appearing between his eyebrows. "New rules, new level of caution. I'll stay away from the Santa Monica store. If the opportunity arises to, say, attend a photo shoot together, one of us declines."

She nodded slowly. "We become extravigilant."

"Exactly." But he didn't meet her eyes as he said it.

It seemed surreal to be talking about this, to be more attracted to someone than she'd ever been but discussing ways to not act on it. Though it was the strength of that attraction that was the exact problem.

Hope was dangerous.

"So," she said, seeking to disarm some of the tension that had grown between them in the last ten minutes, "I guess standing around in your kitchen early in the morning is probably not something we should be doing, either."

"Nope," he said, his lips curving in a tight smile. "Especially with the way my thoughts are heading, seeing you leaning against my cabinetry."

She stepped away from the counter, which only brought her closer to him. In two steps, she could be in his arms again...

She bit down on her lip. He was right—there was no safe way to spend time alone together.

"Okay," she said, feeling as if she was signing her own death warrant. But she wouldn't give up this job or the opportunities Hawke's Blooms could offer her at this stage in her career. And if she wanted the job, she couldn't sleep with the boss. "I agree to your new plan."

He held out a hand for her mug, and as she gave it to him, his hand closed around hers for a long moment. "Even though we're trying to avoid repeating it, I want you to know I've enjoyed every moment I've spent with you, Faith Sixty-Three."

A ball of emotion rose up and lodged itself in her throat, and she had to swallow to get her voice to work. "I've enjoyed the time I've spent with you, too."

"Come on," he said, his voice rough. "I'll drive you out to get your car."

He grabbed his keys from the end of the counter, and she followed him out, stopping only to pick up her handbag and, one last time, to look around the apartment where she'd glimpsed heaven.

Eight

Dylan knocked on the door of Faith's ground-floor apartment and stepped back to wait. It had been almost a month since the night she'd stayed at his place. The night that had rocked him to his core. In that time, they'd seen each other at Liam's research lab and in meetings about the launch, but, as agreed, they hadn't spent any time alone together. And every day it had been a little more difficult than the day before to keep himself from calling her.

But that third date had been weighing on his mind. It was a loose end that needed clearing up, and it was time he did just that. The closure would help him move forward. Maybe he was grasping at straws, but nothing else had worked so far to help him forget her and move on.

The apartment door opened to reveal Faith in shorts and a T-shirt, her face makeup-free and her curling hair loose around her shoulders. She stole his breath.

"Dylan," she said, her voice betraying her surprise.

"Sorry for the unannounced visit." He smiled and dug his hands into his pockets. "Do you mind if I come in for a couple of minutes?"

She blinked and then opened the door wider. "Sure."

Once inside, he turned to take in the decor. Or lack of decor. The place was beyond minimalist—it was practically bare. There was an old sofa, a coffee table and a TV. The coffee table had a small pile of floristry magazines sitting haphazardly on it, and an empty mug. No bright cushions on the sofa, no colorful paintings on the walls. No collections of eccentric odds and ends, no surprises at all. It was like the anti-Faith apartment.

There was a kitchen beside the living room, with a counter acting as a divider between the rooms. Except for a chrome toaster and a mismatched wooden knife block, the kitchen counters were bare, echoing the interior design of the living room. He'd expected flair. Color. Personality. Faith.

"Can I get you a drink?" she asked, her features schooled to blank.

He shook his head and brought his attention back to the reason he'd come. "No, I won't be here long."

"Even so, maybe we should have this conversation outside." She headed out through the door she'd opened for him and stood in the small courtyard at the front of the apartment block. There were a few dry-looking shrubs enclosing a paved square that was heavily shaded by the building, and it looked about as wrong for her as the interior did.

"Is there a problem with the launch?" she asked, crossing her arms under her breasts.

The launch was only a week away and plans were

in full swing, but it was running as smoothly as could be expected. But it was connected to why he'd knocked on her door this morning.

He cleared his throat. "We need to talk about the auction and our last date."

He'd wanted to bring it up again for a while now, but it didn't seem right to talk about it when they were at work. Where he was the boss and she was his employee. Those roles didn't disappear simply by talking to her here, obviously, but at least by discussing the situation when they were on her turf, it felt a little more equal.

She snapped off a leaf from a nearby shrub and crumpled it in her fingers. "I've told you we can let that slide. I've already got more than I expected from the auction with this assignment working with the Ruby Iris."

That sounded fine in theory, but he needed the closure, so he ignored her objection. "And I've told you that I won't let it slide. You paid to have me look more closely at your floristry skills and I did, but I want to make sure you've had the opportunity to say all you need to about where you see yourself in the company." He offered her a smile. "Since we're both going to the launch anyway, I thought we could go together and it could serve as our final date."

She shifted her weight from one leg to the other. "I seem to remember we decided to keep our distance. To go cold turkey. In fact, those rules pretty much exclude you even being here today."

"It's been almost a month without incident. I think we're fine." Well, *she* seemed fine, anyway. He was still kept awake at night, replaying memories of their night together. Of the feel of her skin, the touch of her lips as she kissed him in desperation.

She, however, seemed unaffected, which was more than a little annoying.

"So how would you see this working?" she asked, sounding unconvinced.

"I'll pick you up, like a date. We've never had any problems being alone in a car together, so that should be fine. Then we'll attend the launch together. Perhaps dance, but since we'll be in public, surrounded by Hawke's Blooms staff and management, there won't be any chance to get carried away. Then I'll drop you home."

"That last point sounds like a danger area," she said as she ran her hands over a branch near her shoulder.

"Good point." In theory, it would only be the same level of temptation that they had right now, but on the night of the launch, they'd both be wearing their finest, would have danced, perhaps would have had a glass or two of champagne. "I'll arrange a limo to drop you home. It will be on standby so you can leave when you want to. Alone."

She screwed up her nose as she considered. "Okay, that sounds harmless enough. And then we'll be square?"

"Then we'll be square," he confirmed. Of course, he was going to reimburse her the money she'd paid for the dates as soon as they'd had the last one, despite her earlier protests. Eight thousand two hundred dollars was a lot of money for someone on her wage.

And speaking of money, there was one other aspect of this last date that needed addressing. "Also, I'd appreciate it if you'd let me buy you a dress for the launch."

She shook her head. "You don't have to buy me a dress, Dylan."

He'd expected opposition, so it didn't faze him. He rocked back on his heels and laid out his reasoning. "You admitted that you spent almost all your savings at the auction, so yes, I do. Will it help if I promise not to buy you a corsage?"

"Dylan—" she began, but he interrupted.

"Humor me. Let me buy you a dress, we'll have the date, and then we can properly go back to being a boss and an employee."

"You want to take me shopping?" She arched an eyebrow. "Alone?"

Alone would be crazy. Luckily, he'd already come up with a solution. "I've arranged a personal shopper who will take us to a store after closing time. We'll not only have private access to the store and advice but also be chaperoned."

She didn't say anything, but he wanted this closure, so he smiled and said, "Just say yes, Faith."

She blew out a breath. "Okay, sure."

Good. Part of him was glad he'd been able to get her to agree. After this he'd be able to move on. Another part of him was wondering if he'd stepped out of the frying pan into the fire.

Faith pulled up in the parking lot of the upscale clothing store and let out a sigh. She was looking forward to spending time with Dylan far more than she should, and that worried her.

Pretending to be unaffected by him in her apartment had almost cost her her sanity. If he hadn't promised to have a personal shopper here tonight, she would never have agreed. Though he'd seemed remarkably unaffected when he'd made the offer, which was hardly fair. If she was struggling, then it would boost her ego if he'd been struggling right along with her.

Perhaps he'd moved on already? Her stomach dipped at the thought, but it would be for the best. Yes, indeed. It was exactly what they needed to happen. If only it didn't feel like the end of the world to contemplate…

His Porsche pulled up beside her. Dylan stepped out and paused to set the keyless lock. He wore jeans and a white polo shirt—it was the only time she'd seen him in jeans besides the morning after they'd made love. She gripped the steering wheel tighter. The memory threatened to overwhelm her with sensation, so she pushed it to the back of her mind and focused on the here and now. However, the fact that the here and now consisted of Dylan's rear end outlined by soft denim wasn't helping her gain control much.

"Evening, Faith," he said as he opened her car door. The deep, sexy drawl sent a shiver up her spine. She stepped out and Dylan closed the door.

"Hello, Dylan," she said. Then, before she could give herself away, she smiled and locked her car. "Is the personal shopper here already or do we need to wait?"

"She's inside."

"Let's not keep her waiting, then," she said and set off for the entrance.

Dylan was beside her in two strides. "You know, you seem a lot more keen about this than I expected."

Actually, she was keen to have another person in the mix and avoid being alone with him, especially in a dimly lit parking lot. If he'd moved on, she wasn't letting him know she was still back where she'd been the night they'd made love. She straightened her spine.

"The sooner we start, the sooner it will be over," she said over her shoulder.

A middle-aged woman wearing a designer pantsuit, her hair in a sleek silver bob, opened the door for them. "Dylan and Faith?" she asked.

"That's us," Dylan said, holding out his hand.

"I'm Julie." She shook Dylan's hand and then held her hand out to Faith. "As I understand it, we're looking for an outfit for Faith to wear to an event?"

"Yes," Faith said. "So, something formal."

"Lovely. The formal section is this way." She moved away, and Faith turned to Dylan.

"You don't need to hang around," she said brightly. "Or if you want to stay, you could wait over by the doors? You'll get bored looking at women's clothes." The last thing she wanted was to be trying on clothes with him within touching distance.

He grinned. "Not a chance. I'm staying to make sure you don't weasel out."

"What if I promise—"

Dylan cut her off. "I'm staying, Faith, so you may as well catch up with Julie."

"Sure," she said on a sigh. She'd come to learn a thing or two about this man, and she could tell this wasn't a battle she was going to win. She followed the path Julie had taken to the formal wear section, very aware of Dylan's gaze on her as he tagged along.

Once they arrived, Julie made a sweeping gesture with her arm to point out the options. "Did you have anything in mind? Some guidelines so I know where to start?"

Faith chewed the inside of her cheek, trying to come up with some ideas. She'd been too worried about being here with Dylan to think about the actual dress.

"Something bright," Dylan said. "Vibrant."

"Okay, good." Julie nodded. "Anything else?"

Dylan rocked back on his heels. "Perhaps something quirky. She looks great in halter necks, but then, she looks great in everything, so that shouldn't limit you."

Faith watched the exchange, a little stunned. Dylan glanced over and caught her expression. "What? I've been paying attention."

He certainly had. Suddenly this situation they were in tonight felt even more uneven than it had earlier. She lifted her chin. "So what are you planning on wearing to the launch?"

He shrugged. "A suit, I guess."

"White shirt and a random tie from your closet?" she asked sweetly.

"Probably."

She shook her head in mock disappointment. "Conservative choice."

One corner of his mouth twitched. "Is that so?"

"New deal." She planted her hands on her hips. "You get to stay and have input into what I wear if I can choose something for you to wear."

He blinked slowly. "You're changing the rules?"

"I am." She stood a little taller. "You got a problem with that?"

"Nope. I've always liked your attitude. Deal." He turned to Julie. "We'll need time in the menswear section as well."

They walked around both sections of the store for twenty minutes, each handing garments to Julie to take to the other's changing room. By the time they were finished, there were probably more clothes in there waiting for them than left on the shelves.

"We're done," Dylan said.

Julie nodded. "Okay, follow me."

She led them into a room the size of a small store in itself. It was circular, with mirrored doors along the outer wall and a round sofa in the middle. On one side of the room was a long chrome stand on wheels that was full of the dresses Faith had agreed to try on, and on the other side of the room was a matching stand with the clothes for Dylan. There was also an ice bucket on a stand, with champagne chilling.

Julie lifted the bottle. "How about we start with a glass of bubbly?"

Faith glanced at Dylan, and he raised an eyebrow, leaving it to her. The night they'd lost control had started with champagne… But tonight they were chaperoned, and she was having fun, so the champagne would be nice.

She nodded at Julie. "Thank you."

Julie poured two glasses and handed them over. Dylan clinked his to Faith's. "Here's to an interesting night."

"Cheers," she said and took a sip before handing her glass back to Julie and heading for her changing room. There were so many dresses, she didn't know where to start, so she grabbed the first one her hand landed on and slipped through the door.

It was an electric-blue velvet, floor-length number. As she was zipping up, Julie called out, "How's it going? Need any help?"

"I'm fine, thanks. The zip is on the side."

She adjusted the dress and looked in the mirror. The color was amazing on her, and the dress itself made her look more elegant than she'd anticipated. As she opened the door, Dylan stilled, his hand freezing on the shirt cuff he'd been adjusting.

He cleared his throat. "Stunning. But it's not the right one."

Faith looked down at the dress. "I like it."

"I like it, too. But it's not the right one."

She was about to argue when she caught sight of the rack full of dresses still to try. No point becoming attached to the first one, anyway. "Turn around and show me what you're wearing."

He held his arms out and turned, letting her see. He'd chosen the most conservative of all the options— a cream shirt with a black suit and charcoal tie. The colors set off his tan, but she smiled and said, "I like it, but it's not the right one."

Julie jumped up from the sofa. "Good, we're narrowing it down. Next! I'll take those two outfits back into the store when you have them off."

Faith grabbed another dress and slipped back into the changing room. For the next five changes, Dylan's eyes heated with approval, but he said each wasn't the right one, so she kept going, wondering what he was waiting for.

And for each of those five changes, she'd also rejected his outfits. Seeing him in a fitted white shirt that accentuated the breadth of his shoulders and his toned biceps had made her mouth dry, but she was waiting for something a little bit different.

She emerged wearing the sixth dress, a light-as-air

confection in mint green that shimmered like mother-of-pearl and seemed to float and sparkle as she moved.

Dylan's eyes darkened when he saw her. "Now we're getting somewhere." He reached out to touch the sleeve, and the warmth of his hand seeped through the light fabric. "This is more how I see you."

"What do you mean?" she asked, looking down at the dress.

"Let me ask you a question instead." He lifted her chin with a crooked finger. "I've seen your heart. When you make flower arrangements, your heart is on display. Crab apple and mint, the Ruby Iris with pale pink blooms and crystals. You're unique, you're creative and you're effervescent. So why is your apartment so plain that it's practically military issue?"

She moved away, giving herself a moment to think. They'd agreed not to spend time alone together, so where did that leave soul-baring admissions? Maybe it would be best not to get too deep for exactly the same reasons.

She shrugged. "I just haven't gotten around to decorating yet. It doesn't seem as if I've been there long enough."

"It's more than that," he said, moving back into her field of vision. "It's part of not wanting to put down roots, isn't it? Being a rolling stone?"

This man saw through her far too easily. She let out a long breath and told him more than she'd ever told a living soul. "There was one time when I was nine. I was living with my grandparents, and I'd thought I was finally settled, that I'd finish growing up at their house." She'd begun to hope. "I looked through magazines and ripped out posters of bands and actors that my little nine-year-old heart was crushing on, and I covered my walls with them. It was more than just putting posters up. It was about marking my territory. That room was mine, you know?"

"Yeah, I do," he said softly, his green eyes intense.

"I spent ridiculous amounts of time arranging who to put where and who could be side by side with someone else. I was so proud of that damn wall when I was finished that I would lie on my bed and just stare at it."

He ran a hand up and down her back, hypnotizing her into a sense of calm. "What happened to the wall, Faith?"

"Nothing. The wall was fine." She swallowed hard. "But my father called one night and said he was picking me up in the morning to take me out to a theme park. Once we were on the road, he told me he was dropping me off with my mother afterward. She wanted to give parenthood another go."

Dylan's body tensed, but his voice remained even. "What about your things?"

"My grandparents had packed my clothes while I was having breakfast—I didn't have a lot—and they were already in the back of the truck." The betrayal of their not giving her advance warning, of always keeping her in the dark, still stung. "Part of me was happy my mother wanted me, but part of me was thinking about my wall. About where I'd begun to feel settled."

"Oh, baby," he said on a sigh. "You had it all ripped out from under you again."

"I never put anything up on a wall again. And the next time I went back to my grandparents' to live— after my aunt handed me back when I was eleven— I ripped down every one of those pictures and threw them in the trash." She rubbed at her breastbone. That damn memory still had the power to hurt, even after all these years.

"Hey, come here," he said, and wrapped his arms around her.

She just stood in his embrace, not relaxing. "I'm okay."

"I know you are," he said gently. "But I'm going to hug you anyway."

It was the perfect thing to say, and she let herself lean against his solid chest to soak up his strength for just a moment. Then she chuckled—of course it was the perfect thing to say, since he was a known charmer.

He dipped his head. "What's funny?"

"You know, I was warned about your way with words," she said, biting down on a smile and stepping back.

His eyebrows shot up. "Who said that?"

She shrugged a shoulder innocently, enjoying his surprise. "One of Adam's staff members at the photo shoot. She also said the girls in Adam's office have a crush on you."

"Really?" he asked, grinning.

She smacked him on the shoulder. "Yes, really. She also said that you could charm the pants off anyone if you tried."

His gaze slowly made its way from her face to her toes. "Lucky you're wearing a dress, then."

"Somehow," she said, her breath coming a little faster, "I don't think choice of clothing would affect your success."

The green of his eyes grew dark, became full of promise. "There's only one thing that's stopping me from trying right now."

She swallowed. "Our personal shopper?"

"No, she's easy to deal with." His fingertips toyed with the neckline of her dress, sending sparks through her bloodstream.

"Oh." And here she'd thought the chaperone was protecting them. "Then what is it?"

He moved closer, surrounding her with his body heat. "We made a decision. In my kitchen."

"We did." She moistened her lips, and he watched the action as he spoke.

"And nothing has changed in the factors that led us to make that decision." His head dipped to kiss a spot just below her earlobe.

It took several heartbeats for her to remember what they were talking about, since his lips were working magic, drawing her into a haze of desire. "They haven't," she agreed, reaching her arms around his neck.

He kissed one corner of her mouth, then the other, his lips brushing hers, featherlight, in between. "So I won't be trying to charm your pants—or dress—off you. I won't be trying anything."

When his lips brushed past hers again, she opened her mouth, intoxicated by him, and he took the invitation, kissing her once, twice.

"Then why are you kissing me?" she asked, using the last brain cell left working in her head.

He pulled away and looked at her with heavy-lidded eyes. "That's a very good question. One I don't have a logical answer for."

She already missed his touch even though his mouth was only inches away. "Do you have an illogical answer?"

"Several," he said with a smile that melted her insides. "Starting with how you look in that dress."

"You don't look so bad yourself." He wore a lavender shirt and a silver tie that Julie had matched with it. "Speaking of our clothes, where is our personal shopper?"

"She slipped out of the room right about when I started touching the sleeve of this dress."

Faith blinked. "She's been gone all this time? She must be getting bored."

"I'll pay her a bonus for her discretion—it will be worth it." He leaned in and placed a kiss on the curve of Faith's jaw. "It's been a long, difficult month."

It had been a difficult month for him, too? "I thought that was just me."

"Why would you think that?" he asked, his voice low.

How far into her mind was she willing to let him see? She sucked her bottom lip between her teeth. There probably wasn't a point in holding back now. "You seemed so together when you came to my apartment, while I was falling apart from wanting you."

His eyebrows lifted. "I thought the same about you. You seemed unaffected, and I was having trouble keeping my hands to myself. In fact, I was getting annoyed that you were so calm."

"Not even close." She smoothed her hands over the lapels of his jacket. "In fact, I thought you must have moved on."

He let out a wry laugh. "I haven't even been able to contemplate another woman since that first night at the Santa Monica store, when you pretty much ambushed me so I would watch you work."

For a long moment she considered just staying here in

this little world they'd created. It would be like heaven. Well, until it was ripped away. Places she wanted to be were always ripped away in the end. And the longer she let herself become used to this, the worse it would hurt when it was over.

"It's been the same for me," she said. "But we've already discussed this, and standing here, so close, isn't helping any."

He drew in a sharp breath and moved back. "You're right." He scrubbed a hand through his hair and didn't meet her eyes as he said, "I'll find Julie."

Nine

The night of the launch, Faith was a jumble of excitement and nerves as she sat beside Dylan in the back of the limousine. Going on a date with this man felt like standing at the edge of a cliff and hoping she didn't fall.

He glanced over and squeezed her hand. "Did I say you look beautiful?"

"Twice," she said, smiling. "But I don't mind."

The limo driver pulled over a short distance from the hotel. "Apparently I need to drop you here so you can walk the red carpet," he said over his shoulder.

Faith turned to Dylan. "Red carpet?"

Dylan grinned. "After the success of the Midnight Lily launch, and since Jenna has come out as Princess Jensine, we were able to attract a few more celebrities this time."

A thought suddenly occurred to her. "Will it be a

problem if you're seen on the red carpet with an employee?"

"Not in the least." He stroked his thumb over the
back of her hand. "It's perfectly natural that I'd escort
the florist who made the arrangements for tonight."

Put that way, it seemed reasonable, so she let out a
breath and smiled.

The driver opened their door and Faith stepped out,
taking in the scene around her. Paparazzi lined the street
and a crowd had gathered, hoping to catch a glimpse
of someone famous. The atmosphere was like nothing
she'd ever experienced before and was a little intimidating.

Then Dylan was at her elbow, with a warm hand
on the small of her back, grounding her. Keeping her
centered.

"I don't know how Jenna lives like this," she whispered.

"Most of the time, she doesn't," he said. "She spends
the majority of her days with Meg, Bonnie and Liam."

The image of a little family rose in Faith's mind—the
stability, the love. Only in her mind, it wasn't Jenna's
family. It was Dylan surrounded by a bunch of kids with
her curly red hair and his green eyes. The image was so
perfect, so unattainable, her chest ached.

"Dylan," a voice called once they reached the carpet.
"Can we get a quote?"

Dylan smiled and waved, then leaned to Faith's ear.
"Ebony is from a local morning show. They sometimes
do a gardening segment, and I've been talking to them
about doing something with us, so I need to talk to her.
Can you—?" He paused, then grabbed an arm a few feet

away. "Adam, I need to do a bit of media. Can you walk
in with Faith? You're here alone, aren't you?"

Adam offered Faith a smile before nodding to his
brother. "Sure."

He put a hand under her elbow and they walked
through the door, making small talk about the weather.
Once inside, he dropped her arm and asked, "Can I talk
to you privately about something?"

She resisted taking a step back as his expression
changed. There was something serious on his mind.
Something he wasn't happy about. But he was the
CEO of Hawke's Blooms Enterprises, which covered
the farm, the stores, the markets and R&D, above even
Dylan, so she said, "Of course," and smiled politely.

He glanced around and then led her through a door
marked Staff Only into what appeared to be an office.

Then he turned and faced her squarely, face stony.
"I need to ask. What do you want out of this involvement with my brother?"

Her blood turned cold at the implication about her
morals. Then she crossed her arms under her breasts
and matched his stance.

"What does a woman normally want out of an involvement with a man?" she asked, heavy on the sar-
casm.

Without missing a beat, he began to make a list, raising a finger for each item. "Money, promotion, prestige,
access to something, an opportunity to sue or blackmail. I could go on."

She coughed out a laugh, more amazed than insulted
by his cynicism. "Please don't."

"If you're planning to use whatever it is between you
and my brother to get ahead, it won't end well for you."

She cocked her head to the side, examining Adam's face. It was amazing how similar he looked to Dylan, yet how little they were alike. She'd seen a range of expressions on Dylan's face before but nothing this hard, this remote. Adam's green eyes were the cold arctic sea, whereas Dylan's sparked with life and energy. There was no doubt in her mind that Dylan was the better man, and she wasn't going to let his brother push her around.

She narrowed her eyes and poked her index finger into his chest. "Are you always this suspicious of people's motives?"

He looked a little less certain. "I've found it pays to be."

"Well, let me put your mind at rest." She took a step back and folded her arms again. "Hawke's Blooms has been good to me. I would never do anything to hurt the company. And Dylan? He's a good man. I would never hurt him, and anyone who wanted to would have to go through me to do it."

Adam frowned, apparently taken by surprise by her answer. "So you are planning on a future with him?"

"Actually, I'm not. But here's a question for you. How much of this—" she waved a finger, taking in the room he'd corralled her in "—is about the company and how much is about protecting your little brother?"

Adam opened his mouth to answer but then hesitated, frowned and closed his mouth again. Before he was able to find any words, Dylan burst through the door.

"What the *hell* is going on here?" His voice was tightly controlled but his gaze was clearly full of irritation aimed at his brother.

"I was just—" Adam began, but Faith had had enough and stepped in front of him.

"Your brother was grilling me about my intentions. Turns out he was worried I'd sue the company. Or was it blackmail that you were more concerned about?" she asked, moving to stand beside Dylan and smiling brightly at Adam.

Dylan's face turned red. "You said *what* to her?"

Adam held his hands up in surrender as Dylan took a step forward. "It was a reasonable concern."

"Adam, I'm warning you, get out of this room." Dylan planted his feet shoulder width apart and glared at his brother. "Now."

Adam's eyebrows shot up. "Okay, sure," he said and headed for the door. "Look, I'm sorry—"

"Not the time," Dylan said, his voice tight and fists clenching at his sides.

"Right then." Adam disappeared completely from view.

Dylan kicked the door shut behind him and then turned to Faith and blew out a breath. "I can't believe he did that. Sorry doesn't seem enough."

He seemed so tense that she laid a hand on his arm, wanting to reassure him. "No harm done. I was handling it."

One corner of his mouth quirked up. "Actually, when I opened the door, the expression on his face did seem a bit lost."

"Good," she said, satisfied she'd been able to hold her own. "You know, I think he was more worried about us as your brother than he was as the CEO."

A frown line appeared across his forehead. "What do you mean?"

"He's protective of you." Heat radiated through Dylan's

suit coat to her hand, and she rubbed his upper arm, always wanting a little more when she was near him.

He let out an exasperated breath. "He should be more worried about himself."

"Why?" The dynamics between Dylan and his brothers were endlessly fascinating to her, but then again, anything about Dylan fascinated her.

"I can't remember the last time I saw him in a relationship. Or with a woman who made him happy. I don't know why he thinks he's in any position to sort out anyone else's love life."

Her throat was suddenly tight, and she had to swallow before she could get her voice to work. "We don't have a love life. We've put a lot of effort into ensuring that."

"That's true," he said, his eyes pained. "I still love this dress on you, by the way."

She looked down at the shimmering green dress. "Thank you again. It's a lovely present." Then, unable to help herself, she looked back at him, taking in the lavender shirt and silver tie. "And I like you in that suit."

His eyes darkened. "Someone with great flair picked it out for me."

She ran a hand down the front of the shirt, remembering what it felt like to touch him without fabric between them. Without reserve.

He sucked in a sharp breath. "If we're going to leave this room, we'd better go now."

She dropped her hand and took a step back. "I think you're right."

He opened the door and gestured for her to go past, and they walked into the ballroom as if nothing had happened.

* * *

Dylan looked out over the crowd of the fashionable and famous mingling and drinking champagne in honor of Hawke's Blooms. He was still annoyed at his brother but was trying not to let it affect him. He just wanted Faith to have one perfect night to remember, and he wouldn't let Adam ruin it.

She'd bought three dates at the auction—she'd spent the first making flower arrangements at the Santa Monica store and the second making flower arrangements at Liam's research facility. Was it too much to ask that he be able to give her one night when she wasn't working, without his stupid brother ruining it?

He glanced down at Faith and pulled her a little closer against his side as they made their way through the ballroom. They were stopped by several people he knew in the industry, and he introduced Faith each time as the florist who had created the designs that adorned the room. The guests were full of praise, and although Faith didn't say it, he could feel her pride in her work. He smiled inside, knowing he'd become attuned to her feelings.

"Thank you," she whispered just below his ear once they'd moved on from another person who'd been impressed by her work.

He took a moment to appreciate the warmth of her breath on his neck before asking, "For what?"

"I told you once that my dream was to create arrangements that reached lots of people. To spread joy on that larger scale." She moistened her lips. "You've made it happen."

His chest expanded at the expression in her eyes, but he couldn't take the credit. "No, you've made it happen. I might have arranged the opportunity for Jenna, Liam and Adam to see your ideas for the Ruby Iris, but you're the one who impressed them."

"As you said, you arranged the opportunity," she said, clearly unwilling to let it drop.

"Ah, but you were creative enough in your approach to attend the auction and get my attention in the first place." He smiled down into her eyes. "You're one of a kind, Faith."

His mother appeared at his elbow, wineglass in hand. "Here you are, Dylan. I've been looking everywhere for you."

He leaned down and kissed her cheek. "Did you need something?"

"Just to check on you. Adam said something cryptic about wanting me to make sure you're all right. What happened?"

Dylan smiled tightly, not wanting to get into it with his mother. "Just big brother pushing too far."

"Don't be hard on him," his mother said indulgently. "His heart is always in the right place."

Dylan didn't say anything, letting his silence speak for him.

"Okay," his mother said, chuckling. "Sometimes he does take things too far. Now, introduce me to Faith. I've heard such good things about your work from Jenna."

Obediently, he glanced back down at his date. "Faith, this is my mother. Mom, this is Faith Crawford."

Faith smiled and held out her hand. "Lovely to meet you, Mrs. Hawke."

"You, too, Faith. But call me Andrea." She shook her

hand. "The floral arrangements are gorgeous. You've worked miracles with them."

The two women looked over at the closest arrangement, and Faith smiled. "Thank you. I made these final versions this morning out at Liam's facility, so this is the first time I've seen them under the ballroom lights."

The crystals interspersed among the blooms caught the sparkling light and refracted it into little sunbeams across the ceiling. All the guests were commenting on the effect.

"Oh, I meant to say—" Dylan's mother turned to him "—Jenna was looking for you. She wanted you to meet a journalist before you go up on stage. You go and find her and I'll keep Faith company."

Dylan looked from one woman to the other, uncomfortable about leaving them together but not completely sure why. He looked down at Faith and she patted his arm. "Go. I'll be fine."

He released her elbow and threaded his way through the crowd, restricting himself to only one last look back over his shoulder.

Faith watched Dylan walk away with the same wrench in her chest that she always felt when he left.

Women stopped him constantly, sometimes with a hand on his forearm, sometimes by putting themselves in his path. Even from a distance, she could tell he was charming them and then moving on.

"He's good with people," his mother said from beside her. "They like him."

"Yes," Faith said, turning back to face Andrea with a polite smile. "They do."

"Interesting thing is, his brothers are easier to read

than he is. It might look as if Dylan is more open than them, but he manages to keep more of himself hidden. He wears a mask of openness, which tricks people, if that makes sense."

Faith thought about conversations they'd had and the hidden depths he'd revealed. "It does make sense."

"Although he seems different with you," Andrea said casually, and then took a sip of her wine.

Butterflies leapt to life in Faith's belly. First Adam and now their mother—what was it with Dylan's family fishing for information? "You only saw us together for about ten seconds," she said, matching the other woman's casual tone.

Andrea waved the objection away with a flick of her wrist. "A mother can read between the lines. Also, I know my son, and his face is different when he speaks about you."

"He speaks about me?" Faith asked before she could think better of it.

Andrea grinned. "He's mentioned you a few times when giving me an update on this launch and your work with the Ruby Iris."

Faith could see the expectation in the other woman's eyes, the excitement that her son had found someone to settle down with. But it wouldn't be her, and that hurt more than she could let on.

She took a breath and chose her words carefully to ensure there was no misunderstanding. "I feel I need to tell you that nothing is going to happen between Dylan and me."

"Huh, that's funny. I seem to remember hearing the same story from Liam and Jenna a while ago." Her expression said Andrea wasn't deterred in the slightest. "Is this because you work for him?"

"Yes, partly. But it's more than that." Would a woman with a loving, close family even understand Faith's issues with love if she told her? Regardless, this was Dylan's mother, and it was up to him to share the parts of his life with her that he wanted.

"I'll leave it alone, then." Andrea looked up at the stage, where the tech guys were switching on microphones and getting ready. "I think the speeches are about to start."

Faith turned so that she could see the stage, her eyes easily finding Dylan in the group. He glanced up and caught her watching him, a slow smile spreading across his face. Then Jenna tapped him on the shoulder and he turned away.

"Nope," Andrea whispered. "Nothing going on between you two at all."

Faith bit down on her lip to stop the smile and watched the stage. Jenna began by welcoming everyone and gave the crowd a short history of the new flower. When she was done, Liam took the microphone and spoke of his vision in creating the Ruby Iris. Then he handed the microphone to Dylan.

Faith drank him in as he stood tall and confident at the center of the stage, but with that mask of openness, which made it seem he was sharing something with the people gathered. He was a natural, and even before he spoke, the audience was responding to him.

"Hi, everyone," he said, giving them his charmer smile. "I'm Dylan Hawke and I'd like to say a few words on behalf of the Hawke's Blooms stores. We're looking forward to working with this new flower—we think our customers will be excited to have it in their bouquets, and I know our florists are keen to create arrangements that people will love."

He walked a few steps along the stage, ensuring he was including the entire audience in his gaze. "I'd like to thank everyone who's played a part in bringing the Ruby Iris to this point, but I'd especially like to thank one of our florists, Faith Crawford, for working behind the scenes and creating these stunning arrangements we have in the room tonight. Faith, can you come up here for a moment?"

He shielded his eyes from the spotlight with the hand that still held the microphone, then raised his other hand in her direction as a round of applause flowed through the room.

Faith's pulse jumped. She hadn't expected this, but she was touched that he'd think to mention her. His mother gave her a little prod, and Faith began making her way through the crowd until she reached the two steps that led up to the small stage. Dylan reached out to steady her and moved to the side to join in the clapping.

Faith looked out over the crowd and, although the majority of people were strangers, they were smiling at her with approval. They liked her work. She'd achieved another step in her career plan—she'd reached a large group of people with her designs. She'd made them smile. She caught Dylan's gaze and mouthed, "Thank you." He nodded, his eyes sparkling.

Giving Faith's arm a little squeeze on the way past, Jenna took the microphone from Dylan and wound up the proceedings. As the music started again and the people on the stage descended to the ballroom floor, Faith was still on cloud nine. So when Dylan said, "Dance with me," she didn't hesitate.

He took her hand and led her out onto the small dance floor, where a few couples were moving to the music, and then pulled her into his arms. The clean scent of him surrounded her, and she wanted nothing more than to lean into him, to lose herself in his heat. Would she ever be able to be near him and react as if he was any other man? Or would he always have this power over her?

She needed to get her mind onto a normal topic of conversation. She cast around for an idea, then remembered that Jenna had wanted him to talk to someone earlier. "How did it go with the journalist?"

"He was from the same morning show as the woman outside. I've made an appointment to see them both tomorrow, so cross your fingers for me."

"I will." Though she was sure he wouldn't need it. Everything Dylan touched turned to gold. Except her— when he touched her, she turned to flames.

His hand on her back traced a path up, then down, leaving a trail of tingles in its wake. Faith hesitated. "Should we be doing this?"

"It's a date—our last one—and people dance on dates." He pulled her a couple of inches closer. "Besides, there are hundreds of people here. We're in no danger."

"It feels dangerous." Which was possibly the understatement of the night.

"I'll admit that it's lucky I have that limo waiting outside to take you home." His Adam's apple slowly bobbed up and down. "I don't think I could kiss you on your cheek at the door and leave tonight."

She couldn't imagine letting him walk away from her

door tonight, either. In fact, she was starting to think she would have just as much trouble leaving him here and getting into the limo.

"Speaking of the limo," she paused, moistening her lips, "I'm thinking it's probably time I went home."

"Now?" he said, coming to a standstill in the middle of the dance floor. "We haven't been here that long."

In some ways, any amount of time on this date was always going to be too long, especially now when they were touching again.

She drew in a breath, pretending this wasn't going to wrench her in two. "I was here for the speeches, I saw my arrangements in the ballroom full of people and I've danced with the most eligible bachelor in the room. What more could the night possibly bring?"

He grinned and his eyes sparkled with promise. "More dancing with that eligible bachelor."

"Yeah, that's what I'm worried about."

He chuckled. "Fair call."

The music segued from one song to another, which seemed like a natural place to end things. She stepped back, away from the circle of his arms. "Thank you for tonight. You've made it magical."

"You brought the magic," he said, his voice low.

It was too much. Being this close to him, knowing she couldn't have him, was too much. She couldn't breathe. She turned and wove her way through the crowd until she reached the door and could fill her lungs again. Dylan followed and spoke to the doorman. Within moments, the limo had pulled up in front of the door, and with a last chaste but lingering kiss on his cheek, she slipped into the backseat and left the launch—left him—behind.

Ten

Faith sat bolt upright on the studio sofa, waiting for *The Morning Show* to start again after the ad break. Her palms were sweaty—a combination of the hot lights and a case of nerves that just might kill her—so she tried to wipe them discreetly on her skirt.

"Hey," Dylan said beside her. "Are you all right?"

"Well, I've forgotten my name. Will that be a problem?"

He chuckled and rubbed a hand up and down on her back. "They have your name written on the autocue for the host, so that doesn't matter. Just tell me you remember how to arrange flowers."

"I can do that in my sleep." Then she winced as she imagined herself fumbling. "Well, as long as I don't drop the flowers with my sweaty hands."

A man wearing a microphone headpiece waved an arm. "And we're back in three…two…one…"

The host, Lee Cassidy, a woman in her early thirties with black hair pulled tightly back from her face, scooted back into the seat at the last moment and smiled at the camera. "We have a treat for you now. Dylan Hawke, one of the brothers behind the Hawke's Blooms, and head of their hugely successful chain of florist stores, is here in the studio to tell us about a brand-new flower they launched a couple of days ago, the Ruby Iris. And he's brought along one of his florists, Faith Crawford." The host turned to them and smiled her megawatt smile again. "Welcome to the show. How are you both this morning?"

Dylan looked at Faith, giving her the chance to speak first. She opened her mouth to reply but no words came out. She closed her mouth, swallowed and tried again. Nothing. Prickles crawled across her skin.

Dylan smoothly picked up the ball. "We're both great, thanks, Lee. In fact, we're still buzzing after the launch of the Ruby Iris on the weekend. It was quite a night."

"It sounds as if it was fabulous." The host turned to the camera, giving her viewers the full benefit of her smile. "In fact, we have some photos."

The big screen behind them suddenly flashed with images from the night, including one of Faith taking Dylan's hand as she stepped up onto the stage. She was gazing up at him with her heart in her eyes. Would anyone else recognize that? Would Dylan be able to read that expression?

"So, Faith," Lee said, "tell me why you love the Ruby Iris so much. What's special about this new flower?"

Faith steeled herself. She had to answer this time.

She needed words. Any words would do. "Well, Lee, it's red."

Lee raised her eyebrows as if to say, *Is that really what you want to go with?*

Dylan leaned forward. "Of course, there are many red flowers, but there haven't been any red irises before now." He nodded at Faith, encouraging her to pick up the thought and run with it.

"That's true," she said, aware she was probably speaking too fast, but at least her vocal cords were working now. "The most popular iris has been the traditional purple, and a customer favorite is the white, and there has been pink—"

"Okay," Lee said cutting her off, "how about you show us more about this flower. We have a few things over here waiting for you."

"I'd love to," Faith said, relieved she could finally do something she was comfortable with instead of mindlessly listing flower colors.

The guy with the microphone headpiece waved at her to stand and pointed to the counter he'd shown her earlier. Lee followed him over, and the cameras panned to track their progress.

Faith stood behind a gleaming white counter with all the flowers and tools they'd brought along with them neatly laid out, and sent up a silent prayer that she didn't mess this up. Hawke's Blooms was counting on her. Dylan was counting on her.

Lee was at her side. "What are you going to make for us today?"

Faith's nerves were rising, threatening to take over; she tried to breathe through it, but it wasn't working. Then Dylan appeared at her other elbow and passed her a single white carnation. Faith took the flower, and the moment it was in her hand, she relaxed. She could do this.

As she trimmed the base of the stalk, she smiled at Lee. "I'm doing a simple arrangement that anyone at home could try. I'm going to use the Ruby Iris, but you can substitute your favorite flower—say, daffodils or tulips."

For the next few minutes, she worked on the arrangement, bringing the vision in her mind to life, giving a couple of easy jobs to Lee to do so the segment was more interesting.

When Faith was done, Lee called Dylan back into the shot and thanked them both for coming in. Then the guy with the headphones told them they were on an ad break. Lee rushed back to the sofa to be ready for the next segment, a girl with a ponytail guided Dylan and Faith off the set and within minutes, they were in Dylan's car.

Faith blinked. It was over. She'd made her first-ever TV appearance and it had consisted of her freezing and generally messing it up. Her head was still spinning.

"I'm so sorry, Dylan," she said as he slid into the driver's seat.

He started the car and glanced over at her. "What for?"

"You worked so hard to get that segment and I ruined it."

"You were great," he said cheerfully as he leaned over and squeezed her knee. She'd never met someone as skilled at manipulating the truth. If she hadn't been in the studio herself to see the train wreck, she might have believed him.

She raised an eyebrow at him and he grinned. "Okay, so you stumbled a couple of times, but your demonstration was great. You were professional, yet you explained things in ways the viewers would understand, and your love for your work shone through."

"I've let Hawke's Blooms down," she said, trying not to grimace as she said it. She didn't want pity. She wanted to apologize. "Let you down."

"Hey, you did us proud." Before he could say anything else, his cell phone rang in its cradle on the dashboard and he thumbed the Talk button. "Dylan Hawke."

"Dylan, it's Ben Matthews from *The Morning Show*. Thanks again for coming on today."

"Thank you for inviting us." Dylan pulled out to overtake a car without missing a beat in the conversation. "Anytime you want someone from Hawke's Blooms back, let us know."

"I was hoping you'd feel that way. I've just been talking to a producer from our network office in San Diego. I'd asked them to watch out for your segment today and they were impressed."

"That's good to hear," Dylan said, sliding Faith a grin.

"They've been considering a weekly gardening segment, but now they're interested in making it about flowers instead. Maybe how to arrange them, keeping them alive longer, that sort of stuff. What would you think about Hawke's Blooms doing that segment? If it goes well, we could talk about other guest spots on our LA show then."

Dylan squeezed the steering wheel harder, but his voice remained easygoing. "We'd be very interested in doing that, Ben."

"There's only one condition they've laid down. You need to have that woman from today's segment as the florist. Our social media went crazy for her when she was on air."

Faith gasped and then covered her mouth with her hand in case Ben could hear her in the background. The producers had liked her enough to make her involvement a condition? It was surreal. And people watching had liked her enough to comment about her?

"I'll talk to her and let you know," Dylan said.

"Well, talk quickly. They want you down there for tomorrow's show. You'll need to be in the studio by five a.m."

"I'll get back to you within the hour." Dylan ended the call and threw Faith a grin. "I guess you didn't ruin it."

"They want me," she said, the awe she felt coming out in her voice.

He laughed. "They sure do. What do you think? Interested?"

"Absolutely." This was the biggest thing ever to happen in her career—in her *life*—and nothing could make her let the opportunity pass.

"Then we'd better start making plans." He turned into her street. "I'll ring Ben Matthews back and work out the details. I'll also have my personal assistant book us flights and rooms in San Diego for tonight. We'll catch a late flight down and one back after the show in the morning."

His voice had been so calm, planning the details it would take to get them there, that at first she missed the significance of what he'd said. Then it hit her.

"A hotel?" she said as she wrapped one arm around herself. "Us?"

Gaze still on the road, he nodded. "They want us on set at five a.m., and I don't want to take any chances on delays. It would be much better if we're already in town."

"But we agreed…" She let her words trail off, wondering if she was making too big a deal out of this since he didn't seem worried at all.

"Don't worry about it," he said, his voice a notch lower than it had been only a minute earlier. "I'll get rooms on different floors. We'll be fine."

Okay, that seemed reasonable. Different floors should be enough distance if they were both on their best behavior.

He pulled up in front of her house. "You pack a bag and I'll let you know the time of the flight."

"Sure," she said and climbed out. As he drove away, she sighed and hoped she could trust herself to be on her best behavior if Dylan Hawke was sleeping in the same building.

The flight to San Diego was uneventful, and as soon as they arrived at the hotel, Faith excused herself to her room. She told Dylan she needed some quiet time so that her head was together for the show tomorrow, and that she'd order room service for dinner and read the book she'd brought.

But it wasn't that she needed quiet so much as a break from the tension of being with Dylan. Or, more precisely, being with him and not touching him as her body was screaming out to do. That particular tension was going to drive her insane.

And going insane just before going on live TV representing Hawke's Blooms would not help anyone. She tried to drag in a full breath but it felt as if there was an iron band around her ribs, stopping her lungs from expanding. It might have been okay to mess up last time, but tomorrow had higher stakes. It was the first of what could become a regular segment. The expectations would be higher. The crew would be anticipating someone professional. Could she be that professional?

Her cell rang, and the sudden buzzing made her jump. She checked the screen and Dylan's name flashed up. She took a breath and thumbed the Talk button. "Hey, what's up?"

"Just wanted to make sure you're okay."

Even over the phone, his voice had the power to send a shiver down her spine. "I'm fine. I've stayed in hotels before."

"About tomorrow," he said, and she could hear the smile in his voice. "You freaked out a little bit last time."

She sank down to the edge of the bed. "I'm older and wiser now."

His voice dipped, became serious. "Honestly."

"Okay." She blew out a breath. "I'm probably not wiser. Though I'm not freaking out."

"Promise?"

She lay back over the hotel bed and covered her eyes with the inside of her arm. "Maybe freaking out just a little bit. But nothing to worry about. I'll have it under control in a moment."

"Try and minimize it in your mind," he said, his voice like warm honey. "It's no big deal."

She snorted. "It's probably not a big deal for you.

You've spoken in public heaps of times. This is still big and intimidating for me."

"If you worry about it all night, you'll have yourself in a state by morning."

"Is it too late to cancel?" she asked, only half joking. "Or fly someone else up here?"

"You're the one they want."

There was something in the way he said the words that made her think he wasn't just talking about the TV spot or about business. It was in the way he said *want*, as if he was on this bed beside her, whispering the word in her ear. Her pulse picked up speed. Part of her was longing to whisper it back. Longing to walk the corridor and stairs to his room and whisper it in person. But they'd made a decision, and she needed to be strong. She pulled herself up to sit against the headboard, piling the pillows behind her, trying to focus back on the real reason for this conversation. Having her eyes closed when talking to Dylan Hawke was probably not the best way to stay focused on work.

"But if I ruin this, it's Hawke's Blooms that will suffer," she said, shifting her weight against the pillows, unable to get comfortable.

"You won't ruin it. I have every faith in you."

He meant it, too. She could tell. What she wouldn't give to have him here beside her right now, sharing his strength, his self-assurance. She always felt more anchored when he was near. Unfortunately, having him near would also kick her libido into action. What she needed was to stay on topic.

"You said yourself I'll have myself in a state by the morning. Maybe I'm not cut out for this. I'd be better off standing behind the counter back in Santa Monica."

"Think about something else." His voice was cajoling, like the devil inviting her to sin. "Go to your happy place."

"My happy place?" she asked warily.

"A memory or thought that always makes you happy. Do you have one of those that you can use?"

Her breath caught high in her throat. *Him.* "Yeah, I can think of something."

"What is it?"

"It doesn't matter," she said, attempting to sound breezy. "I've got one."

"If you tell me, I can talk you through it. Work with me here. I'm trying to help."

"Okay, it's…um…the flower markets."

"The flower markets?" he asked, skepticism heavy in his voice.

Seemed she wasn't as good at manipulating the truth as he was. Maybe more detail would help. "In the mornings, like at about two or three a.m., when they first open."

"Faith, I don't doubt you like the flower markets. But that's not the happy place you decided to use."

"Sure it is."

"Faith," he said, his voice low. "What is your happy place, really?"

"I can't tell you." She hoped that would be enough to make him drop the subject but had a sinking feeling nothing would make him do that now.

"Why?" It was a simple question, merely a word, but when it was him asking, it became more potent, and she lost her will to resist.

"Because it's you," she said on an anguished breath. "You're my happy place."

A groan came down the line. "Hell."

There was a knock on the door, and she wasn't sure if the interruption was good timing or bad. "Hang on, someone's at the door."

"I know," he said, and as she opened the door, she saw him leaning in the doorway as if he'd been there a while, his cell still at his ear, his eyes blazing.

"You're here," she said. She'd never wanted him more than in that moment. She disconnected the call and threw her cell in the direction of a table, but she missed and it fell to the floor. She left it.

Instead of answering, he reached out with his free arm and dragged her to him, his mouth landing on hers with a comfortable thud. Or maybe that sound was his cell phone dropping to the floor. He stepped forward, so she stepped backward, and he kicked the door behind them closed, blotting out all sound except breathing and the rub of fabric on fabric as they moved.

She grabbed the front of his sweater and pulled him to the bed. The pillows were still bunched in a pile at the headboard, so she maneuvered him to lie diagonally across the crisp white cover. Then she followed, not worrying about grace and finesse, just needing to touch him, to be as close to him as she could.

His leg wrapped around hers, pulling her against him, and she almost melted, but she didn't stop her frantic touching, exploring wherever she could reach. It was as if a fire burned deep inside every cell, and the only thing that could relieve the burn was Dylan. Her fingertips brushed over his jaw, his throat, needing to feel the stubble of his evening beard as if the roughness held the secrets of the universe.

As they moved, his fingers worked at her buttons

until the sides of her top fell apart. She shrugged out of it without missing a beat and was rewarded when his large palm covered a breast. She was rendered motionless, absorbing the sensations, the heat, the pure beauty of the moment.

"Dylan," she said without even realizing she was speaking.

He pulled her bra aside and leaned down, covering the peak of her breast with his mouth, using his tongue, his teeth, to make her writhe.

When he began to undo the button and zipper on her trousers, she lifted her hips, glad he was the one doing it, because operating a simple zipper was probably beyond her. Once the trousers were off, she relaxed her hips, but his hand smoothed over the front of her and her hips bucked straight back up again.

"I've been dreaming of touching you again," he said, his voice urgent. His fingers caressed her over the thin fabric, then moved underneath. At the first contact with her skin, an electric current shot through her body and she shivered.

"I've been dreaming of it, too." Fantasizing, hoping, even though she knew she shouldn't.

She tried to wriggle out of the underpants but there were hands and intertwined legs in the way, so she made no progress until he grabbed the sides and pulled them down her legs. Then he moved down her body and rested his face on her hip, his fingers toying with her, driving her crazy. His warm breath fanned over her, and the world narrowed to just this moment. She felt the weight of his head lift from her hip a moment before his mouth closed over the center of her. She gasped and moaned his name.

He moved her leg to accommodate his shoulders, and she offered no resistance—couldn't have if she'd wanted to, since every single bone in her body seemed to have dissolved. His tongue was working magic, and she was on the edge of something powerful, something glimmering in the edges of her vision. When it hit, he rode it out with her, holding her tight, his face pressed against her stomach.

Then he was gone and she heard his clothes dropping on the carpet, his belt buckle clinking as it landed, the heavy fabric of his sweater making a more muffled sound as it hit the ground. The mattress dipped as he came back into view, already sheathed, crawling over her, hovering, his features pulled taut with tension. She looped her arms around his neck and pulled him back to her, reveling in the feel of his body against hers, leg to leg, hip to hip, chest to chest.

She scraped her nails lightly across his back, eliciting a shudder, so she did it again. He reared back, lifting himself above her, and stilled. "I'm not sure I'll ever get enough of you."

A faint sense of misgiving twinged in her chest—she suspected no matter how much time she had with him, it would never be enough. She pushed the thought away. She'd take the time with him that she could get.

He began to move again, guiding himself to her, and she raised her hips to meet him. Then as he slid inside her in one smooth thrust, he held her gaze. His eyes were so dark she couldn't see the green, just an intensity she'd never known. She was trapped by it, could only move in sync with his strokes, becoming more and more lost as if pulled deeper by an exquisite undertow.

He changed his angle and the friction increased,

becoming too much, not enough. He was above her, around her, inside her. Everything was Dylan. When the fever within her peaked impossibly high, she burst free, her entire body rippling with the power of it. And while she was still flying, Dylan called her name and shuddered, joining her, holding her close.

Minutes later, she was still in his arms, trying to catch her breath. After her experience of being with this man twice now, she'd come to the realization that making love with him was nothing short of explosive.

"We did it again," she said, opening one eye to look at him.

He reached for her hand and interlaced his fingers with hers. "Perhaps it was unreasonable to stay in the same hotel and expect to keep our hands to ourselves."

She thought back over the evening, at her attempts to resist. "We almost made it."

He laughed. "We nowhere near made it. But at least you're relaxed now."

"You're right," she said and stretched. "And if I tense up in the studio, my happy place is happier than ever."

"Tense up? Then you're not relaxed enough. How about I do something about that…"

He reached for her again and, smiling, she went to him.

Eleven

Dylan had fallen asleep, sprawled across both the bed and her, but Faith was wide awake. She wouldn't let herself fall asleep with him. She'd glimpsed heaven with him tonight, and it had made her face something.

He wasn't just her happy place. He was more than that.

She was in love with him.

Sleeping in his arms was her idea of paradise, which was why it would be emotionally reckless. How could she stay ahead of the eight ball and protect her heart if she indulged herself in sleeping beside Dylan's warm body? She couldn't let her guard down and lose her independence in whatever it was they had between them.

From the experience of her childhood, she knew she had a tendency to become attached more often and more deeply than other people did, and she'd done it again by falling in love with Dylan. He would be moving on at some point—people always did—and in the meantime the idea of coming to rely on him for anything, including letting herself fall into a routine of sleeping beside him, frightened her witless. Anytime in her past that she'd started to feel that she belonged somewhere, it had all been ripped out from under her. The path toward letting herself relax and get sucked into the belief that this could be permanent held only heartache.

She slipped out from under his arm—pausing when his breathing changed and he rolled over—and picked up her clothes. After she was dressed, she grabbed her purse and, with one last look at his sleeping form half draped by the covers, quietly slipped out of the hotel room.

She checked her watch. Ten past two a.m. The flower market would be open. She headed down to the lobby and caught a cab. Checking out the San Diego flower market had been on her list of things to do while she was here—perhaps not this early in the morning, but she was grateful for this way of keeping her mind off the man sleeping in her hotel room. The man she loved.

An hour later, she had a call on her cell from Dylan.

"Where are you?" he asked, his voice raspy from sleep but with an edge of concern.

She covered her other ear with a hand to hear better. "Down at the flower market."

"On your own?" Suddenly he sounded fully awake. "Jesus."

"I wanted to check them out."

There was scuffling on the line as if he was dragging on clothes. "Why didn't you wake me? I would have come with you."

Because that would have defeated the purpose of finding some breathing space. "I'm fine, and you needed the sleep."

"I'll come down there." From his tone, he was already set on his course of action.

"No need," she said quickly. "I was just about to leave." It was true anyway—she was about done, and she wanted some time back at the hotel before having to head to the studio.

"Hang tight. I'll send a car for you."

"I can catch a cab."

"The car will be there in a few minutes. I'll call you back as soon as I've ordered it, and we'll stay on the line till you're back here."

"You know," she said wryly, "this isn't my first visit to a predawn flower market."

"Indulge me."

She sighed. He wasn't going to give up, and in all honesty, it was nice that he was trying to ensure her safety. "Okay."

By the time she made it back to the hotel, Dylan was waiting in the lobby. He hauled her into his arms and held her until she could barely breathe.

"Hey," she said. "I need a little air."

He loosened his grip and led her to the bank of elevators. "Sorry. When I woke and couldn't find you... and then found you were out in the city in the middle of the night..." He punched the Up button and the doors swooshed open. Once they were inside and he'd hit the button for her floor, he gathered her against him again. "I can't remember the last time I was that scared."

She'd had no idea that he'd be so worried. That he cared that much. She rested her head against his shoulder and let him hold her. "I'm sorry. I didn't mean to worry you."

"Tell me honestly." He tilted her chin up so she met his gaze. "Why did you go down to the markets?"

It was as if she could see the universe in the depths of his green eyes, and in that moment she couldn't lie, not even to protect herself. "I needed a little space."

A bell dinged and the doors opened. Neither of them said a word until they were in her room again. Dylan headed straight for the minibar and grabbed two orange juices. He handed her one, then took a long drink from the other bottle before asking, "Space from me?"

"From us," she said, choosing her words with care. "Sometimes when I'm with you, it's intense."

He thought about that, putting his juice down and taking hers as well. Then he found her hands and interlaced their fingers. "What if we decided to give this thing between us a go? What would you think about that?"

Her pulse jumped. He cared enough to try? Although it was impossible, it meant so much that he wanted to. "We can't." She lifted one shoulder and let it drop. "The fraternization policy."

"Screw the policy," he said without hesitation.

She coughed out a laugh. "It's your company. You can't be that cavalier."

"What's the point of being one of the owners if I can't?"

"You want to change a policy that's doing some good in creating a safe workplace and protecting staff from unwanted advances, just because you want to get involved with an employee?"

"Okay, it doesn't sound good when you put it like

that. But I want to spend more time with you. I want us to be together." His eyes were solemn as he cupped the side of her face with his palm. "Is that what you want?"

Was it what she thought was in her best interests? No. What she thought would last? No. But he'd asked what she wanted. And she wanted nothing more than to be with the man she loved, so before she could stop it, a whispered "yes" slipped from between her lips.

He stepped closer and kissed her forehead tenderly. "Then we'll find a way."

Her heart squeezed tight. He sounded so determined that she didn't have the heart to say it didn't matter. She'd be moving on. Or he would be. One of them would leave; it was the way these things worked.

But maybe she could enjoy the time they had together? Just because she couldn't have forever didn't mean she couldn't have for now.

So she decided to ignore the consequences, and instead nodded and smiled and said, "I'd like that."

Five weeks later, and Faith's life was going well. Almost too well. When things fell into place this easily, it often preceded a fall, so part of her was on guard. The San Diego job was amazing—she'd become relaxed in front of the camera, and had been getting great viewer feedback on her segments. And spending more time with Dylan was her very favorite part of each day.

She was just shoving a vegetable lasagna in the oven when her cell rang. Dylan was due in about half an hour for dinner, so it was probably him letting her know he was leaving the office. Since the first trip to San Diego, they'd fallen into a pattern of spending more time together, usually at his place. They'd order takeout, maybe watch a movie, then make love, and she'd slip out and head home afterward, determined to keep her vow of not getting used to sleeping next to his warm body.

Tonight was the first time she'd agreed to have him visit her apartment. Things had been going so well, she'd let her guard slip and agreed when he'd suggested it. Her stomach was a tight ball of nerves as she wondered how she'd cope when she couldn't leave during the night. Which, of course, was probably why Dylan had suggested it...

She pulled the oven mitts off and grabbed her cell, but it was an unknown number on the screen.

"Hello?"

"Hi, is that Faith Crawford?"

Seven minutes later, Faith disconnected the call and fell onto the sofa.

She'd just been offered a job. A dream job. A nationally syndicated gardening variety show in New York had been looking for a florist to add to their team of gardeners and landscapers, and they'd seen her work on the San Diego show. Her role would be to teach people about flower arranging in a regular segment, but also to travel with a producer and record stories on high-profile floral arrangements—the ones found in the White House, in cathedrals, at big events. She'd be paid to study up close the very designs she hoped to be making one day, make contacts and share her love of flowers with a huge audience.

Yet she'd hesitated. The producer had given her a day to think about it—if she wasn't interested, they needed to know soon so they could approach someone else.

The job was full-time and in New York. She'd have to move across the country. Leave Dylan. A white-hot pain pierced her chest and she had trouble drawing a breath. Could she do it? It was unthinkable. But what if she turned the job down and stayed? When this thing with Dylan fizzled out, she'd be left without him and the dream job. And in the meantime, she'd still be working for him, so they'd have to keep sneaking around so no one guessed they were breaking company rules.

Outside, his car pulled up. She stood, tucking her hair firmly behind her ears and trying to pull herself together. What would she say to him? She'd never been more torn in her life. She might love Dylan, but her career had been her constant, the rock in her life. She *had* to take the incredible job offer in New York. To do anything less would be cheating herself and banking on a dream that could never come true.

She pulled open the front door and was confronted by the only man who'd ever touched her heart. He leaned down and kissed her and she sank into him, trying to create a memory, because she had no idea how he would react once she told him.

When they finished dinner, Faith gathered the plates and headed for the kitchen, almost as if she was escaping. Dylan followed, determined to find out what was on her mind, since she'd avoided his prodding while they ate.

"You've been distracted all through dinner," he said, standing behind her at the sink and massaging her shoulders. "Which is a shame, because that was the best vegetable lasagna I've had—and I'm not sure you even tasted it as you ate."

She turned in his arms, searching his gaze. "There's something I need to tell you."

"I'm right here." He smiled indulgently and smoothed a bright red curl back from her face.

"I had a job offer today." Her gaze didn't waver—she was watching for his reaction.

He rubbed her arms up and down, wanting to reassure her. He didn't own her. The businessman side of him hoped she'd stay at Hawke's Blooms, but the man in a relationship with her just wanted her to be happy.

"I'm not surprised. You've been doing high-profile work—one of our competitors was bound to headhunt you at some stage."

"It isn't one of your competitors," she said, sucking her bottom lip into her mouth.

He raised an eyebrow, curiosity piqued. "Who was it?"

She named the show and he let out a long whistle. "Isn't that recorded in New York?"

"The job is located there. I'd have to move."

His gut clenched as her words hit home. "What did you tell them?"

"That I'd think about it." She looked at the counter as she spoke.

He withdrew his hands and dug them into his pockets, not liking where this was headed. "And have you thought?"

She hesitated, then said, "There are so many factors to consider. I don't know what to do."

He let out a relieved breath and pulled her against his chest. "If you're not sure, then don't take it."

"Why?" she asked, her voice partly muffled by his shirt.

"I think we have something special here. Between us. If you stay, we can see where it goes." In fact, this conversation had been something of a wakeup call. He'd been happy enough going along, spending time together, making love when they could, but now that the possibility of separation had been raised, he was completely aware of how much she meant to him. He wasn't letting her go.

"Dylan," she began, but he cut her off.

"Don't decide just yet." He leaned in and placed a trail of kisses along the line of her jaw. "Give us a chance." He moved to her earlobe. He tugged it gently with his teeth and then pulled it into his mouth. She gasped and he smiled against her skin. What they had was too strong—she wouldn't leave him. And he'd never leave her.

Digging his fingers into her wild curls, he tipped her head back and claimed her mouth. Even though it had been less than twenty-four hours, it felt like forever since he'd kissed her, and he made up for the lost time. Weeks of having her in his bed at night hadn't slaked his desire for her; if anything, they had increased it. Whenever his mind wandered at work, it was always Faith it went to. The sound of her laugh, her dimples, the warmth of her mouth on him, the way her hips moved when she walked.

Her arms snaked around his waist, grabbing fistfuls of his shirt at the back, holding him in place. He loved the way she wanted him as fiercely as he wanted her.

He spun them around, away from the counter, and pressed her against the wall, kissing her, relishing the feel of her curves against him. He hooked a hand under her knee and lifted, pulling her pelvis closer, and he groaned at the delicious pressure. No woman had ever affected him this deeply or made him want this hungrily.

When her fingers worked on the buttons of his shirt, fumbling in her haste, his heart beat so hard against his ribs that she must have felt it under her hands. Finally she made it to the last button and pushed aside his cotton shirt, spreading her palms over his chest. It was as if her hands were magic; everywhere she touched she left a path of sparks, drawing him further under her spell.

Her top had a bow behind her neck, and when he pulled the end, the knot came undone. She wasn't wearing a bra, so as he peeled the front of her top down, he bared her breasts to his gaze. He cupped them with reverent hands, lifting them to meet his mouth, making her writhe against him and murmur his name. His blood heated, his pulse raced, he was helpless and she was everything.

As she undid the top button on his trousers and dipped her hand inside his pants and encircled him, he hissed out a breath between his teeth, then again as she slowly moved her hand up and down. He dropped his head to her shoulder. He was hers. No question, she owned him. After tonight, he'd make sure they were always together.

Suddenly unable to wait a moment longer, he grabbed the condom from his pocket and took off his trousers and boxers before doing the same with her underwear, not bothering to remove her skirt, just lifting it out of the way. She took the condom from him and rolled it down his length, wrapping a leg around his waist again. This time he lifted her hips, supporting her weight so that she could wrap her other leg around him as well, and then brought her down on top of him. Her sharp intake of breath mirrored his, and he paused to take in the beauty of the moment, of the sensations she evoked in his body and in his heart.

Tensing her legs, she moved up and slowly down again, and he whispered raggedly, "I love you."

The only sign that she'd heard was that her movements became faster, and he met her stroke for stroke, telling her how beautiful she was, loving the way the flesh of her bottom filled his hands. He grew more frantic, loving her, feeling the rising tension in his entire body.

He was near the edge, so close to falling over, but he held on, hovering, unwilling to go alone. He reached down between them, found her most sensitive spot and caressed until she exploded, moaning his name, contracting around him so tightly that he couldn't hold a moment longer. He let go, calling out the name of the woman he loved.

When Faith woke the next morning, she was alone. She reached out to feel the other side of her bed and found it rumpled but cold. Rising quickly, she slipped on a robe and padded through the apartment, finding no trace of Dylan.

A small part of her was relieved. She'd made a decision during the night to take the job and didn't think she could face telling him just yet. She knew that was cowardly—of course it was—but how could she face the man she loved and tell him she was leaving? Instead, when they'd made love, she'd said goodbye with her touch. In every silent way she could.

Maybe tomorrow, or once she was packed and her

flight was booked, she would drop in to see him and try to explain. Maybe by then she'd have found the words.

She pulled on some clothes and dragged the boxes she always kept on standby out of the hall closet. It wouldn't take long—being wary of putting down roots meant she liked to be ready to pick up and travel when the need struck, so packing was easy.

She was on her living room floor, surrounded by sealed and half-packed boxes, when Dylan returned. In one hand he held a takeout tray with two coffees and a pastry bag, and in the other, a bunch of flowers. But his expression…his expression was going to haunt her dreams.

Dylan froze on the threshold to Faith's apartment, feeling as if he'd been sucker punched.

When he'd woken this morning, he'd been so damn filled with love and optimism, all he could think about was waking like this every morning. Of spending the rest of his life with her. He'd slipped out without waking her to hunt down the perfect engagement ring. He knew it couldn't be a standard diamond for Faith, and he'd found a purple diamond in a platinum setting in a window and convinced the owner to open early for him.

He'd been on cloud nine, seeing a rosy future in front of them, seeing everything he'd never known he wanted all wrapped up in one gorgeous woman. Faith. Telling her he loved her last night had felt right, deep in his soul. She might not have said the words back, but he was in no doubt that she loved him. Not after the way she'd been touching him last night.

He'd hoped she'd still be asleep when he got back with breakfast and the ring, but it had taken a little longer than he'd planned. Still, the last thing he'd expected to see was her getting ready to flee.

Again.

Especially after spending a night together that had rocked his world. It was as if all the air in the room—in his life—had been sucked out, leaving him in a vacuum.

"Going somewhere?" he asked mildly.

"Uh, yes."

He took a step inside but couldn't bring himself to sit down or even cross the room. Not when she was surrounded by those damn packing boxes. "You're taking the job, aren't you?"

"It's an incredible opportunity." Her voice was laced with guilt, and she wouldn't meet his eyes. It seemed that they weren't on the same page about this relationship at all.

"When did you decide?" he asked, not 100 percent sure he wanted to know the answer. "Just now, or had you already made up your mind last night?"

She was silent, which pretty much answered his question. He wanted to throw up.

"So you'd made up your mind and were obviously hoping to skip out this morning while I wasn't looking. Were you planning on ever telling me? Or perhaps the plan was a quick call from New York after you'd arrived?"

"I was definitely going to talk to you." She finally looked up and met his gaze, and he could see that much was true. Shame about the rest.

"So," he said and drew in a breath, steeling himself, "telling you last night that I love you doesn't mean anything to you?"

"Of course it does, but love isn't enough, Dylan. It's

not steadfast." She moistened her lips, her beautiful brown eyes pained. "You have to understand that my career is the only thing I've ever been able to count on."

Suddenly Dylan was angry. She was giving up because she didn't think she could count on them? On him? He dropped the flowers on the coffee table and slid the takeout tray down beside the bouquet. Then he reached into his pocket, found the little velvet box, held it up and opened it.

"How's this for steadfast?" he said, forcing each word out past a tight jaw. "I was willing to commit my life to you."

She flinched. "I'm sorry. But you say that now—"

"I said it last night, too," he pointed out, setting a clenched fist on his hip.

She brushed at a tear as it slid down her cheek. "Thing is, I believe you. I promise I do. But once the novelty wears off, you'll be gone. It was never going to last."

"Explain that to me," he said, not caring that his exasperation was coming through in his tone. "Explain how you know what I'll do."

She collected her hair up in her hands, and then let it drop as she sat back on her heels. "One thing I've learned is that love is fickle. All my life I've seen the proof of people's attraction to the next bright, shiny thing. *I* was never enough. My aunt who loved me for a year then gave me up when she got pregnant. My mother who loved me but was always leaving for the next big adventure. My grandparents who loved me but were always relieved when someone else took me in. My father who loved me but wouldn't arrange a job on land so I could live with him. You might love me, Dylan," she said, her voice cracking on his name, "but something else will come along, snag your attention and drag you away. I will never allow myself to be in the position of thinking I'm not enough again."

He'd known she had a rough childhood and that made trust difficult for her, but he couldn't believe she thought their relationship wasn't worth fighting for. Wasn't worth giving a chance. She didn't think he was worth taking a risk on. Weariness suffused every cell in his body.

"You know, you say people leave, but you're the one leaving. It's always you leaving, either sneaking out of my place after we make love, or leaving early from the launch, or going to the flower market at two in the morning."

Then he dropped the ring on the hall stand and glanced over his shoulder. "Ever heard the phrase 'Be careful what you wish for'? You've been expecting me to leave since day one, and here I go."

He walked out the door and across the small courtyard to his car without once looking back.

Twelve

Faith sat on a plastic chair at the window of her tiny New York apartment, chin in her hands as she looked down at the street below. She'd been here for only two weeks, so it wasn't strange that it didn't feel like home yet…though when had anyplace ever felt like home?

She loved the new job, but deep in her soul she'd been numb from the moment she'd arrived. No, before. She'd always been alone, but this loneliness was different—it was a yearning for one person. A tall, flirtatious man with sparkling green eyes and hair like polished mahogany.

Since she'd learned the hard lessons about life as a child, she'd always been emotionally self-sufficient, but something had changed. She'd developed relationships. She'd never let a person get as close to her, under her guard, as Dylan had. But it wasn't just him—she'd become friends with Jenna.

Jenna had called to congratulate her when she'd heard about the job, and they'd kept in touch since she moved. They'd spent a lot of time together while organizing the launch of the Ruby Iris, but at the time, Faith had thought of them as colleagues working together. Now she realized what Jenna had known then—they'd become friends.

Somewhere along the line, Faith had learned to believe in people again.

Desperate to hear a friendly voice, she picked up her cell and dialed Jenna's number.

Jenna picked up on the first ring, her lilting voice a little breathless. "Hi, Faith."

"Is this a bad time?" Faith asked. She was acutely aware that Jenna had two babies and her time was often not her own.

"Now is good. We're out back in the double stroller, walking along the flower beds. As long as I keep pushing them, I can talk to you until snack time."

Faith's mind drifted to when she'd worked on-site at the flower farm and could wander along those same flower beds during her lunch break, sometimes chatting with Jenna or carrying one of the babies on her hip. "Give them both a cuddle from me when you get a chance."

"Will do. How are you?"

"It's all good here." Faith smiled as she said it, hoping it would make her voice sound happy. "Just home from work and felt like a chat."

There was a pause. "Have you talked to Dylan lately?"

By an unspoken rule, they'd never spoken about Dylan, and Faith wasn't sure how much Dylan had told his sister-in-law of what had happened between them. "Um, no. I don't think we've had a chance to touch base since I arrived."

"A chance to touch base? That sounds as if you're talking about an acquaintance."

"Dylan and I worked together," she said carefully.

Jenna laughed. "You're not honestly going to try to tell me that nothing happened between you two. I haven't pushed you on it because I realize things must have been messy, but I've never seen two people who looked at each other the way you guys did. It was intense."

Faith's eyes stung with tears that she wouldn't let fall—they *had* been intense. She swallowed before she could reply. "So Dylan hasn't said anything?"

"No, which isn't like him. I can usually wheedle information out of him, but when your name comes up, he clams up. Come on," she said, her voice ultrasweet, "tell Aunty Jenna what happened. You know you want to."

Jenna was right—having no one to talk to about it had made her heart feel even heavier. "But Dylan is your family…"

"Don't worry about that. If he's treated you badly, I'll be mad at him, but he'll always be Bonnie's uncle and soon he'll be Meg's uncle too. There's nothing you can say about Dylan that will ruin my relationship with him. Tell me what he did."

"He didn't do anything," Faith admitted. "It was me." She curled her legs up underneath her on the hard chair and told Jenna the whole story.

"So," Jenna said when Faith was done, "Dylan loves you but you won't trust him to stick around?"

Already feeling raw from reliving everything that

had happened, the words hit her hard. "It's not about trusting him—it's about relationships in general. I... have trouble believing in them."

"Faith, Dylan is the most steadfast man you're ever likely to meet. He's devoted himself to his family's business since he was a child. He's always there for his brothers, for his parents, for me. You might have trouble believing in relationships, but if Dylan offers a commitment, he means it."

The floor was falling away from under her feet, and all Faith could do was squeeze her eyes shut. He'd been prepared to commit to her as well, but she'd thrown it away. Had she made the biggest mistake of her life?

A man who was committed to all the things in his life that were important to him was nothing like her own family, yet she'd been expecting him to behave the way they had. She'd taken her issues with her family out on him.

She hadn't been fair to either one of them. Her stomach clenched and dipped.

Unfortunately, even if it was a mistake, it was too late. After their last morning together, he wouldn't ever want to see her again. The pain in his eyes when he'd seen her packing her things had felt like a slap.

He would never trust her again, and she couldn't blame him.

Dylan sat in a wingback in his pristine white-on-white living room and swore. Then he took another mouthful of the beer he'd been nursing for a good ten minutes. This room was mind-numbingly dull. How had he never noticed that before? The interior designer who'd done the place had told him it would look modern, crisp and fresh. But it looked bland.

Like his entire life.

When Faith left, she'd taken all the damn sunshine with her. He hadn't found the energy to get excited about—or even interested in—anything for weeks. Maybe he never would again.

He took another swig of the beer.

Regardless, he shouldn't be giving her another thought. She'd given up on what they had, on their future. Hell, she'd left the state without a second thought. The best thing he could do was forget her. Which, naturally, was easier said than done.

There were voices at his door, and then the sound of people letting themselves in. Only his housekeeper, parents and brothers had their own keys. His parents had enough manners not to use them, and it was his housekeeper's day off. Which left his brothers. He sighed. He was in no mood to see them or anyone.

"I'm not home," he called out.

Ignoring him, Adam and Liam headed through the entryway, straight for him.

"So this is your answer," Adam said, shaking his head. "Drinking on a Saturday morning."

"I'm not *drinking*. I'm having a beer and watching football."

Liam made a point of looking around the room. "Are you doing it telepathically? Or hadn't you noticed the TV isn't on?"

"Not yet, smartass. I was about to switch it on when you barged in here. Also, I want the keys back."

Adam crossed his arms over his chest. "We're worried—this isn't like you. Tell us what you're going to do about your relationship."

Dylan looked away. "I don't have a relationship."

"With Faith," Adam said with exaggerated patience.

Dylan pointed a finger at his brother. "I seem to recall you were the one constantly telling me not to get involved with her."

"True." Adam nodded, seemingly unperturbed. "And my word should be law to my younger brothers. Yet you ignored me and went ahead anyway. What does that tell you?"

"That you're deluded about the extent of your power over us?" Dylan looked down at his beer. There was only half left. He was going to need a lot more alcohol to make it through this conversation.

Liam dropped onto a sofa across from him. "That's a good point, and we'll return to that later. But Adam's right. You broke company policy for this woman. I wouldn't have believed it if I hadn't been there watching the whole thing unfold."

"I made a mistake," Dylan said and took another swig of his beer, hoping they didn't see through him, because he'd make that same mistake again in a flash if it meant more time with Faith.

Adam blew out a breath. "I saw the way you and Faith defended each other at the launch. You're in love. Both of you. So why are you drinking here alone?"

Dylan flinched. That was a hell of a question, but not one he wanted to get into with his brothers. "She's gone. Feel free to follow her lead, and make sure you close the door on the way out."

Propping one ankle on a knee, Liam leaned back in the sofa. "Did you ask her to stay?"

Did he ask her to stay? What sort of idiot did they take him for? He drew in a measured breath before replying. "Of *course* I asked her to stay. I even bought her a damn ring."

Liam rubbed a hand over his jaw. "I've come to know Faith, and I think I understand her."

Adam and Dylan both turned disbelieving eyes to him.

Liam shrugged. "Okay, Jenna understands her. But still, she told me a couple of things."

Adam sighed. "If Jenna had some ideas, out with it."

"Faith didn't need a ring," Liam said, leaning forward and resting his forearms on his knees. "She needed you, you moron. Words have always come easy to you, and she knows that, so how would she know what to believe?"

Dylan frowned. "Jenna called me a moron?"

"No, that part was me. But listen up. You have to do something to *show* her that you're in it for the long haul. That you'll stand by her." Liam's eyes narrowed. "You are in it for the long haul, aren't you?"

"Would I have bought her a ring if I was going to bail out?"

Adam nodded. "So if you want her back, you won't be able to rely on your gift of gab. You can't just talk—you'll have to show her."

For a long moment, Dylan was speechless. They were right. He'd known her childhood had been full of promises that had quickly been broken—how had he not realized he'd need to do something more?

People had loved her in the past only when she fitted into their lives, and he'd pretty much asked her to say no to a new job for him. He rubbed his hand down

his face. Hell, he'd asked her to give up a great opportunity because he lived in LA—to fit in with his life.

Adam dug his hands into his pockets. "Final question, then we'll leave. Is what you had with Faith worth
fighting for?"

Dylan stilled. Was it too late to show her that his love
didn't depend on anything else? That he'd take her on
her own terms? And how would he show her? He'd have
to make a change in his life *for* her. So she wouldn't
simply have to fit in with him ever again.

He reached for his cell. "Let yourselves out," he said
without looking at his brothers. "And leave your keys.
I was serious about that."

He didn't have to look up to know his brothers were
smiling, but he ignored them and made a call. He had
several calls to make and was impatient to get going.
The sooner he started on the plan that was forming in
his mind, the sooner he could see Faith.

Excitement bubbling away in her belly, Faith checked
the address again and looked up at the building. Yes,
the gorgeous apartment building on the edge of Central
Park was the right place.

Jenna had called a couple of days ago, saying she'd
be in New York for a few days visiting a friend and
would love to meet up, and Faith had jumped at the
offer.

A doorman asked if he could help, and Faith said
she was visiting a friend in 813. The doorman smiled
and said she was expected, and then ushered her to the
elevator.

Once she'd found the right floor, she buzzed the button outside apartment 813 and waited. But when the

door swung open, it was Dylan on the threshold, not Jenna. He looked so tall and solid and gorgeous and *Dylan* that Faith's throat tightened too much to speak. So she just stood there and drank in the sight of him.

After what seemed like an eternity, he cleared his throat. "Come in," he said.

Still without speaking, she walked in, and he closed the door behind her. Such simple actions, but weighted with so much meaning. Expectation. Hope.

The apartment was empty of furniture, but it was beautiful—huge, filled with light, and with great views of the park through floor-to-ceiling windows. But as soon as Dylan was in front of her again, she couldn't look at the room. Or speak.

"Hi," he said eventually, his voice raspy.

"Hi," she whispered back.

Being this close again, it seemed natural, necessary even, to reach out and touch him…but she didn't have that privilege anymore. He'd offered it to her and she'd declined it. She'd left, just as he'd accused her of doing.

She dropped her gaze to the floor. "I came to see Jenna."

"I know." But he didn't make any move to summon Jenna or do anything else. The tension in the room was thick enough to press down on her, make her want to run. But she wouldn't leave this time, not when she had this chance to be near him, if even for a few minutes.

She took a breath, steeled herself and looked at him again. "How are you?"

He lifted one shoulder and then let it drop. "As well as can be expected. You?"

"Good," she said, but her voice cracked, so she added, "I'm good." Her hands trembled with the intensity of seeing him and not touching him, not being able to speak freely. Of being alone with him. "Is Jenna here?"

"No," he said simply.

Suddenly the strangeness of the situation hit her. Seeing Dylan again had fried her brain, so she hadn't put two and two together right away. "Whose apartment is this?"

"Yours." His expression didn't change, giving nothing away.

She took a step back. "What do you mean?"

"I've had a contract for this place drawn up in your name—" he gestured to some paperwork on the kitchen counter through an archway "—but if you'd rather have a different apartment, we can tear this contract up and keep looking."

"I already have a place to live," she said warily.

"It's a present. Although," he said, casting a quick glance around, "if you wanted, this place is big enough for both of us."

"Both of us?" she repeated, not daring to believe he meant what she thought he was saying.

He nodded, his beautiful green eyes not sparkling now—they were too somber. "If you'll have me. Or you can have it for yourself if you choose not to invite me back into your life. No strings attached. A parting gift. Completely your choice."

"My choice?" She circled her throat with a hand. He really wanted her back?

"Or if you don't like the city," he said with a casual shrug, despite his entire body being tense, "we could move farther out, and you can commute for your job. Whatever you want, I'll make it work."

She paused as the pieces of what he was saying

clicked together. "Hang on. You're willing to move to New York?"

"In an instant," he said without hesitation. "If that's what it takes."

It was so unexpected, she couldn't get her head around it. "What would you do here? Your company is on the West Coast."

He rubbed his fingers across his forehead. "I've been thinking that I could open some Hawke's Blooms stores on the East Coast. It makes business sense."

She checked his expression more closely and realized he was sincere. "That's quite a change in your role—moving away from managing the existing stores to starting small again."

"We can employ people to oversee the existing stores to free me up to start the new ones. I've realized that's what I love doing—the buzz and excitement of starting something new. You gave me that by pushing me to think about my own dreams." He reached out and cradled the side of her face in his palm. "Have I thanked you for that?"

She leaned into his palm and laid her hand over his, pressing in, making the contact more solid. "You just offered me an apartment, Dylan. I don't think you need to do anything else."

He took a small step closer. He was so close, she could feel his body heat. Her lungs struggled to find enough air. She released his hand from her cheek, and he let it fall to his side.

"Loving you means I like to do things for you."

"You know," she said looking up at him from under her lashes, "all of this is a big risk for you, given you don't even know if I love you back."

One corner of his mouth turned up in a cocky grin. "Are you going to deny it?"

She was immediately sorry she'd teased. She sucked in her bottom lip between her teeth, trying to think of the best thing to say. She couldn't lie, but it didn't feel like the right time to tell him that she loved him for the first time. It should be special.

His grin stretched wide. "No need to say it. I already know you love me, despite your unwillingness to admit it."

"You always were confident." She wanted to chuckle, but a thick ball of emotion had lodged in her throat and she was worried that if she tried to laugh, she'd cry instead.

He took her hands and held them between their bodies. "You can keep leaving, Faith, but as long as you love me, I'll keep following, even if I have to open stores in every damn state."

His words were the last straw—she burst into tears, and Dylan drew her against his body. Everyone in her life before had found a loophole to get rid of her. By leaving, she'd given Dylan a huge loophole—and he simply went around it to follow her. Jenna was right—he was the most steadfast man she was ever likely to meet. He was a man she could trust to stand by his word.

She pulled back so she could see his eyes, still hiccupping as the tears pressed in on her. In his gaze, she saw his love, his commitment, and she knew she could finally completely trust that he really wanted to be with her and would stay for the long haul.

"I love you, Dylan Hawke," she said, her heart full to bursting.

He lifted her off her feet and spun her around. "I can't tell you how glad I am to hear you say that."

"Hey," she said on a surprised laugh, "I thought you said you already knew."

He gently set her down and tucked her hair behind her ears. "I did, but it's still nice to hear it said aloud."

"I'll be sure to say it often, then." Her voice was barely more than a whisper.

He leaned in and kissed her. She wrapped her arms around his neck, pulling him closer. Weeks of not seeing him, not touching him, not kissing him, had built into a need that she was finally free to let loose.

When he pulled back, his breathing was heavy, but he was smiling. "Do you still have the ring I left on your hall stand in LA?"

She reached down to grab her purse where she'd dropped it, and then dug around before producing the precious little velvet box. "I've had it with me every day."

She passed it to him with an unsteady hand. When he'd left it in her apartment, she'd closed the box and hadn't opened it again, so she'd had only the one fleeting glance at the ring from across the room when he'd shown it to her in anger. She might have carried it with her ever since, but she hadn't given in and peeked inside. Technically it was still Dylan's ring, and she'd known she should give it back, but she hadn't been able to bring herself to do it.

He took the box from her, opened it and retrieved the purple diamond ring.

"More than anything in the world," he said, his voice low, "I want to be your husband and you to be my wife. Faith Crawford, will you marry me?"

"I want that so badly." She swiped at the tears still rolling freely down her cheeks. "Yes, I'll marry you."

He slid the ring onto her finger and then kissed her slowly, reverently. As he pulled away, he whispered against her mouth, "I think this is the start of our biggest adventure yet."

* * * * *

LET'S TALK
Romance

For exclusive extracts, competitions
and special offers, find us online:

 facebook.com/millsandboon

 @MillsandBoon

 @MillsandBoonUK

Get in touch on 01413 063232

MILLS & BOON

Desire

Indulge in secrets and scandal, intense drama and plenty of sizzling hot action with powerful and passionate heroes who have it all: wealth, status, good looks…everything but the right woman.

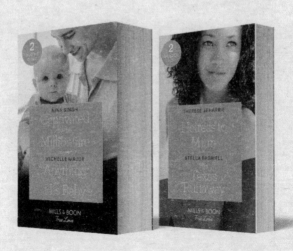

MILLS & BOON
MEDICAL
Pulse-Racing Passion

Set your pulse racing with dedicated, delectable doctors in the high-pressure world of medicine, where emotions run high and passion, comfort and love are the best medicine.

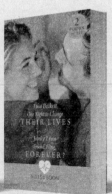